Brian Hess is a graduate of Southwestern Michigan with an associates in Art and Humanities, and studied literature under the guidance of Professor Michael Collins. He is a father of three and currently lives in Southwest Michigan with his wife. His published works include a number of poems, short stories, and a (YA) novel entitled, *The Legends of Lynquest*.

This book is dedicated to any and all people who have taken on the burden and responsibility of an ethical life. The true measure of love is found in our treatment of others. Those of you who have taken on this task are the true healers of this world. Yours is a heart most courageous.

B. F. Hess

AMERICAN ODYSSEY

THE DEVIL'S HAND

AUSTIN MACAULEY PUBLISHERS™

LONDON • CAMBRIDGE • NEW YORK • SHARJAH

Ordering Information
Quantity sales: Special discounts are available on quantity purchases by corporations, associations, and others. For details, contact the publisher at the address below.

Publisher's Cataloging-in-Publication data
Hess, B.F.
American Odyssey

ISBN 9781649799883 (Paperback)
ISBN 9781649799890 (ePub e-book)

Library of Congress Control Number: 2023907079

www.austinmacauley.com/us

First Published 2023
Austin Macauley Publishers LLC
40 Wall Street, 33rd Floor, Suite 3302
New York, NY 10005
USA

mail-usa@austinmacauley.com
+1 (646) 5125767

I want to personally thank Mrs. Loreta Lontayao Hess, author Silvia M. Holloman, Artist Alison Elrod, Patti Blanchard and a host of friends and lost acquaintances who took the time to build in me the foundation of self-love.

Table of Contents

Prologue

Every mountain stream, no matter how small, carries the hope of a mighty river in its trickles. Follow any stream down, and it may become the torrent you would expect, but in the end, you will undoubtedly find it calmly greeting the sea, and so it is with the human spirit. We start our lives in a restless fervor, like a leaf caught in a current, pulled to the bottom and up again, but eventually, we greet the ambiguity of life with calm, clear resolve. The human spirit is buoyant. Or, more specifically, someone's fortitude can be plunged to the depths of despair, but if they can hold their breath long enough, they will rise again elsewhere in life a stronger and, hopefully, wiser person.

This was the case with Uriel Jacob Sullinger, an upwardly mobile lawyer from Manhattan, who followed the swift currents that flow in high places. The silent demons of his childhood created an undertow that left him questioning his life, his loves and even his reality. Now, anxious and bewildered, he holds his breath and waits. He hangs, as only a human could hang, in a state of purgatory—suspended between heaven and hell.

Michael Calling

The spent and battered husk of a man in his early thirties stood awkwardly at the base of the steps to the Clay County Home for the Mentally Ill. The fine Armani suit that had once distinguished him among men now hung on him like a fallen banner. His broken nose, bruised face and swollen jaw bore witness to the twisted road that had led him to this point. Nervously, he scratched his thin strawberry blond hair and took one last look back.

A beautiful Italian woman sat in the driver's seat of a Lincoln Continental convertible parked outside the gate. A young black girl sat in the back seat. She smiled and waved to the man. Though her smile was warm, her eyes spoke a firm and silent admonishment. A reluctant smile crossed his face and he wiped his sweaty hands on his shirt. He nodded his head in a solemn surrender to the moment and then turned to start his long ascent up the steps. At the top, he paused before reaching for the door. The thumb of his right hand caressed the tips of his fingers as he took a moment to reflect. His shoulders drooped and he scuffed at the concrete threshold in front of the door with the sole of his right shoe.

At that moment, the shadow of a large bird crossed the ground before him and disappeared into a roost in the crest of the building. He again nodded to himself, snatched open the door and stepped into the lobby, joining the handful of other nameless people there that day who had found themselves refugees from their own reality.

He took a seat in the back of the room and watched the receptionist as she worked. She was a middle-aged woman with large horn-rimmed glasses and gray-black hair tied into a tight bun atop her head. He sat there tapping his right foot nervously, watching her type at the computer. From the corner of his right eye, he saw a woman in light pink paisley pajamas with disheveled light brown hair. She was sitting in a plastic chair rocking forward and backward, talking to herself and counting on her fingers: "One—no other god, two—his name in vain, three—keep the sabbath, four—Mom and Dad, five—don't kill, six—adultery, seven—stealing, eight—false witness, nine—no lust, ten—don't covet," she said softly. "Rape, isn't there. It's not. Why? Why isn't it there? It should be there, it should be…wait maybe I made a mistake. One…"

Nervously, he began to pick at his thumbnail with his teeth. He turned his attention back to the receptionist. After a few more moments of listening to the woman babble to herself, he mustered the courage to approach the receptionist. He rose to his feet and silently crept up to her desk and stood there, hoping she would look up. She was a fastidious woman. She had a smug way about her. She looked down her nose through her bifocals as she typed, as if the job was beneath her. She reminded him of someone. A memory rattled loose and he let out a snicker. She looked up from her computer.

"I'm sorry," she said. "Do you have an appointment with one of the doctors?"

"Uh…no, I…I don't, but I think I have a problem. I need to see someone," he stammered.

Her eyebrows raised slightly. "I see. Well, you will have to make an appointment with one of the doctors before I can—" she stopped short and raised her index finger. "I'm sorry, I will have to put you on hold…wait, I mean…wait one minute, won't you?" she blathered. "Dr. Kessler! Dr. Kessler!" she shouted down the hall.

A man wearing a gray-brown tweed jacket, wingtip shoes, and gray slacks stopped short in the hall to the right of the lobby. He turned and approached her desk, carrying a clipboard under his right arm. He had a warm, friendly smile and a timeless demeanor. "Good afternoon, Alice," he said. "What has the wheel of fate spun for my schedule today? Wait… Don't tell me… Mrs. Buchanan has canceled once again," he said with a sigh.

"Yes," she said, "she had a previous appointment to have her hair done for her sister's wedding."

"Hmm," he said as he rolled his eyes. "I thought all of her sisters were married off by now."

Alice smiled gently. "You know your patients well, Dr. Kessler."

The doctor simply smiled and said, "It's all part of the job, Alice." Then he glanced over at the man with the bruised face and torn Armani suit. "Who is this?" he asked.

"I'm sorry," said Alice, "I don't exactly know. I didn't get that far." Alice turned to the gentleman. "What did you say your name was?"

"Sullinger. My name is Sullinger," he said plainly.

The doctor's face perked up. "Sullinger? Your first name wouldn't happen to be Uriel, would it?"

"Actually, I go by my middle name, Jacob, now—too many fights in school, you know? It's just a little too close to urinal for my taste. Only my great-uncle called me by my first name."

"Your great-uncle didn't happen to be Walter Sullinger, did he?"

A warm smile flushed the man's face. "Yes, he was my great-uncle," he said softly.

"Ha!" crowed the doctor. "Michael's calling card! This is your lucky day, Mr. Sullinger. Alice, if you would, give me five minutes and then send Mr. Sullinger to my office."

"Yes, Dr. Kessler," said Alice. Then she turned to Mr. Sullinger. "Take a seat in the lobby and when I say so, it's the third door on the right, right down that way," she said, gesturing in the direction the doctor was walking.

Mr. Sullinger gave the receptionist a gentle nod and took a seat nearby. It was fifteen minutes later when she looked up from her computer in his direction and pointed with her nose to the doctor's office.

Mr. Sullinger rose to his feet and ambled down the hall to the third door on the right. He gazed at the door knowing full well that to pass through the door meant going back; back to the beginning. *Oh, how far he had come to find himself here, and yet, how far would he have to go to find the answers he sought?* He knocked ever so gently three times. "Come in, Mr. Sullinger," came a voice from the other side. He turned the knob slowly and took his first apprehensive steps into the room.

"Come in, come in. I've been waiting for this moment for quite some time," said the doctor. "Please sit down. Your great-Uncle Walt was a patient of mine for many years. You could even say, I cut my doctoral teeth on his case," he bristled with pride as he rose to shake the man's hand. "Yes, I was right out of med school when I was first introduced to Walter."

Mr. Sullinger walked across the room, shook the good doctor's hand, slid the chair back from the front of the desk, and quietly sat down. "Usually, I would ask you what brought you here, but I don't think that's necessary in this case," said Dr. Kessler. Mr. Sullinger blushed and raised his eyebrows. "So,

Jacob, is it now? Okay. It's a pity, though, because if you did use your first name, your initials would be *US*, and that's bigger than both of us, but if you feel more comfortable with Jacob?" Mr. Sullinger gave a nod. "I imagine you have many questions. Where shall we begin?"

Jacob took a moment to think… "Michael's calling card," he said. "That's my first question. I have never heard that phrase before."

Dr. Kessler plopped down in his thick leather chair and smiled, and then gestured with his hand. "When fate hands you a full house and life has only a pair showing. You know…Kismet. You walked in on the same day that I had a cancellation; it's fate."

"Fate?" asked Jacob. "You mentioned the archangel Michael, do you believe in angels, Dr. Kessler?"

"Do you mean, do I believe in God?"

"Well, I'm not familiar with the Bible, doctor, but I do know about angels." Jacob blushed a little as the words left his lips.

"Fate, God, the Holy spirit, Karma, Allah…It's all the same thing, Jacob. They are merely the same thing seen from different cultures. To quibble about details is to play a fool's game. If you like, your Great Uncle Walt would have said, 'Only the gardener knows the right time and place for the planting of a good seed.'"

A big warm smile graced Jacob's face. "Yep, sure enough—he would have put it just that way."

"You know, he spoke of you often. He was very fond of you," said the doctor.

Jacob's face sank a little and his eyes glanced at the floor. "I was very fond of him. I should have visited him before…" He paused. "Before he died."

"Why didn't you?" asked the doctor.

"I…I don't know…there was…I mean, well…I just couldn't after…" The doctor waited patiently for him to find the courage. "You'll have to excuse me, doctor, I'm new at this. I've never…I mean…" Jacob took a deep breath. "I never thought I would find myself in this position." There was a hapless smile on his battered face.

The doctor smiled warmly. "No one does, Jacob. We all have trouble with the past. We all have ghosts in our heads that we struggle to understand."

"So, how do I start?" asked Jacob.

"Well, you can start by telling me about your lapel," said Dr. Kessler.

"Huh, what?" puzzled Jacob.

"Your lapel. The initials on your lapel are ME. Yet yours are US or JS, if you like."

Jacob looked down and laughed. "It's a long story, I'm afraid," said Jacob.

"It looks like it was once a nice suit."

"It was," said Jacob. "It's not mine, of course, but well…that's *ME*, isn't it? …or at least it was *ME*," he said with chagrin. "Actually, I'm not sure any more who *me* is."

"Did you steal it?" asked the doctor. Jacob just looked away. "There are no secrets you can't share here, Jacob. Think of my office as a sanctuary. You are safe here."

"I don't think I'm ready for that yet," answered Jacob.

"Okay, tell me about your relationship with your Uncle Walter. How much did you know about him? Let's start there. Tell me about your first meeting."

Jacob sat in silence a moment and clenched his jaw. He turned his attention to the woods outside the office window. There was something about the way the trees' branches seem to reach out for each other. It gave him comfort. He bit his lower lip and shook his head as he struggled with his words. The doctor waited patiently in silence.

The Sprig

Jacob took a deep breath and sighed. "Some of my earliest memories are of when I was six; we lived in Jersey," he began.

"We lived in Essex, in a run-down apartment building on the Southeast side. Thanks to my father's addictions, we were perpetually poor. It was some time shortly after my sixth birthday when my father and Uncle Matt began taking long trips. My father and Uncle Matt would disappear for a week or so, once a year. My father said it was to help old Great uncle Walt with work around the house, but when he returned, he would spend the next two weeks grumbling, about how *That rich old bastard wouldn't come up off of any real money.*

"One day after my eighth birthday, my uncle Matt had a bright idea. 'Let's bring the kid and the little woman along. It might soften the old fucker up,' he said. So, my father piled all of us into our 1979 Volkswagen station wagon for the eight-and-a-half-hour ride to Clay County, Virginia. I sat in the back seat with Uncle Matt. He sat almost the whole way with one arm stretched out along the back of the seat, glassy-eyed, staring at me, twirling my hair with the tips of his fingers. It was a very long ride.

"After what seemed like a lifetime to my eight-year-old mind, we arrived at the sprawling estate and grand old colonial house of my Great uncle Walt, AKA, the "Rich Old Bastard." If I think really hard, I can still see him sitting in his full-backed wicker patio chair with a tall glass of spiked tea. He always wore a thin-rimmed fedora and carried a walking stick. I wasn't quite sure whether he needed it, or whether he just liked the way it looked. Either way, his ruddy face didn't seem pleased to see our car pull up the long winding dirt drive.

"Then we came to a stop, the car door swung open and I slumped out. His eyes lit up like a street lamp and a half-smile half-smirk graced his face as he rose to his feet to greet us. "What's this? What's this?" he exclaimed. 'Well,

well, well! What do we have here? A young traveler? Kindred spirit perhaps?' Uncle Matt glanced over at my father and grinned a devious grin.

"I remember distinctly, he was a roly-poly gentleman with an infectious laugh that sounded like a goose chortle, a bone white mustache which curled into his mouth and a lap that disappeared when he sat down. He had a love of fine things and it had taken him around the world. Through the course of his life, he had made a handsome living off the sales of these goods; mostly rare books and art, but on occasion, he would return with rare plants to place in his garden.

"The Tanglewood estate had a rather large garden and green house full of all sorts of strange and wonderful plants. As a child, I couldn't have imagined a man's life could be reflected in the scenery of a garden. But as Great uncle Walt once said, 'The landscape of a man's deeds is rooted in the dark fertile soil of his mind.' At eight, I didn't understand the special significance of these words. How could I have possibly known?

"My father called up from the driveway, 'We thought it was time for Uriel to meet his Great uncle Walt.' My father glanced over at my mother. 'Well, don't just stand there, take him up to see Uncle Walt.' My mother was never keen on my father's schemes, but she always played along, for fear of reprisal.

"She took my hand and gave it a squeeze before dragging me up the steps to his porch. Except for his right hand, which rocked the head of his cane from side to side, Uncle Walt didn't move. He stood expressionless, examining me. He wore large baggy plaid trousers and suspenders over a clean white long sleeve shirt. There I stood, toe to toe with what seemed like a towering red-faced carny. We both stood in silence for an awkward moment looking each other over. 'So, this is the famed Uriel Jacob Sullinger,' he said.

'Mama? Are we at the circus?' I asked cautiously.

"Uncle Walt looked down at me with one raised eyebrow, scratched his chin and twisted his mustache, and then took a deep breath. 'Ha!' he laughed. He poked me in the stomach with his cane. 'Hmm, what a strange sprig you are,' he said. 'I shall have to plant you in my garden and see what grows, ha, ha, ha!' he chuckled to himself.

I squeezed my mother's hand. 'Mom?'

'Yes dear?' she answered.

'What's a sprig?'

"'Never mind, honey, it's just a saying,' she said. 'Well, we'll just freshen up a little before dinner, it was such a long drive down.' She pulled me into the house and let the screen door slam behind us. 'Georgia! Georgia!' My mother called out. 'You can prepare the guest rooms. We will be staying for a week this time,' she said as we made our way through the house toward the kitchen.

"Georgia was a tall, slender, thirty-year-old black woman with short cropped hair and a flair for sarcasm.

'Mrs. S, y'all shoulda told me you were bringin' the youngin',' she said flippantly. 'I would have brought my floppy shoes and clown nose, so as I could entertain him for the week.'

'Oh, come now, Georgia, he won't be any trouble. Besides, I'm here too. I'll look after him,' said my mother.

'So, you say, Mrs. S, but they ain't nothing for a child to do, but get in trouble in this big old place...Why, he could get lost in the woods out back, you know?'

"Uncle Walt's voice came from behind us. He had quietly followed us inside. 'Don't fret too much, Georgia, I'll keep an eye on him. I haven't shown anybody around the old place in years. It'll be nice to have some company on my walks after dinner.'

'Well, all right then, Mr. Sullinger. You watch over him, I got too many things to do around here to keep my eye on him.'

"Uncle Walt smiled and patted me on the back. 'Come with me, lad, we will go exploring whilst the grownups unpack.'

"My mother let loose of my hand and gave me a gentle nudge in Uncle Walt's direction. He and I walked slowly through the old house, out the back door to the yard and to the terraced garden beyond. Instantly, my senses were met with the full-bodied smell of rich dark earth and fresh grass clippings. The pallet of my great uncle's garden lacked nothing for color. Every shade of every color seemed to be represented in a panoramic banquet for the eyes.

"His garden was carefully manicured by two Hispanic men, Juan and Pedro. Their endless labor had molded the landscape into a stairway of hedgerows and flower beds which stretched backward and upward to a plateau where an enormous greenhouse stood, with vines of fruit laden grapes which hung like a heavy green tapestry before it.

"Uncle Walt spent the afternoon teaching me the names of each plant and where in the world he found it. He sipped his spiked tea gingerly from a glass held between his middle finger and his thumb and pointed to each plant in the row, as if he were on a first-name basis with it. I listened and marveled at the old man's passion, a child learning to love the meaning of life.

"Once we had strolled the length of his terraces, we arrived at the double glass doors of the greenhouse. He pulled on a chain which ran into his right pocket and a ring full of keys rose into his hand. He then paused, and took a long slow look at me. A melancholy smile swept across his face. 'No,' he said. 'I dare say, you're not ready for this garden yet.' With that, he stuffed the keys back into his pocket. 'Come,' he said. 'We should get ready for dinner; Georgia will be calling us soon.'

"As we turned back toward the house, I looked over my shoulder one last time at the muted green calling to me from the other side of the glass; what mysteries of the darkened corners of the world lay beyond those doors? I could only wonder.

"Just as he had said, as we neared the back door, Georgia was approaching from the other side. 'I was just comin' to call ya'll ta dinner. Did you and the youngin' have a nice talk, Mr. Sullinger?'

'Yes Georgia, I talked my heart out at the young lad and he took it like a man.' Uncle Walt winked at me and smiled. 'He might be a fruitful kind of seed after all, Georgia,' he chortled.

"'That's good, Mr. Sullinger. That's good,' said Georgia, as she set about putting the finishing touches on the table. 'Now, if you and your kin are ready, ya'll can eat. I'll just call 'em in from outside.'

"Georgia swept passed me down the hall and outside to call my father and uncle Matt in for dinner. 'Ya'll can come eat, Mr. S! Vittles is on the table!' My father and uncle Matt were standing near the car having a lengthy discussion about money and the cost of the trip. My mother was upstairs unpacking and partaking in the *potpourri* and other *medicinals*, for her nerves, of course. Georgia called up from the base of the stairs, 'It's time for dinner now, Mrs. S. Ya'll can come down now.'

"We stayed for dinner that night, and two more. Then I saw Uncle Walt give my father a big wad of money and with that, my father packed us all back into the car and we returned to Jersey. As we pulled away from the drive, my father blurted out with a smile, 'Good news, Jake, you will be spending your summers with Uncle Walt for a while!' My mother shook her head and rubbed her temples, which usually meant she was really uncomfortable with the whole situation.

'Do you really need me to come next time?' she asked.

'Never mind that,' said Uncle Matt. 'Where's my cut. It was my idea to bring the kid.' My father reached into his pocket and handed a big roll of bills to my mother.

'Here,' he said. 'Count out a thousand for the miserable parasite in the back seat.'

"'Hey! I resent that,' said Uncle Matt. 'I'm not miserable! I'm a very lovable parasite and you know it!' My mother handed the bills over the seat and Uncle Matt laughed like a hyena as he took the money.

"I, on the other hand, watched Uncle Walt's house get smaller and smaller behind us. 'Do I have to wait until summer?' I asked. My mother shot me a worried glance over her shoulder and then glared at Uncle Matt in disgust as he counted his money.

"When summer break came, I was dropped off at Tanglewood, bags in hand and sporting a new suit complete with suspenders, bow tie and Hush Puppies shoes. My mother and father stayed long enough to negotiate a price and left without saying goodbye. They sped away with a fresh new wad of money and a question of impertinence in the mind of their only son.

"That summer, Uncle Walt taught me how to play poker. We played with different coins from around the world. He taught me about the different countries of the world and all their strange customs. He had a map of the world lacquered into the mantle of his desk. We would spend endless hours pouring over it and talking about all the cultures. With each new country, my world grew larger and more complex. The boundaries of Jersey were stretched to the Far East and India as well as to Africa and the Isle of Madagascar. As far north as Siberia and Mongolia, and south as far as New Zealand and the Isle of Tasmania.

"With every visit to the grand old house, I grew closer and closer to the old man and further and further from my father and mother. The distance, to my young mind, was measured by a growing sense of distrust of my mother and father. Theirs was a world of drunken debauchery, drugs, endless days of sleeping, and sprawling nights of argument. I found myself spending many tumultuous nights in wistful thought of the Tanglewood estate.

"The following summer was spent on tending his gardens and on long walks through the woods. There was an old cemetery bordered by a short stone wall which lay way back in the woods. There, the Sullinger family was laid to rest. Uncle Walt shared with me the history of our family name. It was a history my father never cared about. My grandfather and grandmother, two of my great aunts and both my great grandparents on the Sullinger side, lay side by side beneath the sweeping limbs and shadows of four giant willows. In all, there were three generations represented there.

"Uncle Walt spoke with reverence about their lives and sacrifice and with a deep respect for the family name. The cemetery had eleven graves in it, some dating all the way back to 1834, and he had something to say about each and every one—save for one. It was a grave and stone separated from the rest by one plot. He took me from grave to grave, carefully avoiding that one. He clutched his cane tightly in his right hand and pointed with it to each stone in the yard.

"After he had reached the last grave and still hadn't spoken of the solitary grave, I felt compelled to ask. 'What about that one?' I said as I pointed to the plot. As the words left my lips, I longed to take them back. Uncle Walt paused in silence a moment. He bit his lower lip as he stared over at the standing stone. His eyes fell and he glanced down at the soil beneath his feet and lightly kicked at the loose earth.

"'You know, Uriel, there are many kinds of gardens,' he said, lightly twisting his walking stick into the ground. 'This, too is a garden—of a sort. But this garden hides a demon in the weeds.' He paused and looked at the head of his cane. He took hold of it by the shaft and lifted it to his eyes and gazed at the intricate carving which made up its crest. He rolled the cane between his fingers and pondered its hidden meaning. 'Yes indeed,' he said. 'Satan himself hides among these flagstones.'

"For the first time, I realized that his cane bore a strange significance to him. It was only then that I bothered to examine it closely. The carving was of a naked man wrestling a white serpent. The man's face was twisted in rage as the snake coiled around his body and trailed on to the point. The man held the snake just behind the head in an everlasting struggle for control.

"'There is a sickness in our family, Uriel. A curse within the blood. It took my son from me, and I can only hope he will be the last.' His jaw clenched in a defiant grimace as he stared at the lone flagstone. Time stood still as I waited for him to elaborate…He shrugged his eyebrows and yielded to the bitter truth. 'But that's a subject that will have to wait until you are a little older, I think.' Uncle Walt took a deep sigh and turned back toward the house. I stood there a moment and stared at the distant grave. The awareness hit me like a water balloon. The old man's pain was marked by loss and loneliness, and I represented the hope of a second chance.

'Are you coming?' he asked. 'You know, Georgia is making her famous cornbread. You don't want to miss that, do you?'

'I'm right behind you, Uncle Walt,' I said. 'I can't let you eat it all.' He let out a laugh and we walked side by side in the solace of our kinship. We tracked the heavenly scent of fresh cornbread, through the woods and down the garden path like a couple of bears following their noses.

"That night after dinner, I disappeared into the woods unnoticed and sought out the cemetery, in particular, the solitary grave. There I read the inscription. Robert Sullinger from 1957 to 1983. *A distant star shines thrice as bright.* I heard a woman's voice come from behind me as I read the words.

'Robert was his son, Uriel,' Georgia said, standing at the entrance to the yard. 'He was sick, you see? And no one could help him.'

'What did he die of, Georgia?' I asked.

'Well, if Mr. Sullinger wanted you to know, he'd a told ya himself. It would be disrespectful of me to say—ya'll be'n kin and all.'

'But he died so young, it must have been something bad,' I said, staring down at the grave.

"'Oh, it was bad all right, he fought it for years. But it took him, all the same. He was always a strange boy, smart as a cracker,' Georgia said with a far off look in her eyes. 'He's not sufferin' now, though. He's finally at rest. So, let's not dig up old sorrows. Come on, youngin', let's get back to the house. I got to give Mr. Sullinger his medicine.'

"I turned to her full of questions, but her eyes shut me down. She shook her head with a somber face and said, 'In good time, child, he will tell you everything, when he's ready. He loves you, you know? That old man loves you very much.' She wrapped her arm around me as I drew near and we walked slowly back to the house. 'Whatcha say to a piece of my famous Key-lime pie?'

'Do you mean another piece? I snuck a piece before I came out here,' I said, laughing.

"'Why, ya sneaky little wiggaboo,' she said, laughing. 'Well, I guess another slice won't kill ya. It might fattin' ya up some though. You know, other than Robert, you the only kin to Mr. Sullinger I ever considered liken.' You alright wit me.' Georgia laughed and pulled me in close. 'We family now, boy.' At that moment, I felt a bond for family I had never known before; a kinship with all life and with those who shoulder the vulnerability of sincerity and the costly devotion of love."

"Okay, Jacob, I'm afraid I'm going to have to stop you here for now," said Dr. Kessler. "I am going to make arrangements for you to stay here for a week and we can continue with your Great uncle Walt in the morning; say, at ten o'clock?"

Jacob froze and looked down, and then back up at the doctor. "Do I have to?" he asked.

"Well, no. You don't have to, but my schedule is much less demanding tomorrow and I want you to devote some time to putting your memories together. You can relax and consolidate those memories that stand out in your mind as significant."

Jacob drew a deep breath and nodded. "I have a lot to think about, don't I?"

"Remember, Jacob, it's not as important to me that you recall as it is for you. Take your time and try to see the past as it was; unvarnished, as they say." Jacob gave a resolute nod and rose from his chair. Dr. Kessler walked Jacob back out to the lobby and presented him to Alice. "Alice," he said, "would you please reserve a room for Mr. Sullinger?" The good doctor leaned in and whispered into Alice's ear, "Walter's room was 207, I believe. If it's available, give him that one." He then turned and smiled at Jacob. "Alice will take care of you. I want to see you first thing after breakfast at ten o'clock, I think. You know where my office is."

Jacob tilted his head and said, "I will have to make a call before I can stay. Do you have a phone I can use? It's a local call, of course."

Alice raised an eyebrow. "There's a pay phone in the lobby you can use."

"I don't have any money on me right now," said Jacob. "Is there any way you could…?"

"Come on, Alice, have a heart," said Dr. Kessler.

"Oh, okay, but only because you're one of my favorite doctors," she said with a smile. "You can use my phone. I will give you an outside line, but you better make it short. You know Mrs. Fontaine doesn't like private calls on the hospital's lines?"

"You can tell her it was my idea, Alice," said Dr. Kessler.

Alice rolled her eyes. "Oh, I'm sure that will calm her right down. You know how she is."

Alice led Jacob over to her desk, picked up the receiver and handed it to Jacob. She pressed the line he was to use and then she walked away.

Brrrrrrr…brrrrrrrr…Click, click… "Hello," a woman's soft voice spoke on the other end of the line.

"Hello Rose, it's me, Jacob. I'm still here at the hospital."

"Oh, Jacob, how did it go? What did the doctor say?"

"The doctor thinks I should stay here for a week or so. Would you ask Georgia to keep hope? You are welcome to stay at Tanglewood until…until the doctor thinks I am ready to leave."

"Oh, I see. Don't you worry, Jacob, I have always kept hope."

"You can return to Angelo's, if you want. You don't have to wait for me or anything. I will call you when I get out, I mean when I'm ready to leave, if you still want me to."

"Oh Jacob, don't be ridiculous, of course, I want you to. Take your time, I will be waiting for your call."

"Thank you, Rose, you're a saint. I'm sorry I never…I mean we never…"

"Jacob? I will be here when you are ready. Until then, take care and I will keep hope."

"Thank you, Rosa, goodbye," Jacob held the receiver close to his face for a few seconds after she had hung up, hoping the words which ached in his heart would fall out of his mouth. His breath shortened in a feeble effort to spit them out, but he could only muster a whisper. "Jacob, you coward," he said. Silently, he placed the receiver down and looked around the lobby. Alice was helping another patient gather her things and finish filling out her paperwork. She glanced over at Jacob standing quietly by her desk.

"Okay, stay right here, Mrs. Shumer. I have to show a gentleman to his room. I'll be right back. In the meantime, you can finish filling out your information. We will need your medical history and the history of any family members."

The woman fumbled a bit with the pen in a state of confused apprehension. "But, but, but I don't think I can—"

"Yes, I know it's a lot to remember. Do the best you can dear, and I will help you when I get back." Alice smiled gently at the woman as she turned her attention to Jacob. She looked Jacob up and down as she crossed the lobby. "I suppose you didn't bring anything else to wear, did you?"

Jacob cringed. "No, I didn't, I'm sorry. I wasn't planning on staying."

"Naturally," Alice grumbled, "they never do…okay, I will check the lost and found. You may have to wear a belt. Maybe your roommate, Boo, will have something you can wear. You look about his size." Alice noticed the worried look on Jacob's face. "Oh…You'll like Boo, he's a hoot. Ha! At least that's what he answers to anyway. He suffers from PTSD. You should know that upfront. All I will say is, be prepared for anything and you won't be disappointed." She shook her head and laughed to herself as she walked.

Jacob followed her down the hall to the second wing and up the stairs to the second floor. Jacob took note and counted the doors as they passed them. "Your room will be 207," said Alice. "It was your uncle's room, though it was a private room then." She paused for a moment at the door. "Go on in and meet your new roommate," she smirked.

"Thank you—I think," said Jacob.

Jacob entered the room slowly. A rather gaunt man stood silently staring out of the room's big double-paned glass window. Jacob heard the door squeak closed and latch behind him. He stood quietly in the spacious room. A TV that hung from the ceiling between the two beds squawked out the theme song of *Wheel of Fortune*. Pat Sajak's voice rang out and immediately faded into the background, as Jacob noticed the man before him was standing at attention.

"So, you are my new infantryman," the man blurted out without turning around. Jacob studied the back of him. He was a tall, thin black man in his late thirties with short cropped hair and a full-length nightgown. His shoulders were broad and cocked back, as if he were ready for a fight. His night clothes were striped up and down from shoulder to ankle hem in thin blue lines on an off white, or eggshell cloth. "What took you so long? I've been expecting you since those *turban-ites* took the high ground. They're holed up out there in those cliffs."

Jacob looked out of the window to the forest of elms, oaks, and poplar trees that sloped down and away just beyond the grounds. He smiled and stood at attention. "Do you mean up there, sir?" The man spun around on his heels.

"Yes, I mean up there. The enemy has been hunkered down up there for weeks. I am Captain Luemarius Glass, your direct commanding officer. You can call me Boo. That's what they all call me around the base. It confuses the enemy."

"Yes sir," said Jacob. "Private J. Sullinger reporting for duty, sir. If you don't mind, sir, which bed is mine? Sir."

"They're both mine!" snapped Boo. "But you can use that one until your replacement comes," he said pointing at the bed closest to the door.

"My replacement, sir?" Jacob's voice was apprehensive.

"Yes, your replacement! They never seem to last long under my command."

Jacob stifled a laugh. "I see, sir. Perhaps you are underestimating me, sir."

"Not an underestimation really, but making you aware of what you are in for, private. There are a lot of enemies in there that we are going to have to deal with."

"Yes sir. I see there are, but you are not alone, sir. I am with you…sir."

Boo paused and a confused look crossed his face. He blinked a couple of times and then gave a stern nod.

"Sir," said Jacob. "Permission to stand down, sir. I have to prepare for tomorrow's battle."

"Yes, yes, of course. Dismissed, Private. Ready your things. Second Lieutenant Jefferies will take the watch tonight," said Boo, as he turned his attention back to the window. "As you were."

"Yes sir," said Jacob as he unbuttoned his coat and kicked off his shoes. He slid the coat off and hung it on the bed post by his pillow. He rummaged through the drawers of the night stand and found a nightgown identical to Boo's. "Perfect," he whispered to himself as he laid it on the bed. He then got undressed and slid the gown on over his head. Although it was only eight thirty, he climbed into bed and stared up at the ceiling. The television blathered on into what became the sound-scape to his thoughts.

His uncle Walt, Rosalinda, Gabriel, Monsieur Diabolus, and even Hope wrestled around inside his skull. There were so many shattered pieces to his life. What seemed real might not be and what was a dream could have been real. He glanced over at Boo diligently staring out of the window and thought, *how is it that the mind can so easily alter our view of the world?* His memories were so vivid, so lucid. *How could they be anything but true?* He could still hear Satan's laughter and the incessant ringing of the bell.

He could still feel the warmth of Michael's arms wrapped around him as he was pulled from the water, and yet, he couldn't remember how he found himself on the dock. It made him question his whole life and everyone in it. Then a memory of when he was eight floated up from the depths of his heart. It was one of Uncle Walt holding a fist full of cards. He was sitting across from a pile of Egyptian coins, smiling in his thin rimmed fedora and bushy mustache. "It's your turn, Master Jacob," he said with a devious grin. "Lay your cards down. I paid to see them," he chuckled.

This was Jacob's last thought, as slumber stole the night away. Boo quietly turned and watched Jacob fall asleep. The subtle look of apprehension on his face gave way to a humble look of hope, then he quietly turned back toward the window.

The Tree of Being

The next morning dawned bright as the sun streamed in from their eastern view. Jacob squinted and covered his face with his arm. He laid there for several minutes before realizing where he was. He felt the presence of someone standing beside his bed so he turned to find Boo inches from his face. "Are you coming, Private? Mess is being served. Reveille has come and gone, soldier."

Jacob let out a soft groan as he succumbed to the morning light. "Yes sir, Boo," he said softly. "I wouldn't want to miss the pleasure of your company, sir."

Boo took a step back and Jacob rose slowly to sit on the edge of the bed. "You're not going dressed like that are you, Private?" asked Boo. "No self-respecting soldier would be caught in public wearing his nightgown," he grumbled as he walked to the closet. He riffled through the clothes and then spun around and handed a pair of blue and white pajamas. "Here, you can wear one of my uniforms."

Jacob opened his eyes wide at the sight. "These?" he exclaimed. "These are pa—"

"Now there's no need to thank me," said Boo. "You make a good decoy dressed in my uniform. Put it on and let's go to breakfast."

"Yes sir," said Jacob as he rubbed his eyes. He put the pajamas on and followed Boo as he shuffled out of the door and down the hall in a kind of soft march to whatever passed for a cadence in his head. Boo led him down the wide stairs and then turned right at the bottom and crossed the hall. There was a set of double doors that led to a courtyard. Once beyond those doors, he found a fair-sized courtyard under an opaque glass roof. Tables were set discreetly among the grass and low hedges. The air was thick with the smell of bacon and eggs, syrup, coffee, and toast.

Jacob's stomach grumbled at the thought of breakfast. He hadn't eaten since three o'clock the day before. Boo grabbed a tray and got in line with the other patients, and Jacob followed suit.

"Lieutenant Jefferies has already eaten. He likes to start early and return to his post," Boo said with a smile. "He's the finest example of a soldier I've ever had under my command." Jacob looked around the yard for anyone who might look like he belonged in the military. The courtyard was full of people, young and old, but no one that even remotely looked of a military background. In fact, Boo seemed to move through the crowd completely unnoticed. There wasn't a friend or compatriot who recognized him.

Boo quietly filled his tray with a roll, a small portion of eggs, two slices of bacon, and some grits. The tray was conspicuously bare. He gazed across the courtyard and found a table in the corner where he could watch everyone cautiously. Jacob matched Boo's movements almost to the letter and took a seat right next to him facing the whole of the room. Boo snatched up his fork and stared at his food as if he were looking at a plate of garbage.

"What's the matter, sir? Aren't you hungry?" Jacob asked.

"Not really," said Boo. "I lost my appetite years ago. Don't know why I even bother, some days." He scooped up a modicum of eggs and sniffed at them and then slipped them gingerly into his mouth, all the while with his eyes fixed on the movements of the crowd. "I like to sit in the corner and watch for interlopers."

"Interlopers, sir?" asked Jacob.

"Yeah, you know…possible spies, or traitors. One can never be too careful down here on the front line."

"Oh, I see," said Jacob. At that moment, Jacob noticed Dr. Kessler enter the courtyard and head toward their table. As he approached, he acknowledged Boo with a nod. Boo's movements froze, his fork poised before his mouth. He glared up at the doctor.

"I've come to talk to Private Sullinger here," said Dr. Kessler.

"Shock," said Boo.

"And awe," answered the doctor. Jacob choked on his eggs when he realized Boo had just made their table Checkpoint Charlie. His hacking split the soft chatter of the other patients and for a moment, the courtyard fell silent.

Boo resumed eating. "Okay, you're cleared. What is the news from headquarters? Are you removing my private from his post already?" asked Boo.

"No, no, nothing like that. I want to schedule a rendezvous with him on the Southeast veranda of the hospital…ehm…I mean base, if you don't object, Captain."

"Of course not, Doctor. He seems to have developed a nasty cough," Boo said, glancing over at Jacob still struggling to swallow. "We have to keep our men healthy. Put your report on my desk when you're done."

"Absolutely, Captain. As soon as we're finished," said Dr. Kessler as he smiled at Jacob. "I'll be waiting there when you are done with breakfast, Jacob." Jacob smiled back and gave a nod.

"I'll be there shortly, doctor," he said.

After breakfast, Jacob and Boo parted ways and Jacob crossed the hospital to the veranda on the southeast side. Dr. Kessler was waiting on a bench overlooking the green sloping hills and elm woods. "Ah, good," he said as he saw the blue stripes of Jacob's pajamas. "You made it. I trust you had a good breakfast with Boo."

"Ha! yes, he's an interesting kind of person," said Jacob as he approached the bench.

"That's putting it mildly," said the doctor. "Please, have a seat. I'd like to hear more about your memories." Jacob took a seat at the other end of the bench.

"Boo keeps mentioning a Lieutenant Jefferies. Tell me, Doctor, is there anyone here that might answer to that name?"

"Well, of course, I don't have the registry here at my disposal, but I don't recall any Jefferies being admitted."

"Hmm…Whoever he is, he must have been important."

"Why do you say?"

"Because I've only been in that room one night and I have heard his name five times. That tells me this Jefferies is one important person—or at least, he is to Boo."

"That would be a good guess, I would say," said Dr. Kessler. "None of his other roommates mentioned a Jefferies. I wonder why he chose you to confide in. At any rate, we're not here to talk about Boo. I don't have many appointments today, so I want you to pick up where we left off yesterday."

"Okay, I'll try to remember where we were. Let's see…We talked about the family plots and Uncle Walt's son Robert. That was on my third visit to Tanglewood. Well, by my fourth summer at Tanglewood—"

"If you don't mind me asking, how old were you then?" asked Dr. Kessler.

"Oh…twelve, I think. That was the year we moved to the Bronx, my uncle Matt got out of prison for B&E and aggravated assault that year," Jacob said scratching his chin.

"If you don't mind me asking, what prompted the move?"

Jacob gave a half smirk, half smile. "Oh, it was child protective services," he said plainly. "We always seemed to move whenever they appeared at the door. Sometimes in the middle of the night."

"And your uncle Matt sounds like a real character."

Jacob looked down and nervously picked at the paint of the bench. "Oh, he was, that's for sure. He was the devil's own." Dr. Kessler took note of Jacob's response.

"Anyway, you were saying…"

"Oh yeah…Well, by that time, I had become right at home. Juan and Pablo called me *Spanky* and Georgia would cook whatever I wanted. Uncle Walt spoiled me with trinkets and candies from around the globe. There was an unspoken feeling that I belonged at Tanglewood and an increasing sentiment to avoid talking about my life beyond the stone walls of the estate. It was a sentiment which I encouraged with a full and fattened heart.

"This was the year the seed of greed was planted in my heart. I got a taste, just a taste mind you, of what it would be like to be wealthy. It left me with an addiction to money and power, a hunger which could not be satisfied. I'm afraid at this point, the stage was set for the bartering of my soul."

Dr. Kessler tilted his head a little and raised an eyebrow at the notion. "Interesting," he said.

"What's interesting?" asked Jacob.

"Oh, it's probably nothing. Please continue."

Jacob slunk back on the bench and looked across the horizon, as if he were gazing back in time. "Okay…Let's see…It was mid-August when Uncle Walt asked me to tread the garden with him after lunch. 'I've got a house full of tales to share,' he said. So, we walked the garden once more—down the hedgerows and through the rose beds to the top of the yard. There, a Japanese pagoda stood three feet tall between two short bonsai trees to the right of the double doors of his greenhouse. His face beamed with an impish pride; as if he had stolen the Hope Diamond. 'This,' he said with a whisper, 'this is my special garden. Only the most rare and unusual plants thrive here.'

"There was a thick chain and lock wrapped through the handles of the double doors. He pulled the key from his pocket, took hold of the heavy lock, inserted the key and turned. The lock clicked and fell open. I felt my heart swell within my chest. He pulled the chain from the handles and then looked down at my eager face and smiled. 'This will be our secret, you understand. Some of these plants are not allowed in the US. I have to keep them under tight control.' He placed his finger over his mouth. 'So Mum's the word, okay?'

"I nodded my head in nervous anticipation of what lay inside. He pulled the lock loose and opened the doors. My eyes were met by a thousand shades of green, a dash of red, white and orange, blues and even purple. The air was thick and moist like a tropical jungle. A solar heater kept the building at just the right temperature and a sprinkler system set on a timer provided the right level of moisture.

"Uncle Walt stood there gloating like a proud father, smiling at his crowning achievement. 'Look around you, Master Uriel, these are the rarest plants in the world. Flowers from Madagascar, figs from Indonesia, carnivorous plants from the depths of the Amazon, and wild Cassiopeia acuminata from the Congo. One by one, I have brought them here and carefully nurtured them.'

"He introduced me to his cherished ones, and each came with a story of their meeting, each story more colorful than the last. Some were full of drama, some were full of intrigue and sometimes even danger, but one story in particular interested me more than all the rest. It was the story of the rare and beautiful flower known as the scorpion orchid, a flower he acquired in Papua New Guinea. It was a story which was spun like a web, with a beautiful woman, a headhunting tribal chief and, like any good web, a poisonous spider was at the center of it all.

"We turned a corner and the thick foliage opened to a clearing with a concrete bench and a cobblestone floor. We were surrounded by cascades of flowering wisteria vines, Casablanca lilies and moon flowers not yet open. There was a conspicuous hole dug in the ground beside the bougainvillea which he stared down at momentarily (as if to honor some future moment) and then moved on. He approached a thicket of small white orchids and took one delicate flower into his fingers. His face shone with a melancholy light, as if the sight of the orchid had evoked some sacred ghost from the past. He plucked the flower from its perch and strolled over to the bench which sat before his holy place.

"'This is my most cherished flower, though it's not the rarest by far,' he said. 'No. Not the rarest at all, a mere segregate for that flower.' He smiled as he gazed at the speckled white beauty. 'The rarest flower I was forced to leave behind.' Uncle Walt bit his lower lip and sighed as the flood of memories swept him away. 'It was in early summer, before the monsoons, you see, when we trekked into the mountains of New Guinea,' he began his tale with some trepidation."

Jacob paused for a moment and looked at the doctor across the bench and said, "You know, doctor, reflecting on this story I am about to tell makes me wonder where my angels came from." The doctor took note of Jacob's reference to angels but quietly listened as Jacob continued to share the words of Uncle Walt.

'We crossed the lowlands where the nights were hot and the mosquitoes were unbearable. The jungle was thick with moss and vines and the volcanic mud swamps bubbled like cauldrons of the underworld.

"'Once we had ventured a week into the interior, the gentle sloping forest met with giant limestone cliffs, spires and gullies, caves and crevasses nearly impossible to forge. We slowly made our way across the Ramu River and neared the headwaters of the Kratke range. There we camped for the night. We were searching for a rare night blooming Jessamine that grows on the cliffs of the Finisterre mountains.' Uncle Walt's eyes burned like embers with the memory and I, like a moth, was mesmerized by their light.

"'It was there in our camp that I noticed the scorpion orchid. A small patch of them lay hidden among the ferns surrounding our tents. Foolish me. I knew the orchid hid the venomous Tabuina Varirata, a jumping spider known for the delirium and fever its venom causes just before death. I was so enamored by the orchids—by their speckled white beauty—I just had to walk among their numbers.

"'When I dared to cup one of them between my fingers, I felt the tickle of something crawl up my sleeve. I froze where I stood. The sweat that saturated my shirt made the garment heavy, but slowly, I pulled it up. When the cuff tightened around my forearm, I got the most incredible pain, as if someone stuck a red-hot poker in my arm.

"'I yanked the sleeve up and for a split second, saw the furry legged creature, fangs still buried in my skin. Its eight eyes looked directly into mine before it jumped off my arm into the surrounding shrub. Immediately, my arm began to swell. I cried out in pain and Yagonie, my guide, and the Sherpas came running to my aid. They led me back to camp and prepared food and tried to keep me as comfortable as possible. The med kit was useless. It only held antidote for snake bites, broken bones, and malaria. The fact that we were so far up in the mountains held out little hope for my recovery.

"'What was worse was the native belief of the mountain being cursed. The Sherpas began to get spooked. They spoke of the tribes which lived in the area and how a powerful chief put a curse on the mountain. The tribe that lived on the mountain were fierce and were known to be head hunters.

"'By evening, a fever set in and the sounds of the jungle echoed inside my skull like a symphony of dissidence. The restless chatter of the Sherpas worsened when one of them spotted a honey glider in the tree above my tent. Yagonie tried to calm them down. "Saamantayao! Saamantayao!" they shouted. It was no use, one by one they all began to leave. Yagonie came to me; "They are all leaving,' he said. 'They have seen the spirit ancestor of the local chief and are too frightened to stay."

"'Don't leave me here, Yagonie,' I muttered. 'Don't leave me to die.'

"'I have to go. I must get help. Perhaps I can reach tribe that lives in the next valley. I will return, two or three day,' he said. 'It is your only chance.'

"'If you must go, you must. Leave me with water and go with God's speed,' I said.

"'I will, Mr. Sullinger. I will return as soon as I can.' Yagonie filled my canteen and handed it to me, and then he vanished into the jungle. He never returned.

"Uncle Walt took a deep breath and sighed. His reddish face was softened by his melancholy mind. 'These memories, you see, hang in my head like thoughts of a childhood fun-house as seen through smoked glass and mirrors.' He stopped to take a handkerchief from his pocket and wipe the sweat from his forehead, and then he continued, 'The sounds of the night that surrounded me, the birds and nocturnal creatures squawked like laughter from the depths of the cold dark jungle. Every joint in my body ached with the fever and each beat of my heart was echoed by a sharp throbbing in my arm.

"'My senses wove a thin veil of reality into the fabric of a dream. I heard a bird of paradise calling from the tree above my tent, or perhaps it was the cry of a salutary cassowary. The shadow of a woman danced across the tent wall and stepped in front of the open flap. I saw feathers which looked like tufts of fiery orange and white down tossed into a frenzy of motion and framed by black glistening streaks, feathers that were splayed out in a fan of seduction before the campfire light.

"'There was no way to tell whether what I was seeing was real or imagined. The shifting shadows swirled around me and I felt my body hit the ground with a thud. I was dragged outside to the edge of the fire. I could scarcely open my eyes, but through the haze of my delirium, I saw a scantily dressed woman with light brown skin and black stringy hair. Her large deep brown eyes looked down on me with mercy.

"'There was the sound of a rip and my wounded arm lay swollen and bare. "Ohco monammy biaghow!" she said. Shadows surrounded me on all sides; black faces painted white shifted in and out of the darkness like ghosts of New Guinea. She placed a sharp knife of volcanic glass into the fire. Looking up, I saw the feathers of a bird of paradise cast against the trees and midnight sky. The native chatter echoed from all around, drowning out the buzzing in my ears. The woman turned to me wielding the knife. She looked down, with the reflection of the fire in her eyes. 'You must hold still,' she said plainly.

"'You…you speak English…oh thank god,' I mumbled.

"'Shhh,' she said, 'save your strength…Sigma yao, tayao awyee!'

"'Dozens of hands pinned me hard to the ground and she came down fast with the knife. 'Ahhhhhh!' I screamed. My body writhed beneath the burden of their hands. 'Wha…? What have you done?' I yelled. Her bloody knife laid the skin of my arm open like I was made of tissue paper. She cut the poisoned flesh from me and threw it into the fire. The knife cut and cauterized the wound with two clean slices.'

"Uncle Walt rolled his sleeve up to show me the scar which bore witness to his tale. It was five inches long and an inch wide, but as straight as an arrow. Whatever made the cut, had to be razor sharp.

"There was one lucid moment in the midst of all the anguish. My eyes opened wide and I stared up into the face of compassion. Behind those eyes was a strange and wonderful woman. I knew instantly. I couldn't say how I knew, but I knew. I loved her like no woman on Earth. There is a saying which I heard once in France: "If the poem is deep, complex and beautiful yet hard to define, then she is divine." She was the rarest flower I had ever seen. I spoke the words, 'What a rare and beautiful flower you are,' and then collapsed unconscious. I saw her smile warmly as I slipped into the black of sleep. God only knows how long I lay there sleeping; it felt like weeks.

"'In the mountains of New Guinea, the campfire smoke mingles with the morning fog among the trees creating a veil of white wet smoke laden dew. The voice of the cassowary, rainbow lorikeet, or a great cuckoo-dove seemed to rise from the mist on the mountains like the spirits of the islands calling me back to the realm of the living.

"'For me, this was a gift, the gift of life. It came with the first sight of a spindly plume of white-gray smoke twining its way up from the smoldering coals next to my head. The spirit of life and clarity of mind returned to me. I looked down at my feet and then around the camp on all sides. There was nothing but jungle and the smell of rotting leaf litter mingled with the smell of the campfire. My body ached like I was an old man, but I was alive and felt a strengthening of spirit confirmed by a grumbling in my stomach. My arm was wrapped with leaves and tied off with cloth from my own sleeve.

"'I lay there staring up at the morning light streaming through the canopy. The glistening strands of light shifted ever so slightly back and forth with the movement of the listless leaves. Then a shadow fell over me. I found myself puzzling at what I was seeing.'

"Uncle Walt's face turned cherry red and he let out a chortle. He shook his head from side to side and started laughing to himself.

"'What?' I asked. 'What was it?'

"'You know... Now that I think about it, it wasn't until I noticed his feet on both sides of my head that I remembered that some aborigines wore a koteka...Haha!' He laughed out loud.

"'A ko...ko...texa? What's that?' I asked.

"'Koteka. It's the New Guinea word for penis sheath. Hahahaha!'

"'A what?' I exclaimed.

"'A sheath, a gourd or bamboo stick worn over a man's willy whacker. Hahahaha!' Uncle Walt slapped his knee and wiped a tear from his crested eye. 'So, there I was. Lying flat on the ground staring up at a man's jungle berries and a long bamboo shaft. It looked like a fat brown tick on the end of a stick. If I wasn't so frightened, I probably would have rolled right into the firepit.'

"'What happened next, Uncle Walt? What happened next?'

"'It was Chief Saamantayao. He called out to his warriors and they tied my weakened body to a bamboo pole and carried me through the jungle to their village. They sat me against a large rock and argued back and forth—over what to do with me, no doubt. I watched them banter back and forth until I noticed a pair of eyes staring at me beneath a furrowed brow.

"'It was a young warrior sitting in the shadows of a giant mahogany sharpening his arrows and mumbling to himself. He glared at me with a look of utter contempt. A shouting match broke out between the Chief and one of the elders and the spirited young warrior charge forward yelling, pointing and shaking his bow in the air. The Chief barked out a command and snatched up his machete.

"'Shoving two men aside, he stormed over to where I lay, still tied to the pole. His painted face glared down at me and he mumbled something as he raised his blade into the air. Then his attention was drawn to something. It must have been something which worried him, because his face changed. There was someone standing behind me, the sight of whom stopped him just short of the kill. He lowered his knife and backed away.

"'It was the woman who saved me. She stepped out of a dream and down from the hillside behind me. Quietly, she stepped between the Chief and me. I couldn't know her intentions, but she moved like a panther, slow and deliberate. "Ahkonie bahnatallani ko," she said. I could only decipher her movements. She was defiant, with her shoulders back, her chin up and a deliberate menacing tone in her voice. "Abokatow!" she yelled. "Abokatow kyaya batatii! Ohh, yat to gonia gowana ko."

"'Saamantayao stood there, pondering her words. He raised his chin and gave a nod. "Malana mok taguru ga botii mo," he said, and waved his machete in the air. "Ga botii mo!" he shouted once more.

"'She moved quickly and knelt down beside me. "I bought you some time. Look angry at them—at all of them," she whispered as she untied my hands. "They have never seen a white man with a red face before."

"'So, I glared as angrily as I could across the whole of the group. Not a single man was impressed, I'm afraid,' chuckled Uncle Walt."

"Somehow, I just couldn't imagine Uncle Walt being angry at anyone; he just wasn't that kind of man."

"'At any rate,' he continued, 'she freed me and escorted me to her *menchati*, or stilt house. It was separated from the tribe by a good hundred meters or so. Once we were there, she spoke freely. "My name is Marta," she said. "I am a doctor and a botanist from Spain. I was sent with Father Shapiro and two nuns, Sister Mercedes and Sister Angelina, on a mission to this region. They are all dead now and if you don't do exactly as I tell you, you will be too."

"'I'm all ears,' I said without hesitation.

"'The young warrior that so fiercely stated his case is the chief's son. He wants your head as a trophy. It would make a nice prize, the head of a red-faced white man."

"'What did you tell them?'

"'I told them you were the red-faced spirit of the volcano, come to avenge the murder of the Chief Araboti. He was the man Saamantayao slaughtered three weeks ago."

"'Good gracious!' I declared. 'Is there any hope of me getting out of here?'

"'Yes, but not without me,' she answered. 'We will wait until nightfall and slip away into the jungle. Saamantayao knows these jungles well, so we will have to stay one step ahead of him. I know of one place he is reluctant to go.'

"'What about you? You don't have to do this. You are jeopardizing your own life as well.'

"'I've been with this tribe for nearly five years now. I've been waiting for a good chance to get away and this is as good as any. Besides, you wouldn't stand a chance without me.' She smiled and I fell in love a second time. She was dark, mysterious, and enchanting. She moved like the spirit of feminine grace as she shuffled about the hut. She kept one eye on the open-air window, diligently watching the movements of the chief and his men. There was something in her motion which spoke to me; it spoke to me of love or perhaps it was the chemistry of science.

"'She was a botanist, and I a gardener, by grand design. I couldn't help feeling it was meant to be. Either way, I was her willing and loyal subject— not to mention, she was my only chance of survival. We ate taro root, sinigang, and wild pork, and quietly waited for nightfall.

"'As I glanced around the hut, I noticed she kept a honey glider in a cage that hung from a cord in the corner of the main room. There were several containers with different plant leaves in them, a microscope, a mortar and pestle beside a thick leather notebook. She wasn't a good housekeeper, but her hospitality was grand. She seemed to like sharing the stories of the past five years and we even found cause to laugh at the behavior of the tribe, but were still ever mindful of our predicament.

"'As the sun set in the west, I was treated to her brilliant ingenuity and the finer details of her master plan. For you see, she had kept the honey glider for a reason. She knew that the tribe considered it a spirit of their ancestors and they knew she kept one. Therefore, in their eyes, she maintained a close connection to the underworld. That night, she tied the honey glider to a string and that string was tied to one end of a six-foot pole which hung balanced from the ceiling. On the other end of that pole was a dark dress on a clothes hanger.

"'When the honey glider was left to roam the hut, the dress would move about the hut on the other end of the staff, thereby making it look like she was still awake and moving about the hut. *It was sheer brilliance.* We slipped away through a hole we cut in the woven palm fronds of the northernmost wall. To the best of my knowledge, they didn't know we were gone until morning.

"'She took me deep, deep into the interior, through paths of jungle and mountain range only the bravest would dare travel. There beneath a giant dark tree was a plane fuselage. It was a WWII bomber that was gutted by the jungle and utterly consumed by the tree. I remember the tree had no birds among its branches and bore no fruit or flowers, but gave off an awful smell and dominated everything in the surroundings.

"'Quite literally, the roots of the tree had resurfaced and choked the life out of every other plant in the area. The plane was a prisoner of the twisted mass of vines and roots which grew from it. She cleared them away on the inside of the plane with a machete she had brought and we made a home right there. That first night, we sat up late by the fire and she told me about the tree.'

"'The natives call it *Otomi-Ullasa*, the tree of being. This particular tree is the tree of Saamantayao. That is why he won't seek us here. He fears the tree,' she said as she gazed up at it. 'It's ugly, is it not?'

"'It's hideous,' I replied. 'And it's killed off every other plant.'

"'Just like him, wouldn't you say?' She had a strange smirk on her face.

"'Why do they call it the tree of being?' I asked.

"'When the boys of the tribe turn twelve, the—how do you Americans say—the witch doctor brings the boy into the jungle and the boy is told to plant the sapling. As the boy grows, the tree grows. If the boy turns out to be a good man, the tree will bear the most amazing fruit and birds from all around will nest in its branches and all will be well with nature and the boy.'

"'And if the boy becomes someone of malevolence?' I asked.

"'You see no fruit in this tree, do you?' she asked.

"'No, I don't,' I said. 'Not a single one. It just has these rancid black seed pods. In fact, if I didn't know better, I would have guessed the tree was dead. It looks withered and weak, but it still grows.'

"'It is dead, but surviving,' she said softly. She then looked deep into my eyes. 'Like a man without a soul, would you not say?'

"'So, you are saying we are hiding from Saamantayao under a tree that bears his…his terrible nature…his malice?'

"'His personal truth—the truth of what he has become. That is why he won't search for us here; every man fears the truth of his soul." Marta poked at the fire with a stick and stared into the flames. She set the stick down and placed her hand on my shoulder and smiled. "He will continue to search for us until he has exhausted everywhere else. We will be safe here for quite some time.'

"'I took hold of her hand. 'I want to thank you, Marta, for saving my life. If it weren't for you—'

"'Shhh, don't,' she said. 'You saved mine as well. I had all but given up hope of ever escaping the tribe. I had forgotten what it was like to have a conversation with an educated human being. And you? You are like manna from heaven.' She smiled and rose to her feet. 'I will make a place for us inside the plane.'

"'Wait…Wait a minute! Uncle Walt?' I exclaimed. 'Does this story have the big "S" in it?'

"Uncle Walt's face turned tomato red. He tried to wipe the grin from his face with his hand, but couldn't. His eyes beamed with muted laughter. He coughed into his closed fist to conceal his amusement and a nervousness settled into his posture on the other end of the bench.

"'You're not going to tell me, are you?' I grumbled.

"'Well…you know, of course,' he stammered. 'I would have to resign my gentleman status if I were to reveal any details, but it should suffice to say, the eleven months we spent beneath that tree were, without a doubt, the best of my life. I can say that without any reservations.'

"'Oh, come on!' I whined. 'For crying out loud! You told me all of that, but you won't give me the dirt? What a crock of shit!'

"Uncle Walt slapped his knee and chuckled. 'Ha!' he croaked. 'I'm afraid you're not old enough for those parts yet, but be patient, you will learn about the big 'S' soon enough.'

"'Okay, okay, fine! Don't tell me. Keep all the good stuff to yourself...so what happened next?'

"'Well, as I have said, we spent the next eleven months under that tree. We spent our days roaming the jungle cataloging plants and flowers. She sketched them in her journal and I foraged for more samples. It was absolute Paradise; I almost forgot we were hiding from a bloodthirsty headhunter. There were long afternoons of love and passion intermingled with the bliss of discovery. I swear, we were like two teenagers turned loose in a world we had yet to discover. She taught me the wonderment of jungle medicine, a practice I still dabble in today. I shared the history of each flower we came in contact with; we were a perfect pair.

"'After a month of hiding, the inevitable happened. She woke up one morning and walked into the brush and vomited. Her face upon her return was one of ambivalence, but oh, how she glowed. I shall never forget the glorious light in her eyes that morning.'

"'What was it, Uncle Walt, what was it?'

"Uncle Walt's face drifted off with a smile, his eyes filled with a warmth only love can explain. He looked at me side-ways and said plainly, 'She was pregnant, Uriel. My flower had propagated.' He took a moment to reflect on those words. 'I'll tell you, Jacob, if there is any feeling which can make a man feel like a god, it's fatherhood. It's a feeling that only a woman can endow you with and it is grander than any accomplishment you can attain on your own.'

'What's it like, Uncle Walt?'

"He smiled warmly and answered, 'It's like being promoted to the bomb squad, but for some reason, you can't wait to start. Nine months becomes too long to wait for that unpredictable bundle of need.' He then turned to me with a stern admonishment. 'You remember this, Uriel, life is not about sex, money, or the paltry things we own. It's about the few fleeting moments in which we are allowed to glimpse the almighty in ourselves.' Uncle Walt's eyes drifted away and down. 'In the end, we all fall short, but the effort must be there to be sincere.'

"He took a deep breath and sighed. 'I have something for you,' he said. His eyes glanced over at the conspicuous hole in the ground.

"'What is it, Uncle Walt?" I said as I followed his eyes.

"He bent down and reached behind the bench and produced a sapling; it was a small tree about ten inches tall in a pot. 'It is your own Ullasa tree. I've had it shipped all the way from New Guinea. I want you to plant it. It will help you find a good path for your life. Plant it and care for it and others and you will always be happy.'

"I sat there for a moment, stunned. At age twelve, I wasn't exposed to superstitions, nor had I any notions of God or Satan, or any religion for that matter, so there was nothing but the wide-eyed naiveté of a young boy and all those wonderful stories. I took the tree from his quivering hands and approached the hole. I knelt down and took hold of the spade that laid next to it.

"Uncle Walt rose to his feet and stood behind me as I removed the tree from its pot and placed it in the hole. I filled the dirt around the roots and patted it down. 'Here,' he said, handing me a watering jug. 'Give it a little water to get it started.' I whetted the ground around the sapling and marveled at the old man's faith in the superstition. 'Done,' said Uncle Walt, proudly. 'Now we will have such a grand tree. Yes, a grand tree indeed.' He chuckled and extended his hand to help me to my feet. 'Now when you stay with me, you can look in on it and see for yourself what a fine young lad you really are,' he said with a wink.

"'Does it really work, Uncle Walt? Will I be able to see myself in the tree?'

"'Indeed, it does, Uriel. Now, we still have an hour or two before dinner and I have some Chinese yen in my pocket and a deck of cards that tell me I can win back the francs you won last summer. Did you bring them this year?' he smirked.

"'What, you mean these?' I said, producing them from my pocket and waving them in his face.

"'Oh…you cheeky devil,' he chortled.

"We rose to our feet and shuffled out of the greenhouse and as he pulled the thick chain through the door handles and clasped the lock upon his secret place, I asked, 'But what happened to Marta, Uncle Walt?'

"He paused and looked down. 'Oh, she left me for another adventure in Venezuela. Some flowers were meant to be wild. If one tried to plant them here, they would die.' Uncle Walt turned his face toward me and smiled. 'You know, Uriel, part of being a good gardener is knowing when to pick a flower and when to let it grow.'"

"You know, Doctor?" said Jacob. "I wish I could say those words lived in me. I wish I could say they weren't lost to time, but a child's attentions don't dwell on things of importance; theirs is a world of endless amusement and wonder."

"That's the thing, Jacob," said Dr. Kessler. "A child is not expected to remember those things. They are only expected to be children. Besides, they will learn them for themselves soon enough."

Jacob bowed his head in silence. "How long have I been prattling on? It's almost noon, isn't it?"

"Almost one," said the doctor. "What do you say we pick it up again tomorrow, same time?"

"All right, doctor," said Jacob as he rose to his feet. "I think I will do a little detective work and see if I can't track down this Lieutenant Jefferies."

"I don't know if that's wise, Jacob. You never know what might be a trigger with a PTSD patient."

"Don't worry, I'll be discreet about it." Jacob smiled and trotted off across the terrace.

Leap Year

After lunch, Jacob traced his steps back to Alice's desk. Alice was busy typing up the next week's schedule: arts and crafts on Monday—West wing, Group discussion on importance of family, Tuesday at 2 pm—commons, Origami Wednesday at 1 pm—courtyard…

"Excuse me, Alice," Jacob said softly over her right shoulder.

Alice looked up from behind her glasses. "Yes?" Her voice bristled with a mild annoyance.

"Yes, I heard through some discussions that an old college mate might be staying here, a man by the name of Jefferies. Would you be kind enough to look him up and tell me which room I might find him in? I want to get reacquainted with him," Jacob spoke softly and with some trepidation.

"Hmm…well now, let me look." Alice slid open the bottom drawer of her desk and pulled from it a black binder. She flipped it open, sifted through the pages and ran her finger across the names. "Jefferies you said his name was? Hmm… Jefferies, Jefferies… Jamison, Jackson, Johansson, Johnson… No, I don't see a Jefferies here, Mr.…Sullinger? Wasn't it?"

"Yes ma'am, Jacob Sullinger. They must have been mistaken. Thank you for taking the time. I didn't mean to interrupt you, but he was a good friend I had lost touch with and I thought it would be nice to catch up with him."

"I wish I could have been more help to you," said Alice.

"Not at all, you have been a great help," Jacob said with a smile. He then turned and headed off to his room. Alice shrugged her shoulders in puzzlement and turned her attention back to the task at hand.

Once he reached his room, he found it empty, or so he thought. The TV was still on but the volume had been turned all the way down. There was a Bible and a photo album on the floor along with Boo's hair brush, razor and shoe polishing kit. Photos from his past were strewn about the room. Jacob knelt down and sifted through the photos. They were black and white pictures from the fifties.

He recognized Boo's young face standing next to an old Chrysler Imperial holding a young boy in his arms. There was a striking family resemblance between Boo and the child. There were other pictures with his family and no doubt the boy's mother. One of the photos had been torn into pieces. Jacob carefully collected them and put them together. When the pieces were placed end to end, they revealed a very special moment in Boo's life. There he stood outside the recruiting office with a young private in full dress—his son, all grown up now!

Boo's right arm hung on the young man's shoulder; their faces beamed with pride and patriotism. It was at this moment that Jacob became aware of breathing coming from the other side of Boo's bed—from the corner beneath the window. It was a man's voice, hushed and muttering, as if someone was speaking only in breath. Jacob froze stone still and listened.

"Oh…Sis, Sister…I'm sorry. I'm so sorry. Thomas…was…was there that day. He wasn't supposed to be. Why…why was he there? They got him…there was nothing I could do." Boo's quivering breath was saturated with bitter weeping. "We were ambushed. Ambushed…and, and they took him, I mean they took us both…but, but I couldn't…I couldn't. God, they were cruel…"

"He screamed, Sis. God, he screamed so loud. I heard him…everywhere. I heard it. It followed me around. In the morning when I woke…and, and at night. Oh, how they made him scream. I heard him in my dreams…They thought they could break him, you see, but he…he t…took it. He took it all until…until I couldn't any more…I, I…Oh God, what have I done? Sis…I can't take it…back. I can't…"

Jacob quietly gathered up the photos and slipped them back into the album. He placed it into the top drawer of Boo's dresser and carefully stepped around to the other side of the bed. There, in the corner, below the window sill, Boo was curled up with his arms around his knees gently rocking. His eyes were wide and glassy and he stared straight ahead as if he were looking down a long dark tunnel. At first, he didn't seem to notice Jacob, but then his eyes floated up as if Jacob's presence was calling him back from another world.

"Sullinger? Is that you? Get down, get down, man. They'll see you," he panicked and his leg kicked out and swept Jacob's legs out from under him. Jacob's body hit the floor with a thud. Boo snatched hold of Jacob's arm and pulled him close and then he wrapped his arm tight around Jacob's neck. Jacob struggled get out a few words.

"What's out there, sir? What did you see?" asked Jacob.

"Sniper, maybe two or three. They have us pinned down at this position."

"Us?" Jacob asked softly.

"Yes, it's just Jefferies and me. They split the unit. Watson and Bishop took the others to recon the situation and that's when those bastards attacked."

"I see," said Jacob. "What if I draw their fire and you and Jefferies make a break for the door, sir?"

Boo pondered the notion for a moment. "You, you would do that? You would risk your life for me?"

"Absolutely sir, you're the finest Captain I've ever had the pleasure to serve under. I will crawl over to the other side of the window and draw their fire from there and you and Jefferies can slip away. I will follow as soon as I can."

"That just might work, Private, you're still wearing my uniform. They will be distracted and think you are me. Good plan, Sullinger, good plan."

Jacob scooted across the floor beneath the window and then looked back at Boo's terrified face. "I will count to three, sir, and stand in full sight of the snipers. You and Jefferies make a break for the door."

"Roger that, I appreciate what you are doing, Private, it really means a lot to me and my sister."

Jacob gave a nod and counted down softly and slowly. "Three…two…one…go!" he shouted and he jumped up and stood in the window as Boo scooted around the bed and crawled out into the hallway. He stood just outside the door.

"Get down, Private! Get down! We're clear, run for it!" Jacob dropped again to the floor and scooted out of the room. "That was damn fine thinking, Sullinger. I'm going to recommend you for a medal for bravery. Truly, you were born with balls of steel."

"It was nothing, sir. You would've done the same for me. Now you and Jefferies can fall back to a safer spot, sir."

"Jefferies? He's already gone to find the others. You can't stop that one. He is always on the job. A remarkable soldier, he is. I tell you, every time I look, he's already gone off…sssomewhe…" Boo's sentence slowed to a halt. His eyes drifted away and down, as a horrific reality sank in. His eyes began to tear up and his lower lip quivered. He placed his left hand on Jacob's shoulder and then let it fall. He turned and slowly walked away.

"Boo?" Jacob exclaimed. "Boo, are you alright?" But his voice went unanswered. Boo quietly shuffled down the hall. The distinct cadence in his step was conspicuously gone. Jacob didn't dare follow, but watched as Boo's beleaguered form disappeared around the corner. Jacob slipped back into the room and put the rest of Boo's things away. He spent the rest of the day wandering the grounds of the institution, searching for anyone who might fit the description of the young man in the photo. He would be an African American male in his late twenties. Jacob found no one that remotely fit that description.

After dinner, Jacob went to the game room on the second floor. At the end of the west wing, there were a couple of bookcases on opposite sides of two French doors. The doors led to a balcony overlooking the west-wing patio and four busts of various prominent psychologists, but Jacob was more interested in the books. He was looking for a distraction, something to help him escape the awkwardness of his predicament. He slowly scanned each bookcase for something of interest.

The shelves were laden with paperbacks and magazines families had donated. There was even a copy of the *Adventures of Huckleberry Finn*. He plucked the book from its resting place and sat down in a big armchair close to the window and began to thumb through the pages. It brought a smile to his face to reacquaint himself with Tom Sawyer and old Huck Finn. It took him away from all of his thoughts.

Before long, he found himself straining to make the words out in the fading light from the window. Jacob looked up at the clock to find it was already 8:37. He closed the book and stretched. *That was relaxing*, he thought. As though the act of not thinking of why he was there was something his soul was crying out for. He then rose to his feet, refreshed, and ambled the short distance back to his room with the book tucked under his arm. Once there, he found Boo standing in front of the big window. Jacob slipped into the room quietly, set the book down on the nightstand and slid between the sheets of his bed. Boo never moved. Jacob listened for a few minutes to the sounds of the orderlies outside in the hall until his eyes grew heavy, then as he turned his back to Boo, Boo spoke.

"They're coming, you know," he said softly.

"Who, sir? The enemy?" ask Jacob.

"Huh—no. Not the enemy—my family. They'll be here in a couple of days."

"Really? That's fantastic. When was the last time you saw them?" Jacob asked as rolled back over to face him.

"I don't remember; it seems like a lifetime."

"So, what's the problem? You don't seem happy."

"I…I don't know what to say. What do I tell them? I have been gone for so long. How do I begin to say what really happened in Afghanistan?" he began to sob. "I am such a coward. In the field, I fought my way through countless situations and faced death on each street corner and at every doorway, but this enemy isn't flesh and bone, it's the truth within me. How do I face them knowing what I know?"

"I think I know what you mean," said Jacob.

"You do?" Boo turned around to face him.

"Yes," said Jacob, "when I was fourteen, something happened to me and a family member. Something I couldn't tell. When something like that happens, you are changed in many ways forever."

"Yes…Yes, that's it. I'm not the man I used to be," Boo exclaimed. "So, what did you do when you had to face your family?"

Jacob took a moment and thought back. A feeble look and a wrinkled brow said it all.

"I see," said Boo. "You never found an answer, either."

"No, not really…sorry. I'm not much help to you, am I? Even so, it's nice to know we're not alone in our search."

"Maybe," said Boo. "I hope we find an answer soon; I only have two more days." Boo turned back to face the window.

Jacob closed his eyes. His mind was a blur. A flurry of memories called out from the depths of his past. He could still feel Uncle Matt's presence hanging over him, still smell the stale cigarettes on his breath, still hear his grating ragged voice, *Take it! Take it, you pussy, or I'll do it again.* Jacob took a deep breath and sighed. "I guess there are some things we are doomed to live with alone," he whispered to himself. The terror of those words sank in and sent a shiver though him. "Boo?" he said softly.

"Yeah," Boo replied.

"Can I still call you Captain?"

Boo smiled to himself. "Sure," he said, and then he gave a snort. "You can hitch your wagon to a falling star if you want to."

Jacob smiled, "At least it's not a fallen angel," he whispered and he settled in beneath the sheets and drifted off to sleep.

When he awoke the following morning, Boo had already gone, so Jacob pulled the sheets off and placed his feet on the cold tile floor. He rubbed his eyes and listened for a moment to see if he could hear Boo marching outside in the hall. His shuffle was unmistakable.

All he heard was the sound of Mrs. Tuttle hacking up her morning phlegm in the hall. It seemed to be a regular morning occurrence. Jacob remembered hearing it the morning before. He stood up and approached the big window. There, on the lawn below the window, Boo paced back and forth, treading the same line between two imaginary points, shaking his head and mumbling to himself. Jacob scratched his chin and ran his fingers through what was left of his hair. He knew something had to be done, but he didn't know what that was. He shook his head in frustration and turned away from the window.

Jacob sauntered through his morning routine in a listless fashion. His thoughts of Boo seemed to affect his appetite. He was only halfway through his cold eggs when Dr. Kessler approached his table. "Shall we take up where we left off?" he asked.

"Sure, I guess," said Jacob, "I don't know what good it will do."

"Just the same, I want to hear more about your youth. It gives me a deeper understanding of what triggers...um...your problem?"

"My problem? I'm not sure there was any *trigger*, doctor. Just genetics, and you can't do anything about that."

"Maybe, maybe not. Meet me in the gardens on the south side of the hospital. I want you to see something."

"Okay, my curiosity is piqued," said Jacob.

"Say twenty minutes?"

"Maybe thirty, I want to talk to Boo before we meet."

"Okay, thirty then, it's your dime." Jacob gave a nod and the doctor trotted off toward the door.

After breakfast, Jacob rounded the corner of the east end of the building. There was Boo, treading between the same two points he had been walking between before. His face was grim and his fists were clenched tight and swinging left to right. He was caught up in a full-fledged argument with himself. Jacob's first thought was, *Maybe now is not a good time to disturb him.* But then he thought, *maybe that's just what he needs.*

So, Jacob walked up to Boo, saluted and said, "Sir...Private Sullinger reporting for duty sir." Boo stopped in his tracks and looked at Jacob.

"Yes? What do you want? I'm busy," Boo grumbled.

"I have a riddle for you, sir," said Jacob.

"A riddle?" exclaimed Boo.

"Yes sir, a riddle."

"Okay, what is it?"

"What do you call a lesbian dinosaur, sir?"

"A what? A lesbian dinosaur? Okay, I don't know, Sullinger. What?"

"A lick-a-lot-a-puss, sir."

Boo looked down and shook his head. A reluctant smile stretched across his face and he laughed. "You came all the way out here to tell me that?"

"Yes, sir. You needed to hear it, sir. Sometimes, we forget the best medicine."

Boo paused and blushed a little. "Point well made, Private."

"It's not a defeat, sir, just falling back. I have to meet up with the doctor now. Will I see you later?"

Boo nodded and shook his head once more. "A lick-a lot-a-puss. Ha, that's a good one," he laughed.

"So, I'll see you after, then?" asked Jacob.

"Oh, I'll be around," Boo said with a smile.

"Good," said Jacob, and he turned and crossed the lawn toward the south side of the building.

Once there, he found Dr. Kessler standing on the patio beneath an arch of vining pink and yellow roses. The sight of the arch made Jacob smile. "That's the kind of thing Uncle Walt would've loved," he said as he approached. Dr. Kessler smiled back.

"He did. That's why he built it."

"He did?" Jacob asked.

"Yeah, and he planted the roses and dedicated them to his son Robert." Dr. Kessler pointed to an inscription at the pinnacle of the arch which read, *To Robert, the rarest of hearts.* "Actually, your uncle planted almost everything in the garden you're about to see. It seems there was no place he could go without bringing a bit of life to it." Jacob paused and reflected on these words a moment. "Shall we?" asked the doctor as he gestured to the path beyond the arch. Jacob nodded and they began to walk.

"So, I heard about your relationship with your Great uncle Walt and all about his travels. Tell me something about your relationship with your parents."

"My parents? There was hardly anything which you would call a *relationship*. But if you're asking when my childhood came to an abrupt end— it was on my thirteenth birthday."

"On your thirteenth birthday? Why your birthday?" asked Dr. Kessler.

"Well, on my thirteenth birthday, my father, mother and uncle Matt drove to Tanglewood and spent the day celebrating. Georgia baked a cake and made fried chicken, collard greens, mashed potatoes, and gravy. We all ate until we were sick. My father and uncle helped themselves to Uncle Walt's aged Scotch and soon after, the argument started.

"Apparently, only a month earlier, a social worker appeared at the house to look into my *living* arrangements and found them to be unsatisfactory. The social worker mentioned that someone had petitioned the courts for custody of me. In all likelihood, it was Great uncle Walt. This meant my father's cash cow was about to dry up. I stood to one side of the front window behind the curtains and listened to them quarreling on the front porch.

"'I know what you're trying to do!' My father yelled. 'You're not going to get away with it. He's my son, not yours.'

"Then why don't you clean yourself up and get a job. You haven't done one thing to secure that boy's future. Not one!' Uncle Walt rebutted. 'Here he is thirteen, almost a man, and no future to speak of. For god's sake, Frank, do the right thing.'

"'Don't preach to me, old man, we are not all blessed like you! You're all fuckin' high and mighty in your big house. Your brother didn't leave me with the kind of wealth you got left with.'

"'Your father got the same inheritance I did. The exact same! Only, he chose to gamble rather than invest. He had his chance and I laid him to rest out yonder,' said Uncle Walt, pointing toward the hills behind the house. 'At the rate you're going, I'll be laying you right beside him before long.' Uncle Walt regained his composure and choked back his frustration. 'Look,' he said. 'Your father had his chance and you've had yours, but Jacob could have a real future if you gave him to me. Come now, Frank, give the lad to me and he'll have all the opportunities you didn't.'

"My father paused a moment and thought. I could see his body sway back and forth through the sun-laced curtains as the scotch did its work. Then the words boiled up from within him, his right hand clenched tight around the glass. 'No! God damn it, no!' He hurled the glass at Uncle Walt, barely missing his head. 'Jacob!' he shouted as he stormed into the house. 'Jacob get your things, we're going home. Where's your mother?' he slurred.

"I slowly stepped out from my hiding place behind the curtains and walked toward the door. Georgia's worried eyes watched from the darkened hall as my father swept past me and flew up the stairs, yelling, 'Maggie? Maggie, get your ass down here, we're leavin'!'

"Georgia stepped out of the shadows and embraced me. 'Shhh,' she whispered as she pulled my head in close. 'It's all right, child. Don't you worry. You know you still got family here, no matter what happens, we still kin.' Then she turned me loose and stepped outside to check on Uncle Walt.

"When my father and mother appeared, my father had a hold of my mother's arm and he was pulling her along. 'Come on, damn it, I'm not stayin' in this fuckin' house another minute,' he said.

"'Okay, okay I'm coming. Just let me get my purse,' my mother grumbled.

"I reached up next to the door and grabbed my coat and my mother's purse, which hung side by side. When they approached, I handed the purse to my mother and shot her a look of disappointment. 'Some birthday,' I muttered, as I followed them out to the car.

"Uncle Matt had been watching the argument and decided it was wiser to just get into the car and wait. The three of us climbed into the car and the last door was shut, like an exclamation point at the end of my childhood. I took a long last look out the rear window as we pulled away. Uncle Walt and Georgia stood at the top of the steps lost in that moment."

"I tell you, doctor, I could literally feel the strands around my heart stretch with every inch of distance my father put between us and that house. That was the last time I saw Uncle Walt."

"How come you never went back?" asked Dr. Kessler.

"Well now, I'm not really sure," Jacob remarked.

"Why am I not convinced?" smirked the doctor.

Jacob rolled his eyes as they stepped out from behind a line of fir trees. "Wow! That's beautiful," he exclaimed. "Is this the garden you were talking about?"

The doctor's face lit up. "Yes, isn't it, though? Your Uncle Walt selected all of the flowers. He really had a talent for gardening. Did you notice how it seems to jump out at you once you pass the standing fir trees?"

"Yes, yes, it caught me totally off guard," Jacob said with a laugh.

"He planned it that way. He wanted to create a secret garden, a sanctuary of beauty and light. He called it his garden of life."

Jacob stopped to take it all in. It was a large circle with bands of blue and red tulips around the outside edge. The border was marked eight times with billowing tufts of pink hydrangeas. Pathways of cobblestone one foot wide ran like ant trails between the flower beds. Daisies and daffodils, hyacinths and hibiscus crisscrossed in a tangled pattern of pink, yellow and fiery orange. A central fountain overflowed its basin across rock beds into twelve narrow troughs, which ran like the spokes of a giant wheel toward the hydrangea beds. Jacob shook his head in astonishment. "I'm speechless," he said.

The doctor smiled. "It was his version of the Buddhist Mandala circle of life." Jacob's face almost turned in on itself at the thought of such a task. "Well, he did have help, you know?" said Dr. Kessler. "Some of the patients and groundskeepers worked together to make it, but the idea was all your Great uncle Walt's."

"Uncle Walt never did do anything small, did he?"

"Nope," the doctor said plainly. "That's what I liked about him. He was like his beloved flowers; blissfully unaware he was inspiring others by doing what he loves. I tell you, Jacob, one would have never known he had the daemons he struggled with."

Jacob paused and looked at the doctor. "Was he a bad case? I mean, how often did he have to stay here at the hospital?"

The doctor raised his eyebrows, "I'm not supposed to say, but ten, maybe twelve times. He was as bad as I've ever seen, at times. Georgia was the rock who kept him steady, really. She used to work here and well, they just hit it off. He seemed to like her sarcastic sense of humor."

"What's that? A lake?" Jacob asked as he pointed to a body of water beyond the garden.

"Ah, now that is our duck pond. Your uncle came down here often. It's quiet and nobody bothers you—except the ducks, of course."

"Nice!"

"Let's have a seat on the bench down there and you can finish telling me about your childhood."

The two men ambled down to the water's edge. Jacob picked up a flat stone, reared back and slung it low across the water. It skipped once, twice, three times and finally a fourth before disappearing into the dark green water. "They have good stones here. I like this spot, it feels…umm…*Zen* to me."

"Zen?" Dr. Kessler exclaimed.

"You know…welcoming…like I belong. Or maybe it's the garden," Jacob laughed at himself.

"No, no, that's good," said the doctor, "that's a good thing, let's run with it. Tell me what happened after your thirteenth birthday."

"Well, after that I started to get into trouble at school. You know, fights, bad grades, drugs and alcohol. And when I was fifteen…"

"Fifteen? What happened when you were fourteen?"

Jacob glanced over at the doctor with an awkward look. "You know? I don't remember too much about my fourteenth year. It's kind of a blur, to tell the truth."

"Well, that's an interesting note, don't you think?"

"Yeah, maybe. Ha." Jacob laughed and rubbed his forehead. "Maybe it was a leap year," he chuckled. The doctor shot him a look of skepticism. "Well, like I was saying," he continued,

"when I was fifteen, I stole a Cadillac coupe and got caught. I did nine months in juvie for that one, and had six months of community service. I remember seeing the district attorney pull up in a sweet-looking Alfa Romero; cherry red convertible, suede leather seats. Man! How I wished I had stolen that car! They would've never brought me in alive.

"His name was Adam Kovatski. He wore a button-down vest pinstriped three-piece suit and walked like he had a stack of silver dollars shoved up his ass. God, was he cocky! He delivered the state's case against me like he was teaching me a lesson in humility, like I shoulda paid him for making him come down there. He was truly the master of his own world. I decided right then, I would become a lawyer. But it took something my family never had—money—lots of it.

"Now, my father had once told me, if I ever contacted Great uncle Walt again, he would cut off my ears. He may have been drunk when he said it, but that didn't matter, he wasn't a kidding kind of man. So, I did what any kid in my position would do. I wrote Uncle Walt a letter and posted the return address from a friend's house. Uncle Walt was true blue.

"I received a letter two weeks later saying he would foot the bill from any college I chose, but I would have to get scholarships, too, to hide the fact he was paying for it. My father would see the scholarships and Uncle Walt would pay the rest. I was on green street. All I had to do was buckle down, and buckle down I did. The following year, I made straight A's.

"I channeled some of my frustration into wrestling, football and weight lifting, to deter my father's heavy-handed parenting. Spending my weekends at the library kept me out of trouble and none of the friends I used to hang out with ever went there. Things started to go right for me. I could feel a spring in my step. "Ha!" Jacob laughed. "A small stack of silver dollars in my own ass, so to speak."

"After high school, I went to Colombia for my undergraduate and got my master's. I passed the bar on my second try and landed a job downstairs at Simon & Neubauer. Three years later, I made it to junior associate; had an office on the first floor."

"That's great! So, if everything was good, what led you here?" asked the doctor.

"Angels," said Jacob. He blushed a little as the words left his lips.

"Angels?"

"Yep, angels and devils. Actually, it was Satan himself."

"You don't look like a religious kind, if you don't mind me saying so."

"That's just it, I'm not."

"I'm afraid I'm not following you," said Dr. Kessler. "It's really uncommon for someone with little or no religious back ground to suddenly start believing in angels and devils. Did you go to church at all as a child?"

"Nope, not once. Not even when I visited Uncle Walt." There was a strange lull in the conversation.

"Did you read the Bible at some point in your life?"

"Nope." Jacob shrugged his shoulders. "I shy away from that kind of thing."

The doctor shook his head. "What was it that changed in your beliefs?"

"When did I start believing in angels?" Jacob repeated. "Never. I still don't believe in angels or devils."

The doctor's face grew grim and he stared blankly over at Jacob. He took a deep breath and asked, "Then what are we talking about here? Why are you here at the hospital?"

"Okay, I guess I should go back to the beginning of my...*problem*. That was about a year ago. It all began with a strange conversation involving an old acquaintance from college. You have to understand, I was a different man a year ago."

The Lamb

"It was a Tuesday morning, I think, when he came through the doors of Simon & Neubauer. He looked haggard and beaten down by life, but strangely happy. Until that day, I hadn't seen him since college. God, what a rube he was in those days. A mediocre business major in a second-hand suit, no doubt from his old man's closet. About the only thing I did respect him for was his ability to play a great game of poker. He had a strong poker face that took my drinking money on more than one occasion. Still, a big-hearted bloke like him has no place on Wall Street.

"I recognized him straight away when he came in. Those big dopey eyes and casual friendly smile gave off the scent of weakness, that scent of easy money. He spoke to Beatrice at the front desk and she pointed to my office and then, as she often does, told him to take a seat in the waiting room. I watched him fidget through the slits in the blinds of my office widow for a few minutes as I pretended to look busy. He didn't take his eyes off my office as he nervously clenched his brown leather brief case. When I felt sure I had tortured him enough, I paged to Bea to show him in.

"He jumped to his feet and moved toward my office door. I sauntered toward the door to greet him. 'Daniel, my good man, how long has it been?' I said, stretching out my hand.

'Hello, Jacob,' he said with a firm handshake.

'I heard through Todd from our old fraternity that you did well for yourself on Wall Street.'

'Yes, yes I did actually, but that was several years ago and I have had a turn for the worse, I'm afraid.'

'Well, come in and sit down and tell me the situation. If the price is right, I'm sure I can help,' I said, gleaming as I closed my office door behind him.

"He sat down slowly in the big leather chair opposite my desk, still tightly clutching that brown briefcase. He shot me a worried look, one that let me know that the money was going to be the issue. If he still had a poker face, he wasn't wearing it today.

"I casually slid in behind my desk and sat down. 'Well, tell me the situation anyway, maybe I can give you some advice.'

'Well, as you said, I did do very well for myself on Wall Street. The firm I was working for, Steinman & Becker brokerage, set me on their biggest accounts. I caught a windfall situation, shall we say, and netted myself a substantial commission. I think the number was 5.2 million.'

'Wow,' I said. 'That's a healthy sum.' The thought of 5.2 million dollars made my palms sweat.

'Unfortunately, my now ex-wife had made plans with that money that didn't include me.'

'Aww, lucky at cards, unlucky at love,' I smirked.

"He shot me a grimacing look and said, 'Not exactly. That was five years ago. I have remarried since then. She's a wonderful woman who loves me for me, not my money.' He paused to bolster his courage a bit. 'The sad fact is, I took a job at a lesser firm to spend time with my new wife and baby. That's when it all went south. The market turned and the firm went under, leaving me swimming in debt and at the mercy of my ex-wife's extravagant life style. As you know, I have two children by my first wife. She has custody and makes damn sure I spare no expense for her living arrangements.'

'Okay,' I said. 'This is all sad stuff, but where do I come in? You know I don't do pro-bono work. It sounds like you wouldn't be able to pay my fees, and I'm not a charity lawyer.'

'I know,' he said. 'That's why I came to you. You are the most ruthless and heartless son-of-a-bitch I have ever met. More than a match for my ex-wife.'

'Flattery will get you nowhere,' I said, as I reached for my phone to buzz Beatrice.

'Wait!' he exclaimed holding up his hand. 'I have a proposition for you that could make you a rich man.'

'Okay,' I said. 'You've got exactly three minutes to impress me, then it's back to whatever ghetto you crawled out of.'

'I have in this briefcase five insurance policies. I have one for each of my children, one for my new wife and one for you. Yours is for twenty-five million dollars. The money will be paid to you should I die in an accidental death.'

'Do you plan to have an accident?' I said laughing. 'How do I get paid?'

"Daniel looked at me as serious and as sober as a hanging judge on sentencing day and calmly said, 'In one month's time.'

'What? You're not serious. Come now, man, things haven't gotten that bad, have they?' I said with a smirk.

"His brow lowered in a defiant glare. 'Don't start pretending that you give a fuck now, Jacob. We both know you couldn't care less about what happens to me. The only family I had to fall back on was my father, and he died years ago. This is the only way I can provide for the ones that I love and make no mistake; I do love them that much. The only thing you have to do is set up the trust funds so that that goddamn succubus doesn't get her hands on the money and you walk away with a cool twenty-five mil.'

"Well, he was right about being heartless, I haven't cared about anyone since my mother died and, come to think of it, I'm not too sure I cared about her either. Daniel sat there with a firm conviction on his face waiting for an answer. 'So, you've got it all figured out, have you? You whack yourself and I clean up the mess. And if you don't do it right, what a mess that will be.'

"He opened the briefcase, pulled out the policy he spoke of, and plopped it on the desk in front of me. 'Don't worry,' he said. 'Monsieur Diabolus promises to deliver an unquestionable accident.'

"'Monsieur Diabolus?' I scoffed as I picked up the stack of papers and scanned the fine print. 'Darkstar Life and Trust…? Who ever heard of this insurance company?' I skimmed through the fine print. 'Well, it looks legitimate enough, I guess, though there is no name under the beneficiary.' The thought of twenty-five million dollars began to make my heart race. With that kind of money, I could open my own office, set my own hours and be a power player; maybe even buy a politician. The prospect began to appeal to me.

"'His name is Minos Tauri Diabolus,' said Daniel. 'But he prefers to be called Monsieur Diabolus. Let's just say I have already made a deal with the devil.'

"'I guess so,' I said, as I sat the papers down and slunk back in my seat. I stared at him intensely. His big brown eyes firmly fixed on my expression. *He seems so much more confident than when he was in college. Wall Street must have made a man of him.* 'You know,' I said, 'with all this talk of suicide, someone might think you've gone strange.'

'Don't patronize me, Jacob. I am still in my right mind, although I can see how it would sound to someone who doesn't know.'

'Who doesn't know what?'

'Who doesn't know Monsieur Diabolus.'

"We both paused a moment as we wrestled with the situation. I lightly tugged at my goatee and stared across the desk at him. 'You realize, of course, that this would put me in an awkward position.'

'Well…what's it going to be? You know, if you don't want the money, there are plenty of heartless lawyers in Manhattan,' he said, as he picked up the policy and slipped it back into the brief case.

'Wow, playing hard ball, I see. Okay, I tell you what…Give me twenty-four hours to come up with an answer; until then, don't do anything rash.'

'Okay, here's my address,' he said, handing me his card. 'You can stop by tomorrow night to give me your answer. It wouldn't be prudent to discuss this matter over the phone.'

'You know, by law I am required to turn you in to the authorities. It's a good thing I'm a lawyer—otherwise, I would feel obligated to uphold the law.'

'Just be there tomorrow night, or say goodbye to twenty-five mil,' he said.

'You really know how to drive a deal home.'

'I have one more hand to play before it's all over,' he said.

'And what hand is that?' I asked.

'The devil's hand, Jacob, the royal flush.'

'You're really going to go through with this, aren't you?'

'It's a done deal, I have but to board Monsieur Diabolus' yacht and play one last game of seven card draw. I could win big for the ones I love.'

"We both rose to our feet and shook hands once more, before he headed toward the door. I followed him out past the front desk to make sure his crazy ass left and to make damn sure he didn't run out into traffic. If he was going to do it, I wanted to make sure he didn't do it before my name was on that dotted line. Before passing through the double glass doors which led to the street, he looked at me and said firmly, 'Remember Jacob, twenty-four hours. That's all you have.'

"I gave a nod and watched him descend the steps and get into a black limousine that awaited his return, which didn't make any sense to me; he said he didn't have any money. As the limo pulled into traffic, I noticed Mardi Gras beads hanging from the driver's rear-view mirror and the Louisiana license plates.

"I also had to ponder the audacity of someone bold enough to have his driver park in a no-parking zone on a busy Manhattan Street on a Tuesday morning. I turned around to find Beatrice's big blue eyes staring up at me inquisitively through her large-framed glasses. 'This is shaping up to be an interesting day,' was all I said as I strolled back to my office.

Smoldering Embers

"It was a quarter to four when I left the office and walked the two blocks to the parking garage. The day was warm and sunny with a westerly breeze. It was a perfect day to drop the top on my Aston Martin and troll for clients at the Chamberlin club on the waterfront. The Chamberlin club is an upper-class club for the business and political elite. With a long list of power brokers and their soon to be ex-wives, it is an excellent place to drum up some business.

In fact, it is the kind of place I used to get thrown out of, that is, before I helped Louie the maître d' with his little cocaine problem. Ever since I got him off a ten-year stint in the New York penitentiary, he has been setting me up with a table that overlooks the river.

"When I got there, I slipped the valet a five spot and told him to park next to the door. I wasn't planning to stay. Just a few martinis and a couple of business cards and I'll shake off the stuffy crowd for some real fun. Louie greeted me at the door in his usual nervous style.

'Ah, Mr. Sullinger. Greetings. Here to capitalize on old clients again, I see.'

'Hello Louie. Yes, and maybe score some new ones.'

'Haven't I paid all my fees by now?' he quipped. 'You know, some would call this extortion.'

'It's not extortion when a lawyer does it,' I said.

'One of these days you are going to get me fired.'

'Come on, don't get selfish on me, now. Remember, you owe me.'

'Oh, how could you ever let me forget,' he said, as he snatched up the wine list. 'Very well then, right this way.'

"We meandered through the dimly lit aisles past the private smoking rooms and the lounge to a small table along the big picture window overlooking the harbor and the Staten Island ferry. I looked around the place to see what high rollers, if any, had shown up. It was the usual senior citizen set picking the bones of their T-bone steaks and lobster bisque. A tall, thin waiter with a silver tray approached me as I pulled a pack of cigarettes from my pocket.

'Would the gentleman like a drink to go with that cigarette, sir?' he said as he snapped a lighter open and placed it a safe distance from my cigarette.

'Yes, get me a dry martini with two olives, and when I say dry, I mean wave the vermouth bottle over it.'

'Very good then, sir, one Dean Martin special coming up.'

'Very funny, just bring it to me on the veranda; I want to enjoy the view.'

'As you wish, sir.'

"I strolled through the open French doors to the wide long deck it revealed. An intoxicating panorama of the East River, the Brooklyn Bridge and the meandering streets beyond met my eyes. *God, I love living like the rich,* I thought as I took it all in. *Twenty-five million dollars could buy me a table here permanently.* I snickered to myself when I thought what Louie would think about that.

"My eyes were drawn to a tiny light blinking pink and blue in the distant cross street beyond the bridge. I knew the light well and couldn't keep the melancholy spirit of my youth from conjuring up her young face. A shy specter as a preteen in her junior high prom dress and an awkward dance had planted a seed that never got the chance to grow. The blinking light was an all-night diner named Angelo's that her family owned and a sanctuary to my adolescent love.

"She, now twenty-eight, had grown into an Italian beauty the gods had named Rosalinda Galotti. Her three brothers kept a constant watch over her and subsequently made her single by default. I drop in from time to time to taste her magnificent linguine clam sauce and her seafood fettuccine, but most of all to bathe in her radiant beauty and try my luck at seducing what had been rendered too holy for my bed, a heart of gold, a heart which could not be stolen. Somewhere in me, a young boy sighs a sad and rather naïve surrender to her good nature.

"A young couple shattered my reminiscing when they stepped out on the veranda laughing and carrying on. They took their place along the rail a few steps away. Both looked to be in their early twenties. They had the look of old money about them. Probably from one of the rich families of upstate New York that dabbled in the New York night life this time of the year.

"The girl was cute, dishwater blonde with hazel eyes, costume jewelry, and a faux Gucci handbag. The young man sported a designer haircut, an Armani suit, and a flagpole you could play the Star-Spangled Banner to. It was obvious; she was digging for gold and he was looking to score. I glanced at their hands and saw no wedding bands, so there was no immediate prospect of a paycheck in that situation for me.

"The waiter finally caught up with me, carrying my martini on the silver tray.

'Here is your martini, sir. Will that be all for now?'

"'Yes, but stay close, I may want another,' I said, plucking the glass from the tray. I turned my attention back to the couple that was playing out their passions silhouetted against the Brooklyn Bridge. Their image seemed to fade to black and white when I caught a glimpse of a skin-tight emerald green silk dress and long shimmering black hair dancing in the afternoon breeze.

"There was someone standing just beyond the couple, and from what I could tell, it was a woman of exceptional beauty. Like a blip on the radar of my subconscious, she came as a presence. I could feel her long before I ever got a good look at her. Her skin was like ivory, soft and creamy. I could see open toed sandals when she kicked up one heel behind her and the thin gold bracelets around her wrists glistened and jingled like money as she grabbed hold of the rail. It was music to my ears.

"The cooing of the lovers reached a fevered pitch as the young man took his girl's hand and led her inside to a more private retreat and I was left alone with a vision from my deepest fantasy. There she stood, in full view now, a slender young Asian woman with her hands on the rail of the deck leaning into the wind. Her face shown like gossamer clouds in the afternoon sun and the curve of her body in that dress branded an image of carnal desire into the back of my brain. I watched intently as she followed the slow-moving ships with her eyes. Then it happened. She looked down briefly and then raised her eyes to meet mine. It was a long, powerful gaze, as if she was speaking to me with those emerald green eyes.

"I felt my mouth fall open and my lower lip began to quiver. The sweet smell of her perfume wafted over and filled the air around my head. The intoxicating aroma of honeysuckle and lilacs found its way under my skin and suddenly my tie was too tight and my drink far too dry. She never blinked, but held me fast, frozen in that eternal second.

"I could feel her beckoning me to approach without uttering a word. My nerves faltered and my hand wavered, spilling vodka all over my wrist. 'God damn it,' I said out loud to myself as I looked down at my vodka-soaked Rolex. I quickly tried to regain my composure by laughing at myself and saying, 'You know I hate these martini glasses. I'm not even on to my second one yet and I'm already spilling them.'

"I chuckled a little and looked up to find myself standing alone on that open veranda in the twilight of dusk. Suddenly, that veranda felt like the loneliest place on earth. *How long had I been here? Where did she go? Where did she come from? How did she get out here without me seeing her?* My mind was a blur with questions. I felt like a ridiculous school boy ditched after his senior prom.

"The waiter quickly approached from behind, 'I see you spilled your drink, sir; can I get you another.'

'No, that's all right. The glass you gave me is faulty. You can tell me, though, where that beautiful Asian woman went.'

'Asian woman, sir?'

'Yes, she was standing right there just a moment ago.'

'I'm afraid I didn't see her, sir. I was standing just inside the doors as you had requested and all I saw was the young couple, but they left two and a half hours ago.'

'What?' I said, rubbing my brow. 'What time is it? How long have I been out here?'

'It is a quarter to nine, sir. I have been watching you stare at the bridge alone now for nearly two and a half hours.'

'What? That can't be true. Are you saying that I have lost all track of time? You must be mistaken.'

'I don't believe so, sir. Shall I bring you a seltzer to clean your jacket sleeve?'

'No, I don't think it reached my sleeve, but my watch has had enough to drink.'

'Let me take your glass, then. I will bring you another.'

'No, look...just forget the hard stuff. Bring me a glass of Moscato, put it in a normal glass, and if I start seeing Asian women, come take it away.'

'There is one other thing, sir; Mrs. Embers is waiting for you in the lounge. She sent me to give you the message.'

'Then you can bring me the wine there. Can you do that right?'

'Yes sir,' was all he muttered as he stormed off.

"I went back inside and found Mrs. Embers simmering in her gin and tonic in a corner booth at the back of the lounge. Her name was Fran. She was a 56-year-old wife of an insurance assessor. Her husband worked for one of the largest, if not the largest, insurance companies in New York. He was on a perpetual business trip and she was diagnosed terminally horny. Far be it from me to let a situation like this go uncapitalized on. I met her a year and a half ago when I helped her with a drunk and disorderly charge and had been providing services, shall we say, ever since. She looked up at me as she calmly stirred the ice in her glass.

"'Good evening, Jacob, care to join me?' she said with a coy smile. She was obviously on her third or fourth drink by now and was slightly listing to one side. You could tell by the streaks of blonde amongst the gray and her stark blue eyes that she was once a very attractive woman. But the ravages of time, alcohol, and rich food had long since robbed her of that beauty. Now she spends her time stewing in a cocktail of gin and loneliness. Like a hound on the hunt, I caught the smell of opportunity and took advantage of it.

"I slid in next to her and slipped my arm around her shoulders. 'Good evening, Fran,' I said softly giving her a light peck on the cheek.

'What is that called? A teaser?' she said with a smile.

'I like to think of it as free sample.'

'Mmmm,' she moaned as she leaned into me. 'I've missed you, you know?'

'Where have you been lately? You aren't trying to avoid me, are you?' I asked snuggling onto her ample body.

'No, they had to move my mother into a nursing home, so I had to take a trip to Florida to get her things squared away. But now I'm back and in need of some quality time with you and your friend.'

'My friend?' I asked with one raised eyebrow.

'Yes, just the three of us,' she said with a sultry gleam in her eye. 'You, me, and that fat cock of yours. That adds up to one good time.'

'Ha, ha, ha, I see… Well, I'm sure I can work something into your busy schedule,' I smirked. 'Let me get something to drink first. I haven't had much luck with the waiters in this place tonight,' I said raising my voice. 'Where's that goddamned glass of wine?'

"The waiter suddenly appeared holding the Moscato. He placed it before me and tried to leave before I could say anything.

'What took you so long?' I snapped. 'Christ, I could have grown my own grapes by now.' The waiter tried his best to ignore me as he turned away. 'Just bring me the damn bottle and I'll pour my own, you putz.'

'Calm down, Jacob, it's only a glass of wine,' said Fran.

'Yes, but this is supposed to be a four-star joint, I shouldn't have to wait.'

'Do I have to remind you, Jacob, you're not a member here? If he knew that, you wouldn't even get a drink before they carted your ass out of here. So, shut up and plant one right here,' she said pointing to her lips.

"I smiled and leaned in pressing my lips to hers. I pulled her body into me with my arm and held the kiss long enough to feel her body relax, then I grazed her mouth with my tongue as I pulled away.

"'Mmm, that one's going to cost me, I bet,' she said.

'You know me so well,' I replied with a smile.

"She looked into my eyes with a vulnerable, but helpless expression. She knew what a scoundrel I was, but like me, she also loved to gamble on a long shot. What a bittersweet paradox the heart makes of life. It's better in my mind not to have one.

"She placed a hand on my thigh under the table and gave it a squeeze. 'Are you coming over tonight?' she asked softly.

'I'm planning on it,' I said running my fingers through her hair.

'I think my husband has a few old suits that might fit you. You can wear one of them to work tomorrow and I will have yours sent to the cleaners.'

'It sounds like you've thought this out carefully,' I said.

'I told you, it's been a while and I have needs.'

'I know,' I said. 'I'm lucky your husband keeps a full closet.'

"We whiled away the next hour catching up on her husband's travels over a few more glasses of wine and gin. By the time we left, she was good and tight. I had to get into her purse to pay our tab. She had four hundred dollars in there. I took sixty to pay our bill and pocketed forty for my own troubles. She wouldn't miss it, her husband pulled in six figures easy and right now she was in no shape to argue. I helped her to her feet and we strolled out to the reception area. 'Louie,' I said, 'have Mrs. Ember's car brought around?'

'Louieeee!' Fran shrieked as she stumbled around the foyer.

'Shhhh,' I said softly to her. 'We don't want to draw attention to ourselves.'

'The lady arrived by taxi, Mr. Sullinger. I think she was anticipating you being at the Chamberlin Club tonight.'

'Oh, sorry,' Fran whispered. She then leaned toward Louie and whispered, 'We are trying to be incomsp...income...inconspicumus, because we are going to have sex. Heh, heh, heh. Shhhhh.'

'All right, then,' I said. 'Have my car brought around. I will take her home.' I pulled Fran back, away from Louie's face.

'I know!' she suddenly blurted out. 'Louie can come too! We will have a threesome! That will be funnnn! I like you, Louie, you're a good guy,' said Fran as she caressed Louie's face with her right hand.

'Shut up!' I barked as I jerked her back by her left arm.

'Are you sure that's wise for you to take Mrs. Embers home?' Louie inquired.

'Someone has to make sure she gets home all right.'

'You're not really concerned for her safety, are you? She must be another one of your so-called former clients,' Louie said with a smirk.

'Keep your nose out of my business, Louie, or I'll cut it off,' I said as I struggled to keep Fran on her feet.

"The valet pulled my car up and jumped out as Louie opened the passenger side door. Then I poured Mrs. Embers into the car seat and shut the door. I quickly ran around to the other side and climbed in behind the wheel. Without as much as a kiss my ass, Louie, I pulled out of the drive and into the evening traffic. Fran was slumped over the arm rest with her head on my shoulder, drooling. 'Hey,' I said. 'Wake up! Stop drooling on my jacket, bitch.' I tried to shrug her away but she just fell back onto my shoulder and passed out.

"Fran's apartment was on the west side of Manhattan in Greenwich Village. It was a tenth-floor corner apartment with a grand view of Washington Square Park and the Hudson River. I, on the other hand, shared a flat with a roommate in Brooklyn way over on Fillmore and Flatbush, a twenty-minute drive on a good day when traffic was light. It's not much to call home, but I don't plan to stay there long, either. I usually only crash there when my list of numbers in my cell phone fails me. The New York night life has provided me with my own little phone book full of women I can sponge off. I rarely need to go home except to pick up my mail.

"We caught every green light until we got to Church Street. At the corner of Church and Maiden Lane, we caught the one and only red light on our ten-minute journey across town. As I waited for the light to change, I entertained myself with an electric billboard on the side of a high rise across the street. It was a gigantic sign with dancing flames over a devil holding a martini. The sign was advertising a new nightclub called the Inferno Room. *Wow,* I thought. *That looks exciting. I bet I could score on a few phone numbers there.*

"It was at that moment that I became aware of someone standing beneath the sign. There, below a street light in the midst of a throng of faceless people shuffling, was a woman in an emerald green dress. She was standing sideways to my position and I could see her long black hair draped down to the small of her back, and the steam rising from the subway grate beneath her obscured the detail of her appearance in a white haze. The light of the street lamp hit the steam about her and gave off a soft glow like a halo in the night.

No, it can't be, I thought. *I'm sure I just imagined her this afternoon.* I squinted my eyes to try to get a good look, but as I did, there came a 'honk' from behind and a voice calling out, 'Hey buddy, move your ass! I got a flight to catch!'

"I looked up at the green traffic light and started down the street slowly. As I passed her to my left, she followed me with her eyes and I caught a glimpse of her face and those startling Asian green eyes. *It is her*, a voice screamed inside my head. *I didn't imagine her this afternoon.* I felt downright giddy that I wasn't losing my mind. I looked back in my rear-view mirror to make sure I wasn't seeing things, but to my dismay, she had vanished.

"The streetlight showed nothing more than steam escaping from the subway vent and the restless bustling of the masses on a lonely street corner. I scratched my head. 'What the hell?' I said to myself. 'I gotta get more sleep. I'm having recurring daydreams.' I looked over at Fran still slumped over on to my right shoulder and the small wet spot of saliva on my jacket forming under her chin. With my left hand against her forehead, I shoved her away toward the passenger car door. She fell backward with a thud.

"It was only a matter of a few more moments and we were pulling into the parking lot of the 21 Washington Square North—apartments for the wealthy. Fortunately, I found a visitor's parking spot close to the door. I pulled into it, parked, and flicked the switch to put the top up. Once it had finished reaching the windshield, I latched it down and ran around to Fran's side of the car. When

I opened the car door she was leaning on, she poured out backward with her arms hanging down toward the ground. I looked down at her half-opened eyelids and drool-soaked chin staring up at me. 'You're pathetic,' I said as I bent over to pick her up. Wrapping her arms around my neck, I slid the rest of her out of the car and stood her on her feet.

"She briefly woke from her stupor long enough to realize she had her arms around my neck. 'You...'" she said as her head bobbled around. 'You are such a scoundrel...I'm gonna fuck your...' she paused a moment as she tried to bring the sight of me into focus. Then she uttered the words, 'Lights out,' and fell backward across the hood of my car with her arms splayed out and her dress hiked up all the way past the top of her stockings.

'Good, stay there,' I said, 'while I lock up the car.' I pushed her car door shut with my foot and with a chirp, chirp, secured it for the night.

"I took a quick look around to make sure no one was watching and then went rifling through her purse again to find her security card. The Washington Towers didn't have a doorman, thank God, but I would have to find her security card. I found her lipstick, a pocket purse, a compact, a half a pack of Rollo's, tweezers, four condoms, a tin of breath mints and, of all things, a men's razor; for that stubborn facial hair, no doubt. What I didn't find was a security card.

"I dumped the contents of her purse on to the hood of my car and other than some pocket change, her apartment key, and her wedding ring, I saw nothing else. It wasn't until I looked over at Fran's bare thigh did I see the shiny blue and white card sticking out of the top of her panty hose. I snatched it up and frantically threw her shit back into the purse.

"Holding on to the purse and apartment key in my left hand, I threw Fran's right arm over my shoulder and hoisted her to her feet. We swaggered across the parking lot, up the stairs to the door. I swiped the card, waited for the buzz and with my left hand still holding her purse, I flung the large glass doors open and dragged her inside. I made my way up to the elevator landing, pressed the button and waited impatiently for the elevator to arrive.

"Hanging on the wall of the elevator landing to my right, of all things, was a huge print of Salvador Dali's painting, *The Metamorphosis of Narcissus*. To my left was a small waiting area with a coffee table, a loveseat, and a couple of large leather chairs.

"There was a gentleman with a thin-rimmed fedora sitting at the end of the loveseat reading a newspaper that was splayed out on the coffee table and talking on his cell phone. He seemed completely engrossed in what he was doing and didn't even look up when Fran, for some reason, fell forward. Her high heels buckled beneath her *ankles* and the arm that was keeping her standing slid off my shoulder and she rolled over right in front of me as she headed for the floor.

"I acted fast and threw my arms out and around her before she hit the ground. It wasn't until I looked down that I realized that though my left hand was wrapped around her waist, my right hand was firmly holding on to her left breast that had fallen out on the way down. At that moment, the elevator opened and I dragged her inside. Fortunately for me, there wasn't anyone inside to tell the tale of our pirouette.

"I set her on the floor of the elevator at my feet and tucked her breast back into her bra. At this point, I had given up on any notion of having her walk the rest of the way. I was just going to have to drag her down the corridor to her door. Fortunately, her apartment was only three doors from the elevator. When the elevator stopped and the door opened, I had my back to the door. I leaned backward out into the hall and looked both directions. *Ah, the coast is clear,* I thought. *I'll just scoot her down to apartment 2041.*

"I snatched her up under the arms and dragged her down the hall as quickly as I could, but as I reached the service closet, I heard a door latch click and a man's voice, 'Okay, okay,' he said as he stood in the doorway of apartment 2045. 'Okay, okay. I'll get the ice cream; I'll get the ice cream. Go ahead and get undressed and I'll be right back. Christ, I'm not paying you by the minute.'

"As the man stood there squawking in the doorway, I opened the service closet and shoved Fran in, threw her purse on the floor and tried to close the door, but her legs were in the way. I gave them a shove with my foot and closed the door before the gentleman turned around. I left Fran in the closet and passed the man as he walked down the corridor toward the elevator. Standing at the threshold of Fran's apartment just two doors down, I watched the man board the elevator and the door close.

"Like a flash, I shoved the key into the lock and opened the door. I left the door standing wide open and went back to retrieve my lush. Fran must have moved some from when I left her just moments before, because when I tried to open the door, her body was now in the way.

"I pressed my shoulder against the door and threw my entire weight into it. Her heavy body slid across the linoleum with a squeak as the fat on her legs had stuck to the linoleum floor. I grabbed her purse and the first part of her body that I came to, which were her legs. I tucked them under my arms and dragged her feet first down the hall. Her dress slid all the way up past her underwear and piled up under her armpits as her now disheveled hair trailed along behind her.

"We crossed the threshold of her door with a bump, bump as her head bounced across the threshold. I dropped her legs with a thud and slammed the door behind us. *There, I think I pulled it off*, I thought, setting the purse on the table in the entrance hall.

"Fran was sprawled out on the floor with her arms over her head and a comical smile on her face. 'Well, old girl,' I said as I looked down, 'we made it. Let's get you into bed.' As I bent over to pick her up by the arms, the ridiculousness of the situation began to wear on me and I started to grumble. 'Every fucking time,' I grumbled to myself. 'The old bag gets plowed every fucking time. Why can't rich old women come in a smaller size? Jesus, I'm getting a hernia here.'

"I dragged her the rest of the way into the bedroom and peeled her dress off over her head. I unbuckled the clasps of the thin straps that kept her shoes on and tossed them into the corner of the room. Wrapping my arms around her, I hoisted her up and let her body fall onto the bed. I looked down at her half naked body sprawled out on the bed. *What a sad sack of shit she was*, I thought. *Here she has the kind of life I have always dreamed of, and all she can do with it is drink. Oh yeah, drink. That reminds me.*

"Her husband kept a bottle of 50-year-old scotch on a curio at the end of the bed. I grabbed a rock glass and filled it up halfway, took a seat in the corner of the room and stared at how the moonlight hit her pale white body fat. It was truly unflattering, but this is always how an evening with Fran ended. In all the time I have known her, I have never had to do the deed. How she knows I have a fat cock, I'll never know.

"I sat there sipping my scotch and watching the mischievous smile on her face. I can only imagine that she is dreaming about that fat dick right now. I shook my head at the prospect, rose to my feet, and strolled over to the balcony door. The night lights playing on the Hudson River and the street lights below turning green danced around in my head and conjured up the image of those brilliant emerald green eyes. She was such a vision to behold. Unlike any woman I had ever seen. Even the smell of honeysuckle and lilacs seem to stay with me, as if her scent was trapped within my skull. I caught a glimpse of my own reflection in the glass of the balcony door; it looked like a transparent ghost moving through the room.

"*Such a travesty of fate*, I thought. *I was meant for a life like this, a life full of the finest things it had to offer. In one month's time, it will all be mine. Once Danny whacks himself, I can finally live like I was meant to.* The thought of twenty-five million dollars brought a smile to my face and I could have sworn that last taste of scotch was the sweetest I had ever had.

"I set down my glass and turned my attention back to Fran. I positioned her body on the left side of the bed and laid her head on the pillow. I then pulled her panties off and dropped them on the floor revealing her well-maintained bush. It was obvious that she was planning to get laid tonight. I spread her legs slightly and pulled the bedding back before I took the now empty glass I had set on the curio and walked into the bathroom.

"I filled the glass a quarter of the way with warm water and re-entered the bedroom. There, in the space between her thighs, I poured the warm water and then covered her up. "Sweet dreams, old girl," I said softly. Then I got undressed and slid in beside her. When I closed my eyes, I saw a vision of the Asian woman's face as I drifted off to sleep."

Angels and Demons

Jacob looked over at the doctor still leaning back on the bench and carefully listening. "This is when my troubles really began. It all began with a strange dream."

"I see," said the doctor. "Was there an event in your life which might have presaged this dream?"

"No, not that I remember. I had recently gotten the promotion to junior associate at the firm, and it wasn't long after that, I heard of Uncle Walt's passing. Six or eight months maybe."

The doctor nodded. "I see, please continue."

"Well, as I've said, I don't remember falling asleep, but I remember feeling sick to my stomach as I stood on the tenth-floor landing waiting for the elevator. I guess my dinner of vodka, wine, and scotch didn't set too well. It was morning, but there was something odd about it; the elevator was taking longer than it should to get to the tenth floor. I watched as the numbers above the door climbed slowly. Finally, they settled on ten and there was a 'bing.'

"As the doors of the elevator opened, I lowered my eyes to greet what I thought was going to be an empty elevator, but found myself looking straight into the face of that Asian beauty. Time seemed to grind to a stop when she looked up and smiled at me. I boarded the elevator, and as she stepped past me onto the landing, she reached up with her left hand and softly caressed my right cheek.

"The tips of her fingers burned like a hot rake across my skin and immediately sank into the center of my being. Her eyes held me fast like a strand tethered to my heart, which she tugged at as she pulled away. The doors closed behind me. I was left alone on an elevator descending and the image of her scorched into my mind.

"Once again, the elevator seemed to take forever to reach the first floor. Then, as before, my eyes were drawn to the display above the doors as I impatiently waited. 8th, 7th, 6th, *come on,* I thought. *Maybe there is something wrong with the lift.* 4th, 3rd, 2nd, 'Finally,' I said to myself when the first floor arrived, but the elevator didn't stop. 'B,' read the display above the door. B1, B2, B3, *What the fuck? I didn't know they had sub-floors in this building.* B6, B7, B8, *God damn, how far does it go?* B10, B11, B12. 'Holy shit!' I exclaimed. 'I'm going to be late for work!' At B13, the lift came to a stop, the bell rang, and the doors slowly opened to reveal a sight straight out of Dante's *Inferno.*

"In the distance, blurred by waves of heat rising from a scorched earth, I could see a great fat Minotaur lounging on a bejeweled throne of gold and gems. It was as tall as a six-story building with mounds of fat across its entire body. There were four or five cherub daemons with cloven feet and arms like monkeys feeding the beast with tridents. They stabbed at a banquet of cut up cow, goat, pig and human bodies and shoved it into the mouth of the great beast.

"The Minotaur showed no sign of stopping as it gorged on everything and drooled the waste upon his chest. My stomach turned within me when I saw a half-cooked slab of cow slide off its belly and hit the floor. It was then that I realized the throne he was sitting on had no legs, but was held up by a great multitude of people. Thousands and thousands of people were hunched over, crying and screaming in pain as they bore the full weight of the humongous beast on their backs.

"Two small daemons appeared in the doorway to the elevator. They were carrying tridents and chattering to each other as they glared up at me with eyes of fire. I stepped backward into the lift. One of them stepped into the lift, chattering as it came. It poked at me with his trident, beckoned the other with its monkey-like hand.

"Without hesitation, the other daemon leaped forward on to the back of the first and thrust his trident into my chest. I awoke and grabbed my chest and sat up gasping for air. I looked around and realized I was still in bed. Fran was to my left still snoozing off the effects of her gin and tonic while I lay in a pool of sweat, my heart pounding within.

"The clock on the night stand read 6:45, but it felt like I had been asleep for days. I sat there a moment, regaining my sense of reality. There was no way I was going back to sleep after that, so I shook off the remnants of the dream as best I could and quietly slipped out of bed.

"As quickly and as silently as I could, I showered, shaved, and dressed before Fran awoke. It is lucky for me she is a heavy sleeper and usually doesn't get up until after one o'clock. I scoured her husband's walk-in closet for something to wear. There was a sleek pinstripe suit that looked about my size. *This, with a light blue shirt and a red power tie for effect, ought to do nicely,* I thought. I looked at the lapel; there was a small *ME* below the buttonhole. *See,* I thought, *even the monogram says me. I like the sound of that. If I am going to meet Daniel on his home turf, I wanted to dominate the proceedings.* In my business, appearance is the key to all opportunities.

"I stood before the full-length mirror in his closet and tied a single Windsor into the red pinstriped tie I had selected. That's when I noticed the subtle lines across my right cheek. My memory flashed back to the dream of that nameless beauty and the burning sensation that had so completely held me spellbound. 'What's wrong with you, Jacob?' I whispered to myself as I ran my fingers across my cheek. 'Have you forgotten who you are? You are Jacob Sullinger, mover, shaker and heart-breaker. There isn't a woman alive that can reach your heart of stone. Don't forget where you came from.'

"A disenfranchised childhood and tutelage at the school of hard knocks in the Bronx was enough to teach me it's either play or be played. I didn't make it into that law office by accident. No indeed, it was by sheer will alone that I ascended to where I was, and I wasn't finished yet. The thought of the twenty-five million dollars brought a sinister smile to my face as I put the finishing touches on my appearance. *There, not a bad fit at all*, I thought, staring at the dapper young man in the mirror.

"I returned to the bedroom and looked down at Fran still silently sleeping. *Now where did I leave that purse?* I pondered. *That's right; it's in the entrance hall.* I found the purse and took the remaining three hundred as well as retrieved one of the condoms from it. I peeled the wrapper open and unrolled the condom, then I mustered up as much spit as my mouth could make after a night of drinking and dribbled it into the condom. I then tied it off at the top and returned to the bedroom to leave it and the wrapper on the nightstand. *You were such an animal last night*, I thought, as I chuckled to myself. Then I left by way of the staircase to the first floor. There was no sense in tempting fate.

"It was 8:03 when I found my car and started off to work. I made a quick stop at the Brandy Hills Bakery on the corner for a cup of coffee, a bear claw, and a newspaper before going to the office. There on the corner, amidst the morning commuters that shuffled in and out the bakery stood an old man with disheveled white hair, tattered military pants, army boots, and a London fog jacket. 'How will I know him?' he said to himself as I sauntered by. 'I never seem to recognize them when I am in a crowd. I mean, here I am at the corner right on time like I am told, but all's I ever hear is, you will know him.'

"I shot him a worried look as I stepped past the babbling lunatic. When he realized I had made eye contact, he reached out his hand toward me and asked, 'Excuse me, do you have the time, sir?'

"I pulled my arm away before he touched my coat. 'Time to back the fuck off, old man. If you know what I mean?' I glared at him with eye of steel.

'Ah, in that case,' he said with a smile, 'it's later than you know. I will pray for you.'

'Whatever gets you off,' I said as I walked toward the bakery door.

"Once inside, I ordered my bear claw and large latté, paid the girl, and strolled over to the news stand by the window. Dropping my change in the slot, I opened the machine and pulled out a copy of the Journal and stepped to a table to set my latté down. *Hmm, the DOW Jones is on the way up,* I thought as I studied the cover story. *I should give my man Jack a call and see how my money is doing.*

"I perused the headlines a bit and quickly sifted through the pages before glancing up to see the old man outside washing the windows of my car with a cup of water and a newspaper. Folding my new paper in half, I stuffed it under my arm, snatched up my coffee, and bolted for the door. I shoved my way through a group of people standing by the door and jetted outside. 'Hey! Hey! Hey!' I yelled. 'What the fuck do you think you're doing? Back away from the Martin, old man. Do you have some kind of death wish?'

"The old man pulled away from my car with his hands in the air still holding the newspaper and cup of water. His face was stuck in an expression of confused astonishment. He immediately started to babble to himself. 'B...b...but I thought he would like clean windows,' he said to himself. He turned his head slightly to the right and down and whispered. 'Mikey, you did say he would be angry, but you...you didn't say he was violent.'

'Who are you talking to? Get the hell away from my car, you lunatic, before you wind up hurt,' I said as I moved to place my body between him and my car. 'You're still standing too close to my car!' I yelled. 'I said back the fuck off!' He took two steps backward and looked at me like a scolded puppy.

I took the newspaper out from under my arm and shook it in his face. 'Remember, old man, if you see this car again, you give it a wide berth. You got me?'

"He just nodded his head in compliance with a wide-eyed look of innocence, mumbling, 'I don't know about this one, Mikey, it might be too late. Well, if you say so…but, but I…well, yes…yes, I have seen worse.' I watched, bewildered, as the old man quietly babbled to himself, walked across the parking lot and slipped into the anonymity of the crowded city streets and disappeared. A handful of people had gathered at the entrance of the garage and stood there gawking at me. ""Does anyone else want to make me late for work?' I snapped at the crowed.

"'What was that all about?' I heard one of them say. I shot a cold stare at anyone who might want a piece of me and then shook my head and waved them off with my newspaper before I climbed into my car and headed to work.

"The incident really got under my skin as I thought about the crazy old man. *What a lunatic. I could have kicked his teeth in, and what the hell did that guy mean? Who is he yelling at?* I could feel my blood pressure rise. Grinding my teeth and pounded my fist on the steering wheel didn't seem to help. *That crazy old man, I'd better never see him near my car again,* I thought as I reached for the radio to distract me. The song that was playing was Billion-Dollar Babies and my thoughts floated back to pile of money that had become the focus of all my daydreams.

"After that, the sounds of Korn, Nine Inch Nails, and Five Finger Death punch rocked my skull until the thought of that old man was as far from my mind as ethics from the White House. It was just a few city miles, and a modicum of traffic lights, and I was pulling into the 12th Street parking garage. Today was the day I was setting in motion the events that was going to lead me to my pot of gold. *Wahoo! Yeah, twenty-five million dollars*, I thought. *I bet my man Jack on Wall Street could double, or even triple that amount.*

"It was a ten-minute walk to the office from the garage and I don't think my feet even hit the ground. 'Mmm, mm, m, m, m. I'm in the money—I'm in the money,' I began to sing to myself as I ascended the steps that lead to the law offices of Simon & Neubauer.

'Good morning, Mr. Sullinger,' said Beatrice as I sauntered past her desk singing. 'Usually, I only hear the senior partners singing that song,' she said chuckling to herself.

'Yes well, today the song belongs to me. Tell me, Bea, are you going to come to work for me when I open my own office?'

'I will have to check the weather report first,' she said with a smile.

'Why is that?' I asked.

'Because, it might be a cold day in hell before that happens at the rate junior associates get paid. Ha, ha, ha. Don't forget, I stuff all the pay envelopes around here. I know how much you make.'

'You just wait. Things are turning in my direction. I can smell the winds of change and it smells like money.'

'Yes well, I hope you don't mind if I don't climb aboard the good ship *Pipe Dream* yet, I still have a lot of work to do around here.'

'Suit yourself,' I said. 'Oh, and while I'm thinking about it, could you get me the numbers for the New York trust we use for our terminal clients. I have some trust funds and a will to set up, and I am going to have to make some calls.'

'Of course, as if I didn't have enough to do. I'll get right on it.'

'I appreciate that,' I said with a wink and a smile.

'Don't you know from sarcasm?' she said shaking her head.

'I knew I could count on you,' I said, closing my office door behind me.

"The morning sped by as I set my wheel of good fortune in motion. I made several calls and drew up the contracts that afternoon. I would need a few copies from the copy machine before I could stuff my briefcase for my meeting with Daniel that evening. Another intern was in the copying room when I entered, so I had to wait my turn. His name was Robert McCarver, but the guys call him Bobby Mac on the golf course. I call him Mac for short.

'Hey Mac, are you sure you know how to work that thing?' I chided as he hovered over the copier.

"He shot me a disparaging look and said, 'Just wait your turn, Jake.'

'Hey, did you hear about that new club, the *Inferno Room*? It sounds like my kind of place. I'm thinking of checking it out this weekend, are you in?'

'Hell no,' he said. 'The last time I went to a nightclub with you, I had to sleep on the couch for three weeks.'

'Ah, come on man, where's your sense of adventure? What's the matter, didn't Mrs. Mac take to you coming home at four in the morning?'

'No, I think it was the smell of Jack Daniels and cheap perfume that did it. At any rate, I can't take that risk again—Jesus man, I almost became one of your clients.'

'That's not such a bad thing, I'm a good lawyer.'

'I guess we would have to better define the word *good.* Anyway, count me out. I want no part in your next safari into the Manhattan night life.'

'Suit yourself,' I said as I watched him hastily gathered up his stack of papers. 'Just more women for me.'

"He shuffled out the door with his payload of paperwork, and I set about making the copies for my files, then it was lunch at *Alfraito*'s, and back to the office to look busy until three o'clock. When three o'clock hit, I closed up shop, left word with Beatrice, and hit the street like a kid on the last day of school, with wide-eyed optimism and an endless summer in the forefront of my mind.

"On the way to the parking garage, I plucked Daniel's business card from my pocket and glanced at the address. *Jersey? Shit it will probably be late before I get back*, I thought to myself. I quickly dialed the number on the card and waited for someone to pick up.

'Hello?'

'Daniel?'

'Yes.'

'This is Jacob, I have those papers you wanted and I'm on my way to your house now.'

'Good. When you get here, use the intercom and I will buzz you in.'

'I will see you in about an hour.'

'Great, I will see you then.' *Click.*

"Well, he doesn't mince words when there is money on the line, I thought as I slipped my phone back into my pocket.

"Once I had located my car, I was on my way toward the Holland Tunnel and the endless suburban streets of Jersey City. Forty-five minutes later, I found myself turning onto a street of modest but well-cared-for apartment houses. A conspicuous black limousine with Louisiana license plates sat in front of the address I was searching for. The dark-tinted windows left me wondering whether this Monsieur Diabolus was residing inside; even the driver's door left me with an uneasy curiosity about the occupants. The Mardi Gras beads hanging from the review mirror and a bumper sticker that read,

"Devils do it with a smile at the *Inferno Room*," were the only clues to the owner's nature.

"I parked across the street where I could keep an eye on my Martin and made damn sure to lock it up, and then I started toward the front steps carrying my brief case. As I reached the bottom of the steps, I had the strangest feeling of dread come over me. The heat of the sun seemed to intensify, as if something terrible were about to happen and the light breeze that had blown just moments before came to a dead calm.

"The front door to the apartments swung open and a stately gentleman stepped through it and paused a moment on the landing. The man was completely overdressed in a bright white three-piece suit complete with cape, a walking cane, and a white fedora topped with a small black feather that gleamed blue and purple in the afternoon sun.

"The man gracefully caressed the length of his mid-length white beard and surveyed the neighborhood. He stuck his nose in the air, as if he were the king of the world and then plucked a pocket watch from the breast pocket of his vest. As he did, something fell to the ground, rolled around, and came to rest by his left shoe. Oblivious to the fallen object, he glanced at the watch, and then stuffed the watch back into his pocket and sauntered down the steps as I ascended.

"When I came to the place where he had stood, I looked down. There on the ground was a single red poker chip. I picked it up and looked back at the gentleman as he reached the bottom of the steps. 'Excuse me,' I said catching the man's attention. 'You dropped this.'

"The man paused and stared up the stairs at me. 'Sir? I beg your pardon?' he responded.

'I said you dropped this. It's a poker chip.'

'It is but a trifle, sir, you may keep it if you want,' he said nonchalantly. Then an eyebrow raised and a slight smile wrinkled his face. 'Do you play, sir?'

'I used to when I was in college; was damn good at it too,' I said smugly.

'Then we must play some time, sir, I am always looking for a challenging player.'

"His thick Louisiana accent brimmed with southern propriety. I was immediately taken by his presence. *This was a man in total control of his life*, I thought. 'Of course, it's been years since I have played,' I said.

"'Then you should prepare yourself, sir, and we can discuss this at some later date. When you feel you will be—up to the challenge, shall we say?—there is a number on the back of the chip where you can reach me. Now if you'll excuse me, I have pressing matters to attend to. I bid you a good day, sir.' With that, he turned and disappeared into that ambiguous black limousine.

"I paused a moment and looked down at the chip. Sure, enough there was a number on the back of it. It read 1800-666-7777. *What kind of man has his own 1-800 number?* I thought. I slipped the chip into my left jacket pocket and turned my attention to the intercom. *Let's see—Stevens, Kroach, Jessup, Lamb, here it is, Daniel Lamb.*

"I pressed the button next to his name and his voice rang down from the apartment.

'Hello.'

'It's me, Jacob,' I said. 'I've got the papers you wanted.'

'Come on up, I'm on the second floor, third door on the right at the top of the landing.' Then the buzzer sounded and I opened the door and made my way upstairs.

"At the top of the stairs, I turned to my right and sure enough, the third door was left ajar. I crossed the landing and gently swung the door open. 'Hello,' I said as the door creaked open.

'Come on in,' he said. 'I'm in the kitchen.'

"Closing the door behind me, I crossed the living room and turned the corner. I saw him wiping the kitchen table with a dish towel. 'We had a little mishap,' he said with a smile. "Monsieur Diabolus accidentally broke a glass while he was here. Of course, he offered to pay for it, being the man of integrity that he is.'

'What's another glass?' I said placing my briefcase on the table.

'Exactly,' said Daniel.

"He finished drying the table off and sat down and stared up at me with those big doe eyes. 'So, you've got the trust funds set up?'

'Of course, I don't waste any time when there is twenty-five million riding on the line. All I need from you is your signature on the dotted lines and the *deal will be done*, as they say.' I pulled the stack of papers out and plopped them on the table in front of him.

'Right,' he said picking up the pen I laid in front of him. 'You know,' he proceeded cautiously, 'there is the off chance I could win the card game.'

'And what does that mean to me?' I said, scowling at him.

'It means, I walk away unharmed and set for life. When you win with Monsieur Diabolus, you win big; either way, you'll get paid.'

'That's all that concerns me,' I said.

'Playing with Monsieur Diabolus is still a gamble, the stakes are just higher,' he said as he calmly scanned the fine print of the documents.

'Whatever. Just remember the important part of all of this is, I get paid,' I said glaring at him. 'What was he doing here anyway?'

'He was witnessing all of the insurance policies. He is a notary public.'

'Of New York?' I scoffed. 'What is a Louisiana gentleman doing as a New York notary public?'

'Monsieur Diabolus has, shall we say, a lot of vested interests in New York and is intricately tied to the politics and commerce of the city and even the state.'

'So, what you are saying is, he is a high roller,' I remarked.

"Daniel paused from reading and looked up at me with one eyebrow raised and said with conviction, 'Very high.'

'Hmm,' I said, 'I may have to get to know this Monsieur Diabolus a little better. He sounds like my kind of guy.'

"A few nervous moments later, he finished reviewing my work and tapped the pen on the table, clicked the point out with his thumb, and said, 'Okay, it all looks legit.'

'Did you doubt me?' I asked.

"'No—I know you too well,' he said rolling his eyes as he began sifting through the papers and sign them. Once he was done, I took the stack of documents from him and made sure he had signed every line. 'Now,' he said. 'I have something here for you to sign.'

"Me?"

'Yes, you,' he said firmly. 'You wouldn't begrudge me a little protection of my family's interests, would you?'

'What exactly are you talking about?'

'I chose you, Jacob, because I know you are ruthless, heartless, and will do anything to get rich. I know I can rely on your greed to get the job done, but I am also aware that as soon as I am gone, you will set your sights on the money in my family's trust funds. I have no intention of letting that happen.'

'Just how do you think I would manage that trick?' I said, hoping my slight grin didn't give me away.

'Come now, Jacob, we are not naïve college kids any more. In fact, I don't think you ever were. I know you would simply raise your rates and service fees until the funds were gone. I took the precaution of having this drawn up,' he said, handing me a contract. 'It's a contract that locks in the rates that you can charge the trust funds for the legal protection you provide and prohibits any surcharges you might have thought of.'

'You have thought of everything, haven't you? And what if I don't sign?'

'Then the deal is off. I'm not fucking around with you, Jacob. You will just have to settle for the twenty-five million. Besides, if you can't make that work, you don't deserve it.'

'Okay, okay, calm down. I was just testing your resolve. The agreed upon twenty-five mil is more than enough.'

"He sat there with a stony look upon his face as I read through the contract. The tension mounted as I nervously scratched my chin and looked back at him. 'What is this Latin at the bottom here?'

'I don't know,' said Daniel, 'it is something Monsieur Diabolus put in. I'm not the lawyer here, you are.'

Damn, I knew I should have paid more attention in my Latin class, I thought, as I read the passage again:

Consensio damnatorum; ab anima offertur occasio vincere. Stipenduum peccati gravis est, in sanguine suum sim entombed. Abyssus abyssum invocate abyssus.

'Hmm,' I said scratching my chin. 'Latin was not one of my best courses and some of these words are not legal terms.'

'You mean you don't know?' Daniel scoffed.

'Well, Consensio is to give consent to something and damnatorum, if I am not mistaken, is the Latin word for Damnation. So, just those two words give me cause for alarm. It means the consent to be damned.'

'Sounds like someone has your number, Jacob. Hahaha!' He laughed.

'And here, *Abyssus abyssum invocate abyssus?* Hell, calls hell? What kind of contract is this?' I slapped the papers with the back of my hand. 'What the fuck are you trying to sell me here?'

'I told you, Jacob, this is something that Monsieur Diabolus has insisted on. If you don't sign, there will be no money.'

"'Well, you can fucking forget…' as the words left my lips, I felt a heavy weight on my shoulders. It was as if something heavy was draped across them. My neck suddenly felt tight and I couldn't get the words out. Gasping for air, I threw the document on the table and steadied myself against the table's edge. Still clutching the pen in my right hand, I choked and coughed and wheezed the word, 'Water.'

'Are you all right?' he asked. 'Yes, yes, I'll get you a glass of water.' He jumped up and ran into the kitchen.

"I glanced up at the big mirror in the living room and saw my reflection showed a great albino python wrapped around my neck and draped down my right arm. I could feel it tighten around my throat. I clawed at it with my left hand in a feeble attempt to breathe.

"The serpent's head hung above my right shoulder. It turned slightly toward me and wound its way down my arm and around my wrist. It raised its head and looked me in the eye and with a jolt, came down hard, sinking its teeth into my hand. I felt a sharp pain in my finger and blood began to trickle down into a pool upon the contract. The serpent then forced my hand against my will to scroll out my name upon the page. As soon as the last letter was formed, it was gone and I was left hunched over my left arm while my right hand dripped blood upon the page.

"Daniel returned with a glass of water in his hand. 'Here you go, your water. Can you stand up?' He grabbed my arm and helped me to my feet.

'Wha…wha…what the hell was that?' I exclaimed.

"'What?' he asked. 'You were choking on something, so I brought you a glass of water.' He set the glass on the table next to the papers covered in my blood. 'What happened here? You cut your finger? There must have been a shard left over from Monsieur Diabolus' broken glass.'

'You mean you didn't see it?' I exclaimed.

'See what?' said Daniel puzzling.

"I glared at him intensely and realized that he hadn't seen what I saw. There was an awkward moment of silence as we stared at each other. *If I were to tell him, he would think I was crazy*, I thought, so I just shook my head. 'Never mind, jackass,' I said under my breath. Looking down at my throbbing finger, I could see a small piece of glass still wedged within the cut. I placed my finger to my lips and carefully pulled it out with my teeth and spat it out on my opened palm. 'You need to be more careful when you clean up broken glass, numb nuts.'

'Well, you decided to sign it after all, I see,' he said picking up the bloody document.

"I just glared at him.

"'Monsieur Diabolus will be pleased. He was quite adamant you should sign. Here…here is a napkin for your cut,' he said as he handed me a paper towel. He carefully looked over the document and then placed it amongst his things to the side. 'I will give this to him tomorrow when he returns.'

'He is coming back tomorrow?' I asked.

'He is personally overseeing every phase of this transaction. For him to take this much interest in the situation, there must be something, or someone that he has invested a lot of time in.'

'You seem to know him well, Daniel,' I said curiously.

'As well as anybody could, I guess. He is something of an enigma,' he answered. 'Well anyway, you will get your money.'

'I'd better,' I said. 'For that kind of money, I would track you down in hell just for the chance to watch you burn.'

"I quietly pulled my cell phone from my pocket, glanced at the time, and then softly set it on the table next to the glass of water he had brought. 'So, you said he'll be back tomorrow, then?' I asked.

"'Yeah, he'll be here to pick up the papers and arrange the card game. Yep, in two weeks' time, I will be boarding his private yacht for the game of my life.' Daniel fell silent for a moment and looked down, as if the weight of what he had said had fully sunk in. He raised his chin and nodded his head in a defiant confirmation. 'God save me, it is for the right reasons that I go,' he said. 'Tell me, Jacob, do you believe, if you do the wrong thing for the right reasons, you will be vindicated? Does the end justify the means?'

"I watched his resolve, and marveled at the crazy asshole. I didn't know what would come of all this drama, but as long as I was going to end up wiping my ass with hundred-dollar bills—I didn't care. 'Whatever,' I said. 'Let me know when it all goes down; I want to know when I get my money.'

'Spoken like a true lawyer,' he said with a smirk.

"I left after that. There is only so much apathy I can take. I made my way back out to the street. As I opened my car door, I took one last look at Daniel's apartment. It brought a smile to my face to think of my phone still sitting on his kitchen table. Without my phone, I will have to take the long drive back into Brooklyn and stay at my apartment with my roommate Dominic and his annoying lovesick girlfriend, Miranda. Normally, I try to avoid them like the plague, but since Monsieur Diabolus is going to be visiting Daniel tomorrow, I wanted a good reason to call.

"I drove the hour and forty-five minutes to get to Brooklyn. Back to the two-room apartment I shared when I wasn't looking for *clients*. As I pulled up, I could see the silhouette of two people in the kitchen through the big picture window upstairs. I don't know what they were up to, but I could see he had his shirt off, and that couldn't be good. I locked my car up tight and sauntered up the stairs, through the door and up to the second floor.

"As I approached my apartment, I heard giggling and whispers from the other side of the door. I pulled my keys from my pocket and slipped it into the keyhole, pausing a moment, I thought twice about barging in. 'Ehmmm, ehmmm!' I said loudly clearing my throat.

'Shhhh, he's home…shit,' Dominic whispered.

'You said he wasn't coming back tonight,' said Miranda.

'Jesus, he's never home. I wonder what the hell happened,' said Dominic. 'Quick, run to my bedroom.'

"There was some quick shuffling through the apartment as I turned the doorknob and then, silence. I made my way quietly to the kitchen. There on the counter were a spatula and a dishcloth laid out on the counter, my electric toothbrush, and a tube of KY. 'What the fuck!' I exclaimed. 'My toothbrush?' Laughter rang out from behind Dominic's bedroom door.

'We were going to wash it when we were done. Hahaha!' said Dominic. I could hear Miranda stifling her laughter in the background.

'You two are sick! Next time use your own toothbrush, assholes!'

'Mine isn't electric,' Dominic chuckled.

'It doesn't vibrate, hahaha!' Miranda added with a laugh.

"I carefully picked the toothbrush up by the bristles and threw it into the trash. Then, I opened the fridge and peered into it for a moment. There was a jar of pickles, a carton of eggs, a half-gallon of orange juice, an assortment of condiments, a carton of Chang's Chinese takeout, and a pizza box from Dino's pizzeria. I pulled the pizza box from the fridge and opened it up. There were still three pieces inside. 'You're buying me a new toothbrush!' I said loudly. 'And I'm taking your pizza.'

'Whatever!' said Dominic from behind his door. 'Hey, you got the rent, dude? It's three days late.'

"'Oh yeah,' I said. 'Here—it's on the counter next to your ass cream,' I said with a laugh as I took out my wallet and threw the money on the counter. *It's a good thing Fran had that cash, I completely forgot*, I thought. "I'm going to bed. Try to keep the noise down. I have to work in the morning."

'Whatever, dude,' was all he said.

"I took the pizza and disappeared into my bedroom, closing the door behind me. I kicked off my shoes, turned on my TV and fell back onto my bed. *What a day,* I thought as I gently rubbed the tip of my sore finger. I loosened Fran's husband's tie and unbuttoned the top button of her husband's shirt. *Oh shit, I'm going to have to get my suit back from Fran,* I thought. *I might keep this one, I kind of like the way it fits; besides, as many suits as Fran's husband has, he won't miss it.* Once I had finished off the pizza, I felt the heavy hand of sleep take me and I drifted off to the sound of the evening news and slipped into another vivid dream. A dream I can't seem to forget.

"I remember standing in the darkness with nothing but a gleaming star in the distance, so far away. It flickered and glistened like white gold against the black, and I, like a moth, was drawn to it. I stepped forward into the darkness and it got closer. I could almost feel its presence before me, cold and shiny, like a new car. How I longed for the power that it granted the possessor.

"This point in the dark was calling me toward it. Like a bell it rang out from the distance, a resonating voice that moved me forward. It controlled my every action; I behaved the way it wanted me to behave. I smiled when it wanted me to smile and laughed when it was right for me to laugh, as though I had forfeited my own will. I became aware of the hold it had on me, like some master of puppets.

"As I drew nearer to this glistening star, I found myself standing on a street corner at a traffic light. I was waiting for the light to turn green amidst a crowd of people, faceless and gaunt in their absent-minded malaise. I, alone, saw the light turn green. I was the only one the star had beckoned forward. I stepped into the street and crossed without so much as a dog to accompany me. The star, gleaming bright and beautiful in the distance, rang out in the black.

"I stopped on the opposite street corner and looked back at the masses as they waited for the light. Steam rose around me from the subway below, venting its heat through the grate I stood on. Lost within this mist, I could see the dragon lady standing on the opposite corner smiling at me, those deep Asian eyes laughing behind her elegant smile and that emerald green dress, shining like new money amidst the nameless crowd. I looked down at my feet, barely visible in the rising steam and darkness below and again at the star, but could not move. Something insidious held me fast and an over whelming feeling of foreboding came over me as the grate beneath my feet began to sink into the darkness."

Jacob paused and looked out at the ducks on the pond. Dr. Kessler was carefully watching Jacob's expressions and listening intently. "Why did you stop?" he asked.

Jacob tilted his head slightly, but never looked the doctor in the eye. "All this sounds so strange, doesn't it? Dreams, visions? If I were sitting where you are, I would think me mad."

"The mind is a tricky thing, Jacob," said the doctor. "If there is something unsettling in the subconscious, it will often find a way to show itself. Try not to think of them as *crazy* dreams or visions. They are cries for help echoing up from your childhood." The doctor smiled at Jacob. "Do you want to go on or shall we save it for another day?"

Jacob rose to his feet, stuck his hands in the pockets of his pajamas and shuffled his right foot across the ground. "No doc, I think I need more time," he said as he turned back toward the hospital.

"You know, you're going to have to tell someone," the doctor called out, "It might as well be me." Jacob looked back and gave a stiff-lipped nod of his head and turned and walked away. *Maybe he's right*, he thought. *What I need is someone who knows how I feel, someone whom I can trust. Someone I may never see again.*

When he got to the garden, he stopped and gazed at the beauty of his great uncle's work. He pondered who that person might be, this person of singularity. He massaged the back of his neck with his right hand and strained at the thought, then shrugged his shoulders and meandered back toward the hospital.

A Gravis Situation

The following day, Jacob rose early, skipped breakfast, and walked his way back to the garden and duck pond. Jacob sat quietly on the bench and wrestled with his thoughts. His past had led him to this point, to a moment frozen in place. It was just two weeks of his childhood, but it shaped everything he did from that moment to this. *How could I ever find that happy child again?* he thought. He's *gone and there was nothing that will bring him back and no one I trust enough share my story with. Sure, I could tell the doctor, but the doctor has never gone through something like that. Would he understand? He was just trained to say all of the right things.* "No," Jacob said out loud. "I want to tell someone who knows what hell is like."

After sitting for two hours, he heard the sound of someone walking the path toward the garden. Their steps got steadily louder until they stopped behind the bench Jacob sat on. Without turning around, Jacob said, "You found me."

"It wasn't that hard. I knew you would come back here."

"It's a good place to think," said Jacob, as he threw a listless stone into the pond. "You don't have to stand there, Doc, have a seat."

"Thank you, I was waiting for an invitation," said Dr. Kessler. "Are you ready to take up where we left off?"

"Oh, I guess. If you've got nothing better to do with your time."

"Nothing which interests me more." Jacob shot a look of suspicion at the doctor.

"So, you like uncovering people's dirty little secrets then?"

"Secrets? I could care less about your secrets. Everyone has secrets, Jacob; not everyone is able to put those secrets to rest. What I care about is your happiness." Dr. Kessler nodded his head and folded his arms as he settled on to the bench. "So, let's get on with it, shall we?"

"I don't remember where I left off."

"You had gone back to your apartment and confronted your roommate. I believe you were telling me something about a dream you had. The dream about a star, a busy street, and the Asian woman."

"Ah yes, I remember now. I remember what woke me up, too. Ha-ha-ha. I woke to a strange sound of pounding coming from Dominic's room. Thud, thud…thud, thud…thud, thud…" Jacob snickered. "It was the sound of a headboard knocking against the wall. I sat up in bed and looked at the clock. *5:28? What the fuck! It's not even 6:00 yet and they are going at it already?* 'Oh, for crying out loud!' I shouted. 'Can't you guys sleep in for once?' Then I threw the pizza box at the door and buried my head in the pillow. 'Christ, they're worse than lemmings,' I mumbled.

"Well, eight o'clock came with little notice. The banging of Dominic's headboard (though it lasted only twenty minutes) and the strange feeling I was left with after the dream was too much for my head. I finally got up and took a shower, carefully placing Fran's husband's suit on a hanger. It was still clean and I wanted to wear it again. Instead, I picked out one of my suits, got dressed and headed off to work, stopping only to grab a coffee and my morning copy of the Journal.

"I arrived at the office at 9:35 that morning. When I entered the building, I was met by Beatrice's late again face and this time she didn't waste words. 'Don't even bother going into your office. The senior partners want to see you upstairs,' she said.

'What's that all about?' I remarked.

'Don't know,' she said. 'Maybe they want to give you a raise for being late every day.' She shot me a disparaging look.

"I gave her a devil-may-care grin and flippantly said, 'Come on Bee, you know you love it. It gives you something to bitch about.'

'I couldn't care less,' she said. 'You can dig your own grave, as far as I am concerned.'

'In a few short weeks, it won't matter anyway; I'm going to be able to own this place.'

'Ha!' She scoffed. 'Dreamer!'

'You wait and see, Bee, you just wait and see.'

"I crossed the lobby and took the elevator to the eighth floor. *I wonder what the seniors want with me. I haven't been upstairs since my interview two and a half years ago.*

"The marble floors decorated with veins of black and gold paved a straight-line right to Mr. Jamison's office; Mr. Jamison was the most senior partner and VP of the firm. There was only one man above him and that was Simon Neubauer, the grandson of the founding partner. I could feel my tie get tighter as I drew near to his big double doors. When I reached his door, I stopped, took a deep breath, wiped my sweaty hands off on my pants, then opened the door. Leslie, Jamison's secretary, was sitting quietly typing when I conspicuously stepped into the room. She looked up from behind her glasses and without missing a beat said, 'Take a seat and I will let him know you are here.'

"I quietly took a seat and began wracking my brain for excuses for why I was late again. *Hmm, there was a traffic jam in the tunnel. No, he might have watched the news. The fire department was testing the hydrants on my street. No, too complex. There was a car that was double parked, that's why I couldn't get out until I got that bastard to move his car. Yeah, that's it. I think he'll buy that one, if I make it convincing.* I was deeply mired in nervous mental masturbation when I heard Jamison's voice form the intercom. "Show him in and be quick about it, I am on a tight schedule today."

'Yes, Mr. Jamison.' said Leslie. She looked over at me. 'Well? I wouldn't keep him waiting if I were you.'

"I jumped to my feet, walked to the big double doors, took a quick deep breath and glanced over at Leslie. She looked up from her typing and smiled.

"When I entered the room, Jamison was standing at the big picture window behind his grand oak desk looking down at the city streets. Jamison was an imposing man, standing about 6'3", or 6'4", impeccably dressed, and his shiny bald head gave off an air of misogynistic power that had a cold, almost clinical execution to it. He had his back to me, with his hands in his pockets, staring out over the Manhattan commuters. 'Good afternoon, Jacob. It's been a while since you've been up here, hasn't it?' he said still staring out the window at the piss ants below.

'Ha,' I said, 'Oh, it's been two and a half years sir.'

'I'll keep this short,' he said as he turned to face me. 'We have an opportunity for you, Jacob, if you're interested.'

'I am always ready for *opportunity*, Mr. Jamison.'

'That is why the seniors like you; you have an eye for opportunity. There is a large insurance firm that is looking for a good mouthpiece. One that…well, shall we say, doesn't allow the little things like their conscience get in the way of business. It's nothing personal. Just business, you understand?'

'Got it, just business,' I said quietly.

'An opportunity like this separates the men from the boys, you understand.'

'Right…men from the boys,' I repeated. *God! I sound like a goddamned parrot!* I thought.

'New York Life & Trust has been with us only for a short time. Originally, we gave the account to Smithy, but they weren't happy with the way he handled their business. It seems they wanted someone who isn't afraid to get his hands dirty and the seniors think that you would be the obvious candidate.'

'If I might ask, how dirty are we talking about?'

'"Oh, nothing too dark, a half dozen defendants have filed a class action suit against the firm and landed in court.' He gestured with his hand to the case files on his desk. 'Some people in California have filed jointly against the insurance company over a neighborhood disaster that happened and left their houses halfway down a hillside. Apparently, there was a landslide and the homeowners filed their claims at the same time. The company is reluctant to pay and is weighing their options in an attempt to see how serious the claimants were. The claimants filed a joint class action suit. After much deliberation, New York Life & Trust has dug in their heels and changed tactics, and this is where you come in.'

'I see,' I said. 'So, you want me to….'

'I want you to make this disappear,' he said sharply. 'This is a very large and important account and the seniors don't want to lose their business, but this is also something that has to be done with some delicacy. The seniors also don't want to be attached to any high-profile cases that could possibly end up being big news.'

'Hmmm,' I said, fingering my goatee. 'I don't exactly want my name attached to a case like that, either.'

"There was a pause and the air grew stale. His eyebrows lowered and he approached his desk and slowly slid the manila envelope across the surface. 'So,' he said smugly, 'what exactly was it that made you late today?'

'Huh…what…?' I stammered. 'Car…double parked,' blundered out of my mouth. Suddenly, my excuse was rendered useless.

'I see,' he said. 'You know the seniors don't much care for tardiness in their juniors.' He then tapped the envelope three times with his fingers.

'Oh…I see,' I said. 'Okay, well then, in that case, I'll put my best man on it then.'

'And who might that be?' he asked.

'Me,' I said, as I slowly picked the envelope up.

"He looked at me with a smug grin and nodded his head slightly. 'I'm glad to see you are all in on this. It wouldn't do to be half-hearted.'

'Oh, I'm all in all right. Just watch and see.' *I didn't have a choice at the moment*, I thought.

'Good, good. You can show yourself out, can't you?'

'Certainly,' I said as he turned his back to me and returned to his picture window.

"Fuck! What an asshole! I thought as I left his office.

"'Have a good afternoon, Mr. Sullinger,' said Leslie as I passed her with my head down. *Shove it up your ass, you fucking cunt!* I screamed in my head while I smiled back at her.

"I returned to my office and my smart-ass secretary. I have to admit, I was more than a little impressed with the underhanded way he dispatched me. He slipped me the devil's dick as slick as you please. He was ruthless; it is a wonder he didn't take the case on himself, but that fucker didn't want to get his hands dirty, either. *Oh well,* I thought. *maybe there is some gray area I can capitalize on. There must be a detail that I can distort for my own purpose.*

"The first thing I did was to make some calls and beg for more time. *Maybe with a little research I can find a loophole, or better yet, make one.* I set Beatrice on the task of finding my contact person and making the call. *God, I love making people my bitch. The dirty looks I get are just the icing on the cake.*

"After poring over the documents for three hours in my office, I came across the interesting bit, and I began to see the light at the end of the tunnel. It seems that the houses in question were recently built and therefore recently examined by a Mr. Edgar Gravis. I looked at my watch. *Let's see, if it is 2:30 here, what time would it be in California?* With a little research, I had the number to good Mr. Gravis' office. I snatched up my office phone, dialed star 69 to block the caller ID, and made the call. *Brrrrrr…brrrrrrr…brr…Click, click.*

'Hello?'

'Hello. Is this Mr. Edgar Gravis?'

'Yes, yes, it is.'

'Greetings Mr. Gravis. My name is Earnest R. Cain. I am a land developer who is interested in a certain section of land along the coast.'

'I'm sorry, Mr. Cain, but I do not have your number on my caller ID. Where exactly are you calling from?'

'Yes sir, I am sorry about that. I got a new phone yesterday and I'm still working out the bugs, perhaps it is the phone company. I will have to contact them and straighten that out.'

'Oh…I see. Well, what is this call pertaining to?'

'As I said, I am involved in land development. I represent a firm that is intensely interested in a certain property. It is my understanding that this stretch of land has recently had a calamity of sorts.'

'Oh…you must be talking about the West Palm Estates property. Yes, it has had a bad landslide recently… Took out nearly the entire block, too. What is it that you wanted to know?'

'You were the inspector of those homes, were you not?'

'Yes sir… I was, as a matter of fact.'

'I was wondering if I might talk to you at length about the acquisition of that land by a rather large Boston investment group.'

'I'm afraid that is impossible. There is an ongoing court case currently and that property is pending the case's outcome.'

'You don't say. Well, I have been ordered by this investment group to acquire this property by whatever means necessary and as soon as possible.'

'And just what does that mean to me? What am I supposed to do about that? Look, Mr. Cain, I'm not sure I like where this is going. This conversation is becoming a liability. Perhaps you should contact me at my private number and we can discuss your proposal in detail.'

'Absolutely, Mr. Gravis. That is absolutely what I had in mind.'

'"My private number is 714-555-8729. Please contact me after 6 pm. I will be able to speak more freely on the subject.' I quickly wrote the number down on my forearm and slid my sleeve over it. It wouldn't do to have any incriminating pieces of paper lying around.

'Certainly, Mr. Gravis, certainly. I will call you tonight. My benefactors are very eager to close this deal and are prepared to make whatever restitutions are necessary to make it happen.'

'I see…well then…we should probably talk at length about this. I am always willing to lend my services to the more generous clients.'

'Well then…Until tonight sir. Do have a good day.'

'You too, Mr. Cain. I look forward to helping you with your little problem.'

"'Good bye, Mr. Gravis,' I said calmly as I hung up on him. I stared at the phone in my hand for a moment and an uncontrollable smile came over my face. *Gotcha!* I thought. *Everyone responds to the smell of money. This is going to be easier than I thought.* I slunk back into my chair and remembered another call I had to make. *Hmmm, it's only two forty-eight, not late enough for that call yet. I had better wait until six or seven.* Feeling content with the afternoon's proceedings, I left for the day. *I deserve a treat at the Tilted Ladle,* I thought. The *Tilted Ladle* was a small bistro down the street. When the day went well, I liked to treated myself to a double latté with extra cream and strawberry crêpes.

"I grabbed my briefcase and crossed the foyer. Beatrice muttered, 'You lazy bastard.'

"I simply smiled as I calmly sauntered by her and said, 'I'm taking the rest of the day off, Bee.' To throw a little salt on that wound, I added, 'Don't work too late now.'

"To which she gave a resounding 'Harrumph.'

"The sunlit streets of Manhattan beamed a bright and beautiful future as I strode to the parking garage to deposit my briefcase into the trunk of my car and then walked the three and half blocks to the restaurant. Feeling like I had the insurance case well in hand and 25 million dollars as good as in my pocket, I walked the streets as though I owned them, a real cock of the walk you might say.

"I crossed against the light and held out a bold finger to whoever was honking. I muscled my way into line at the restaurant and seated myself at the nicest table alfresco while the waiter glared at me. *What did I care? I was the new king in town.* I placed my order and ate in self-declared splendor. It wasn't until I saw a glint of emerald green amongst the wandering crowds that I fell from my ivory tower.

"I had just taken my last bite of crêpes and was slurping the remnants of cream from my double latté when she came up on my radar. The shine of emerald green silk and soft satin black hair caught the afternoon sun and suddenly the whole world turned gray around her. I was a man who was reduced to black and white with a burning desire to know this emerald goddess.

"I immediately jumped to my feet and sifted through my wallet. There were but a few twenties left of Fran's money. I dropped one on the table to settle the bill and bolted down the sidewalk, keeping my watchful eye on her movements across the street. She didn't seem to notice me when I walked into traffic, "Honk, honk...honk honk...Hey buddy, get out of the street! You moron, what the fuck is wrong with you!" yelled one cabbie.

"I said nothing; my eyes were fixed on her movements as she crossed to the eastbound side of the street. I crossed again, this time between the tightly packed cars waiting for the light. Quickening my steps, I fell in behind her. She moved like a ghost through the crowd, never touching a soul as I clumsily ducked and dodged, bumped and bounced my way through the throng toward her.

"I was only a few steps behind her when she turned abruptly in front of the subway entrance and disappeared behind a UPS truck into the oncoming traffic. A bus came to an abrupt halt at the point beyond the truck and suddenly there was the screech of tires, an enormous crash, and the subway entrance flooded with afternoon commuters. I struggled against the masses until I came to the parked truck.

"Hesitant at first, I slowly made my way to the back of the truck. By this time the sound of sirens could be heard in the distance, growing louder as they approached. Carefully, I rounded the corner and peered at the ground in front of the bus. There amidst the shards of broken head light was a mangled ten-speed bicycle and a pool of blood.

"A cyclist was lying on the ground between the bus and a rather nice-looking Lincoln Continental. He was holding his left leg and crying in agony over what looked like a compound fracture. I cringed a little when I saw the bone. The crumpled front left fender of the Lincoln coupled with the folded hood of a Charger that was still attached to it left no question as to what had happened.

"I was secretly relieved, but puzzled by the absence of that elusive Asian woman. I looked around and saw nothing but chaos and angry drivers yelling obscenities from their cars. As the police pulled up, I sank back into the crowed in an attempt to avoid landing in the police report. I didn't need any unnecessary publicity.

"Slowly, I made my way back to the office, but by now it was closed for the day. With no phone and little money, I was going to have to rely on my wits for the rest of the day. I flagged down a taxi and took the short ride to the Chamberlin club where I was met by Louie once more.

'Louie!' I exclaimed as I exited the cab.

'Oh god, not you again,' he grumbled.

'Is Mrs. Embers here?' Louie just stared at me in disgust. 'Look, I just want to talk to her.'

'Leave her alone, you parasite.'

'Come on Louie… Look, if you let me in this once, I will owe you. Right…? There is a first for everything.'

'I can't believe the balls on this guy,' he grumbled. 'Okay, if I let you in, you got to promise not to come back. Okay?'

'You mean never…?' I exclaimed. 'Come on, get real. I meet all my best clients here.'

'That's the deal," said Louie. "Take it or leave it.'

'Shit… You picked a hell of a time to grow some stones, I really need this.'

'Careful, I could change my mind,' he said, raising one eyebrow.

'Okay, okay… You got it. I won't darken your doorstep again,' I said as I started toward the doors.

'Wait,' he said as he stretched out his arm and pushed me back. 'Shake on it.' He then stuck out his hand.

'What? You're yanking my chain!'

"Nope," he said. "You shake on this one, or you don't get inside.'

'Louie…I'm shocked at your lack of trust,' I said. I took his hand and reluctantly shook it.

'Hmmf,' he said.

"Louie gave me a stone-cold look and said, 'I mean it, if you show up after tonight, I'll call the cops.'

"'Well then, I better make the most of it, hadn't I?' I said with a smile as I sauntered past him. I slipped through the doors like a ghost and made my way back to the lounge, where I found her slumped over her gin and tonic in a dark corner booth. She looked up at me through the haze of her stupor; her eyes filled with an ambivalent anger. "Goddamn you!" she said.

'What?' I replied. 'Are you telling me you weren't satisfied with my...ehm, performance? Oh, come on, Fran! Didn't I leave you happy yesterday morning? Didn't I ring your bell?'

'I don't remember...' she mumbled. 'What you left me was broke. Do you realize I had to leave my credit card number with the cleaners to have your suit cleaned?'

'Yeah, so?'

'What if my husband finds the receipt? You know, he keeps meticulous records.'

'Don't worry, give me the ticket and I'll pick up my suit from the cleaners and pay for it long before your husband returns. What cleaners did you take it to?'

'Wong's on 57th Street. Here,' she said handing me her wallet. 'Let's not waste any time. You can clean me out while I'm still sober enough to know. That's all you really want from me anyway.'

'Actually, what I need from you is your phone.'

'My phone?'

'Yeah, I left my phone at a friend's house and I need to call my own phone.'

'Here,' she said handing me her phone. She then smiled at me gently and said, 'Are you sure that is all you need?'

"I took the phone from her and smiled back, 'Of course not,' I said. 'I need some of what you've got.' Then I slid in beside her, making sure I put my arm around her shoulders. I motioned to the waiter to bring a second gin while I dialed my phone number and waited for someone to pick up. A stately gentleman's voice answered.

'Good evening,' said the voice.

'Ehm...Hello, umm, this is awkward. My name is Jacob Sullinger and the phone you picked up is mine. Is this Daniel Lamb?' Fran looked up from her drink to watch me stumble over my words.

'No sir, my name is Monsieur Diabolus. I am currently visiting a friend by the name of Daniel Lamb.'

'Ahh, Monsieur Diabolus, I am the man you met yesterday outside Daniel's house.'

'Yes, Mr. Sullinger, I know you well,' his voice resonated with delight.

'You do?' I marveled.

'Yes, good sir, it seems your reputation precedes you.'

'Yes, it probably does. Well, as you now know, I have left my phone at Daniel's and now I am stuck with the predicament of trying to get it back.'

'Perhaps I could be of some help to you, Mr. Sullinger. I am about to leave Mr. Lamb's residence and head back to my club in Manhattan. I could possibly have my driver stop and pick you up and return your property to you. Tell me, sir, would you be opposed to a night on the town?'

'Me? Why, I would love to see your new club.' I couldn't hold back my excitement. 'Is it far from the Chamberlin club?' Fran's eyes lit up when she heard the words.

'My good man, it is but a stone's throw from there. Perhaps you have heard of the Inferno Room?'

'The Inferno Room? Is that yours? God yes, from what I have heard it is the newest rage in Manhattan.' At this point, Fran began tugging wildly at the sleeve of my jacket. I motioned to her to stop.

'Ha, you flatter me, sir, though I must admit the attendance at the club has remained high. We are in our third week and we are still turning people away.'

'"What about me?' Fran said in a panic. 'Take me with you, Jacob, I want to go dancing.' As she shook my arm again, I covered the phone with my hand and whispered, 'Okay, okay, I'll see if you can come.' Actually, I was going to take her with me anyway; *someone had to pay for my drinks.* 'Monsieur Diabolus, if it's all right, I am with a friend and she would like to see your new club as well, would it be possible for her to come?'

'Absolutely, Mr. Sullinger, Mrs. Embers is welcome too. You both will be my guests.'

'Thank you so much, Monsieur, we will be waiting for your arrival.'

'Good, good. I should be there within the hour, Mr. Sullinger. I look forward to a stimulating evening.'

'Me too, Monsieur, me too,' I said as I hung up on him and handed the phone back to Fran.

'Oh, Jacob… Dancing? I haven't gone dancing in ages.'

'That was weird,' I said.

'What was weird?' Fran asked.

'I never told him your name, and yet he seemed to know it was you I was talking about.'

'Oh, he probably got my name from the caller ID. Besides, who cares? I'm going dancing.' She glowed.

'Calm down, calm down,' I said, 'not before you buy me a drink.' The waiter arrived as if I had cued him, bearing a tray with two gin and tonics.

'Well, I guess so, since you're taking me dancing.'

"'That's more like it,' I said with a big smile as I took my drink. I coddled her for another hour, until the waiter brought news that Monsieur Diabolus' limo had arrived. Then she paid our bill and I whisked her away like Cinderella. Louie shot me an indignant look as Fran entered the limo. 'Remember,' he said, 'this is the last time. I mean it.' I just smiled, climbed into the limo and closed the door on his cold stare.

"Monsieur Diabolus was reclining on the wide leather seat that faced the front, so she and I took the seat that faced the rear window. Diabolus was a grand sight in his white suit and feather crested fedora. His walking cane rested across his knees and a large cigar burned slowly between his fingers. 'Good evening, Mr. Sullinger, Mrs. Embers.'

'Good evening, Monsieur,' I said nervously. 'It sure is nice of you to do this.'

'Nonsense, it is my pleasure, and you could say I have a vested interest in you both.'

'Both of us?' Fran questioned.

"I paused momentarily from settling into the soft leather seat, as the limo pulled out of the parking lot. 'What do you mean, Monsieur? What interest do you have in me?'

'Oh, I always have need of a ruthless lawyer, ha, ha, ha,' he quipped.

'And me?' asked Fran. 'What interest could you possibly have in me?'

"Monsieur Diabolus took a deep puff on his cigar and smiled as the smoke rolled from between his lips, and then he cracked the window of the limo. 'My apologies for the smoke, I usually travel alone and have grown used to the smell. Actually, I rather like it myself. Do you smoke, Mr. Sullinger?'

'Only cigarettes, from time to time, but second-hand smoke doesn't bother me,' I replied.

"I watched Fran's eyes as she studied him. She seemed to be quite taken by him. He looked back at her as one would a young girl with a misplaced crush.

"'I think it is sophisticated,' she said with a flirtatious smile. He flexed his bravado by teasing his beard with his fingertips. I studied him intensely, His hair was a gray-white curly mane of medium length which tufted itself out from beneath his hat. His eyes were set slightly apart by a broad nose and forehead. His face was distinguished by piercing green eyes and flared nostrils. His thick medium length mustache and beard encircled his full lips, placing an emphasis on the cigar as he puffed.

"He had all the bravado of a Brahman bull in a Spanish bullfight and gave off a self-proclaimed sense of dominance and power. His mystique was unmistakable. It was one of the old world's, when money and testosterone made a heady mix of misogyny and sex. *This is my kind of guy*, I thought. *A real man's man. If I wasn't straight, he could have probably had me.* He looked at me and grinned as if he had read my mind. It made me more than just a little uncomfortable. Then he nonchalantly turned his head to glance out the window. 'I love the city, don't you, Mr. Sullinger?'

'Oh absolutely,' I said. 'There is always something going on.'

'So many souls wandering…searching. It's a paradise to an opportunist like myself,' his words dripped with a certain contempt.

'I see what you mean, Monsieur; it is a good place for your kind of business.'

"He looked deep into my eyes and said, 'I tell you, sir, you have no idea how lucrative it is.'

'I can only imagine,' I said.

"We made a few stops at traffic lights and we were there. 'Ah…here we are,' he said. 'I told you it was but a stone's throw from the Chamberlin.' The driver pulled up outside the club and stopped right there in the street, a feat that would have come with a ticket for anyone else. There was a police officer writing tickets on the opposite side of the street, but she seemed oblivious to us holding up traffic.

"The doors of the limo were flung open and our eyes were met by the neon glow of two enormous signs in the shape of gates that were open wide. There were two scantily dressed women in red sequined devil costumes holding trays of martinis on either side of the four doors. The women were accompanied by one very large gentleman wearing a period costume of a 1920s gangster. The pinstripe suit he wore may have been a costume, but the bulge of a holster beneath the coat left no doubt that the gun he was packing was real.

"The driver held the door of the limo while we exited the car. Monsieur Diabolus smiled, pulled the collar of his cape over his shoulders and gestured with his hands to the giant glowing gates. 'This is my place,' he said with pride. 'I welcome you both to the gates to the underworld, ha, ha, ha!'

'Good evening, Monsieur,' said the gangster as he lowered his eyes to the ground.

'Krouse? Where is your boutonnière? What have I told you?'

"The gentleman nervously looked down at his lapel to see the vacant buttonhole. 'My apologies, sir. Um…please…please, it won't happen again.'

"Monsieur Diabolus gazed down with a sideways glance at the man's obedient stance. He slowly reached up without saying a word and pulled the flower from his own lapel and gave it to the man. ""You are the face of my club! You are the first person the public sees, your appearance reflects *my presence!* Don't let the public see you this way,' he barked.

'Yes sir, yes…It won't happen again, I swear it. Thank you, sir,' he said as he took the flower.

"Turning to Fran and me, he gestured to the ladies holding the trays of martinis. 'Please, have one,' he said. 'Like a drug dealer, the first one is free, ha, ha, ha.'

'Don't mind if I do,' I said as I took one of the glasses from the tray.

'Oh, Monsieur, you are so chic!' Fran exclaimed.

"Monsieur Diabolus extended his hand to Fran in a grand chivalrous gesture and she took it like a giddy school girl. 'Shall we, my dear Mrs. Embers?' he said as he led her into the club.

'Please call me Fran,' she replied, blushing.

"I followed, sipping my martini and ogling the beautiful devils that stood beside the door. I was caught up in the thick of things, overwhelmed by the power and grandeur of it all.

"As we entered, we descended a wide stairway that spiraled down to the foyer where another beautiful brunette was waiting to take our coats and lead us into the pleasure palace that was the *Inferno Room*. Monsieur Diabolus removed his coat and fedora and handed them to the girl. He ran his fingers thought his thick silver-gray hair as lights danced around our heads and music thumped in our chest and my free martini worked its magic on my sense of reality. A playful couple made out in the corner as at least two others stared endlessly into their phones, no doubt waiting for some sign of their love interest's imminent appearance.

"There were two long black curtains that separated the foyer from the party. Once beyond the black velvet, we were led out onto a deck in the shape of a hexagon which overlooked an enormous chess board. Two long curved stairways led further down to the left and to the right. The chessboard, complete with statues of angels and daemons facing off, was absolutely packed with an army of waiters dressed as jesters, waitresses in skimpy devil costumes and dancers and patrons of the young and wealthy Manhattan set. I could almost smell the money and numbers changing hands.

"We descended the stairs and were swallowed up in the swarm of commotion and a crowd of sweat laden bodies, while the intoxicating music tugged at even the shyest of souls to dance. 'This way, Mr. Sullinger,' he called out to me. I followed like the piper's rat across the room on the fringes of the dance floor, until he reached a small staircase that led up to a grotto with a fair-sized table and a plush chair.

"At the base of the stairs, he introduced Fran to a tall dark gentleman with wavy black hair. 'Here, Mrs. Embers,' he said as he took her by the hand. 'This is Mr. Falco. He is from Honduras. He is an excellent dancer.' The man stepped forward and took her hand from Monsieur Diabolus. 'Senorita,' he said and then he bowed and kissed her on the back of the hand.

'Oh, Monsieur Diabolus,' said Fran. 'He's so handsome.'

"'He would love to trip the light with you. Mr. Sullinger and I have some business to discuss, so if you will excuse us.' Mr. Falco led her on to the dance floor and they melted into the throng of jubilation and disappeared. Monsieur Diabolus motioned to a waiter and merely pointed to the grotto at the top of the stairs. 'This way, Mr. Sullinger, this is my room,' he said as he pointed to the private room. 'From here, I can survey my entire domain.'

"There was a sign that hung above the grotto that read, *Diaboli ergo Spelunca* (the devil's den). We ascended the stairs and the waiter brought a second chair for me and held it until I sat down. There was an elegant candelabra on the table and a rather auspicious looking ashtray next to an ornately carved wooden cigar box. 'I remember you don't smoke,' he said, 'but if you would like to try one, please feel free to help yourself. They are Cuban…naturally.' He motioned to the waiter. 'Bring me a cognac and another martini for our guest.'

'Thank you,' I said politely, 'but I should tell you, I can't pay. I have no money. That's why I brought Fran.'

'Mr. Sullinger,' he exclaimed with a sophisticated smile, 'you are a scoundrel.'

"I laughed out loud. 'Yes, yes, I admit I am a man who has a weakness for the finer things in life, but without the means to enjoy them.'

"He shrugged his shoulders slightly. 'It matters not,' he said. 'A man's got to do what a man's got to do.'

'My thoughts exactly, Monsieur Diabolus.'

'I have the best seat in the house, would you not say? From here, Mr. Sullinger, I can see the lay of the land.'

"Land...land, there was something I was supposed to do, I thought. Then I remembered, I was supposed to call Mr. Gravis. 'Tell me, Monsieur Diabolus, do you know the time?'

"Without looking at his watch, he said, 'It is a quarter to nine, Mr. Sullinger. Mr. Gravis is waiting for your call, most assuredly.'

"I froze in a nervous stare. 'How did you know about my call to Mr. Gravis?' He merely gave me a blank stare. Immediately, I retracted my question and summoned an excuse, 'Well, it is for the firm, you see...purely business...I can't discuss it...you understand.'

"He leaned back in his grand tall black velvet chair and calmly rolled his cigar between his fingers, and then put it to his lips and drew in a big puff. The cherry on the end glowed intensely for a brief second and then he gave a sinister smile. 'It's okay, Mr. Sullinger, your—*business*—is safe with me,' he said as he let the smoke roll out of his mouth in a veil that rose slowly. He motioned again to one of his temptresses with a wave of his hand and she approached in costume complete with trident and tail. 'Take Mr. Sullinger to my office where he can have some privacy, he has a call to make. And—before I forget,' he said, reaching into his inside vest pocket, 'this belongs to you, Mr. Sullinger.' He retrieved my phone and placed it on the table in front of me.

'Thank you, Monsieur Diabolus,' I said, as I picked it up.

'Not at all, sir, you are my guest.'

'I will just take this with me,' I said, as I put away my phone and plucked the martini from the table.

"When I stood up to follow, I could feel the effects of the alcohol come over me like a child at the carnival. The music and lights were playing with my head and the room had a slight but definite spin on it. The blue-eyed beauty that would lead me to his office looked up at me with sterling white teeth and a shimmering red teddy with a plunging breast line. She caught me staring at the twins and shot me a devious grin. I looked back at my host in awe-less wonder as he smiled and gently gave a nod.

"I followed her down the short stairs, with martini in hand, between tables and chairs and endless conversations about pointless pursuits. We entered a hall that was hidden in a darkened end of the dance room; I sipped my drink as we went. The hall had several rooms to the left and right with thick velvet curtains and whispers and moans of the secrets unseen. As we passed one to the right, a gorgeous black woman wearing nothing but a G-string appeared from behind the curtain. Her full soft breasts gently swayed with her movements as she brushed past me. 'What room is that?' I asked.

'That is the VIP room, sir,' my guide exclaimed.

'I might have to check that out on my way back,' I said.

'It was reserved tonight, sir. That is by invitation only,' she said. 'Did you get an invitation from the Senator?'

"'Um…Which senator was that?' I asked. She merely looked at me with a raised eyebrow and continued down the hall until we arrived at a door at the end of the hall. The once loud music faded in the background to a tolerable roar.

'This is Monsieur's office; I will wait outside until you are ready to return to the party.'

"'Thank you,' I said, handing her my empty glass. 'This shouldn't take long.' I opened the door and stepped inside, closing it behind me. The room was dark until I entered. Motion sensors caused the lights to come on. Double sconces on each wall and a beautiful chandelier in the center of the room flickered to life with a soft glow that slowly grew brighter until I could see I was in a six-sided room.

"A large oak desk was the main feature in the room and a large elegant portrait of a ship in the New York harbor hung over a fireplace on the wall opposite the desk. There were two tall bookshelves that stood at the back of the room separated by the two sconces that hung at the corners of the room. The walls were adorned with many pictures of famous and infamous people. I saw signed pictures of Barbara Streisand, Frank Sinatra, and Jack Nicholson as well as John Gotti, Ted Bundy, and Charles Manson.

"There was even a photo of Monsieur Diabolus seated between George W. Bush Sr. and Osama Bin Laden as they toasted some agreement. I walked over to his desk and sat down in his huge leather chair; I couldn't resist the allure of so much power. I was so distracted by all of the photographs that I almost forgot why I came to his office. Remembering what I had come for, I pulled my phone from my pocket and dialed the number that I had written on my arm earlier that afternoon.

Brrrrr…brrrrr…Click, click. 'Hello?'

'Good evening, Mr. Gravis. This is Earnest Cain, I spoke with you briefly this afternoon about the West Palm Estates property,' I said calmly.

'Yes, yes Mr. Cain. What can I do for you and your business associates?' he asked.

'Well, as I have told you, my clients are extremely interested in that property and wish for the trials to come to a swift and decisive end, so they can continue with the reconstruction of that property.'

'I see, what exactly do you think I could do to expedite the situation?'

'As I see it, Mr. Gravis, this is a problem of timing.'

'Timing, Mr. Cain?'

'Yes sir, timing. When exactly did you submit your inspection to the county commissioner?'

'I believe it was the 20th of November last year.'

'I see, and at that time, did you declare the foundation stable?'

'I did, sir. Of course, that was barring any unforeseen calamity such as the hurricane that slammed into the coast the following spring.'

'Yes sir, but should there be an inspector that would be willing to procure an amendment that was postdated for the 20th of November that stated the acknowledgement of a fault line along the property, and should that amendment get placed into the filing cabinet at the courthouse in such a way as to lead one to believe it was misplaced, well then, it could be considered evidence in the trial, could it not?'

'I see, Mr. Cain. This course of action could have tragic implications, should this be discovered.'

'True, Mr. Gravis, but the firm I am working for would be willing to hire such an inspector to inspect the reconstruction of the property at twice, or even three times his normal salary.'

'You present a tantalizing prospect, Mr. Cain.'

'Yes, well, it should also be said that this is not the only property my clients are interested in within your area; this just the first of several. Such an inspector could stand to do very well for himself in future transactions.'

'Well, far be it from me to look good fortune in the mouth. I do have a friend at the courthouse who would grant me access to the files and I am always eager to accommodate my future client's needs. I'm sure that something can be done to ensure your client's requests are met.'

'I truly hope so, Mr. Gravis. Should the missing amendment be found by the end of the week, I would be contacting you on behalf of the Edgewood Investment Group as soon as the trials are concluded.'

'Yes, yes, oh my! Edgewood? I have heard of the Edgewood Investment Group. Okay then, I will do what I can, sir.'

'Thank you, Mr. Gravis. When we speak again, it will be a more acceptable situation. I am sorry for the inconvenience.'

'Not at all, Mr. Cain, I am happy to do business with you.'

'Have yourself a good evening, sir,' I said confidently.

'You as well, Mr. Cain,' he answered.

Click, click.

"Damn I'm good. I should get a fucking Oscar for that performance, I thought. I sat back and felt the arms of that big leather chair and gently swung myself from side to side on the chair's swivel base. *Yes indeed*, I thought, *I could easily be a power player with Monsieur Diabolus behind me. I shouldn't keep him waiting.*

"Confident that I had gotten Mr. Gravis to bite hook, line, and sinker, I jumped to my feet and walked to the door. I took one last look around and smiled to myself. *I am definitely going to have to find a way into Mr. Diabolus' good graces*, I thought. *He could be my ace in the hole.*

"I found my gorgeous guide standing right outside the door as she said she would be. The thumping of music and giggles and laughter in the hall brought me back to the land of pleasure. 'Okay,' I said, 'lead me back to the fun; I'm ready to get my drink on.' She smiled up at me and quietly escorted me back out to the dance floor. My eyes were fixed on the gentle swing of her tight little ass.

"When I got there, I found Monsieur Diabolus was gone.

"'This way sir,' the little imp said to me as she turned toward the center of the enormous crowded dance floor. The throng was so thick that I had to hold on to the tail of her costume so that I didn't lose her in the commotion. She looked back at me with a wink and a smile when she felt the tug on her bottom. It wasn't until we reached the center that I discovered a secret that the enormous dance floor was hiding.

"There in the center of it all was a huge circular bar complete with a grill to serve up appetizers. The bar was surrounded by a fluffy tall back sofa in the same shape. All in all, it had to be about sixty feet around. There were many small tables that sat like coffee tables before the sofa and waitresses shuffled drinks and food back and forth from the bar to the people. A great spinning globe in the shape of an apple hung over the bar and a ten-foot marble statue of a fallen angel stood beneath it. I was overwhelmed by the sheer magnitude of the operation.

"As we weaved our way toward the center of the big couch, I caught a glimpse of a white suit and the smell of a fine Cuban cigar through the lingering masses. Finally, my view opened up to reveal Monsieur Diabolus seated at the absolute center of this enormous sofa surrounded by five beauties and basking in the attention of all those who dared to draw near. The women hung on him like a stately robe and giggled as his eyes beamed beneath his swollen ego. I was so jealous.

"Before him on the table lay an assortment of appetizers: duck pâté with water chestnuts, pheasant with caramel and truffles, salmon and cucumber sandwiches, and of course caviar served on a fruited crêpe. 'Ah, Mr. Sullinger,' he said as I stood there, with mouth agape. 'I see you have found the party.' His face was caught in a permanent smirk. 'Come…eat. You must be hungry. The crêpes you had for lunch must surely be gone by now.'

'Please, call me Jacob. All my closest friends call me Jacob,' I said.

"He smiled at me and gave a gentle nod. 'Perhaps I should call you Uriel,' he said.

"I was dumbfounded that he knew my first name. He quickly turned my attention to the food with a gesture of his hand. 'Aren't you going to eat?' I asked.

"'None for me, thank you…I do not need to eat, Jacob. I feast upon the night and all of her pleasures.' He looked up at a beautiful brunette who had leaned over the back of the couch next to him and kissed her hand. Pulling her close, he whispered something in her ear and she departed. He then cast a cold stare to the blond who was seated to his right. Her eyes fell and she, too, left the group. 'Please,' he said to me, 'be seated,' as he pointed to her empty place on the sofa.

"I sat and immediately took up the pheasant and began to stuff my face, never once taking my eyes off him. He drew a long drag of his cigar and exhaled with a look of total satisfaction. There was something about him I couldn't quite define, a confidence that transcended my understanding of security. As if he was not bound by the same rules of life as everyone else. Some austere magic surrounded him and protected him from the thoughts that plague every other man.

"It was only moments later that the voluptuous brunette returned, carrying a watermelon martini. She placed it before me and then took the seat to my right. She ran her fingers through my hair softly, caressing my neck and back. My skin tingled with the thought of her skin on mine. She leaned in close and her breasts pressed against my arm. They were so firm and full that blood beyond my control suddenly surged south and my soldier came to life.

"Monsieur Diabolus watched me intently, still wearing that smirk upon his face as I struggled to hide my excitement. 'Ehmm...So,' I said nervously. 'Have you been in the nightclub business long?' I was desperate to keep his attention off my growing problem.

'Oh, I have been doing this kind of work for a very long time indeed. I have them all around the world, you know.'

'Around the world?' I exclaimed. 'Your accent is only slightly Cajun, but it also sounds European to me,' I said.

'You are very astute, Jacob; I am from the Mediterranean; the Island of Crete to be exact. Tell me, Jacob, have you heard the story of King Midas? My family name reaches way back into antiquity. You could say we have legend and gold in our blood,' he said smiling. 'We have been in the...' he paused to draw from his cigar. 'Um...investment business for a very, very long time.'

'Really? How does someone get into this kind of work?'

'Like you, Jacob, I was drawn to the power and excitement of the gilded age.'

"'Just offhand, would there be any room in your organization for a young lawyer?' It was then I felt the brunette's left hand fall on my thigh and gently caress her way up. I stopped chewing for a second and carefully swallowed my food. I took a gulp of my martini as the heat of her movements intensified.

'My good sir, you are already in my employment to a certain measure.'

'Yes, but…' I stammered as her hand had reached my now thickening, throbbing problem. 'I mean, should you need someone to manage one of your nightclubs, I would be very interested in that line of work.'

'Yes,' he said as he looked down at her hand stroking my swollen groin, 'I can see you are.'

'Should you find…umm…if you didn't want to dick…I mean stick with the management you have already.'

"His face became serious and he drew the cigar to a halt before his lips. 'I will consider your offer, Mr. Sullinger,' he said as he puffed. 'It's true, you are the kind of man I like to have in my employment.'

"Suddenly, the music softened and the bodies on the dance floor melted into a harmonious mass of sweat-covered passion. The lovely brunette who was stroking my lower regions suddenly took me by the hand. I took one last big gulp of my martini and then she led me out through the crowd onto the dance floor. She turned to face me and slid her right hand around the back of my neck running her fingers through my hair once more. She looked up at me with those crystal blue eyes and bit her pouting lower lip in an absolutely devious grin and then pulled me close and slid her leg tight against my hardened appendage. I could feel my lower regions swell against her thigh. She stared deep and restless into my eyes. 'Do you have a name?' I whispered.

"With a tilt of her head and one raised eyebrow, she said, 'Delilah.' She then slid her hands around my waist and pulled my body tighter against her thigh and then rested her head on my chest as we did a slow grind to the enveloping music. I ran my hands over her body. Her soft skin, warm and inviting, played with the lights in my head to create a sublime union, a carnival of the senses full of passion and unbridled desire.

"At the pinnacle of my arousal, my spinning head became aware of a presence amidst the slow-moving bodies. It seemed to follow us across the dance floor, closing in on us as this angel of sin in my arms drove my body ever closer to the very edge of resistance. She looked longingly into my eyes and in a timeless moment drew her lips close to mine and stalled. Out of the swarm of dancers, came a hand and arm of a woman. It slid between her body and mine and pried us apart.

"I stood there slack-jawed when I realized it was the Asian woman I had so doggedly sought. With her right hand on my chest, she pushed me backward. *So, you are real*, I thought to myself as I took the step backward.

The look on her face was as serious as a tombstone. She glared at me with those deep green eyes, holding me fast in her gaze. Her left hand slid up between Delilah's breasts as she took Delilah's chin in the palm of her hand and then turned to face her.

"The Asian woman's face was caught in a look of haughty arrogance as she looked Delilah over. She shot me a cold stare once more and then turned again to Delilah and kissed her deeply on the lips, holding her in this embrace while her right hand slid up from my chest and wrapped around the back of my neck. She dug her nails into my skin at the base of my scalp. It burned like fire in my skull then shot straight to my manhood. I tried to catch my breath before I lost control of my bodily functions.

"The Asian temptress slowly pulled away from Delilah; my imagination swirled around their soft moist lips. Without saying a word, she spoke to her with her eyes. I had never wanted to speak the secret language of woman more in my life than at that moment. Lost to me in that lingering gaze was the meaning and intentions of the woman I so desired. She then looked back at me grinning, knowing she had denied me the pleasure of Delilah's lips.

"Taking a fist full of hair at the back of my head, she pulled me even further away from Delilah and released me. As intoxicated as I now was and on the edge of orgasm, I was helpless when she took Delilah's hand and led her away into the crowd. 'No!' I yelled. 'Wait...I...I...I'm not done! Where are you going? What's your name?' They said nothing as they slipped quietly away. 'Who are you...? Delilah...! Delilah...!' I screamed shaking my fists in the air.

"I stood there dumbfounded, my head ringing with sound, lights, thoughts of her and an all-consuming emptiness. My manhood was stripped away and left throbbing with no chance of release. I pulled at my own hair in frustration as I scanned the crowd for any sign of them. There was nothing but an empty feeling of watching others imbibe of their desires. Shaking my head in disgust, I then slowly turned to rejoin Monsieur Diabolus waiting in the lounge at the center of what now seemed like a hollow pursuit.

"When I returned to the lounge, I saw him standing at the bar talking to the bartender. When he noticed me approaching, he tilted his head and smiled slightly. 'Ahhh, there you are... What's the matter, Mr. Sullinger, you look like a man who has just lost the fight with his demons. Hahaha.'

'I think I did,' I said with a scoff. 'I lost Delilah, anyway.'

'Not to worry, sir, I have here the house special. It's a drink I call the devil's brew.'

'What's in it?'

"His eyes widened and he looked over at the bartender. 'It's 90-proof watermelon vodka and a shot of apple pucker with cherry grenadine and cinnamon candy liquor. Watch out, it packs a punch and has got a lot of fire down below,' said the bartender.

'Well, what do you think? Are you feeling brave, Mr. Sullinger?' quipped Monsieur Diabolus.

"I took the drink from the bar, raised the glass, and said, 'Please call me Jacob.' Then I took a big gulp of the concoction. The cinnamon liquor burned my mouth like a red-hot candy while the bittersweet fruit hit my stomach with all the warmth and power of nitroglycerine. I knew then I was in deep trouble."

That Sinking Feeling

Jacob stopped his story and looked at Dr. Kessler. "From this point on," he said, "the evening took a distinct turn toward the bizarre. The way I remember it, it had all the clarity of a Jackson Pollock painting." He shook his head.

"I'm all ears," said Dr. Kessler.

"You know, we can do this some other time," said Jacob.

"I've got the whole day, Jacob."

Jacob dropped his eyes and took a deep breath. "You know? You're a wicked taskmaster."

"That's sometimes part of the job, Jacob, to get people to talk about all the things they've been hiding from themselves."

"Hiding?" asked Jacob.

"You can't rebuild a life from nowhere, you know? You need to start from due north."

"Due north?"

"Yes, due north, A moment in their life that represents that moment of truth. The place of origin. That place when you realize, you can't turn away from your true self."

"Wow! Am I that far gone, Doc?"

"No one is that far gone, Jacob…Life is all about perspective."

Jacob lowered his head and folded his hands and took another deep breath. A labored moment passed.

"Okay," he said, "here goes."

"'Well…the details of the evening are blurred, but I do remember what Monsieur Diabolus said next.' He said, 'You are a young and handsome man, Jacob, you shouldn't be alone tonight.' He motioned to some of his waitresses with his hand and said, 'Ladies, won't you please entertain Mr. Sullinger. He has no one to dance with.'

"With that, I was surrounded by three beautiful vixens who led me and my drink back out to the dance floor. The last thing I remember of Monsieur Diabolus' face was an arrogant smile beneath his brooding eyes of white as he puffed his cigar and watched me being swept away on a tide of lust. The rest of the night was awash with the scent of woman, of arms and legs and whispers of secret fantasies. The room turned and I turned with it as the ladies danced around me like I was some sacred monolith, touching and kissing me and each other. In this circus of sex, I was center ring and savored every drop of my devil's brew.

"Strangely enough, I don't remember much more of the evening, but I do remember lying back on the giant sofa with Monsieur Diabolus to my right and Fran and Mr. Falco caught in an embrace just beyond. The room was filled with the laughter of the ladies and whispers of the two lovers, Fran and Mr. Falco. 'Come home with me,' she said.

'I can't,' answered Mr. Falco. 'I belong here. I cannot leave.'

'You belong here?' Fran questioned.

"Monsieur Diabolus, paused from sipping his expensive cognac and shot Mr. Falco an ominous glare.

'I can't,' said Mr. Falco. 'My contract.'

'That's quite enough, Mr. Falco,' Monsieur Diabolus said sharply. 'You will say nothing more.' Fran looked across to Monsieur Diabolus with wanton eyes, but they were met by a cold stare.

"'I will bid you goodnight, Senorita,' said Mr. Falco and he kissed her hand and then slunk away into the thinning crowed. I, on the other hand, was rendered speechless by my devil's brew; a lifeless mass of drooling drunk slumped over the Monsieur's shoulder. He looked down at me with a certain endearing contempt.

"'I will have my driver take you and Mr. Sullinger to your apartment. He seems to have had too much to drink.' Fran's face perked up at the sound of those words. He waved his hand and two very large gentlemen appeared and dragged me back upstairs as Fran followed on the arm of Monsieur Diabolus. They held me upright as the limo was brought around and I was poured into the back seat. Then Monsieur led Fran around to the other side and opened the door for her. 'It was an enchanting evening, Mrs. Embers, and I am most glad to have spent it in your company.' He kissed her hand and she took her place beside me. Closing the door, he turned to the driver. 'Take Mrs. Embers and Mr. Sullinger to the Washington Towers, then return with the car.'

'Yes sir,' was all I heard and with the slam of the car door, we were set in motion.

"It was an awkward ride to say the least as Fran slid her arm around me as soon as the car door was shut. She pulled me in tight and began whispering in my ear, 'You are in for the ride of your life tonight, Jacob. I'm lathered up and rarin' to ride.' She slid her hand between my legs and squeezed my inner thigh. I struggled a little, but I was in no shape to argue. She spun my head around and took my face in her hands and launched her tongue down my throat and then pulled away and settled back into the plush leather seat. The weight of my body fell forward until I was face down in the middle of her heaving cleavage. 'That's it, Jacob,' she said. 'You take as much as you want.'

"I didn't know whether she was drunk too or whether she was just enjoying her favorite fantasy, but she didn't seem to notice I was struggling to breathe. Slowly, I pulled myself to an upright position and fell backward against the door. The limo pulled into the parking lot of the Washington Towers. It came to a smooth stop and the driver opened the door for Fran first and then walked around the car and opened the passenger side door for me.

"I looked up at him thought the blur of my alcoholic haze. 'Take me home Jeeves. I don't want to ride the Fran go-round tonight,' I said as my head bobbled around on my shoulders. He smiled back down at me and helped me to my feet. As he did, I caught a glimpse of someone in the park across the street. There was a distinct glimmer of an emerald green dress as a woman disappeared beyond the reaches of the street light. 'There she is!' I blurted out. 'You're not getting away from me this time!' I broke free from the driver and took off running.

'Jacob!' Fran yelled. 'Where in the hell are you going? Jacob! Jacob! Get back here, I'm not done with you!'

"It was too late. I was halfway across the street by the second time she had called my name. Cars honked and sped past me as I stumbled forward to the other side. I paused for a second under the street lamp and peered into the night, leaving Fran ranting behind me. There was a strong half-moon and a break in the gathering clouds that projected soft shadows upon the ground. I could see a woman standing on the bridge that crossed a walkway. *There you are,* I thought to myself. When I took off running again, the woman descended the bridge to the other side, out of sight. The cool of the night air seemed to sharpen the senses in my still spinning head. Her presence hung in the darkness like a beacon, leading me to her.

"Fran yelled, 'God damn you, Jacob, you son of a bitch!' as she waited for a chance to cross the street.

"I reached the bridge and crossed; there I stopped to survey my surroundings. In the distance, there stood a gazebo that was bordered by six full sized bushes. *Now, where would I hide if I were a phantom*, I thought to myself. My intuition led me toward the gazebo, so I staggered across the lawn and up the hill. As I shuffled into the gazebo, a bum that had taken refuge there for the night jumped to his feet and took off, leaving his newspaper blankets to fall upon the dusty concrete floor.

"Carefully, I stepped around the gazebo, checking every shadow. I could feel her as if she was part of the darkness. My clumsy footsteps scuffed the concrete as I searched all corners. The night gave up only the sounds of the breeze, the traffic in the background and the rumble of distant thunder. There was movement in the bushes just outside, so slowly, silently, I stepped toward them. The smell of honeysuckle and lilacs floating in the breeze told me that she was there. She was a fantasy turned obsession. She used all of my senses to draw me to her, infecting my memory with her scent and the softness of her fingertips.

"My passion sparked to life with the mere thought of her silky black hair and those burning green eyes. I rounded the bushes into the shadows, fully expecting to find her waiting to take me, but found nothing. Once again, I was left longing for what I could not find. I stood there thoroughly disgusted with myself and heard a sound of someone approaching from behind. As I turned to see who it was, I was thrown to the ground and my head landed with a thud against a stone.

"I laid there still for a moment and saw myself from above. Like a dream, floating and looking down at that beautiful woman standing over me. She knelt down and softly caressed my face with her fingers. My skin came alive with the feel of her touch. She traced my face, gently following the line of my eyes and my chin and ran her fingers through my hair. I saw her bend over my body as I was outstretched on the ground. There was a rumbling in the clouds above us as if the heavens were preparing for war. She drew her lips near to mine and let them ever so lightly touch.

"A flash of lightning lit the sky around us. Silhouettes of creatures swirled amidst the clouds. I could feel her breath fill my mouth with the fire of her lust and then pull away. It sank deep into my being and filled me with a desire that I had never known. She made me want her more than air. I gasped like a fish out of water, trying to recapture the warmth of her moist breath.

"Her hands moved down to my tie and she began to loosen the knot around my neck. She gently pulled and it gave way as it slid smoothly from my collar. Still floating in a dream, I watched from above as she fashioned it into a noose and then tied it tightly around my wrists, leaving enough to pull on if she so chose. She rose to her feet and stared down at me reclining back on the ground. I could see my own face staring drunkenly upward with a smile. It was a look of a man lost in total bliss.

"She straddled my body with a leg on either side, pulled her dress up to her thighs and squatted on top of me pressing against my crotch with only a thin layer of silk and gabardine between us. Taking my face into her hands, she drew near and thrust her tongue into my mouth, swirled it around, and drew from me the passion of my kiss while her fingers began to unbutton my shirt. There was a splash of lightning across the sky and a low rumble just a few seconds later. She had only gotten to the third one when she pulled the rest of them apart, revealing my chest. Her nails clawed and scratched at my skin, sending the fire down below.

"I could feel my manhood engorge beneath her soft slow grinding. She kissed and bit her way to my nipples and breathed hot waves of moist air across my skin, letting her lips graze the very tip of my left nipple. Her hands then went to work on my belt, turning loose my trousers and unzipping my fly. Another lightning bolt split the night and a loud concussion of thunder right behind.

"The storm is getting closer, I thought. She made sure to take a mouthful of my chest before biting down and thrusting her hand down my pants. The pain of her bite mixed with the thrill of her grip to produce a cacophony of sensations. This made my muscles twitch and spasm with delight as she sucked and bit while pulling against me.

"The wind began to lash the trees and pulses of lightning lit the sky around us. She wrenched my pants down and exposed my erection to the tempest above. Taking it into one hand, she pulled, not with the intent to create pleasure, but with the sadistic pawing of a cat torturing its prey, all the while watching my face for any signs of arousal. Lowering her head to my mid-section, her face disappeared below. I felt the warmth of her mouth engulf my lower regions and the swelling began. A groan rose from the depths of me as the warmth of her lips sent chills through my body. The sky above was racked with lightning all around.

"I saw within the flashes the clash of a titanic battle of souls. I could swear, I saw the archangel Michael strike his sword against the shield of a hideous two-faced demon. My eyes grew wide at the sight. She juggled my testicles around on her tongue and stroked my throbbing rod until she felt I was good and ready. She licked her way up my shaft and buried the length of me in the depths of her throat. 'Ohhh,' I said softly as she took me down. 'God damn, girl. Save some for your pussy,' I said. Nothing was said, only the sound of her drawing me in again and again. As she did, I drifted down from my lofty position.

"Slowly, I descended back into my body as if she was pulling me down. The clouds rumbled and flashed above us. I bore witness to a titanic battle in the skies above, all the while sinking deeper into my euphoric state. My breathing deepened with every sigh and wave upon wave grew closer to satisfaction. As if this were not enough to set my senses ablaze, she began kneading my scrotum with the palm of her right hand as her left hand crawled back up to my chest.

"She dug her nails into my skin above my right nipple and I couldn't help it; my pelvic thrust forward into her succulent mouth. She took the thrust and returned tenfold as she bore down on my trembling member. My breathing grew shallow and my body started to quiver. 'Oh god!' I cried out, 'you're gonna make me...ahhhh!'

"Suddenly, she came to an abrupt stop. 'What the fuck?' I exclaimed when she rose to her feet. She stood there over me staring down at my trembling appendage. 'Are you going to finish?' I asked. She pulled at the strings at both sides of her silken panties and they fell to the ground. She squatted over me and this time there was no fabric to hinder the sensation of her warm wet lips against my shaft. I could feel her swollen clitoris as it rested against my engorged head. She started moving forward and backward on top of me breathing deep and rocking her hips.

"Placing her hands upon my chest, she forced herself down the length of me, until I was wet from tip to tail with her desire. Leaning forward, she let her breasts drag along my chest as she moved up to greet my face. She kissed me deeply and my member popped up behind her. She dug her nails into my chest, arched her back and looked deeply into my eyes as she positioned herself above my throbbing pole and put pressure on the tip. I felt the warmth of penetration as she held me in that gaze.

"A bright crack of lightning split the darkness. Her hair hung about my face like the sweeping limbs of a willow tree. She said nothing, but a deep satisfied smile came across her face when she eased down on my fullness. Slowly, she moved, and the shadows moved with her carrying my soul adrift in her passions. She tilted her head backward and let her long black hair drape down the length of her back as she forced me ever deeper into her wanton womb, engraved in the ferment of my mind. I could still see those deep green eyes staring me down.

"There was not a moan or whimper from her lips to let me know of her pleasure, only the force of her thrusts, and the sound of her wetness stirred within me a growing darkness. I watched her body rise and fall, her firm breasts heaving in the shadows. I felt the ground sink beneath us as she drove me closer to the edge. The trees seemed to stretch upward and the earth sank deeper and deeper. I became aware of heat rising from beneath me as if the soil seemed to burn under us.

"Flames sprang up around us to our left and our right and danced higher and higher, yet she did not stop, but drove my body ever onward. I marveled at her features; they seemed to changed right before my eyes, with every thrust her skin grew darker and her nails grew longer, sinking deep into my chest. I cringed when the blood began to trickle down from the holes that she was making. 'Ahhh!' I screamed when the pain shot through me.

"There were sounds of cracking and popping, as her bones stretched and moved to accommodate her new form. Her eyes arced to life and a flame flickered green, burning into my mind. Every hair on my body was alive and tingling. She stared down at me with an arrogant smile as she thrust her body on to my swollen manhood. The ends of her hair turned upward toward the sky and her lips grew as thin and dark as burnt bark. The look of true evil reflected in her face. I saw a thin line of red blood trickle down her chin and my fantasy turned to nightmare.

"Two enormous wings unfolded from behind her and stretched like sails before the storm. The lightning that splashed across the sky was blotted out by their shrunken flesh. Her body drew from me that which it craved. The depths of her spasmed and tightened around me as her body trembled violently when she peaked before me. A torrent of her passion gushed, soaking me. I couldn't hold back the surge of sensations. My balls swelled beneath her weight and hearkened the flood into her. 'Oh my god! I...I...I can't hold it!' I screamed writhing against the knot that held my wrists.

"My heart pounded wildly inside me as I stared up at her hideous smile. 'Say something, damn you! Talk to me! Oh God help me...I'm gonna...I'm gonna...I can't hold it! Say something, you bitch, say something. WHAT THE HELL ARE YOU!' My body stiffened under hers and convulsed wildly as it released its bounty. There were no misgivings, it was a done deal. I was fucked.

"She paused a moment and watched my body finish convulsing. 'Did you think I wouldn't get what I wanted, Jacob?' she said, staring down at me.

"The words fell familiar on my ear. *She sounds like someone I know*, I thought. *Wait a minute...*

"I opened my eyes and looked up at Fran's abundant butt-naked body sitting on top of me and the overwhelming awkwardness of the remnants of our union now draining beneath me. 'What the hell?' I said. 'A dream? It was all a dream?' I struggled against the knot that bound my hands. The sound of the ensuing rain could be heard in the distance and the first few drops of the deluge fell upon my face.

"Fran looked toward the sky. 'Quick Jacob, we better go before it pours on us,' she said as she bent over and grabbed hold of the end of the tie that still bound my hands and pulled me to my feet, and then she led me back through the park with my pants around my knees. The rain came down in sheets and we traversed the bridge and across the street with my cock flapping from side to side the whole way.

"Into her apartment building we went, up the stairs and through the doors. At the elevator landing, she pushed the button and then turned and grabbed hold of my dick. I vaguely remember a man seated in the lobby to our left and that ridiculous Salvador Dali painting which took up the whole wall to our right. The man seemed busy searching his cell phone for information; I don't even think he noticed me standing with my pants down and my flagpole at full salute.

"When the doors of the elevator opened, she used my own cock to shove me inside. She flung me against the back of the elevator, pressed the tenth-floor button, and as the door closed, she dropped to the floor and began sucking me off again. I took a deep breath when my head hit the back of her throat. The sensation of the lift rising as she quickened her strokes was intense. My knees weakened beneath me as the force of gravity pressed me toward the floor. There is no feeling that can quite compare to the one of losing your stomach going up, while someone is going down. I had to brace myself against the rail to keep from collapsing to the floor.

"Once we arrived at the tenth floor, she snatched hold of my cock and dragged me down to her apartment, opened the door and forced me backward into the entryway, down the hall and into the bedroom, slamming the doors behind us as we went. She forced me onto the bed, straddled me once more and tied my hands to the head board. She ripped my pants from my ankles and then she quietly stared down at me like an animal.

"With my head still reeling from the alcohol, the rock and the vision of that Asian beauty, I wrestled to comprehend what had just happened. 'So, what was that? Was I dreaming? One minute there were angels and demons and…a battle and…I was…um…So, it was all a dream?'

'You were passed out so I just…helped myself,' she laughed. 'It must have been a damn good dream.' She turned and went into the bathroom.

'Hey!' I yelled as she walked away. 'Untie me!'

'I will,' she replied. 'When I'm good and ready, now just relax, we're not done yet.'

"I struggled with the knot, frantically trying to loosen it, but it was no use. She must have been a Boy Scout when she was young, because my shit was in lockdown.

"'Did I ever mention my father was a boson's mate in the navy?' said Fran when she heard me struggling. 'He taught me every knot he ever knew, ha, ha, ha!'

"She returned from the bathroom with something in her hand and a glass of water. She stuck a pill in my mouth, plugged my nose with her fingers and poured the water into my mouth. I gagged for a second and then swallowed. I had no choice. 'What was that?' I said gasping.

"'Viagra,' she said casually. 'You owe me four hundred dollars, remember; I've come to collect.' A big smile crossed her face as she turned to set the glass on the nightstand. She waited until it took effect and mounted me. Her large frame sagged over me like a man in a fat suit.

'Oh God,' I said as the weight of her pulled against my arms.

'Just relax,' she said, 'and enjoy the ride.'"

Jacob glanced back at Dr. Kessler, who was trying not to laugh by shrouding his smirk with his left hand. "Well, I can tell you, Doc," said Jacob, "that rodeo lasted until sometime before dawn."

Dr. Kessler stifled a snicker. "Indeed," was all he said.

Jacob stared out at the trees across the pond from where they sat. "I remember the pale blue light of the morning sky streaming through the sliding glass doors when she was finally finished with me. She rolled off to the left side of the bed, kissed me on the forehead and then rolled over and fell asleep. I followed her into slumber, still bound to the headboard and thoroughly worn out.

"When I awoke, it was after one in the afternoon. My hands were loose from the headboard and she was still fast asleep to my left. I managed to loosen the knot around my wrists and get my hands free. *That's it*, I thought. *I'm going to start wearing bow ties from now on. Clip-ons.* I slipped out of bed and tiptoed into the bathroom and closed the door. The image in the mirror was frightening. The night of drinking, lack of sleep and midnight rodeo had left me with bags under my eyes like the Golden Girls. I looked like Bea Arthur.

"I was completely dehydrated, my body drained of its fluids. I struggled to produce even a modicum of saliva. Staring down at the wear marks left on my wrists, I noticed the remnants of Mr. Graves's phone number as a black ink smudge on my left arm. I poured a glass of water, and drank my fill and then slipped into the shower. The hot water felt good on my throbbing headache, but did nothing to remove the image of Fran riding up and down. Like the ink on my arm, the memory of her beating me senseless with those huge breasts of hers and calling out, 'Yeeeehawww!' will be hard to erase.

"Once I was clean of the persistent ink spot and the memory, I dried off and slipped back into the bedroom to collect my clothes. I got dressed and stood at the sliding glass doors which led to the balcony. It was a sterling bright day. The few clouds there were hung in the distance over the river. I looked down at the park across the street and remembered the black-haired beauty. I shook my head in disgust at the thought of how foolish I had become. *What a rube I am. They ought to give me the golden ass award,* I thought.

"I turned and looked at Fran still sleeping off her night's exercise. She was dead to the world. A night of dancing and debauchery had left her, no doubt, dreaming of Mr. Falco and my fat cock.

"Her purse setting on the table at the foot of the bed drew my attention, and I caught the smell of money. I sauntered over to it and took a peek inside. She had taken all the money out of it. *Hmmm*, I thought. *Now where would I hide my cash if I was Fran?* I glanced at the ice bucket that sat next to her husband's single-barrel scotch. One quick look inside brought a wicked smile to my face. There was a wad of twenties rolled up in a rubber band. *That ought to just about cover the cost of the chiropractor I'm going to need*, I thought.

"As I plucked the money from the ice bucket, I noticed my shadow on the floor as it struck me dark and brooding in the afternoon light. Faint splinters of light seemed to shoot out from its edges. I don't know why, but it seemed strange to me. It looked taller and wider than it should be. Then it moved without me and slowly widened across the floor. It stretched out on both sides, as if two large wings were preparing to swallow me in their darkness. I spun around to see what was standing behind me, but there was nothing there.

"Again, I looked at the floor and the two wings raised up on either side of me like a phoenix. My memory flashed back to the dream of that Asian demon and how she changed before my eyes. That was all it took. I bolted for the door and beat feet out of Fran's apartment down the hall to the stairwell and out to the street. My mind was resolute, Fran's apartment was strictly off limits from then on. I would have to find another woman to sponge of.

"Once my feet hit the street, I flagged down a taxi and headed back to the parking garage. It wasn't until I was in the taxi that I counted Fran's money and tucked it away in my wallet. There was six hundred dollars in that wad. Her husband must have left her a thousand to play with and I stumbled on her stash. *Well, I'm definitely not going back now*, I thought.

"That particular Saturday I spent hiding in the library reading archives of old newspapers and articles of landslides along the California coast. It was my hunch that an area that had one landslide was more than likely prone to them. If I could establish that the West Palm Estates had a history of landslides, it would strengthen my case. Sure enough, there had been a landslide along that stretch of coast in 1922 and again in 1965. I made copies for my files and retreated to my apartment in Brookland for some R & R.

"Dominic had taken his little fuck doll upstate for the weekend, so needless to say, I finally got some sleep. Over the next two days, I booked a flight to California and prepared for the trip to Oakland County. I probably didn't have to go, but I didn't want to leave anything to chance. This was my shot at showing the seniors at Simon and Neubauer what a brilliant young intern they had working for them. Jamison was going to look at me differently after this.

"When Monday came, I had to justify my trip to Jamison. He put up a fight, but I was able to persuade him to allot money for the plane tickets and an overnight at a Best Western from the law firm's budget. He agreed, but not before letting me know that he "had better see results and receipts."

"My flight left out of JFK Airport on Thursday morning at 7:50 and, if all went according to plan, I would have that amendment in my hot little hands and back on the plane home by ten o'clock the next morning. Yes, things were lining up quite nicely and I haven't even hit my stride yet. The rest of the week was spent on the details of my elaborate plan. One phone call to Mr. Gravis on Wednesday night assured me that all was in place.

"I put three hundred of Fran's money in a manila envelope and sealed it and then wrote the name Edgar Gravis on the front and placed it in a backpack I stole from my roommate. The hardest part was forging the Edgewood Investment Group logo in the upper left-hand corner of the envelope with a fine point black ink pen. I'm not an artist, but it looked pretty good for an amateur, even if I must say so myself.

"Thursday morning came early, cold and rainy. I got dressed in street clothes, so as to not look too conspicuous. The hang ten t-shirt, blue-jeans, converse shoes and A's ball cap would make me look like one of the locals. My roommate's backpack completed the look. My plan was to take the subway to the airport. I stopped at the local bakery on the way for my usual latté and copy of the Journal before heading to the subway. The weather had forced the homeless people into the subway terminals for shelter, which made for a crowded and uncomfortable start to a long, arduous trip.

"As I descended the steps down to the subway landing, I caught a glimpse of a crazy white-haired old man slipping away into the crowd. I began to feel like I was being followed by that crazy fuck. If I had more time, I would have tracked him down and beat his ass, but not today. Today was a day for executing my Machiavellian masterpiece.

"When the train arrived, I boarded in a throng of people. An old guy was eyeballing the only seat on the opposite wall, so I spoke up quick. "Move off, grandpa, this seat is mine." He shot me a dirty look, but then moved toward the other end of the car. I claimed my seat, slid my backpack under it and stretched my paper out in front of me. A moment or two had passed when I heard the sound tapping on the window opposite my seat.

"Glancing up, I found myself face to face with that crazy old man tapping on the glass from the outside of the train. He waved and smiled at me as the train pulled away. I shook my head in disgust and waved him off. *He doesn't know how lucky he is*, I thought as I turned my attention back to my paper.

"The paper was full of the usual tripe, an article on the layoffs at DuPont and some scandal about phantom shares and lost pensions. *Ha! Poor suckers, there really is one born every minute,* I thought. On the third page, I found an article about my man Jack. *Jack White lands a windfall on foreign trade and opens his own brokerage*, the headline read.

"'My man Jack,' I said to myself. 'I know where my 25 mil is going when—' I stopped, and looked around to make sure no one had heard me. The crowd of unfortunates were milling about as they clung to the train and swayed back and forth. No one seemed to notice my stifled enthusiasm. Nevertheless, a big smile sank down behind my poker face and reveled in its secret glory. All I had to do was to wait until the money rolled in. The rest of my trip was filled with fantasies of what I was going to do with my twenty-five million.

"When the plane touched down at LAX, it was 6:20 pm. I caught a puddle jumper to San Francisco and checked into my hotel by 8:30. It was a late dinner, a call to Mr. Gravis and a few drinks in the lounge and then right to bed. The transaction between Mr. Gravis and myself had to be quick and, if at all possible, without any direct contact. On the phone, he told me he had the envelope for me. My plan was simplicity itself.

"I would take the BART to Oakland and once there, I would get a locker and place my envelope inside. I would place the key to the locker behind the toilet in the first stall of the nearest bathroom. He would leave the key to a locker holding my *amendment* on the top of a vending machine that was close to the car rental kiosk. Barring any catastrophe, I should be boarding the plane with my prize in hand by 9:15. The fact that I had never seen the good Mr. Gravis and he had never seen me was part of the beauty of my plan; it was just a good business practice as far as I'm concerned. We could make the transaction in total anonymity.

"I took a shower, climbed into bed and took one last look at the clock. It was ten-thirty when I turned off the light and rolled over."

Jacob paused his story and looked over at Dr. Kessler. "I know, you know what happened next, don't you?"

"Okay, let me guess," said the doctor. "You had another dream."

"Kind of, I'm not sure it was a dream. That's how these things are. I don't remember falling asleep."

Dr. Kessler chuckled. "Most people don't remember falling asleep, Jacob. I know I don't."

"Well, it didn't feel like a dream, anyway," said Jacob.

"I do remember laying there in the dark and feeling the presence of a man sitting in the chair beside the bed. A thin white strand of smoke rising from the soft glow of a lit cigar was all I could see in the black of night. He said nothing at first, but raised the cigar to his lips. The silhouette of his face shown briefly in the cherry red glow of that drawn cigar, and there was a subtle smile.

'So,' he said softly. 'You want to be a player, do you?'
Motionless, I lay listening to his breathing.

"'Are you sure you have what it takes…Jacob? Sure, you can con the weak ones in the flock, but are you up to the big game? Hmmm?' His voice resonated within my skull. Whispers of other voices danced around my bed. Fran's and Graves's, Jameson's and Louie's filled the air like the smoke from his cigar. 'You are such a little shit. I taught you how to lie and this is what you've become…a pathetic little gutter snipe, stealing from women and conning the weak ones?'

"He paused to take another drag. 'Still, you have brought me souls, nevertheless. You are the door by which they come to me. You've not been completely useless…Tell me, Jacob, do you have what it takes to be the real Devil's spawn? Do you revel in the suffering of others? Have you vanquished all conscience yet? Could you see yourself as a CEO, politician, or a lobbyist perhaps…hmm?'

"He leaned in close to me. I could almost feel his breath on my face. 'I could give you the world,' he whispered. 'But would you know what to do with it?' He paused a moment and then settled back into his chair. 'I think not, but I love the long odds, so I tell you what; I will raise the stakes by five hundred thousand dollars to see what you do. I'm betting you fuck it up, but I'm willing to pay for that show. Tell me, Jacob, is that spot on your arm growing darker?' His chuckling turned to laughter and like thunder, it rumbled away into a distant storm outside my window. It left me small inside somehow, curled up like a chastised child brooding in my suspended sleep.

"Beep, beep…beep, beep…BEEP, BEEP, rang the alarm clock. Startled, I rose from that wicked sleep, my eyes still heavy from a restless night. I sat up on the edge of the bed and rubbed my eyes. As I pulled my hands away from my face, I looked down at my arm and saw the black ink that was once Graves's number. The edges had become smeared and faded, but the center was still a dark black spot. I could almost hear his laughter ringing in my head. 'God damn it! What's up with these fucked up dreams!' I said out loud as I shut off the alarm. 'I got to stop drinking right before bed.'

"The urgency of why I was there flooded back into my brain. *Oh yeah, the amendment*, I thought. *I gotta take care of business.* Throwing off the blankets, I rolled out of bed and got dressed. A quick continental breakfast and a coffee, and I flagged a taxi to the Bay Area Rapid Transit station. My watch read a quarter to eight when the driver dropped me off at the station. I made my way down into the terminal and boarded the train.

"As calm as you please, I waited out the 20-minute ride across the bay and sauntered out the train doors into the Oakland terminal. Making my way to the map of the terminal, I waited until the last of the train's passengers wandered off toward the exit to the street. Once the crowds had thinned, I worked my way to the D section lockers and selected one that was out of the way and placed the envelope with the money in the locker, turned the key and placed the key in my pocket.

"Making my way to the bathrooms, I pretended to be busy washing my hands while two men finished their business and left. Once everyone had gone, I slipped into the first stall and placed the key behind the toilet and then exited the bathroom.

"I made my way to the rental car kiosk and the vending machines that were to the right of it, pulled some change from my pocket and selected a cinnamon roll from the selection. Before I reached into the machine to retrieve the prize, I took a quick look around. The few people that were milling about seemed to be preoccupied, so I glanced at the top of the vending machine and saw the key resting at the front right corner on the edge. I nonchalantly placed my right hand on that corner and reached into the machine to retrieve the pastry with my left, making sure to scoop the key up as I pulled away.

"I meandered over to a bench that was close by, sat and unwrapped my cinnamon roll and looked down at the key in my hand; the number on the key read 2479B. *I'm almost home*, I thought, as I snacked on my roll. The sweet taste of a well-executed plan filled me with confidence. I returned to the map to find the (B) section of lockers and then strolled over until I was standing right in front of 2479. It was in a corner of the terminal behind a pillar, out of sight of the main thoroughfare.

"Opening the locker revealed the manila envelope that was the answer to all my Jameson problems. Within it was a one-page document that I quickly scanned through. Sure enough, he had kept his word. There at the bottom was the signature that will make it all come together. I slipped the envelope into my backpack, closed the locker and made a hasty retreat up the stairs to the street and hailed a taxi. 'San Francisco airport,' I said, 'and don't waste any time getting there either. Your tip will depend on it.'

"'Right, the airport,' was all he said. He took the Bay Bridge back into the city. As we crossed the bridge, I took out my phone, dialed Edgar Gravis' number and tried to leave a message. After the beep, I said, 'The key is behind—'

"Click, click. 'Hello? Mr. Cain...? What is the meaning of this? I thought we agreed on a much more substantial sum than three hundred dollars. This amount is completely unsatisfactory, it's marginal at best!'

'Hold on there, Gravis. The reimbursement of your efforts is completely dependent on the outcome of the trial. I thought I made that clear.'

'You did not, sir! This turn of events could have some serious ramifications for you, if you know what I mean?' he threatened.

"'Look Edgar...can I call you Edgar?' I said scrambling to regain control of the situation. 'Think of this as a small retainer for your future services. The Edgewood Investment Group has big plans for several large businesses in your district. You wouldn't want to jeopardize all that for this miner disagreement, would you?'

'Well no, I suppose not. Perhaps this matter can wait until the trial is over,' he grumbled.

'Good,' I said grinning to myself. 'You will thank me when the trial is over and you get that call from the Edgewood office. They can be very grateful to people who assist them with these difficulties. I am going to put in a good word for you when I get back to Boston, Mr. Gravis.'

'Well, I do appreciate that, Mr. Cain,' he said politely.

'Just be patient and you will see big dividends, I promise."

"Will you be in correspondence with me again, Mr. Cain?'

'No, I'm afraid not, Mr. Gravis; from this point on, you will be dealing with the Edgewood office directly. A Mr. Tony Somata is in charge of the requisition of properties. I will refer your name to him.'

'Oh, thank you, Mr. Cain. I will await his call.'

'Good, I bid you a good afternoon, Mr. Gravis. Take care.'

'You as well, Mr. Cain. It was a pleasure doing business with you.'

"After hanging up on him, I highlighted his name on my phone and pressed delete. *Sucker!* I thought. *Mr. Somata...ha, ha, ha. Where in the hell did I get that name? Ha! I sure pulled that one out of my ass. Sometimes I impress even myself.*

"Twenty minutes later, I was in line at gate 11A boarding a 9:45 flight back to New York. I had plucked the envelope from the backpack and disposed of the backpack outside the airport. There was no need to give the airport security anything to search. I had what I came for and now felt the urgency of my flight.

"Travel-weary and hungry, but feeling my own swag, I landed at JFK and grabbed dinner at the airport pub before taking the subway home. I spent the rest of the weekend preparing the bombshell I was going to fax to the law office of Tyrone & McMarrin, a law firm that was ironically based in Santa Cruz, California.

"Monday morning came and I was at the office early. My early arrival prompted the usual sarcastic, 'Is it the end of the world already?' from Bea.

"To which I answered, laughing, 'It is for some poor unfortunate souls in California.' Closing the door to my office, I broke out the case file and actively began typing up the manifesto for the week. I also put together a list of demands I was going to hit Jamison with once the deal went down. *I was going to get a promotion out of this, or they can kiss my lily-white ass goodbye,* I thought.

"Once I had double checked my work and felt confident that it was all there, I walked it out to Bea's desk. 'Oh, I forgot to tell you,' she said. 'Tyrone & McMarrin set a trial date last Thursday while you were playing in California. You are due in court at the end of the month.'

'I'm not worried,' I said calmly. 'That will all change when they get a load of this,' I gloated as I plopped the stack of papers on her desk.

'What's all this then?' she groaned.

'That is the result of my frolicking good time in California, now suck it up and fax those to Tyrone & McMarrin.'

'But they have all of the case files already,' she exclaimed.

'Not all of them. Just trust me, give them about thirty minutes to look them over and they will be calling us. When they do, transfer the call to my office and I will take it from there.'

"'You're delusional, you know that? Absolutely delusional!' She shook her head in disbelief as she scooped up the paperwork and trotted off to the copying room.

"I returned to my office, took a seat at my desk and waited for that call. I could see Beatrice when she got back from faxing the papers. She shot me a scolding look when I kicked my feet up on my desk, folded my hands and twirled my thumbs while I watched her through the glass. I casually looked at my watch and marked the time. It was 9:53. At 10:25, her phone rang. When it did, she looked at me with astonishment. Her eyes grew wide after she answered it and found it was indeed the office of Tyrone & McMarrin. I smiled confidently back at her, lightly tugged at my sleeves and prepared to take the call; a small perk paid for by weeks of planning.

'Tyrone & McMarrin on line 3, Mr. Sullinger,' the intercom rang.

'Thank you, Bea, I know how much it hurt you to say that.' I winked at her though the glass and then put on my game face.

'Hello, this is Jacob Sullinger, what can I do for you...? Yes, yes, I was made aware of the trial this morning. Well, I sent you all the information that I had on the case... Yes, I was aware that Smithy handled the case originally. The firm wasn't happy with the way he handled the case. I did a little more research and sent you my findings...Was there something of concern to you?"'

'I see...Well that amendment turned up after a considerable amount of research on my part. I flew back to the county seat and retrieved it from the files at the county courthouse myself. Apparently, it was stuck to the back of the filing cabinet. That is why it never made its way into the shared information. That's not my fault; your lawyers should have done a better job. You can look at the paper trail all you want; I think the signature on the bottom of the page says it all. I have reams of evidence that reveals that that property has had a long history of landslides.'

'If you want to go to court, it is up to you, but I assure you, it won't end well for your clients. They could end up paying as much as twice what they paid for the homes plus court costs. I think you should reconsider the trial and settle for what the insurance company is offering you, twenty thousand per home…I know…I know…it's true, it is only a tenth of what they paid for the homes, but needs muster the Devil's drive.'

'The insurance company has assured me that it is willing to draw this case out as long as it has to. Are your clients prepared for a lengthy trial? Maybe they should reconsider. Hello…hello. Are you still listening? Well, I will give you time to talk it over with your clients. I will be here all day should you change your mind. Okay, later then, I will talk to you then. Good day, madam.'

"I hung up the phone and shot Beatrice a sinister grin. 'Bea?' I said through the intercom.

'Yes, Mr. Sullinger,' she replied.

'When they call back, put them on hold for 5 or 10 minutes before transferring the call. I want to make them sweat it out.' *They will remember my name when I am done with them.*

'Yes, Mr. Sullinger,' she grumbled.

'Thank you, Bea, I like it when you call me Mr. Sullinger.'

"She flipped me off through the office window while she muttered to herself in the lobby. I just shook my head and laughed. I did enjoy fucking with her.

"It took the rest of that day for the lawyers at Tyrone & McMarrin to get back to me, but eventually they did and the fruits of my well thought out plan paid off. They pulled the court case off the docket for that month and settled for 50 thousand per home, a price the insurance company was willing to pay. Actually, they would have paid as much as 75 thousand, but there was no need to tell them that. I told them 'I will see what I can do,' to make it sound like I gave a shit about their clients.

"Over the next five days, the agreement was hammered out, much to the satisfaction of New York Life & Trust. Before I knew it, the week had ended, Friday morning was upon me and I expected Jamison to say something about the case to me, but nothing was mentioned. That son of a bitch walked right by me at the elevator and didn't even say good morning, good job or kiss my ass.

Beatrice snickered at my frustration; it must have been visible on my face. I shot Jamison a dirty look as the doors to the elevator closed and then mumbled to myself, 'Cocksucker,' as I walked away.

'What did you expect?' muttered Beatrice. 'A raise, perhaps? It was about time you did your job around here.'

Dark Star Rising

"That weekend, I spent with Sheila, a cute little waitress at a bistro downtown. She was always a good romp in bed, but never too serious. Still, it was a pity that I left my wallet in my other suit. I told her the next time, it was on me. She was a good sport."

"Another woman?" asked Dr. Kessler. "Isn't that hard to keep track of?"

Jacob smiled and blushed slightly. "Not too hard, actually, I am always reminded of the fact they are merely surrogates for the one who won't have me."

"Oh? And who might that be?"

Jacob took a deep breath and sighed. "That would be Rosalinda. A sweeter name I have never heard."

"Why haven't you spoken of her yet?" he asked.

"Because, I told you, Doc. She won't have me. There is no sense dwelling on something you can't possess."

"Jacob," said the doctor, "no man *can* possess a woman. They can only love and accept them. It sounds to me as if you found a strong woman to fall in love with."

"Ha," laughed Jacob. "Lucky me."

The doctor smiled and nodded. "Please continue," he said.

"Monday morning came and I went through my morning routine of stopping at the bakery for a latté, a bear claw and a copy of the journal. As I approached the news stand, the headlines of the New York Times caught my eye. *Yacht Sinks off Coast. One Man Found Dead, Crew Missing.*

"I purchased the paper and read on. In a freak storm that pounded the coast Saturday night, the 50 ft. yacht the Dana Paz took on water and sank below the waves. All hands were lost and the body of 38-year-old Daniel Lamb was found washed up on the coast. The vessel was registered to a Mr. Minos Tauri Diabolus. Mr. Diabolus is an international entrepreneur responsible for the nightclub, the *Inferno Room* in down town Manhattan. The crew is still missing and an extensive search of the area has produced no leads.

"Stunned, I stood there with my mouth wide open, 'The stupid son of a bitch did it,' I said to myself. 'I can't believe he went through with it.'

'It's a pity about your friend,' someone behind me said.

"I turned to see who it was and there was that crazy old man staring at me. 'What?' I said, still reeling from the news.

'I said, it is a pity about your friend Daniel,' the old man repeated.

'He wasn't a friend. He was just another client to me,' I mumbled.

'Still, it was such a loss to his family, don't you think?' the old man's sincerity resonated with some inner voice of mine, small though it might have been.

'I suppose,' I said, briefly pondering Daniel's wife and kids.

'Just think how this will devastate them,' he said. 'Yes, just think of what this means for them.'

'Yeah,' I remarked. 'This will be devastating for them.' As the notion sank in, I realized. 'Hey, this means I'm rich!' I blurted out.

'What?' questioned the old man.

"'Haha!' I laughed. 'This means I am worth 25 million dollars, old man,' I exclaimed. 'That is the best news I have ever heard.' I rolled up the paper and tapped him on the chest. 'I don't even think I could get mad at you today.' I said as I stepped past him. 'Oh, and by the way,' I added. 'Stop following me before you get hurt. This is your last warning, old man.' I shook the paper in his face to emphasize my point.

"The old man stared at me in astonishment. 'I don't believe it, Mikey,' he muttered to himself. 'He doesn't seem to care at all about those people.'

"I stepped outside the bakery a new man, *today I am going to work and do absolutely nothing and I'm not even going to try to look busy,* I thought. *That will chap Bea's ass. Haha!*

"I Jumped into my car and sped off to work. I was late again and I didn't even give two shits, but I was going to spend the whole day torturing Bea. I meandered up the sunlit steps, opened the doors and sauntered by Beatrice. 'Hold all my calls today, Bea, I'm not taking any today,' I smirked.

'You're late…again,' she remarked.

"'Yeah well, you're ugly…and your breath smells like butthole, so I guess we're even,' I cajoled as I strolled passed her. Closing the door of my small office, I sat down at my desk, stretched my paper out and spent two hours enjoying my coffee in plain sight. I spent another 45 minutes flirting with Carol, the new intern from downstairs. She was one of the newbies that works out of cubicles in the basement. It was where I had started two and a half years before.

"When I finally returned to my office, I pulled out the latest copy of Stephen King and began reading. Bea was really struggling to contain her frustration. She kept dropping her pen, fumbling with the drawers of her desk, and muttering to herself as I watched her from behind my unfolded book. Halfway through chapter six, my cell phone rang. The caller ID read Darkstar Life & Trust. That was the name of the insurance company that Daniel had the policies with. I quickly took the call.

'Hello,' I said eagerly.

'Yes, is this Mr. Jacob Sullinger?' the voice on the line asked.

'Yes, this is Sullinger?' I answered nervously.

'Mr. Sullinger, my name is Alexander Shlaymen. I am with the Darkstar insurance agency and it has appeared that one Daniel Lamb has listed you as the beneficiary of a policy worth a considerable amount of money,' his voice was curt and to the point.

'Yes, Daniel and I have been very close since college,' I said, barely containing my enthusiasm.

'I don't know if you were told or not, but Daniel was the victim of an accident last Saturday night and is no longer among the living.'

'Yes, I only just found out this morning, I am absolutely devastated by the turn of events. He was such a big part of my life. I feel certain that my life will forever be changed by the loss.'

'That well may be, sir, but I have to inform you that the company has a check issued to you for the sum of 2.5 million dollars.'

'Excuse me,' I enquired, 'don't you mean 25 million dollars?' I asked as calmly as I could.

'No sir, I stated the sum correctly. 2.5 million dollars. Darkstar does not offer policies for sums that large, sir,' he said plainly.

'Oh, I must have misunderstood Daniel, I though he told me the sum was for twenty-five million,' my teeth ground as I chewed my way through the sentence.

'At any rate, there is a check here for you, should you decide that 2.5 is enough for you…sir,' I could feel the stinging sarcasm through the phone.

'I will be there within the hour, what is your address?'

'2567 Mortis Drive, it is at the corner of Riggs and Mortis.'

'Hmm, I don't think I have ever been that way before,' I said. 'I will have to look it up.'

'I await your arrival, sir. Good day.'

"'Yeah right, whatever,' was all I could get out. As soon as I hung up the phone, I tossed the phone on the desk and started cursing out loud. 'That god damn stupid son of a bitch couldn't even die right! The deal was for 25 million, 25 MILLION! Ahh!' I yelled and I shook my fists in the air. 'No wonder he failed on Wall Street; the man was a complete imbecile! Tell me, what college graduate can't find the proper place for the decimal point? I bet he thought his dick was twenty-five inches long!'

"Now headlong into my rant, I had forgotten that Beatrice could now see me pacing back and forth, cussing and swearing and flailing my arms about in a full-blown tantrum. I must have looked like a lunatic. I looked up at her long enough to catch her laughing to herself at my expense. Bursting out of my office, I blurted out, 'I'm taking the rest of the day off!' And I sped past her desk like my ass was on fire.

'What should I tell the seniors?' she called out laughing.

"'Tell them that New York Life & Trust called. They said that they will be taking their business to whatever law firm I next work for!' and I left her in a fit of laughter. It wasn't until I got to the bottom of the steps that I came to my senses. *No*, I thought. *It ain't going down like that.* So, I turned myself back around and marched back up the stairs, flung open the doors and marched back into my office.

"Bea watched closely as I picked up my phone and slipped it into my pocket and then walked over to my filing cabinet, pulled it open, and plucked out the thickest file I could find and calmly walked it out to her desk. Dropping it right in front of her, I said, 'I want these files copied in triplicate by tomorrow morning there,' I croaked. 'Now both of our days are fucked up!'

'Why, you son of a bitch,' she growled.

'I'll see you tomorrow, Bea. And I want those organized by the dates they were filed with the county as well.'

'It will be a cold day in hell before I will organize anything of yours,' she howled.

"There! That felt right, I thought. *Now I can get my money. I guess 2.5 mil is better than nothing. I'll just give it to my man Jack and he can triple it for me.* I walked the two blocks to the parking garage, found my Martin and started off to find the Darkstar insurance agency on the corner of Riggs and Mortis.

"After an hour and a half of search and turning around a couple of times, I found the office in an unassuming neighborhood in Eastchester. It was an out of the way location for an insurance company, but then again, Darkstar was not a typical name for an insurance company, either.

"Locking up my car, I entered the building. There was a rather attractive brunette sitting behind the front desk. She wore a business suit and had the cold stare of a veteran lawyer; I was immediately impressed. 'You can take a seat, Mr. Sullinger, Alexander will be with you in a moment,' she said. I was compelled to oblige.

"I took the first seat and waited…and waited…and waited. The woman took no more notice of me than if I were a fichus tree in the corner of the room. 'Ehmm,' I coughed, attempting to get the young woman's attention. Her typing paused and she glanced up over her glasses at me with one raised eyebrow and then continued typing. *Hmm…*I thought. *It's like being in the room with Bea.*

"A few more minutes dragged by and then the moment of truth arrived; Alexander entered the room through a set of double doors that led to the meeting rooms. Without as much as a handshake, he said, 'This way, Mr. Sullinger.'

"I followed him through the doors, down a hall and down two flights of stairs. There, I was shown to a meeting room with a long table, six chairs and a very conspicuous Monsieur Diabolus sitting in a tall backed leather chair at the end of the table. 'Wait here, while I go get your file,' said Alexander.

'Monsieur Diabolus,' I exclaimed. 'I am surprised to see you. How on earth did you survive the loss of your yacht?'

'How indeed,' he replied. 'Ugly business that. Daniel was a challenging card player. I will miss his poker face.'

'Yes, he did play a good game of poker,' I replied.

'Yes, he did, but not good enough, I'm afraid,' Diabolus beamed. 'Please sit down, Mr. Sullinger. The proceedings will commence momentarily.' I took my seat at the end of the table opposite the good Monsieur Diabolus. He leaned back in his chair, reached into his coat pocket and produced a lighter and, of course, a cigar. Smelling the cigar brought a smile to his face. 'I love a great cigar, Mr. Sullinger. Do you know why?'

'No,' I said. 'I couldn't imagine why, Monsieur.'

"He rolled the cigar in his fingers and looked at it as if he were about to consume a fine glass of wine. 'Because, Jacob, I draw from it what I want, I get to watch it burn slowly and the burning is a sweet smell to me.' He slowly put the cigar in his mouth and lit it. The tip sparked to life and glowed brighter with every puff he drew. The silence that followed was crushing and awkward. He stared across the table at me with a coldness that seemed to penetrate my skull.

'Why are you here?' I asked. 'What is your part in all of this?'

'I am here, because this is my insurance company, Mr. Sullinger. How do you think I paid for the nightclub? I want you to imagine, if you can, all of the ships, planes, buildings, cars, dams, bridges, cargos and even people that are insured. Someone is paying, on a monthly basis mind you, for the possibility of a disaster. It is an industry derived from fear. Even if a catastrophe does happen, the vast majority of things that are insured will never be collected on. It is the perfect business to be in. Money for nothing…you could say.'

'But you are paying me, aren't you?' I smiled. 'And I barely had to do anything to get it.'

"Diabolus grinned, 'Yes I am, it seems.' He put the cigar to his lips then hesitated before taking a drag. 'Yet, this is but one hand from a full deck of cards, Jacob.' He then drew a long puff and released it. 'Tell me, how much was it? You know…the amount you agreed to?'

'25 million was the deal,' I mumbled.

'And how much are you getting today?' He was truly enjoying the game of words we were playing, while I, on the other hand, squirmed like a worm on a hook.

'Two and a half mil,' I said under my breath.

'What was that?' he gloated. 'I didn't quite hear you.'

'Two and a half million, okay? Two and a half fucking million!' I snapped.

"He took a nice long drag and I watched the cherry glow and recede as the cigar grew shorter. 'Kind of makes you wonder which end of the deck they are dealing from, doesn't it?' he chuckled.

"Finally, Alexander returned with a stack of papers and a silver briefcase. He placed the briefcase on the table between Diabolus and myself and carefully laid the papers in front of me. He pulled a pen from his shirt pocket. 'This is the document declaring that you received the check for 2.5 million dollars,' he said.

'It was supposed to be 25 million,' I grumbled.

"Alexander pointed to the amount on the page. 'Read that amount out loud,' he demanded.

'Two million, five hundred thousand,' I said reluctantly. Diabolus sat there with a content little smirk on his face.

'And is that or is that not your signature right there?' insisted Alexander.

"I looked down at my signature on the bottom of the page. I might have been able to deny the signature, but I couldn't deny that that was my blood next to it. 'It is,' I said in defeat.

'Then if you want your two and a half million dollars, you will sign right here,' he said, as he slid his bony finger down to the line that read, received by.

'This is not your first time around the block, is it, Alex?' I remarked as I took the pen from him and signed on the line.

'That's Alexander to you, Mr. Sullinger,' he scolded. He then lifted the page. 'Sign here and here,' he said pointing to lines on the second page. 'And finally, sign the last page here.'

"I quickly signed and handed the pen back to him. He reached into a file folder and pulled a cashier's check and set it before me. There it was, in black and white: 2.5 million. That wasn't even going to cover the driveway of the house I was going to build. Bye, bye, senators. I might be able to open a small office in Yonkers, but certainly not the high-powered law office that would give Jamison a run for his money.

'You can leave us now, Alexander,' said Monsieur Diabolus calmly.

"After Alexander closed the door behind him, Diabolus rose to his feet and approached the briefcase that lay on the table between us. It was a small briefcase, maybe a foot and a half square. It had two laches beside two combination locks. He carefully spun it around so that it would open facing me. He flipped the latches and then opened the lid. My eyes stretched wide to take it all in. There were stacks and stacks of fifties, hundreds, and thousands, all bound with rubber bands and neatly placed in rows. A prettier sight I had never seen. 'Go ahead, Jacob, touch it. It's real,' he chuckled at me ogling all the money. I picked up a stack of fifties and fanned through it.

'What's this for?' I asked.

'Let's just say, it's a bonus, shall we?'

'There must be a hundred thousand here, I've never seen this much cash in one place before.' I fondled the bills like I was at the drive in with my first date.

'There's five hundred thousand, actually, like we had discussed,' he said puffing on his cigar.

'Discussed?' I questioned.

'Don't you remember?'

'Yes, yes, but I thought it had been a dream.' I scratched my head while I tried to remember.

'Perhaps you did,' he said. 'Perhaps—you are dreaming now.'

'God, I hope not,' I exclaimed. I threw the fifties back into the briefcase and he closed the latches, spun the combination locks, and then took a deep drag on his cigar and blew the smoke on the locks.

'What was that for?' I asked.

'Oh—for good luck,' he said with a smile. 'I have always been a little superstitious. There you go, Jacob; you have your check and five hundred thousand dollars. Do you think you know what to do with it?'

'I'm sure I can think of something,' I said as I rose to my feet.

'Until we meet again, Mr. Sullinger.'

'I'm not so sure we will, Monsieur,' I said.

'I would wager we do, Jacob. I would lay money on it,' he said smiling.

"Not if I can help it, I thought as I headed for the door. 'Good day, Monsieur Diabolus,' was all I said as I exited the room carrying my check and briefcase full of money. Following up the stairs and down the hall, I broke free through the double doors and shot a dirty look at the secretary as I raced past her. Once on the street, I opened the trunk of my car and threw the briefcase in, then closed the trunk, neatly folded my check and stuffed it into my pocket. I jumped into the driver's seat and you could hear a definitive chirp from my tires in my haste to put him well behind me.

"Producing my phone, I quickly highlighted the name of Jack White and hit dial. The line rang only two times and then he picked up. 'Hey…Jacob!' he exclaimed. 'How the hell are you?'

'Jack!' I bellowed. 'God man, have I got some news for you.'

'Okay then, what's the scoop?' he inquired.

'Well, I recently came into a chunk of money. Not the kind of money I was expecting, but a good-sized amount nonetheless, and I read in the Journal that you had started your own brokerage, so I figure you are my best bet to build this money into a real sizable sum.'

'All right, how much are we talking about?' he asked.

'Two and a half million,' I said frankly.

'Wow! That is a fair amount to work with. Let's see, I have had my eye on a certain stock that shows all the signs of extraordinary growth. It has trended well over the last twelve quarters and with the upturn in the market lately, the holidays looming still and the collapse of two of its competitors, it should be poised to net any investor an enormous return on their money,' said Jack.

'That's what I'm talking about!' I exclaimed. 'You know your shit!'

'They don't call me the Great White for nothing,' he boasted.

'Now, if I give you this money, you better not do me dirty, I mean it, man, I would fuck you up,' I warned.

'Jacob, I'm surprised at you, brother...come on man...It's me!' he exclaimed. 'You and I are from the same clan, man. You know...from the Bronx, the old school. I wouldn't do you like that. But I do have to give you the usual disclaimer. It is the stock market and that alone means that it comes with certain risks, but I'm telling you, this stock is HOT. I haven't seen a trend like this in years.' His voice bristled with excitement.

'You make it sound good, what is the name of the stock?' I asked.

'Donte Enterprises Inc., they are a large capital investment group that buys up retirement properties around the world for the wealthy, as well as resorts and casinos. You know...the high end of the market.'

'Sweet! Sounds like my kind of company,' I said. 'I am on my way to your new office now, where exactly is it located?'

'It will be the on 1300 block of 18th Street, near Lexington Avenue, a couple of blocks from the Gramercy Park,' he said.

'Ahh, not too far from the action, I see,' I snickered.

'Close enough to get rich, but far enough away from all the bullshit. I don't want to get caught up in any political scandals. You got to keep those ties neatly hidden, you know,' he said. 'It wouldn't do to let any cats out of the bag.'

'I gotcha, I gotcha… Well, I'm on my way, I should be there in about twenty minutes or so,' I said.

"'Okay then, I will see you and your money when you get here,' he said, then the line fell quiet. Putting my phone away, I leaned into the gas. It was two o'clock and I wanted to make this transaction before quitting time.

"When I arrived at his office, I found a parking spot in front of the building. It seemed remarkable to me that I even found a place to park so close and so quickly. All the lights seemed to turn green as I approached them and the traffic moved freely, not as congested as it usually is.

"I entered his office like Attila the Hun walking into Rome, with all of the swag and pomp of a conqueror of worlds. I had 2.5 million in my pocket and I was about to score big. Jack was standing beside the receptionist's desk giving her some details on one of his new accounts. He was an imposing man, at least 6'4" with broad shoulders, a full head of pepper gray hair, a clean-shaven chiseled jaw and a tailor fitted shark skin suit. The suit had become his trademark on Wall Street. 'That's right,' he said. 'It was the offshore stocks with high yield dividends for the Landswick portfolio.' He looked up at me as I approached the desk. 'Jacob!' he exclaimed. 'You made it! And in record time too.'

'Yeah, kind of weird, isn't it? I even got a spot outside,' I said.

'Must be your lucky day! You caught me at a good time, I am just finishing up here. Thank you, Janice. That will do, for now,' he said gesturing to the file he laid in front of her. He then turned to me and pointed to his office. 'It's not the penthouse, but it is a corner office.'

'Nice,' I said as I followed him to his office door.

"Opening the door, we both slipped inside and he closed the door behind us. He settled in behind his desk and I took a seat and pulled the cashier's check from my pocket. 'So, what do we have here?' he asked with a grand smile.

'I have just come into a large sum of money. It's not as large as I had hoped, but it is enough to make me a very wealthy man, if you are as good as you say you are,' I said grimacing across the desk.

'Jacob, Jacob…I'm stunned… Who got you the money to buy that Martin out there, huh? And you know we go way back; I got your ass covered. Now let's talk business here. You said something about two-point five mil. I did some quick research on that company, Donte Enterprises, and found that their holdings have been sound for the last twelve quarters. That is a three-year trend and as I told you on the phone, two of their largest competitors filed for bankruptcy at the beginning of this year. That means Donte is poised to take over eighty percent of the market at the beginning of next year. You are getting in on the ground level here, brother. You could stand to earn your money back ten times over.'

'Damn! That sounds too good to be true!' I exclaimed.

'I'm telling you, I could take your money and roll it over a couple times into several investments I have lined up and before you know it you would be worth maybe fifty mill,' he sat back in his chair and folded his hands behind his head.

'I don't know, Jack, wouldn't it be wiser to put it into some mid-risk funds and sit on it for a while?' My apprehension started to show.

"Looking into my eyes, he shook his head from side to side. 'Why would you do that? Man, I am telling you, you got to strike while the iron is hot, and it is flaming here, man. How do you think I got this office, hmm? I took the aggressive route; I took the bull by the horns!' he gestured with his hands in the air for dramatic effect. 'Do you want to have the money when you are sixty-eight, when you are too old to enjoy it, or right the fuck now, when you are young enough to know what it is worth?' He reached into his drawer and pulled a pen out and handed it to me.

'Yeah, you're right…I've got some things I want to do before I get old, like own a few politicians,' I said as I reached for the pen.

'Hahaha…That's the spirit, Jacob, fortune favors the bold. Now I just need you to sign that check for me and I will fax a copy of it to the bank to make sure they will back it and you will be on your way to a lifetime of ridiculous opulence and luxury.' His eyes opened wide as I slathered my name on the back of the check.

"He swiftly plucked the check from in front of me as I finished signing and examined it. 'We still have an account with your name on it, though it doesn't have much money in it. You just had to have that car.'

'Hey, hey now, you are what you drive. Besides, it was you that found me the car in the first place. Mr. Salvador Maycha was one of your Ecuadorian millionaires, wasn't he?'

'Actually, he lives right on the border of Peru and Ecuador. The man has extensive Peruvian political ties and that is all I'm at liberty to say, but you got the car for cheap, didn't you? Where else can you get an Aston Martin for twenty-five grand?'

'Yeah, what did you have to do to get it so cheap anyway? You didn't have to sleep with anyone did you? Ha, ha, ha!'

'Please Jacob, let's try to be professional here. I told you, we are like brothers, you and me. We came from the same side of that bridge. Give me a moment to have Janice fax a copy of this check to the bank and get it cleared.'

"He disappeared beyond the door for a moment or two and then returned. 'This should just take a couple of minutes. This bank does large transactions like this for me all the time,' he said nervously, rubbing his hands together.

"I sat there in silence wondering whether the check would clear or not. It had occurred to me that Monsieur Diabolus would be the kind of guy that would pass off a rubber check. We sat there staring at each other in that awkward void, with grim expressions on our face, until the intercom broke the silence. 'The bank called, Mr. White; the check is good and secured for the transaction.'

'Great!' he said as we both rose to our feet. Jack leaned into the intercom, "'Thank you, Janice, good job.' Jack came around the desk and slapped me on the back. 'Well, old friend, that went well, now you just leave the rest to me. Before you know it, you will be slurping down martinis on the French Riviera.' He shook my hand and walked me to the door. 'Don't you worry about a thing; Janice and I will take good care of you.' I nodded quietly as if I were in a trance or something, stunned by how easy the transaction was to make.

'That was almost too easy,' I said.

"'Well, things run smoother when the proper hands have been greased, if you know what I mean,' he said with a wink. He opened the door and said good bye and retreated back into his office and closed the door. Janice just looked at me with a smile. 'Have a nice day, sir,' she said as she scribbled something down on a pad she had in front of her.

'Thank you, I think I will,' I exclaimed.

"I left that office a new man. For the next three weeks, I was riding on the crest of my own accomplishments. No longer worried about money, I felt I could even afford to cut Bea a little slack, so I bought her some cheap perfume at the department store to smooth things over between us. She accepted the gift with a gracious, but worried stare. I guess she knows me a little too well. I figured it was wise to put on my best behavior, at least until I was rich enough to dump the job and open my own office. Then, all hell was going to break loose.

"I spent my afternoons reclining in my small office daydreaming about life after my ship came in. When that time came, Jamison will find out, I make a better ally than an enemy. He doesn't know, but I have made a collection of all the contact information for all of the firm's biggest accounts, and after the exceptional job I did for the New York Life & Trust, it shouldn't be too hard to walk away with at least some of his major accounts.

"My plans were shaping up nicely, I thought. *Hey, once I start collecting on my money, I can apply for a full membership at the Chamberlin Club. That should really steam Louie's cummerbund. He will not only have to let me in, but also get the door for me. That's a perk I will savor with devilish delight.*

"It was the third Friday of September when I received a call at the office which seemed to bring a smile to Beatrice's face. 'A distraught woman is on line three for you, Mr. Sullinger,' she chortled. I shot her a smirk through the glass and picked up the phone.

'Simon & Neubauer, Jacob Sullinger speaking.'

'Jacob, you ass,' a woman's voice broiled on the other end of the line. 'You little shit,' she continued. 'You really did it now! You fucking forgot and now my husband is home from Thailand and has collected his things and moved out!'

'Whoa, whoa, whoa…Slow down, you're not making any sense. Who is this?' I asked.

'Who is this? Who the hell do you think it is, you little fucking leech! It's Fran! I told you to pick it up, but you forgot, and now it's all in the shitter!'

'I forgot what? Easy, easy…the money I took was just a loan…I was going to pay you back, honest…I…I—'

'The money? The money is the least of my problems. What I'm talking about is the suit, you idiot, the suit!'

'What suit?'

'Your suit, you fucking dumbass! You forgot to pick it up at the cleaners and they charged it to my husband's card! How could you be so absolutely fucking brainless? I told you, if you didn't pick it up then they will charge his account. GOD, you are thick!'

'He collected his stuff?'

'Yes, goddamn it! And he said he is filing for a divorce!'

'Does he know that the suit was mine?'

'No, I'm sure he doesn't, not unless you write your name inside your suits.'

'Don't be ridiculous. It's not like I still live with my mother.'

'Well then, there is no way he could know it is your suit.'

'Good, then I'm your ace in the hole.'

'What? What do you mean?'

'I will represent you in the divorce and we will squeeze him for as much as we can get out of him. I'm sure you have a good case on grounds of abandonment. Trust me; with me as your lawyer, you've got nothing to worry about.'

'Do you really think so? I'm too old to go back to work; I wouldn't even know how to begin to start looking for a job.'

'Relax, what I want you to do now is get one of your gin and tonics to calm your nerves, sit down, and make a list of all of the traumatic emotions that you have had to deal with because of his absence; play it up; make it real dark with depression and counseling and drug addiction and alcohol, and I will do the rest.'

'Well…I guess…are you sure this will work?'

'Absolutely! We have to let the courts know how long you have suffered, because of his selfish work habits. He's the one who left you alone, didn't he?'

'Well yes, but I do still love him, Jacob. We have been together for thirty-five years and that's a long time. I'm not sure I want to throw all of that away, because it was really my fault.'

'Nonsense, he shouldn't have taken your love for granted. He left you alone for too long. He should have made time for you. You shouldn't have to put up with that kind of abuse!' I raised my voice a little. 'Why, if I had a wife that loved me as much as you do him, I would do whatever it takes to make her happy!'

'Yeah, I…I suppose you're right. I do deserve a little happiness. I have been alone for too long. He should have made time for me and with even half of his money, I could live very comfortably.'

'"That's my girl…You deserve it…why not…? Get all of the money that you can; he can always earn more. He makes more than enough to support both of your lifestyles.' A demonic grin crossed my face and I felt the overwhelming satisfaction I get when I have landed another pigeon. 'Besides, it's not like he has given you a choice; if you don't countersue, you could end up destitute.'

'Okay…I'll do it; I will sit down today and write down all of the things that I can.'

'Good, good, and don't forget to have that drink; it sounds like you could use it.'

'Thank you, Jacob—for being there, I mean—I know you are only looking after my best interests.'

'Not at all, that's what I'm here for. Any lawyer worth his salt cares about his clients. Now, you just calm down and do as I say and I will take good care of you.'

'Okay, okay, I will calm down now.'

'Good, you try to have a nice afternoon and I will take the rest of my day and start preparing our case.'

'Okay, goodbye Jacob. I'm glad I called you.'

'Me too, Fran…me too.'

"As I hung up the phone, I rubbed my hands together in delight and smiled confidently through the office window at Bea. My cold eyes conveyed my victory over yet another ambiguous situation. Bea simply shook her head in disgust, mumbled to herself, and sorted the files upon her desk in a mêlée of suppressed aggression, which, of course, made the victory all the sweeter. At this point, I was feeling so full of myself, even the lovely Rosalinda couldn't refuse me. There was a certain aura of success around me; she would have to be mad to refuse me (and my eminent wealth) now.

"I spent the remainder of my day preparing Fran's case and dreaming of my soon to be pile of money. I'm sure Bea simmered in her disgust when I placed Fran's counter divorce file on her desk on my way out at the end of the day. I shot her a wink and a smile before I turned away. 'We'll see if you are smiling on Monday,' she said.

'Why, what's happening on Monday?'

'Oh, didn't I tell you? How clumsy of me. You have a meeting with a client in Jamison's office on Monday.'

'Really? Who's the client?'

"Her lips curled over the biggest smile I have ever seen on her face. 'Oh, someone from New York Life and Trust, I think.'

'Brilliant!' I cheered. 'They're happy with how I handled the West Palm Estates case, no doubt.'

'No doubt,' said Bea with one raised eyebrow as she watched me saunter out the big glass double doors and down the steps.

"A quick walk to the parking garage and I was on my way to Angelo's to try my luck with the fair Rosalinda. It had been two and a half years since I had stopped in for linguini and her aromatic garlic bread made fresh every day by her loving hands. It's strange how a childhood love affair can make for such a strong appetite.

"The sunlight gleamed on the hood of my Martin as I rode, top down, triumphantly across the Brooklyn Bridge. Back, back I drove, back in time to a former version of myself. As I ventured across that iron umbilical cord which still connected me to my fading childhood, I felt a strange need to visit the old neighborhood, so I took the long way and drove though the Bronx past my childhood home.

"Pulling up to the curb, I parked and quietly sat, watching the children play stickball in the street. There were many summer days I spent on these streets whiling away the hours with my friends. I could still hear my mother calling me in for dinner and my father warning me about my friends wasting my time. *Couldn't he leave me to my childhood just once?* I thought. *And Uncle Matt, that fucked up excuse for a human being.*

Jacob stopped his story and looked at Dr. Kessler. "You know, some ghosts deserve to be dead," he said without hesitation. He paused a moment to reflect on those words and then he nodded and continued his tale.

"At the end of the street, facing me, stood a tall house still painted tan with brown trim and shutters. Grapevines twined their way along the rod iron porch rails that ran the length of the porch and down the waist-high lattice on the right side of the house. This was the Galotti home, the place where I could run whenever my uncle Matt...Well, when I needed to get lost.

"It was a magical place. The kind of place where kindly old ladies try to fatten you up with soup and garlic bread. It was where the shy ghost of a little girl still waves to me from a dimly lit hall and then runs away, and the muffled voices and sounds of her brother's scuffling upstairs bled through the kitchen ceiling. It became the place of my only fond memories when I lived at home. And the place where I had left what was afforded me of a heart.

"If there ever was a time in my life when I was given a slim last chance of knowing what love is, it was there. The sight of the old house crystallized their faces in my mind until it settled on hers. I breathed a deep sigh, and then turned the key and drove on toward the water front to Angelo's, to my beloved Rosa."

Jacob paused his story and lowered his head. Dr. Kessler waited for him to continue, but his words were not forthcoming.

"Tell me about this uncle of yours, Uncle Matt," said the doctor.

"Look," Jacob blurted out, "I'm not sure I can do this. I'm not proud of who I've become. I'm not sure I'm ready—or even if it's you I want to tell."

Dr. Kessler's shoulders recoiled. "I see. Perhaps it's still too early."

"Maybe, or maybe you're not the person I want to open up to."

"Look, don't get mad, Jacob. I'm just trying get a sense of your youth," Dr. Kessler replied. "Besides, your great uncle trusted me; why won't you?"

Jacob lowered his head as his words boiled over. "My great uncle didn't live with my family," Jacob's voice rumbled, reflecting the conflict in his heart. "He had the luxury of separating himself from the cancer that was my family. He was *the rich old bastard*, remember?"

"You don't mean that," remarked Dr. Kessler.

"Money can do that, you know?" Jacob scowled. "It can protect you from all of the unpleasantness of life. While I, on the other hand, had to survive, survive the screaming and the beatings…and the…the…the…ahhhgh!" Jacob clenched his fists and pounded on his forehead. "I don't know why I even came here," he snapped. "I thought maybe I could find some answers. Maybe I could separate myself from these things that are following me around! Maybe I could find a place in my life when I was still happy."

"You can, Jacob, and you're right; maybe I'm not the one you are supposed to open up to. But in order to find the place you're talking about, you will have to talk to someone and I'm—"

"Can we stop now?" Jacob cut him short.

"Of course," answered Dr. Kessler.

Jacob rose to his feet, turned, and walked away. Dr. Kessler watched as he walked stiff-legged back up the hill toward the garden.

"I'd like to continue tomorrow," Dr. Kessler called out, "at ten o'clock, if you don't mind. I'll be in my office if you're interested." Jacob made no attempt to answer. He just mumbled to himself as he marched the trail back to the hospital.

Zed Wing

By the time he had reached the building, Jacob was in a fit of rage. The thoughts he had been left with churned like magma within his skull. Thoughts of his uncle Walt, the angel Gabriel, his uncle Matt, and Monsieur Diabolus swirled around his imagination, conjuring from its depth's images and memories of pain and feelings of love and loss. His mood drove his feet and his feet drove his fury, until he had walked the entire circumference of the hospital grounds three times.

When he had rounded the back of the building for the third time, he noticed something about the building he hadn't noticed before. From the inside, the building was shaped like a giant "H" but from the back of the building between the two two-story wings, there was a third wing on the first floor. It was a short, inconspicuous wing off the building, possibly only six rooms. The dark brick walls and some of the windows were covered in ivy.

Jacob drew near to one of the windows and peered in. He could see only the padded white walls and the feet of a patient against the foot of the bed rail. He stepped back from the window and scratched his chin and then walked the rest of the way around the hospital and entered the front doors.

Jacob quietly and calmly walked through the lobby, down the right service hall past the courtyard to the service hall that connected the four giant wings. He stared down the hall to see if he could see any sign of the smaller corridor. There were two double doors halfway down the hall, but they turned out to be the doors to the employees' break room. He looked into the windows and saw no one there, so he quietly pushed the door open and stepped inside. He could smell stale coffee and tuna fish from someone's discarded sandwich. The room was clean, but the tables and chairs were left in a random fashion, as if a group of nurses had just left the room.

There was one door at the back of the break room. The sign on it read Security Office and once again, when he looked through the window, there was no one there. "Must be my lucky day," he whispered to himself, and he quietly slipped through the door. It was a small office with a desk and two chairs. There was a newspaper on the desk, a blank book of shift reports, two pencils, a pack of Marlboro Menthol cigarettes and some Hustler magazines partially hidden by a copy of Psychology Today magazine, but what interested Jacob was the sign over the narrow open hall beyond the office. It read *Zed Wing.*

He approached the wing and peered down the hall. As he had previously surmised, there were indeed six rooms; there were three doors on the left and three on the right. Five of the doors had clipboards which hung on the wall to the right of each door. A seventh door at the end of the hall was clearly marked 'Emergency Exit.'

Jacob's curiosity overwhelmed his fear; though he knew there would be someone coming soon, he also knew this would most likely be the only chance he would get to see this part of the hospital. The doctors had gone to great lengths to hide this part of the building from the other patients and he wanted to know why, so he slunk down the hall and, one by one, looked into each room. The first room on the right was obviously a room for procedures of some kind. The door was open so Jacob stepped inside.

There was a gurney in the center of it with leather restraints for both the upper and lower body, as well as a thin strap for the head of the patient. The sight of the table made Jacob cringe at the thought of not being able to move and the overwhelming feeling of powerlessness. Two straitjackets hung on a coat rack behind the door and a rolling tray displaying syringes, tongue depressors, and a set of strange-looking clamps—which looked like they were used to pry someone's mouth open—sat next to the gurney.

A feeling of dread came over him as the thought of the room's purpose sank in. The sound of a faucet dripping into the stainless-steel sink caused a chill to run through him and the hair on the back of his neck stood on end, so he didn't linger in the room any longer.

He moved to the next door on the left. It was locked and the small glass window was of shatterproof glass with wire mesh embedded in it. The clipboard next to the door read, *Vacant.* When Jacob looked in, he saw no bed or sink, or TV, or furniture of any kind. There was only padded walls and the floor with a small high window partially covered by ivy. The next room on the right, however, had a bed with an occupant securely strapped to it. The clipboard next to the door read, *Joseph Boyhar: Severe schizoaffective disorder, keep sedated for four hours daily, exercise for an hour after breakfast. Keep strict regimen of paliperidone every 6 hours.*

Jacob couldn't see his face, but he could see the handle of a tongue depressor sticking out of the person's mouth. There was light streaming in from the window and the shadow of Joseph's body was cast upon the wall like a cadaver that didn't know it was dead. There seemed to be no movements of any kind. Jacob drew a deep breath and moved to the next locked door across the hall.

It held a woman in a straitjacket in blue pinstriped pajamas slumped down on the floor. Her legs were slightly folded but set apart like she had been on her knees for some time. Her face was caught in an empty, distant stare of endless sorrow. Jacob's heart sank within his chest at the sight. He imagined emotions of despair so dark, so morose they could rise from within as a voiceless moan and be drawn into the black holes her eyes had become.

Though she seemed to be looking right at him, there was no awareness or recognition in her face. He was as transparent as glass to her and she, otherworldly to him. He read the adjacent clipboard on the wall, *Mabel Olivetti: dissociative identity disorder with violent displays of self-abuse. Mild sedative four times daily and close observation.*

Jacob found it hard to pull away from the window of her room. Her silent surrender to the void and hopeless separation from the world by her clockwork mind held her spellbound in a permanent state of flux and confusion. The walls which made up her padded room didn't really need to be there. She had been trapped long before she came to the hospital and had become a fugitive from herself.

Jacob stood there in silence for a moment and stared at the empty clipboard across the hall and then he glanced at the clipboard hanging beside the final door. The paperwork hung on it like a well-worn novel, with the corners curled and the pages scribbled on. *What misery was held behind it? What poor wretched lost soul had been left behind in this oubliette to slowly disappear?* He thought. *Still, he had to know, even if he was the only one to bear witness to their fate. He had to know.* He drew near to the clipboard and read: *Alister Stromwell: paranoid schizophrenia—delusions of Holocaust victims, departed homeless and deceased orphans. Plagued by guilt and fear of reprisal. Prone to fits of rage and self-mutilation.*

Jacob approached the window and peered inside. At the window stood a man of average height with light brown-gray hair. He was staring out of the only hole afforded him by the ivy at the window's edge. He stood with his back to the door in a hospital gown which had been shredded at the sleeves and hung open at the back. He stood in the three-foot-by-three-foot square of the window light on the floor, as if he were anchored there by some unseen force. His arms and legs were badly bruised and faint deep scratches scarred his skin. There were leather mittens upon his hands that were latched into place with small locks and a hospital band on his right wrist.

As Jacob stood there looking, he placed his hand against the glass, as if to feel some subtle vibration from the other side. Then he closed his eyes, rested his head upon the window and wept. A flood of tears rolled from his face. He was overcome with a longing for his Great uncle Walt; it was a longing to be free from his tainted memories, to set free the caged spirit of his childhood and live in the full light of a new day. When Jacob looked up into the room once more, he was shocked to see the man staring back at him from the other side. He had come within inches of the glass and Jacob was now gazing at the image of his bruised and battered face.

The man's eyes scanned the window, as if he were looking for a lost friend in a crowded room. He called out from the other side, with throat raw and veins bulging. His words, muted to a faint cry by the thick glass. "Rebecca...Sonia...Momma...Where are you? I can't see you anymore." He pounded his fists on the door crying, "Papa...Papa...don't go! Don't leave me here! Don't leave me..."

Jacob rolled to one side of the door and grasped at his hair as his heart pounded within him. He looked down the hall at the door of the vacant room and the clipboard hanging next to it. He could hear footsteps coming from the security office and the laughter of some distant conversation. As the security guards returned to their office, they hear a sound. It was the sound of the emergency exit door closing behind Jacob's fast-moving footsteps.

Outside the door, Jacob sprinted across the grounds to a place near the woods. He stopped at its edge and leaned against a large elm tree. Out of breath and sick with empathy for the inhabitants of *Zed Wing*, he stood in the shadows staring back at the door, waiting to see if anyone would emerge. A security guard opened the door and looked around, but Jacob stood silent behind the tree hoping he wasn't seen.

After a few moments of waiting, the guard shrugged his shoulders and closed the door. Jacob caught his breath and reconciled himself to his own personal problem. He was going to have to open up to someone or he might soon find himself staring back from the other side of his own padded cell—be it literal or not. Now more than ever, he felt the need to lay his demons to rest and set out to slowly walk the grounds again.

Finding Jefferies

It took several hours for Jacob to calm himself. After he had walked the perimeter of the building once more, he stopped at the patio outside the west wing. It was a large cobblestone patio in a half circle with four short pillars and busts of prominent psychologists. Jacob walked among them. Freud, Skinner, Piaget, and Pavlov stood like overlords of the insanity they came to represent. There was a balcony on the second floor directly above the patio. It was a small balcony with a short cement rail about two and half feet tall and ten inches wide. Four flowerpots filled with geraniums were placed along the rail, three feet apart.

He pondered the position of the balcony and remembered the double French doors in the game room at the end of the west-wing. Jacob glared at the busts around him. He didn't trust psychologists. They were too clinical, too detached to really care about his pain. It was then a thought began to sink in. He was going to have to find someone to confide in, someone who might understand, someone he could relate to. He turned his attention back to the grounds in quiet contemplation of who that person might be.

He quietly strolled along the wall watching the other patients. His stroll took him by the hedgerow which grew along the wall near the front gate. As he passed, he noticed a soft shadow among the thick green oleander leaves. The apparition evoked a snicker, but his curiosity stopped short of investigating and he made his way back to Alice's desk. When he got there, Alice was engaged in a conversation with a black woman in her middle forties.

"No Ma'am, I haven't seen Boo all afternoon. Have you checked his room?"

"Yes, I just came from there. His things are all in order, but he's not there."

Alice's face turned serious and she reached for the phone. As her hand raised the receiver, Jacob stepped forward and placed his hand on hers. "Wait," he said. "I think I may be able to shed a little light on the situation."

Alice smiled. "Oh, thank God, do you know where he is? No one can find him on the grounds and there is a strict rule about going beyond the grounds."

"Oh, I'm sure he's still on the grounds, but you won't find someone who doesn't want to be found," Jacob said with a warm smile.

"I see," said the woman. "Then I will just come back in another six months. He's not ready to come home yet."

"Wait," said Jacob. "You wouldn't happen to be Mrs. Jefferies, would you?"

"Why yes, yes I am. I'm his sister. Who are you?"

"I'm Boo's roommate, Jacob Sullinger. May I talk to you for a moment? Boo has mentioned you, or rather, your son." The woman's face fell and a somber note filled her eyes. Alice watched the conversation, but said nothing. Her hand slowly placed the receiver back down. "Will you come with me?" he asked, and he took the woman's hand and led her out the front doors and down the steps of the hospital. There by the gate, next to a statue of the martyred disciple Paul, they stood in its shadow and spoke freely.

"What is it?" she asked. "What can you tell me about my brother?"

"Well, not much, I'm afraid, but there has been a change in him lately."

"A change? What kind of change?"

"Hmm," said Jacob scratching his chin. "How can I say this? When I first came to the hospital almost a week ago, he acted like he was still on duty. He was a proud Captain still fighting the war in Afghanistan. And now..."

"And now, what?"

"Now he's remembered everything and is facing the fight of his life. I can't tell you what he wrestles with. Only he can do that, but I can say he is not far away from coming home. He's long overdue."

Mrs. Jefferies clasped hold of Jacob's hand and pulled it to her face and began to cry. "I have missed him so; you have no idea what this means to me. We were close, you see, and...and...that god damned war...It's not right for a family to lose two loved ones in one battle for no good reason."

"I can't promise you any miracles. He will never be the Boo you once knew, but he is closer to the answer he seeks than he knows. Please stay hopeful." Jacob smiled and placed his hand on her shoulder. "I have grown very fond of Boo in the last few days and strangely enough, we have a great deal in common. Please be patient with him."

"It is all I've ever done," she said. Then she reached into her purse and pulled out a scrap of paper and a pen. She scribbled down her phone number and handed it to Jacob. "Here," she said. "Call me when he is ready and I will be here the next day to pick him up. He means the world to me. Do you understand? I would do anything in the world for my baby brother."

"Yes Mrs. Jefferies, I understand, I wish I had someone like you waiting for me."

She caressed his cheek with her gloved hand. "Oh, I'm sure you do. You may not know it, but I bet you do." Then she turned away and strolled out of the gate and got into the passenger door of a large white Mercedes.

Jacob watched as the car pulled away and disappeared beyond the wall. He smiled to himself and glanced past the statue to the hedgerow beyond. There were a conspicuous pair of slippers on a conspicuous pair of feet below the boughs of the hedge. "You can come out now, Boo. She's gone," said Jacob. The feet shuffled in a moment of awkwardness and then slowly stepped from the hedge. His face was swollen and care-worn. His hands, fists tightly clenched, hung at his sides. "Don't worry Boo, I won't meddle in your family business. It's not my place."

Boo stepped up to Jacob, without looking up from the ground. "I'm not ready to face her yet. I...I just can't. Not yet."

"Believe me, I totally understand," said Jacob. Boo stood there trying to summon the words to open the door to his cage. They were words of shame and rage and frustration.

"If...If I could just...just get it off my chest," he growled. "Jacob, I don't think I can do this alone." Boo's eyes looked into Jacob's and released a silent scream. Jacob flashed a beleaguered smile and he shook his head in dismay.

"I don't know how much help I would be, I have the same problem," he said.

Jacob scratched his thinning scalp and stared at the ground. The soft shadow of Saint Paul sharpened on the lawn as the sun broke through the clouds. Jacob could feel his spirit begin to rise. "Boo, my friend, it seems we are meant to be here."

"What? What do you mean?"

"We both are carrying bags of a life we've once lived. Neither of us has told a single soul and neither of us ever will." Jacob threw his arm over Boo's shoulder, "I've got a proposition for you, but I have to ask you first, do you trust me?"

Boo looked at Jacob and smiled. "Strangely enough, I do. There is definitely something of me in you, I can see it."

"Well then, I have some bags I have to unpack, but you have to promise me you will take it to your grave, and in return, I will bear your story the same courtesy." Boo's face lit up and he laughed. It wasn't a laugh of mockery, or scorn, but of blissful enlightenment, as if the door to his cage were kicked open and he was suddenly free. "Come on," said Jacob. "I know a place where life grows in a circle. There we can find our way back to the beginning." The two strolled off quietly but cheerful, and time was theirs to do with as they pleased.

"Hey wait," said Boo. "I've got one for you."

"One what?" asked Jacob.

"How do you know you're in a really tough lesbian bar?" Boo asked.

"Ha! Okay, I don't know; how do you know you're in a tough lesbian bar?"

"Even the pool table doesn't have any balls?"

"Ha, ha, ha!" they laughed as they crossed the lawn. Shoulder to shoulder, they disappeared into the woods.

The following morning, an orderly met Dr. Kessler at the gate when he arrived at the hospital. The orderly's concerned face and hasty walk let Dr. Kessler know something was amiss. As he approached the doctor's BMW, the driver's window glided down.

"What's the matter, Brady? Did we have a suicide last night?"

"No, no nothing like that, doctor, but we…umm…we lost some patients."

"Lost some patients? Which ones?"

"A Mr. Luemarius Glass and Mr. Sullinger," he stammered. "They weren't in their room at lights out and we searched the whole hospital and found no trace of them."

The doctor smiled and shook his head. "Jacob and Boo. What a pair of miscreants," he mumbled.

"What's that, sir?"

"Oh, nothing Brady—nothing at all—I hope," answered the doctor.

Once inside the hospital, the doctor went directly to his office and put his papers in the top right drawer of his desk. He sat in his fat leather chair and stared out the window tapping his fingers on the desk. *They wouldn't leave the grounds*, he thought. *Though they might have taken something with them or left something. Maybe there's a clue in their room.*

So, he made his way to their room. Everything was untouched, their beds were neatly made, their clothes were folded and placed at the foot of their beds. *Nope, everything in order,* thought the doctor. *Just like good soldiers.* He stepped toward the window and stared down at the grounds. *Could they have spent the whole night outside on the grounds?* The doctor spent the next several hours like the orderlies, walking the grounds and trying to think like Jacob and Boo. It wasn't until he rounded the south side of the lawn and saw the arch of roses standing in the late afternoon sun did it hit him.

A big smile came to his face and he began to walk the trail down to the garden and pond. As he approached, he could hear the sound of laughter. He slowed his steps and quietly rounded the fir trees into the garden. In the distance, he saw the two figures of Boo and Jacob. They were laughing and skipping stones across the water like a couple of kids.

A sheepish smile swept the doctor's face and without making a sound, he quietly headed back to the hospital. Once there, he found Alice preparing to make a call to Boo's sister. She paused before dialing the number.

"Did you find them?" Alice asked frantically.

"Yes, yes, I found them. They're still on the grounds."

"Oh, thank god!" exclaimed Alice as she set the receiver down. "Where are they and I will send Brady and Hatch to fetch them."

"Now, let's not be too hasty, Alice. They're not hurting anyone. Let's just give them their peace. They'll come in when they're ready."

"Are you sure, doctor? We've never allowed patients to stay out all night before."

"Yes, I think we can make an exception—just this once."

"All right, if you insist. But if they're not back by dinner, it will be your ass, doctor, not mine."

"All right, Alice, I get your point. I'll take the heat on this one. Trust me, though, they'll be back by then."

As the day wore on, the look on Dr. Kessler's face began to show his concern. The lines on his forehead grew deeper and the corners of his mouth sagged. By the time Mr. Johansson finished his hour in Dr. Kessler's office, the good doctor could hardly keep himself from looking out the window. After dinner, Dr. Kessler rounded up a couple of orderlies and walked the path down to the duck pond, but this time Boo and Jacob were nowhere to be seen. He heard a bird calling out in the distance as the sun softened the evening shadows. "Damn it!" said the doctor. "Where in the hell could they be?"

"Maybe we missed them when we came down," said Hatch.

"They would have had to climb that embankment over there to avoid being seen by us," replied Brady. Dr. Kessler searched the hill with his eyes, looking for a path which they might have made, but there was nothing. The rich dark earth and grass seemed untouched.

"Come on, let's search the grounds one more time before it gets dark," said Dr. Kessler.

The three men made their way back to the hospital and walked the grounds until dark before conceding defeat. Dr. Kessler led the two men back to Boo's room where they stood in the doorway. "Wait," said the doctor. "They're in the building."

"How do you know?" asked Hatch.

"There were fresh clothes folded on the bed when I was here last, and now they're gone. Hmm—I wonder," said the doctor.

"Wonder what?" asked Brady.

"Come on. Let's go down to the laundry," said the doctor. The three men crossed the hall and took the stairs down to the basement where the laundry was done. Except for the stacks of folded linens and the standing washers, it was quiet. Across the room was a wheeled canvas cart set beneath the dirty laundry chute. Dr. Kessler calmly strolled over and looked into the cart. There on the top lay two pairs of pajamas soiled with dark earth and grass stains. The doctor smiled. "Just as I thought," said the doctor. "They came in for a change of clothes."

"And something to eat, I imagine," said Hatch.

"Let's search the building again, now that we know they're here. Brady, check all the first-floor doors and make sure they're locked. Hatch and I will check the kitchen," said the doctor.

When they ascended the stairs to the first floor, Hatch looked down the hall in the direction of the kitchen and noticed the door to the pantry was ajar. "Doctor! Come quick, they've broken into the pantry," he called out. The doctor quickened his steps.

"Of course," said the doctor. "They are probably hungry by now. Let's see what they've taken." The two entered the pantry and searched the shelves.

"It does look like they were in a hurry, they knocked over the flour tin and rummaged through the sack of potatoes," said Brady.

Hatch strolled over to the refrigerator and opened it. "The cook has gone home for the night, so there is no way to be sure, but there do seem to be things missing," he said.

"Thing? What things?" asked the doctor.

"Well, I like to make myself a sandwich from time to time, so I know the cook keeps a loaf of bread and bologna in here. Both are gone. Not only that, but there are no eggs to speak of. There were two flats of eggs in here after lunch. Now they're gone."

"Look around," said the doctor. "Is there anything else missing?"

"Well, there's usually a box of zip-lock bags on that shelf by the door," said Hatch. "Uh-oh," he said. "Mrs. Highlany's not going to like this. There is usually a whole vat of tapioca pudding in here. You know how she loves her pudding."

"Pudding? Zip-lock bags? Ha! What in the hell are those two vandals up to?" chuckled the doctor.

Brady approached the pantry from the hall. "I've secured all of the first-floor doors, doctor. You can go home now; Hatch and I can take care of this mess. We'll find them."

"Not on your life," exclaimed the doctor. "I'm responsible for those two. I'm not leaving until those two are accounted for. I will just have to sleep on the couch in my office for the night." There was a moment of silence and the sound of a door closing in the hall. "What was that? Did you hear it?"

"It sounded like it came from the meeting room, or Dr. Malinowski's office down the hall," said Hatch.

"Hatch, you check the doctor's office. Brady and I will check the meeting room. Let's be quick. Maybe we can catch them," said Dr. Kessler.

The three shuffled out the pantry and down the hall as fast as they could. Hatch checked the door of Dr, Malinowski's office, but it was locked. "It must have been the meeting room," he said. "This one's locked." Dr. Kessler turned the knob of the meeting room door and flung it open. He peered into the emptiness of a darkened, silent room. He felt along the wall for the light switch. Click, went the switch, but nothing happened. Click, click, click.

"There's no power," said the doctor.

"But the lights in the hall are on," said Brady. "It must be in the room."

"Hatch, bring a flashlight. We need to check this out," said Dr. Kessler.

"There's one in the janitor's closet, I'll be back in a flash," said Hatch as he took off down the hall.

Dr. Kessler stepped into the room and felt along the wall with his left hand. "Jacob," he said softly, "are you in here? Boo? If you are, answer me." He listened, but heard nothing. He felt his hand touch one of the light sconces on the wall. Slowly, he traced the length of the sconce with his fingertips. When he reached the light bulb, it felt strange. It was bigger than he remembered and more oblong. He twisted it to secure it in its socket and it rolled right out of his fingers and hit the floor with a splat. "That didn't sound right," said the doctor.

Brady stood in the doorway waiting for Hatch to return with the flashlight. "Why don't you wait for the flashlight, doctor? It's probably safer." he said.

"No, they're not here, I'm sure of it," said the doctor.

"Wait, here comes Hatch now," said Brady. Dr. Kessler listened to the sound of footsteps getting louder as they came up the hall. Hatch arrived at the meeting room door panting. He flicked the light on and pointed the beam in the direction of the doctor.

"Come here, Hatch. I want to shine the light on something," said the doctor. Hatch walked over to where the doctor was standing. "Here, let me have the light a moment," said Dr. Kessler. Hatch handed him the flashlight and the doctor shined it on the wall sconce. The sconce was a small two-candle candelabra, which should have had two flame-shaped light bulbs. Instead, one candle was bulb-less and on the other, there sat an egg. "Ha, ha, ha," laughed the doctor.

"What? What is it?" asked Brady, still standing in the doorway.

The doctor shined the light on the floor to find the other egg splattered across the tile. "It's an egg," he said.

"An egg?" asked Hatch.

"Yep, they're all eggs—look," said the doctor as he shined the light on all of the sconces around the room. "They've replaced all of the light bulbs in the room with eggs. What in the hell are those two up to?"

"Well, I'll be damned." said Hatch. "Why do you suppose they wanted the light bulbs?"

"I couldn't even begin to imagine," answered the doctor.

"Hey, Dr. Kessler," said Brady. "Look at these lines on the tiles in the hall."

"What lines?" asked the doctor. The doctor and Hatch returned to the hall and looked down. Sure enough, there were thin black lines running up and down the hall, crisscrossing in all directions. "Oh, for the Son of Sam!" exclaimed the doctor. "I've had about enough of this charade. I'm wiped out. Why don't you two follow these lines and see where they lead and report to me in the morning. I'm too tired and I have an appointment with Mrs. Alister at nine in the morning. If you need me, I'll be in my office."

"Good enough, Dr. Kessler. We'll track them down. They got to be in here somewhere," said Hatch.

"Yeah, we'll find them, doctor. The doors are all locked, they can't get out, so it's just a matter of time now," exclaimed Brady.

"Fine, if you don't find them, let me sleep, won't you?"

"Oh, we'll find them," exclaimed Hatch.

"So you say, but keep in mind, gentlemen, you are dealing with a highly trained commando. I'll just leave you with that thought." Brady and Hatch looked at each other and then down at the lines on the floor. The doctor trotted off toward his office and Brady and Hatch began following the thin black dotted lines in opposite directions.

When the doctor arrived at his office, he checked the room thoroughly before settling in on the couch that sat against the bookcase. He unbuttoned the top buttons of his shirt and tucked his hands beneath his head and tried to let go of the events of the day. His last thought before drifting off was whether or not the lines on the tiles would lead to the second floor.

The Stand

The following morning came crashing through Dr. Kessler's restful slumber in the form of Hatch's fist pounding on his office door. "Pow...pow...pow, pow! Doctor, come quick. We've found them. They've barricaded the first-floor doors to the patio on the west wing."

"Huh, what? What time is it?" asked the doctor as he rubbed his eyes.

"It's 5:40 doctor, just before sunrise," Hatch answered.

"5:40?" the doctor exclaimed. "Good grief, what could they possibly be doing at this hour?"

"You'll have to come see this for yourself, doctor. They've piled all the furniture up against the west wing doors on the first floor," said Brady.

"All right, all right, I'm coming," said the doctor as he opened the door to their bewildered faces. "Well, let's go see what they're up to."

"Hatch and I followed the lines until 3 am, then we took a break. The lines didn't lead anywhere," said Brady, walking briskly down the corridor.

"Yeah, they went everywhere, doctor. We never found an end," remarked Hatch.

"Then about fifteen minutes ago we did a door check, and found this," said Hatch as he pointed down the west wing hall.

There at the end of the hall was a pile of three sofa chairs, two book cases, four tables, two benches and a gurney upside down. "Look," said Dr. Kessler as they approached the barricade. "They stacked them carefully, so if you pulled the gurney off the top, the whole thing would collapse. Those smart little SOBs."

"Yeah, but why?" asked Brady. "The door was locked anyway."

"Well, they obviously didn't want anyone else using the door, either," said the doctor.

"Wait a minute," said Hatch. "This door leads to the patio. There's another door on the second floor just above this one. Brady, when you locked up last night, did you also lock the second-floor doors?"

"Oops," said Brady. "I didn't think about that."

"Shit!" exclaimed the doctor. "Come on, let's check the second-floor balcony." They took the stairs up and tumbled onto the second-floor landing. There, only a few steps away, were the French doors that opened up to the balcony above the patio. They could see Boo and Jacob kneeling down behind the cement rail beyond the doors. They had used a cane to bar the door and were hunkered down as if they were defending a stronghold.

"Do you want us to kick the door open and take them, doctor?" asked Hatch.

"Why?" asked the doctor. "They can't go anywhere. Let's see what this is all about, shall we? Take a seat and we will wait them out." Brady, Hatch, and the doctor all took seats in the reading area just inside the doors and watched.

On the other side of the glass doors, Boo and Jacob whispered to each other. "We have 12 explosives, 8 tapioca bombs, and two dozen grenades, sir. Do you think it will be enough to take the enemy?"

"It should be, Private Sullinger, if we take them by surprise." Boo raised up quietly and peered down at the four busts below. "They don't seem to be aware of our position, Private. Ready the tapioca bombs."

"Yes sir." Jacob took the vat of tapioca and spooned the pudding into the zip-lock bags, sealed them and set them to one side. He carefully laid the last flat of eggs and the twelve lightbulbs out and waited for Boo's command.

Boo glanced over the rail a second time. "It's them all right," he said. "Al-Kasim Gihadi, his two bodyguards, and your uncle Matt. They are completely unaware of our presence. We will start with the smoke bombs and follow it up with a volley of explosives. That should completely take them by surprise. Then, we will finish them with grenades."

Jacob snickered and handed Boo six lightbulbs. "On my mark," said Boo. "Okay, three, two…one. Go, go, go!" he shouted. They both jumped to their feet and hurled the light-bulbs at the four statues below. "Pop, pop, pop-pop, pop-pop-pop…pop-pop-pop, pop-pop." The bulbs exploded on the pillars and busts below. "We've got them on the run, private, quick! The bombs, launch them!"

"Yes sir!" yelled Jacob as he handed Boo a bag full of pudding. Boo hurled it at the bust of Sigmund Freud. "Splat" went the pudding across the forehead of the bust.

"Another!" said Boo. "They haven't had enough!" Jacob handed him another and he threw it as hard as he could at the bust of Skinner. "Take that, Al-Kasim, you worthless dog!"

Jacob rose to his feet and slung a bag at the statue of Pavlov. It landed with such force, it nearly knocked the bust off its pillar. "Fuck you, Uncle Matt, I'm not yours any more, you sorry piece of shit!"

After all of the bags were gone, Boo yelled, "Now let's finish it! The grenades!" They both snatched up as many eggs as they could hold and pummeled the busts below until they were a dripping mess of egg, pudding and shards of glass and then Boo threw his arm over Jacob's shoulder and shook him, laughing, as the sun began to hit the tops of the trees in the distance. "Look at that," he said. "I bet they never saw that coming."

"Ha, ha, ha, they never had a chance." exclaimed Jacob.

"Let's go to breakfast. I'm starving," said Boo as he pulled the cane from the door handles and flung the doors behind them open. Boo and Jacob stepped through the door, only to be met by the cold stares of Dr. Kessler, Hatch, and Brady.

"Breakfast?" questioned Dr. Kessler. "You two vandals want breakfast now?" Brady and Hatch made a move toward the two. Dr. Kessler threw up his right hand. "Wait," he said. "I want to talk to these two in my office. But before I do, they are going to clean that mess outside up and put the furniture downstairs back where it belongs. Then, we will consider your breakfast."

"Man, this sucks," exclaimed Boo. "I'm really hungry too. A great big omelet sounds good right about now."

"With what eggs?" snapped Dr. Kessler. "There isn't but maybe a half dozen eggs left in the whole hospital, and those we collected from the meeting room. Everybody in the hospital is going to have to eat either oatmeal or cold cereal this morning, thanks to you."

Jacob looked at Boo and grimaced. "Oops, I didn't think about that."

"Brady and Hatch here will escort you to the janitor's closet, where you'll find a mop, bucket, and broom to help you clean up. Once you have done that and taken care of your barricade downstairs, I want to see you both in my office."

"Oh, all right," said Jacob, "but they had it coming to them." He smacked Boo on the arm and they both snickered.

"Okay, okay, let's not take all morning, I've got an appointment at nine o'clock." The doctor shook his head and walked back to his office while Brady and Hatch escorted Boo and Jacob down the hall.

Two hours later, Boo and Jacob arrived at Dr. Kessler's office with the orderlies following close behind. Jacob gave a light tap three times on the door. "Come in, you two," said the voice on the other side. Jacob turned the knob and opened the door. The doctor was seated in his tall back leather chair with an annoyed look on his face. He looked past Boo and Jacob. "Brady, Hatch, thank you for your help last night. You can go home now, I'll take it from here," he said.

The two orderlies left the men to the doctor's care. "Well, come on, let's get this over with," said the doctor. Boo and Jacob stepped into the room. "Do you realize how much trouble you two have caused? Boo, Alice nearly called your family, and Jacob, a stunt like this could change your status here at the hospital from voluntary to mandatory. This is some serious shit."

"What do you want us to say?" asked Jacob. "It was something we felt we had to do."

"Yeah, and now the hospital is clean and no one got hurt, so there's no harm, right?" asked Boo.

The doctor looked down and scratched his chin. "I suppose," he said. "But if you two pull a stunt like this again, I'll have you both washing out bedpans." At that moment, Mrs. Baglova went scooting past his office doorway with her walker. Dr. Kessler looked down at the legs of her walker. His face turned bright red and the veins in his temple rose to the surface. "Excuse me, Mrs. Baglova," he said, catching her attention.

Mrs. Baglova stopped and looked up, her face caught in the same distant expressionless gaze she always had. The doctor approached her calmly, held out his hand and placed it on her walker, and then knelt down and pulled something off one of the legs. "Thank you, Mrs. Baglova," he said standing up, "you can go now. Have a nice day." As the woman scooted away, Dr. Kessler turned toward Boo and Jacob and held up the object he had pulled from her walker. His face twisted into a maniacal expression; his voice bristled with frustration as he belted out the words. "Whose big idea was it to tape a felt tip pen to Mrs. Baglova's walker! You know that woman can't sit still!"

Boo and Jacob stood there wearing childish little smirks. "She's made lines all over this hospital's floors," he continued, "Christ, the janitor's going to be buffing those lines out for weeks!" Jacob and Boo couldn't hold back their laughter any longer.

"I guess we should have used a ballpoint," snickered Boo.

"Get out of my office, you two—just get out of my sight—oh, and Jacob, I'm not through with you yet. Tomorrow—my office—ten o'clock."

"Okay, okay, I guess I owe you that much. I'll be here." The doctor ended the meeting by slamming the door behind them as they left. He could hear their laughter resonating through the door as they walked away. He paused a moment and thought about their jubilation and then a soft smile stretched across his face. "Eggs for lightbulbs, ha! That's a good one," he mumbled as he tossed the pen on his desk.

On the other side of the door, Boo and Jacob ambled their way downstairs for breakfast, a triumphant duo riding on a crest of emotional victory. However, when they opened the doors to the courtyard, a hush fell over the other patients and Boo and Jacob found themselves the object of scorn. Jacob quietly took up a tray and got in line. "What's for breakfast?" he asked the patient in front of him.

"Eggs," the man seethed.

"Really?" Jacob eagerly replied.

"Of course not, don't you know sarcasm when you hear it?" He pointed to a sign that read, 'NO EGGS, or anything that requires EGGS…i.e., pancakes, waffles, biscuits, or OMELETS!'

Boo stifled a laugh, but was cut short by the look in Mrs. Carlos's eyes as she stood in front of the heating tray, spooning out the oatmeal. As Jacob and Boo approached her, she turned and walked to the refrigerator and pulled two bowls from it and then returned. "Here," she said. "I've saved these especially for you two."

"But they're cold," exclaimed Boo.

"Yep," said Mrs. Carlos. "So, warm it up with coffee. It's over there where we used to keep the pudding." Her tone was decisively curt.

Jacob looked over at Boo. "I guess we're eating crow for breakfast."

"I guess we are," Boo answered. "But it was worth it," he said with a smile.

The two took their usual table in the corner, but this time they sat laughing and talking about how they watched Brady and Hatch trace the lines through the halls all night.

"Oh, I haven't had that much fun in years," said Boo. "Let's do it again tonight."

"Are you crazy? Dr. Kessler will have you committed. Ha, ha, ha!" laughed Jacob.

"I'm not kidding," said Boo. "I want to fill someone's shoes with this oatmeal."

"You're not serious," said Jacob. "I think you've got bigger fish to fry."

"What do you mean?" asked Boo.

Jacob reached into his pocket and pulled out a scrap of paper. He slapped it on the table and slid it in front of Boo. "It's time, Boo." Boo looked down at the phone number on the slip of paper and fell silent. "Come on Boo, she misses you terribly. At least call her and talk for a while. You don't have to go home yet, if you don't want to."

"I know—it is time," Boo whispered. "I'm ashamed of how long I have been hiding within these walls."

"Don't you think you owe her a phone call, at least?" asked Jacob.

Boo gritted his teeth and nodded. "Yeah—it's time," he said. Then, he picked up the piece of paper and smiled at Jacob, like a child with a secret. "Thank you, Jacob. You are true blue, through and through."

Jacob smiled back and stuffed a spoon full of oatmeal into his mouth. "Crap," he exclaimed, "this shit is stone cold." He glanced over at the smirk on Mrs. Carlos's face. "I think I'll just have coffee and toast," he said, sliding the bowl away. Boo made no complaint, he added sugar to his oatmeal and shoveled it into his mouth. "Suit yourself," he said before swallowing.

After breakfast, Jacob followed Boo out to the lobby where Boo used the phone provided to patients. Jacob stood at a distance to give him some privacy and watched. Boo took out the slip of paper and carefully dialed the number. He tightly clenched the paper in his hand as the line began to ring. Brrrr…brrr…brrr…Click, click… "Hello?" a voice said on the other end of the line. Boo stood there silent for a moment. "Hello?" said the voice a second time. "Boo—is this you?"

Boo stammered at first, trying to collect his thoughts, but then broke down into tears of joy when he heard his sister's voice. He managed to squeak out the words, "Yes, Sis—it's me. I would like to talk if you have the time."

Jacob turned and walked away. With each step, he felt the difference between the man he was and who he had become. It was something his pride couldn't give him and something he couldn't fake or steal. He started to realize that in order to obtain this feeling, he had to give a piece of himself away. This was something *new*, something *profound* and *powerful*, and something he wanted more of.

He walked the halls of the hospital watching the other patients, slowly coming to the realization that each one was living in a world of their own and each one's fears, anxieties, and struggles, though they only existed in the mind, were as real to them as his were. *Perhaps*, he thought. *Gabriel will always be there and that meant, so might Monsieur Diabolus.* There was no healing his problem, no secret psychological answer that will free him from his ghosts.

This thought led him to the conclusion: he would have to change his strategy. *The toughest fight we all face is with ourselves*, he thought. *This must be the human condition.* It was after this revelation he felt the full weight of the night's activities. His wandering eventually took him back to his room where he laid down and fell into a deep restful sleep devoid of dreams or reservations of dreams. It was in this slumber that his soul came to rise the next morning.

"Are you getting up?" Boo asked.

"Huh, what? What time is it?" asked Jacob, blocking the morning light with his hand.

"It's 9:15. Aren't you supposed to be at the doctor's office at ten?"

"Yeah, I guess. I said that I would, but…"

"But what?"

"He just wants me to talk about what he has no business knowing," replied Jacob.

"So, tell him what you think he should know and leave him with egg on his face," Boo said with a smile.

"Ha!" laughed Jacob, "you're incorrigible, you know that? Completely incorrigible."

Boo smiled and straightened his tie and the lapel of his uniform. "Wait," said Jacob. "You're in uniform. What is today, is it a holiday?"

"Nope," said Boo. "My sister is coming today; we are going to visit my nephew's grave. It's time for me to lay something to rest. I think I can now; I had a good long talk with my sister and though we didn't discuss anything specific, I think she understands."

"I'm sure she does," said Jacob. "She struck me as a smart lady."

"Okay, well, I'm off. Good luck with the doctor," said Boo.

"Oh, thanks a lot. I'm sure I can think of something to tell him."

Boo turned on his heels and gave Jacob a military salute. Jacob saluted and threw the covers off himself and prepared to drag his body out of bed while Boo walked, shoulders back and chin up, out the door. Jacob rose to his feet and stepped toward the stainless-steel mirror over the dresser. He looked at himself and ran his fingers through his thinning hair. He had told the doctor a lot, but there was much more to tell.

Surely, there was a way of saying something without saying it, he thought. He shrugged his shoulders and rolled his eyes and then changed into a fresh pair of pajamas before grabbing a cup of coffee in the courtyard. He sipped his coffee until 9:50 and then headed to the doctor's office. This time the door was open. Dr. Kessler sat quietly reading the October issue of Psychology Today. He looked up when Jacob approached his door.

"Ah, Mr. Sullinger, come in. I was thinking you wouldn't show," he said with a smile.

"Well, I'm here, like it or not. I kept my word, didn't I?"

"You did indeed. Come in and have a seat—on the couch, if you like." The doctor walked over and closed the door behind him as Jacob settled on to the couch.

"Where were we the last time we talked?" asked Jacob.

"You were about to tell me about your uncle Matt, I believe," said the doctor. Jacob shot him a disparaging look. "Okay, I see," said the doctor. "Well then, tell me about Angelo's and your Rosalinda."

"Oh yeah, that's right, I was telling you about the Galotti house on the street where I grew up and Angelo's. Angelo's is the Galotti family restaurant."

"Yes, tell me about Angelo's," said the doctor.

"Angelo's?" Jacob stared blankly into space as he lay there and conjured up the past. "Angelo's…I imagine Angelo's is a lot like heaven," said Jacob.

"Like heaven?" the doctor puzzled.

"Yep, like heaven," said Jacob, "when you fall from heaven, it's a long way down."

"Interesting," said the doctor as he settled into his seat.

Rosalinda

"Well...I told you, I visited the neighborhood where I grew up. It may have been as a token gesture to the memory of a little girl I could never get close to, but I often stopped to look at the old place before going to Angelo's. Call it a ritual, if you like. I remember sitting there in my Aston Martin, with the ghosts of my childhood to keep me company before mustering up the courage to face my Rosa. Going to Angelo's always made me feel like a nervous school boy inside, but still, somehow, I was never able to stay away entirely. Something always brought me back. I turned the engine over and headed for the harbor.

"When I turned down the street that led toward the waterfront, the soft glow of pink and blue neon stirred in me an old familiar pang. Dinner at Angelo's was always preceded by a gut-wrenching case of nerves. Rosa was the only woman who could get to me that way. Her smile, big brown eyes, soft olive skin and graceful walk had haunted my fantasies since I was twelve. The food was heavenly, but I could seldom eat it in her presence.

"I parked my gleaming red Martin right in front, steadied my nerves and got into my best game face. I could see her from the street. She was busy busing tables when I pulled up. She paused momentarily to catch a glimpse of this radiant red extension of my manhood. She watched with curiosity as I meticulously put the top up and pretended to check my phone for messages. Then a smile graced her face. She shook her head with a laugh and went back to clearing the table. I slipped my phone into my pocket. I knew she wasn't taken in by my ruse, so I made my way to the door.

"My nervous hand reached for the rail at the base of the steps, and then it hit me, the enchanting aroma of minestrone soup with cheddar dumplings and Italian sausage and garlic and oregano bread. I was snatched back to a day when I was eight and standing outside the back door of the Galotti home. Grandmother Galotti—a large woman in a faded pink gingham dress and cooking apron was busy standing over a steaming pot of soup when she caught a glimpse of me through the screen door.

'Entrare, entrare!' she said. 'Come in, come in!' She flung the door open and ushered me inside. 'Look at you. You are so skinny! Your legs, like a stork's. With legs like that, I should call you spider! Here, you sit. Sit and I give you something to fatten you up.' She poured a bowl of soup and broke off a large piece of garlic bread and placed it in front of me.

"One spoonful and I was hooked, a junky, a sucker, an absolute addict of good Italian food. In all honesty, the woman should have been canonized as a saint by the holy Roman church; she was a master of the culinary arts, a true virtuoso of the delectable delights. The memory left me mute in my tracks.

"I paused and simply breathed in before I entered Angelo's.

"When I stepped inside, she pretended to be busy, quickly snatching silverware and cups from tables Jaco, her brother, had just set. There were only two couples in the place quietly eating in corner booths for privacy. Her brother, a stocky fellow with a thick neck, thinning black hair and hairy arms was setting a table when he saw me standing in my Armani suit with tailored cuffs. 'Hey, Franko!' he called out. 'Look what just slithered in! It's Jake the snake!'

'Hello Jaco,' I chuckled. 'Long time no see.'

Franco and Saul darted into the room from the kitchen. Sal was carrying a dish towel and Franco had a meat cleaver in his firm Italian grip. 'Hey!' Franco yelled, waving the cleaver in the air. 'Look at you! You look like a real person now. Who did you mug to get those clothes? Ha, ha, ha!' he laughed.

"Saul approached me slowly, looking me up and down. 'Not bad, not bad, Jake, but you will need more than a nice suit and a fancy car to win our Rosa.'

'Come on guys, I just came for the linguini and garlic bread,' I said trying to shed their chiding.

'Yeah, yeah. Sure, sure,' said Franco. 'And I'm Pope Benedict. Non si può vestire una scimmia...shmuck.'

'Hey, hey!' said Rosa. 'Leave him alone, his money is good here. Dai andiamo, andiamo clienti, che abbiamo.'

'Ahh!' Saul whelped. 'Once a punk, always a punk,' he said, waving me off with his dish towel as he followed Franco back into the kitchen.

'Thanks Rosa. You still love me, don't you?' I asked with a smile. She said nothing but a raised eyebrow spoke of a secret affliction. She led me to a table.

'Will it be the usual linguini in clam sauce, or will it be the seafood fettuccini this time?'

"'I think the fettuccini sounds good tonight,' I said, salivating at the thought of her moist warm lips. She moved light on her toes like a ballerina with a certain flirtatious style. Her large auburn curls framed her angelic face in an aura of effortless grace. She moved with humble majesty which always left me speechless.

'I'll bring you a nice Pinot Grigio to go with that.'

'You always take such good care of me, Rosa. How is it that you are still single?'

'You know, no one is good enough for my brothers,' she said loudly. "'Christ, the way they carry on, you would think they were going to marry them.' She waited to see if Jaco was listening. He gave no response, but smiled out of the side of his mouth as he polished silverware and laid it on the table. 'What about you?' she asked. 'A nice new suit and an Aston Martin? That must have cost you a good chunk.'

'Well, I got a deal on the car, and I have been keeping busy with legal cases, so I guess you could say I have done well. Actually, I have come into some money recently. Two point five million to be more precise,' I said with some arrogance.

"Jaco paused from setting tables for a split second and shook his head.

'A client of mine died and left an insurance policy in my name,' I said.

'So, you conned some little old lady out of her insurance money this time? Jesus Jake, don't you have any shame?' Rosa scoffed.

'No, no. This was legit,' I said. 'Although, thank you for the idea. That wouldn't be a bad racket to get into.' Rosa shot me a seething cold gaze.

'Whatever happened to you? You used to be such a good boy back in the day,' she said as she felt the fine stitching of my lapel.

'What are you talking about? I am still the same sweet kid from the Bronx, the one who danced with you in junior high.'

'Hardly!' she scoffed. 'I barely recognize you in that suit and your heart is as hard and cold as a tombstone.... No...no, you're not that boy anymore.' There was a definite and sincere sadness in her voice and her eyes.

'It is better than being a drunken grease monkey like my father, or a prison reject like my screwed-up uncle.' I scowled.

'It's not the job, Jacob, or the suit, it's the man in the suit that I'm talking about,' she said plainly.

'You mean you wouldn't have me, even if I were rich? What kind of woman turns down a rich man?'

'The kind of woman who is simply happy to be in love with a good man, and not his money.'

"Jaco's face stretched wide to accommodate his enormous smile. Then he turned to me and said, 'Hey! Romeo! Are you eating or not?'

"I nodded my head in solemn compliance. 'The fettuccini will be fine, thanks Rosa. It will go well with my crow.' I laughed. 'Over the years I've eaten crow at Angelo's more than anywhere else; what can I say? Rosa has a way of serving it so that even crow is palatable.'

"Rosa walked to the kitchen door, swung it open a crack and called to Franco, 'One seafood fettuccini and you better not spit in it or I'll box your ears.' She disappeared behind the waitress station and moments later reappeared holding a bowl of soup and a large crust of garlic bread. She brought them to my table and with a big smile said, 'Here, this is on the house.'

'Rosa!' complained Jaco. 'What are you doin' giving out free food to rich brats?'

'What? He looks skinny to me. Mind your own business,' she rebutted.

'Rosa, you're killing me here,' Jaco grumbled.

'Shut up you,' she said. 'What would Nanna G, God rest her soul, say about you right now.'

"Jaco fell quiet with a simple nod of his head went back to setting tables and polishing silverware.

"I finished off the soup and half of the fettuccini while Rosa sat with me and regaled me with stories of her brother's childhood shenanigans. It felt like I was a kid again. There was something of her grandmother in Rosa, an obelisk of charity and an open-hearted nature that couldn't be corrupted by the world. It was a strength that I had never been exposed to, short of the Galotti home. It left me feeling small and terribly alone. Here was a family, which through all their banter, never betrayed their commitment to each other or respect for what their family name represented. Whatever it was stemmed from their heritage, their religion and their grandmother's strong gift for food and bonding. Watching her and Jaco exchange memories and light hearted ribs, I realized this underlying strength was strangely missing from my childhood. Perhaps it was because I was an only child, or perhaps I lacked something of their faith. An awkward vulnerability came over me. I was out of my element here. I was the only one who didn't get it.

"Like the only child in class who didn't get a card on Valentine's Day, I felt cheated and somewhat an outcast. My conquest of the fair Rosa was routed by this new notion of love and the angel of carnal desire took flight without me. My pants tightened around my gut and my collar around my neck.

Rosa noticed my discomfort. 'What is the matter Jacob? You look like you're not feeling well,' she inquired.

'I…I'm all right. I just have to get going, that's all. I have an important meeting in the morning and need to get to bed early. You understand, don't you?' I said making excuses.

"Her big sad brown eyes cut right through me. 'Yes, yes, I understand,' she said as she began to clear the table. 'I will put this in a box, so you can take it home.' She whisked away my plate and brought it back in a box. Jaco looked over at me with disgust. He sighed and shook his head.

"I, on the other hand, nervously counted the seconds to the door and release from this feeling of abandonment that my childhood and this visit had left me with. Rosa mustered a cordial smile. 'Well, come back and see us, Jacob, don't be a stranger.' she said as she handed me the food and caressed my arm with her left hand.

'I will, I will, ha, ha…you know how I love the food here. Your grandmother would be proud.'

'You are always welcome here,' she added.

'Humph,' Jaco snorted.

'Oh, don't mind him, Jacob,' she said with a wave of her hand. 'Underneath all that testosterone and pasta sauce, they're really big-hearted slobs, once you let them get to know the real you.'

"This statement fell on me like a leaf on water; it hit the surface and slowly sank in. *The real me? Does she see something in me that I am missing?* I thought. I turned toward the door, puzzling over the mystery of a woman who refuses to see the monster in front of her. I looked back at her warm and sincere smile knowing that I couldn't come back as the same man. I couldn't stand in the same room with someone who knows me so well and loves me anyway. Somehow, I couldn't comprehend this. She read the look on my face and deepened her smile. Speaking to me only with her eyes, her thoughts were clear and succinct. She had fallen in love with someone I used to be and would have no other man than him.

"I made my way to the street and as I unlocked my car, I heard a voice call quietly to me from the alley behind the diner. 'Hey monkey boy. Hey melon head, get over here.' It was Saul and Franco. They were standing in the shadow of the diner trying to get my attention without being too loud. I placed the food in the car and walked over to where they stood.

'What do you guys want?' I asked.

'Look,' said Saul, 'I'll keep it simple so youz can understand, okay? We love our sister and we don't want to see her get hurt, so if you know what's good for you, stay on your side of the bridge.'

'Yeah,' added Franco. 'Stay in Manhattan with the other suits.'

'Get hurt...? What are you talking about? I've never laid a hand on Rosa.'

'Jeez slick, you must have ricotta for brains. Everything was going fine until you showed up. Now she ain't gonna to talk to us for a week, because of you,' said Saul.

'So,' said Franco tapping his finger on my chest, 'don't bother coming back until you figure out what your heart is good for, capire?'

'I don't know what she sees in you, but if you come near our sister again, we will pound your face like pizza dough,' said Saul as he patted my left cheek with the palm of his fat hand.

'Franco! Saul! What the hell do you two think you are doing?' a woman's voice rang out over my shoulder. I spun around to find Rosa standing with her hands on her hips tapping her right foot, her face twisted into a grimacing sneer.

"Saul flung his arm over my shoulder. 'Ha, ha, ha!' He laughed. 'We were just sayin' goodbye, weren't we Franky?'

'Yeah, Rose. Just sayin' goodbye, that's all,' Franco added. 'So, take care of yourself, okay Jake? We wouldn't want anything to happen to ya.' Franco patted me on the back.

'Yeah, yeah, you are like uh, family to us, only not as good looking,' Saul chuckled.

'All right, all right you've said your goodbyes, now get back to work, I got a table for six coming in at seven thirty and you guys are designing Hallmark cards out here.'

'Okay, okay! All right already, we're going. Don't get your panties twisted,' said Saul. Then looking me strait in the eye, he said, 'Think about it, Jake, cause that bridge goes both ways.'

"Rosa looked at me with a raised eyebrow. 'What's he talking about?' she asked.

"'Nothing, Rosa,' I said. 'I was extending an invitation to your brothers for a night out on the town.' I winked at Saul and gave a nod in a confirmation of understanding. Saul nodded in return and said goodnight. Rosa simply shook her head and took my arm and walked me to my car.

"'Remember, Jacob, despite how my brothers feel, you are always welcome here. I will always keep a table reserved for that little boy should he ever return,' she said with a kiss on my cheek. I was speechless and she was resolute in spite of my silence. I settled into my car, which felt like a shoe that no longer fit, waved goodbye with a hapless smile, and drove away.

"The road rolled uneven beneath my wheels and jarred my memory from its hiding place. As I drove to my apartment, my mind wandered the haunted hollows of my childhood home, the dimly lit living room of my father's drunken tirades, the shadowy hall where the sound of strangers' voices leaked like poison gas from the cracks around my mother's bedroom door, and of course, the basement stairs in the kitchen that descended into utter black and led to the monster's grotto.

"I can still see Uncle Matt's malevolent smile whenever my mother and father began fighting. He would inevitably say, 'Come on, kid, I'll buy you an ice cream.' This usually meant a trip to Kane's Park and then some seedy hotel for a lesson on the rigors of prison life for anyone with even a snifter of weakness. For my uncle, anyone who showed signs of a soul became his fresh new mark; one way or another, 'Someone is getting fucked,' as he put it.

"The thought of him literally made my skin crawl. It took me the rest of the drive to my apartment to dig a hole in my head, shove these thoughts in, and pack the dirt of my life tight down in on top. After all, *the dead can't hurt you if they stay buried*, I thought.

"When I arrived at my apartment, the lights were off and Dominic's car was gone, so I had the place to myself. I ascended the stairs and unlocked the door. In the fading evening light, I saw the apartment was in disarray with clothes flung around and an empty pizza box on the kitchen counter. I tried the light switch, but there was no power. *That bastard forgot to pay the electric bill again,* I thought. *Oh hell, I'll just hit his liquor and call it a night.*

"I found his bottle of Crown Royal stuck far back in the cabinet beneath the sink. 'Ah, jackpot,' I said, as I snatched it out from behind the box of scrubbing pads. Grabbing a rock glass from the cupboard and some slightly melted ice from the freezer, I sat at the kitchen table and stared out the big picture window as the street lights flickered to life and the car lights cut their way through the ebbing shades of evening. It took three glasses to subdue the jaded child that had been exposed by Rosalinda's stubbornly pure nature.

"What the hell did she mean? I'm still that same kid. How could she love me and still deny me? No matter, I was the holder of the wealth, I thought. *I held the ace card firmly within my hand. Tomorrow will come and I will put my past all behind me and if Rosa is a part of that past, then so be it.* I was deep into the bottle when the last of the neighbor's lights went out and I found the couch in the spinning darkness."

Jacob paused his story and took a deep breath. He looked over at Dr. Kessler, who sat motionless and expressionless in his tall backed chair. Jacob swallowed as if he were choking on the words that were coming. The only sound in the room was the tick, tick, tick, of the clock on the wall. The doctor raised his eyebrows in anticipation of Jacob's words. Then Jacob rested his head back down on the arm of the couch and closed his eyes, He opened his mouth and breathed in and out, hoping the words would follow.

"I…I lay there in that empty apartment, in the darkness with my eyes wide open," he said in a quivering voice, "with the memory of a seven-year-old boy receiving money from his mother for ice cream playing on the big screen in my mind. It was two weeks before my fourteenth birthday and Uncle Matt took me on the Staten Island ferry for the day. The boy quickly snatched the money from his mother's hand and tried to stuff it into his pocket. As he turned to run to the ice cream vender's trolley yards away, the five-dollar bill fell to the ground and scooted to a spot only a few steps away from me. It was in danger of being blown away by the wind. 'Look, Uncle Matt. That kid dropped his money,' I said pointing.

'Grab it, Jacob, his loss is your gain,' he said. I ran to step on it with my shoe before it blew away.

'But it's not mine,' I said returning with the money.

'So,' he said. 'If he wanted it so bad, he shouldn'a been so fucking stupid with it.'

'What? But now he won't have money for his ice cream.'

'So, that's not your fault, that's his. Just stuff the money in your pocket and shut the hell up. Look…' he said. 'There's a baseball shop across the street. I'll take you there after the ferry ride and you can spend it there. What do ya say?'

"I remember looking down at the bill in my hand before making the decision he would later make me regret. Then snubbing my nose at my uncle, I took the money back to the boy. I knew it would cost me, but I didn't know how far he would go to break me of my so-called *weakness*."

Jacob paused and looked at the doctor. Dr. Kessler raised one eyebrow, but said nothing.

"I learned never to question him again," Jacob continued. "This began my tutelage at the feet of the beast. I lay in the emptiness of that apartment and took a deep breath and sighed and prayed my first prayer: 'Dear God, let the morning come quickly.'"

"And then…" asked Dr. Kessler.

"Then, I closed my eyes and slipped into the worst dream I have ever had. Even now, it remains vivid in my mind."

"Really," said Dr. Kessler. "Please, tell me about it."

Jacob hesitated at first, knowing it struck at the heart of his problem, but then he stiffened his resolve and continued.

"It was a calm summer day in this dream, which found my young feet standing at the docks waiting for the Staten Island ferry to settle in next to the landing. My uncle's arm was around my shoulder as he looked down at me and smiled out of the side of his mouth. His thick stubble and wicked grin always seemed to have an air of arrogance. 'You ever been on the ferry?' he asked.

'Nope,' I said. 'This is my first trip. Does it pass the Statue?'

'Yep, we will be able to see it up close.'

"Two men jumped off the ferry, tied it to the pylons and laid down the gangplank. Moments later, we boarded and took our place on the uppermost deck at the bow of the ship. 'Look,' he said pointing. 'Just look at that skyline. You know kid, there ain't nothing like the Manhattan skyline. Just think about all that money. A good lyin' lawyer could clean up in that town.'

"I just looked at him with a strange curiosity and then turned my eyes to the city. 'Do you think so?' I asked.

'Oh yeah, kid, if you knew what you were doin', you could fuck your way right to the top, ha, ha. Keep you from bein' a fucking loser grease monkey like your old man.' I shot him a dirty look and set my feet beneath me when the boat pulled away from the dock.

"The water was smooth, but we held onto the rail to steady ourselves. On the horizon, I could see the statue as a miniature on the line of the water. Clouds began to form above us and a cold wind blew into our faces the closer we got to Liberty Island. The bow of the boat started to bob up and down in the rising swells and Uncle Matt placed his hand on my shoulder as we drew nearer and nearer to the lady.

"The sun seemed to dim with the thickening gray of the brooding skies. I heard a buoy ringing out on the water as the waves began to crash against the bow of the ferry. I looked up at Uncle Matt as he stood there smiling as if it were still a fine calm day. The wind whipped his long stringy hair about his face and eyes, but still he smiled undaunted at the Manhattan skyline like a proud Captain against the storm.

"I began to feel sick in the tossing of the surf, so I focused my attention on the statue looming right ahead. She stood as a majestic matriarch embraced by the city as a symbol of the entire domain, an icon of our inalienable rights to life, liberty and the pursuit of happiness. In her hand, the torch of our promise shone to me as a green light glistening like a distant star.

"The waves at the base of the statue crashed hard against her foundation. I could see the mortar breaking apart in the surf. The bell rang incessantly and the mist of the white water stung cold on our faces. The green star that perched upon her torch moved and I recognized the now familiar emerald green-dressed beauty standing at the rail as lightning split the billowing clouds above her.

"I felt my uncle's hand squeeze my shoulder in a tight grip as he began to laugh. I looked up at him laughing in the madness of the moment. His smile bore the remnants of someone else. His features and voice changed to that of the refined and sophisticated Monsieur Diabolus. He was laughing, laughing at the tempest at the top of his lungs. 'Look!' he yelled. 'Look at your beloved Lady!'

"I turned my eyes toward the statue and to my horror, she began to list forward over the water. The emerald green star too had changed. She had become the dark demon of my twisted dreams perched upon the rail; she sat like a gargoyle at the top. The sound of his laughter melted into the whistling wind and crashing waves to create a mournful howl that sounded like a thousand babies crying, and still the bell rang out over the din.

"In the crack of a jagged streak of lightning, she saw me and flexed her wings; they were wide, black and enigmatic as death itself. I could feel them like a shadow creeping across my heart. With a screech, she took to the sky and my fair lady crumbled and slowly crashed into the depths of the bay. 'No!' I screamed.

"'NO!' Diabolus held me fast in a firm grip around my young neck as I railed against the storm. The winged succubus swooped low and Diabolus shoved my face down onto the forward deck. I felt her talons straddle my shoulders and sink into my chest and back. She snatched me up from the ferry and carried me aloft and circled above the crumbled remains of Miss Liberty, and then tossed me into the swirling waves. I slipped below and saw the broken head and body of our once great icon, her disenfranchised face stared up at me from the murky depths of the bottom of the bay in an almost inexplicable expression of sadness, her image branded by the morning light onto my waking consciousness.

"My eyes opened to the image of the empty Crown bottle lying sideways on the floor; my hand lay inches from it and my phone. A haze drew in around my sight. My dry mouth, parched and reeking of alcohol, smacked and popped as I strained to produce even a little saliva. Slowly, I moved toward the phone and checked the time. 11:48? *Wow! What a night*, I thought.

"I forced my body into a sitting position on the couch and looked around in the light of day. The apartment was in disarray. A pile of papers that once sat on the counter had been blown onto the floor by the morning breeze from the open window. I forced my eyes to bring them into focus. Dominic had scribbled something on one of the papers, so I bent down and picked it up. It was a short note.

"It read, "Moved to Colorado to work for Miranda's old man. I used the money you gave me for the move. P.S. Fuck you, asshole!" *Why, that fucking dick*, I thought. *That's something I would have done.* I crumpled up the letter and threw it on the floor and then made my way to the kitchen sink, snatching the rock glass from the table as I passed. A turn of the tap produced only a drizzle of water into my glass. 'What the fuck!' I screamed. 'No water either? How the fuck am I supposed to take a shower? Grrrrrahhhh!' I screamed and hurled the glass at his door. It shattered into a hundred pieces and the solid base of the glass rolled into the corner of the threshold of my bedroom door. 'Dominic! You son of a bitch!' I yelled.

"There was no answer. I stood in utter silence collecting my thoughts. Returning to my phone on the floor, I picked it up and scanned my list of names and mumbled to myself; 'Chelsy? No, she won't talk to me anymore. Rea? Nah, I can't handle her annoying voice and that mole... Yeah, she should get that thing removed. How about Mandy? I haven't played her in a while. Wait... I can't call her, that's right, I borrowed her car and sold it to pay a parking ticket. How about Candis? Yeah, she always takes good care of me.'

"I highlighted her name and hit dial. Brrrr...brrrr...br...Click, click... 'Hello?'

'Hi Candis, it's Jacob. I am in a pinch this weekend and I was wondering if I could hang out at your place for a few days.'

'Wow! You don't waste words, do you? Well, I was going to my cousin's for the weekend, but I can postpone it until next week, I guess. Why? What is the problem with your place?'

'Oh, nothing really. The landlord is fumigating this weekend and I thought it would be nice to see you again. You know. I loved our time in the Poconos'"

'Of course, you did, I paid for our room because you forgot your credit card, remember?'

'Ah yes, it's all coming back to me now. Well, it won't be that way this time. I have money; we can take in a movie and dinner. What do you say; it'll be just like old times.'

'Yeah, that's what I'm afraid of. Well...I guess so, if you are in a pinch, but just for this weekend. I'll call my cousin and cancel my trip upstate.'

'Great! Thanks, Candis, you're a peach. I'll be right over. I just have to stop by the cleaners to pick up my suits for work. I'll see you soon.'

'Okay, see you then.'

"I knew Candis wouldn't fail me. She is such a sweetheart, I thought as I hung up on her and tossed my phone on the couch.

"I slipped into some street clothes and set about gathering my deodorant, my electric razor, some underwear and socks and some cologne for the weekend. I snatched up my phone on the way out the door, threw my things into the passenger seat of my flaming red chariot and sped off to Candis's. She lived in the first floor flat of a tenement building in Yonkers. It wasn't the Ritz, but any port in a storm, I always say. I made a quick stop at the dry cleaners on Dowry Lane and picked up all my suits for work.

"When I pulled up to her building, I saw her short, stout frame and shoulder-length wavy brown hair wrestling a trash can to the curb. I smiled and waved as I pulled up to the curb next to her. "Ha, ha, I hope that's not where I'm staying tonight," I quipped as I got out of my car.

'I guess it depends on how you behave this weekend whether I put you out with the trash or not,' she said with a laugh.

"I walked around the front of the car and took her arm as I kissed her on the cheek. 'How've you have been, sweety? I'm sorry I haven't been in touch more, but I have been terribly busy at the office and away on business in California.'

'Oh, you smooth-talker you. Come inside and have a beer, we can catch up on old times over lunch.'

'I haven't showered yet, so if you don't mind, I'll get my things settled into your closet and take a quick shower before we eat.' I turned loose of her arm with a slight caress and opened the passenger door of my car. She watched me intently fill my arms with the five suits and my overnight bag full of toiletries and underwear.

'You are only staying the weekend, right? That's what you said; it was only supposed to be for the weekend.'

'Well, I might need to stay on for a little while longer. My roommate didn't pay the utilities and I have to get that mess all straightened out. It might take all week.'

'Jacob! I swear you are the devil's own kin,' she said shaking her head. 'You should've told me. I'm taking care of my boss's cocker spaniels all week while he is on a business trip, I won't be home in the evenings and you're not getting a key. You can forget that right now!'

'You can leave the key under the mat.'

'In this neighborhood? Are you crazy?' she bellowed. 'Why don't I put a sign outside reading free shit? You are incorrigible!' She exhaled a sigh of exasperation and followed it with a hand slap to her ample thigh.

'I'm sure we can work something out,' I said. 'It is only for a week, and think about all the fun we can have. I'll take you out to dinner every night when you get home from your boss's house,' I said. I paused momentarily, contorted my face to a sad and vulnerable homeless man, eyes dipping with disappointment and poor lost puppy dog. 'Okay,' I said with a sigh and a dejected look, 'if the weekend is all you can do, I will have to make another arrangement.'

'Oh…all right,' she exclaimed in defeat. 'You can put away that pathetic look now.'

"'Great!' I beamed. 'I knew I could count on you. Here, help me carry some of this shit into the house.' She shook her head and took my overnight bag and slung it over her shoulder and followed me up the steps and into her apartment. 'Nothing has changed since I was here last, right? I mean, your side of the closet is still on the left, isn't it?'

'Yes,' she said reluctantly. 'You can move my clothes over to the left for the week. You know something? After today, I'm thinking of moving.'

"'Ah, ha, ha, always the joker,' I said as I hung my suits up in her closet. She set my bag on the couch and mumbled something in the living room. 'If you don't mind, I'll take my shower and then we can have that beer.'

"Once my suits were comfortably hanging in her closet, I retrieved my bag from the couch and started off to the bathroom. The thought of a shower was distracted briefly by a blip on my opportunity radar. This came in the form of a corner curio, which held several old photos of her and her father and a baseball in a brass baseball glove stand. The baseball showed signs of heavy use and was slightly brown with age, but the signature on it was distinct and easy to read.

"My heart skipped a beat when I realized she had the signature of Don Mattingly on a game ball. Being that I was a bit of a baseball buff myself, I knew what this was worth. My mind flashed back to a baseball store in Jersey and my hands began to sweat. A quick smile and a raised eyebrow, and I was off to scheme in the shower.

"Twenty minutes later, I was clean, dressed, and fully aware of an itch to get my hands on that baseball. Casually, I rounded the corner into the kitchen. She was sitting at the table twisting the ends of a joint she had rolled. She looked up at me, 'Well, at least you clean up nice,' she said with a smile.

'Thanks,' I said. 'You look as beautiful as ever.'

'Ah, you never stop, do you, you smooth-talker you. Flattery might get you laid, ha, ha, ha.' She laughed.

'How about that beer now?'

"She leaned back in her chair, placed the joint to her lips and lit it. A quick spark ignited a small cherry glow and the smell of cannabis filled the air. Her shoulders dropped in a silent surrender as the stress of the day floated off her in the rising smoke and a smile drifted across her face. She stifled back a cough and squeaked out the words, 'In the fridge...ch...ch...The crisper—in the bottom.' She gestured with her hand still clutching the joint pinched between her thumb and for finger and finally released the mind fog filling her lungs into the room.

"I swung around to the fridge and opened the door, sliding the crisper out and causing the bottles to roll forward with a clank. I snatched one up and twisted off the cap while releasing the door to close. 'So, what's the story on the baseball in the living room?'

"Her smile widened as the question sparked a hidden memory. 'That is the best birthday gift I have ever gotten; summer of '89, my old man took me to a Yankee's game. It was in the seventh inning. Mattingly hit a pop fly into the bleachers on the third base side. My old man caught it while I was in the bathroom.'

'Wow! And on your birthday, too! What are the odds of that?'

"She took another drag on her joint. 'I know—right?' she said from the back of her throat. She blew the smoke into the air and lightly tapped the joint's ash against the edge of an ashtray. 'After the game, while I was standing in line to buy a hat, he found Don Mattingly signing autographs by the locker-room door.' Candis leaned back in her chair and stared out into nowhere and chuckled to her-self. 'My old man...Huh,' she said as if the thought had just occurred to her. 'You know? I must have had the best old man in the world. There wasn't anything that man wouldn't have done for me.'

'Apparently,' I said thinking back on the sorry excuse I had for a father. 'He was certainly better than my old man. How long has it been?'

'Oh, he has been dead now for at least five years.'

"A sudden twinge struck me. It was a feeling I'm not too familiar with. An awkward silence hung like the thin veil of reefer smoke. I looked down at my beer in embarrassment. 'Oh, I'm sorry,' I said. 'I...I didn't mean to...'

'No, it's all right now,' she said. 'I've gotten past the pain. He left me with so many great memories; it would be stupid to be bitter about his death.' She smiled. Her eyes radiated a solemn contentment, a kind of peace with the past that I had never known.

"Once again, I was jealous. 'Give me some of that,' I said as I reached for the joint. She gladly passed it to me and I took a long deep drag. 'Mmmm, nice...ch...ch...ch,' I said choking back the smoke. 'You always did have good taste in weed. Say, what do you say to going out to dinner tonight? My treat, we can go to that pizzeria around the corner.'

'Sounds like a plan to me,' she said.

"We finished our vices and spent the night out on the town. After a medium deep-dish pepperoni, mushroom, and black olive with extra cheese and a few more stories of her comical father, I began to see something in her I had never known. She was a very strong woman, not at all like I had remembered her. Her face lit up like a streetlamp at twilight when she thought of her childhood and there was a happiness that seemed to transcend all the troubles that had beset her young life. There was something buoyant about her personality, something which kept her light hearted and floating above the misery of life. My curiosity was piqued.

"I felt sure there was something about my childhood which was missing, something that had left me (shall we say) poorer in spirit. Candis was a woman who I could learn from. It wasn't until I reached into my wallet to pay the bill that I felt the heavy hand of need. I was down to the last sixty dollars I had procured from Fran and we had just eaten twenty-five of it. My memory flashed back to the baseball in the curio and I felt the pressing need for a plan that would allow me to cash in her memorabilia and still live in her apartment.

"Candis took a compact from her purse and checked her makeup while I set the money on the table. Flipping it open, she glanced into the small mirror and touched up her face with the tan powder. She then looked up at me in curiosity. 'What's that sinister smile on your face?'

'Huh...? I...I...' I stammered. 'Oh...nothing, really. I just thought of something money...I mean, funny,' I said as I cleared my throat.

'Yeah well, knock it off. It's giving me the creeps. You got the look of sin in your eyes.'

'Ha! That's a good one,' I dismissed. 'So, tomorrow, you have to stop by your boss's house on your way home from work?'

'Yeah, just to walk his dogs and make sure they have food and water. It shouldn't take me more than an hour.' She closed her compact and placed it back into her purse.

'So how do we work out the problem of the key?'

'Oh, I suppose I could leave the key under my potted azalea outside. I mean, it is only for a week, right? Just bring the key in and lay it on the kitchen table and *don't* let anyone see you take it. Jeez, this makes me nervous.'

'Don't worry, I'll be discreet. Your neighbors will never even know I am there.'

'Okay, as long as you promise to be careful. I hate the thought of some stranger in my house.'

'Relax, it'll be all right. Come on, I'll buy you a frozen yogurt,' I said as I put my arm around her shoulder.

'Frozen yogurt? You sure know how to win a girl's heart; most guys buy flowers.'

'Would it improve my chances if I did?'

'Nah, you better stick with the yogurt. I know your batting average. Ha, ha, ha, ha!' She laughed and blushed slightly and then pulled her coat from the back of the chair.

"Candis's carefree personality left me feeling very comfortable with her. We shared that yogurt and took a long walk down by the river and talked about our youth; she, about her brothers and I, about the years with my Great uncle Walt. We had baseball, Italian food and that dogged New York devotion to our town in common, but little else. She was infinitely close to her family and had a bevy of friends that would do anything for her while I, on the other hand…

"Well, I had my wit and cunning and an innate ability to get what I wanted from anyone. All I needed was my phone and a sincere smile to open the door to opportunity. That's all I've ever needed. At any rate, with luck on my side, by the end of the weekend, I will have cashed in her baseball and she will be none the wiser.

"I figured, *If she doesn't miss it, then it isn't really stolen, is it?* I checked my conscience. *Yep, still clean, but something wasn't right.* I couldn't quite put my finger on it, but there was something gnawing at my gut. I dismissed it as the combination of pizza and frozen yogurt. *There is no sense in dwelling on undefined emotions*, I thought.

"When we eventually found ourselves bathed in the glow of street lamps and finally succumbed to the awkward silence that fell between our differences, she looked up at me, puzzled. 'You know, Jacob,' she said. 'I think I've seen a side of you I didn't believe existed. I think there is hope for you yet…albeit a very small and distant one.'

'Ha!' I laughed and gave a silent nod and ran my fingers though my thinning hair.

"She noticed my widening cowlick and softly said, 'We are all aging, Jacob, in our own time and in our own way…Maybe that's what I see.'

'Hey, it's getting late,' I said, 'and I have some things to do tomorrow. What do you say, we call it a night?'

'Yeah, sure,' she said, casting a concerned look my way.

"We retreated to her apartment where I spent the night on the couch, despite my many advances. I settled in with my pillow and a comforter she had given me. All the while, I kept a covetous eye on the curio and her prized possession. The image of her putting on her makeup and a cheap baseball from the department store gave me an idea. It settled into my brain like a stubborn splinter under my skin. It was something I had to do, if I wanted to stop thinking about it. Besides, I needed the cash. Pay day was still a whole week away.

Trip Before the Fall

"When morning came, and it was quiet throughout the apartment, which I mistook for smooth sailing, it was really the calm before the storm. Candis ambled through the living room rubbing her eyes on her way to the kitchen. I heard the clanking of a bowl on the counter and the sound of cereal being poured. The smell of coffee roused me from my drowsiness and I opened my eyes to the sight of that beautiful orb in the curio cabinet. It was a thought I was becoming more and more comfortable with. I threw off the comforter and headed to the kitchen, 'Hey, why are you up so early?' I asked.

'Ten o'clock isn't early, Jacob, but it so happens I have an appointment to have my hair done at eleven and then I was going to swing by and walk my boss's dogs again before going to the library. You can come, if you like.'

'Nah, I've got those errands to run, remember?'

'Anything I can help you with?' she asked.

'Afraid not,' I said, 'It's for a case I have. You know, client confidentiality and all. I'll catch up with you after.'

'Okay, I'll be back around three, after children's reading hour is over at the library.' I nodded and stirred the sugar into my coffee.

"After breakfast, Candis dressed and departed for the beauty salon. I watched carefully from the kitchen window until her car was out of sight. Then I casually entered the living room, got dressed and plucked my phone from the pocket of my jeans, tapped the camera app and lined up a spectacular shot of Mr. Mattingly's signature. The picture was perfect. All of the color, the wear, and fading of the ball, captured in perfect detail. *I should be able to make a good copy with this,* I thought. I pulled on the door of the curio. *Locked, I should have guessed,* I thought. *Hmm, now where would she hide the key?*

"A short stroll to her bedroom and a methodical, careful search produced nothing. It wasn't in her night stand, or her dresser. It wasn't in her jewelry box, which was unlocked, or in the music box next to her bed. I slowly looked around the room and I saw it: a seventh-grade softball pitching trophy setting on a shelf with all of her school yearbooks and white pony bookends. The shelf was dusty, from years of neglect, as if it were a forgotten relic. Once I lifted the trophy, I could see the felt had been pealed back and there was something taped inside the base.

"'Ahh, jackpot,' I proclaimed as I reached in and claimed my prize. Just to be sure, I tried the key in the lock and, BINGO!—I was in. I took a look at my watch. From this point on, I was on the clock. Snatching up my keys and wallet, I made a break for my car and the department store down the street.

"Once inside, I perused the cosmetic counter with my phone in hand. I wanted to find just the right shades of browns, tans, and yellows for the wear around the stitching of the ball. I went with the Bohemian Sunset collection; it came with a fine brush applicator, too. Then, it was off to hardware, where I picked up some 1,000 grit ultra-fine sandpaper to provide the used look and then to sporting goods to acquire the ball.

"An official league-sized ball was easy to find, but the stitching was bright red. I was going to have to find a way to fade it a little, if I wanted it to be believable. The goods took all but a few dollars of the cash I had left. The cashier put all my things in the bag and I sped back to Candis's apartment.

"Once I was there, I locked the door and set the makeup and sandpaper on the kitchen table. I took the new ball to the sink and searched the cupboards for bleach. She kept it above the washer and dryer. With the bleach, some water and the sandpaper, I set about aging the stitching. The bleach faded the stitching, the sandpaper gave a coarseness to the leather around the stitching and roughed up the hide. I made a comparison to the real game ball, being careful to notice how the ball was set in the curio.

"After I was satisfied with the aging, I sat down with the game ball in front of me on the table. With a blue ballpoint pen and a piece of paper, I practiced Mattingly's signature, first by laying the paper on the ball and tracing it and then copying it over and over. It took three pieces of paper front and back to get the desired effect, but eventually, it came and I scribbled it on the new ball. Next, I took the makeup case and the applicator and, with the spirit of a Renaissance master, eyed the game ball like I was Rembrandt himself.

"I laid the colors on lightly around the stitching, first the brown, then the tan and finally just a smattering of yellow. When I was done, I was quite happy with the results, but there was a problem. The game ball had a slight sheen to the leather and the makeup had left my baseball looking flat. I sat there scratching my chin, comparing the two and wracking my brain for a solution. A quick look at the clock gave a twinge of anxiety. It was 2:20 and her arrival home could happen at any time. 'Think, Jacob, think,' I mumbled. 'What would give it a little shine?'

"Then I looked past the game ball and noticed the scented candle Candis used to cover up the smell of her pot. 'Wax,' I said to myself. 'Yeah, that would do it.' I took the lighter she had left on the table and lit the candle, let it burn for a moment and watched the wax pool beneath the flame. Then I blew it out and dipped my finger into the liquid wax. I spread it along the stitching until the color was blended nicely and then I rubbed the wax into the hide. Voila, my masterpiece was done. I gloated over it for a moment; it wasn't perfect, but certainly close enough to fool Candis.

"I placed my fake into the curio and set it up in the stand just like the picture on my phone and locked the cabinet. I returned her key to its hiding place, cleaned up my mess and waited for her to return. Then I had a thought. *I don't want the game ball on my person, so I had better put it in my car*, so I put the ball into the bag from the store, stepped out to my car, unlocked the door and slipped it under the seat, and then locked my car. Returning to the apartment, I turned on the TV, lay on the couch, deleted the picture, and casually played on my phone, poised like an actor, center stage, awaiting his opening scene.

"When she arrived at 3:05, I was lounging in a state of confident malevolence, secure in the notion I had pulled it off. 'Now that's the Jacob I remember,' she said as she placed her purse on the table. 'Making yourself right at home, I see. What should we do tonight?'

'Oh, I don't know," I said. "I ran out of money. I had to pay some unexpected bills my roommate left me with.'

'Okay then, I'll just order in some Chinese food and we'll watch TV.'

'Sounds like a plan to me. I have to leave early for work tomorrow anyway. You can pick the show,' I said, focusing on my phone. She made a quick call, jumped into the shower, and we ate to the light of a cheesy sci-fi movie and then called it a night.

"The following morning, I stood before my suits hanging in her closet and for some strange reason, chose the one suit that wasn't mine. There it was, the finely stitched tailoring of Fran's old man's best Armani. I pulled it from the closet and ran my fingers along the lapel. The embossed letters ME in silver added to the appeal of the suit. "He does have good taste," I declared to myself. *Well, with Fran's divorce imminent, I can't take it back, so I might as well call it mine*, I thought. So, I set it aside to wear and waited for Candis to finish in the bathroom.

"When she emerged, she was dressed in a respectable businesswoman's knee-length skirt, pale blue blouse, and dark gray coat with a red and white spotted bow tie. The smell of lilacs wafted from the bathroom in wave of warm moist air, which hit me like a soft sachet of feminine mystic. 'Wow! That smells nice! I forgot how nice it is to bunk with a woman,' I said as I picked up the suit.

"She smiled at me and sauntered past. 'Yeah right, I bet you say that to all your roommates.' She looked at the suit in my hands. 'Is that yours?'

'It is now,' I said with a smirk. 'You could call it a perk from one of my clients.'

'They are either getting more generous, or you have figured out how to steal the clothes right off their backs.'

'I will plead the fifth on that one,' I snickered, 'on the grounds it might incriminate me.'

'I bet it would,' she scoffed. She turned to face the mirror on her dresser and fastened her earrings into place. 'Hey, leave the door open when you're done so it doesn't get musty, and pull the shower curtain closed.'

'Okay, okay…shit, you're worse than my mother,' I said.

"I slung the door closed and emerged thirty minutes later a dapper young man complete with a crimson power tie, ready to take on the world. When I turned the corner into the kitchen, I was met by her ardent stare. 'That's one nice suit, Jacob. You look so sharp in it.'

'Thank you, thank you, save your adulation and just throw money please.'

"Candis laughed and shook her head. I scooped up my car keys and phone from the table on my way toward the door. 'I will see you tonight. Maybe we can do dinner again.'

'Maybe,' she said.

'Well, I'm off, wish me luck. I have a big meeting with Jamison this morning.'

'What's up with that?' she asked.

'Don't know—something about the job I did for New York Life & Trust.'

'Wow—okay, good luck,' she said as she prepared her breakfast.

"I stepped out of the apartment and unlocked my car with a chirp-chirp of my keys. The soft shades of morning still hung on the horizon. I stood for a moment in the glory of that dawn. The thought of my investment and imminent wealth and the prospect of perhaps another case from the New York Life & Trust filled me with such promise, I felt sure I was on the verge of penetrating the glass ceiling in my life. The only thing I needed was a little cash to get me to pay day. Admittedly, there was also some excitement to see what I could get for Mattingly's signature and a little gloating over another caper well done. I slipped into the driver's seat and sped off. There was one stop at the baseball shop across from the Staten Island pier I wanted to make before work.

"Twenty minutes later, I pulled up to the curb outside the Triple Play sporting goods and baseball shop and waited for the door to open. A middle-aged man unlocked the door from inside the shop and I retrieved my prize from beneath my seat and exited my car. I pulled it out of the bag and looked it over and though there was a sense of accomplishment, it came with an uneasy feeling of reluctance. It didn't help to know how much of Candis's childhood was linked to the object. *Still*, I thought. *She doesn't even know it's gone.* It was then I noticed a gray-haired old man standing on the pier across the street. He was watching me intently as my thumb grazed across Mattingly's name. 'Humph,' I scoffed. 'That crazy old man is still following me around.'

"I got out of my car and walked into the shop. 'Hello,' exclaimed the man behind the counter. 'An early riser, aren't we? I wasn't expecting any business until at least ten.'

"I smiled and held out the ball. 'I wanted to know how much this is worth,' I said.

'Well, it depends on whose name is on the ball,' he replied.

'It's Mattingly,' I said with pride. 'How much will you give me for it?'

"The man exchanged his glasses for ones with thicker lenses and bifocals. He took the ball from my hand and squinted down at the signature.

'Hmm, well it is a game ball,' he said, 'it has all the wear of a major league ball, but someone has ruined it by writing on it. I'll give you ten bucks for it.'

'Ten bucks!' I exclaimed. 'That's Don Mattingly's signature on that ball. It has to be worth two or three hundred, if it's worth a dollar.'

'No, no, that's not Mattingly's signature. You see here?' he said pointing to a glass case he had on the counter. 'This is Don Mattingly's signature. Look close at the double *t*'s and the *g*. They are completely different than the ones on your ball. This one was bought at an auction for children's charity for two and a half grand just last year. What you have there, is a fake.'

'A fake? Ah shit,' I said shaking my head. He handed the ball back to me.

'I'll still take it off your hands for two dollars,' he said. 'Maybe I can get the ink off it.'

'Nah,' I said, taking the ball back. 'That's okay. That's not even worth the guilt.'

'Pardon me?' he questioned.

"'Aww, never mind,' I grumbled. I stepped back outside and look at the ball in my hand. *Candis's old man must have penned the signature himself,* I thought, *and all this time she's been living with the memory of a lie. Shit, her old man wasn't much better than mine.* I looked across the street at the pier and open water of the bay. I could feel the anger growing inside and an impulse to chuck that damn ball as hard as I could into the river. I marched across the street, ran the length of the pier, cocked my arm back and lunged it forward toward the bay, but try as I might, I couldn't bring myself to release my grip.

"It was as if there were a string in my heart connecting the ball to my arm. The thought of Candis and her memories weighed heavy on me for some reason. I stood there for a moment and realized where I was. Looking around, I saw the ice cream vendor setting up for the day's customer's and tourists and their children starting to line up near the moorings for the ferry. I was thrust back in time and the sound of a boy asking his mother for money rang in my ears. I could smell the Southern Comfort and Pall Mall cigarettes on Uncle Matt's breath. Even the rustle of the five-dollar bill as it scooted across the ground echoed around me like whispers from the past.

"Then, with a flash of light across my mind, came the brilliance of the young boy's smile when I gave him back the money. In his smile, I recognized true happiness. Actually, his entire face imprinted gratitude and manifested his happiness in me. 'I remember,' I said to myself. 'Yes... I do remember you, Jacob Sullinger.' I looked down at the ball and realized, it belonged in her curio. Her happiness, whether it was based on truth or a lie, was still hers, after all. I heard a voice over my right shoulder. 'Are you going to keep it?' it asked.

"Looking up, I found the white-haired old man standing a few feet away. I shook my head. "No, no, I couldn't do that to her."

'I see,' he said. 'You could sell it to someone else—someone who doesn't know it's a fake.'

'Look!' I snapped. 'It's not about the money.'

'I see. You've come a long way, Jacob.' His smile deepened and took on an air of pride.

'A long way? Only as far as the Bronx, old man,' I replied.

"The old man looked across the bay to the skyline beyond Manhattan. 'From over there?' he gestured.

"I nodded. 'Yeah, somewhere over there.'

'It's a long way down, Jacob,' he said. 'But I'll be waiting there, when you get there.'

'You're as crazy as bat nuts, old man. When I get where?'

'When you get to the other side,' he said and then he turned and walked away.

"I stood there confused in the wake of his statement and watched him walk away, still grappling with the memories and how they were connected to the ball I held in my hand. Finally, I surrendered to the thought of placing the ball back in the curio where it belonged and finding some other way to get the cash. Then it dawned on me what time it was and where I was expected to be at nine o'clock. 'Oh, shit! Jamison!' I exclaimed. 'I can't be late today.' I slipped the ball back into the bag, bolted to my car, threw it on the passenger seat, and sped off toward Manhattan.

The Long Way Down

"When I arrived at the parking garage, there wasn't a single space left in the lot, so I parked out on the street. Before getting out of my car, I took one last look at the ball in the bag and sighed. *Wish my old man loved me that much*, I thought. For some strange reason, I was compelled to bring the ball with me into the office. There was something about it that gave me comfort. Perhaps it had become a symbol of a father's love. So, I locked up my car and slipped some coins into the meter—assuming I would find a space in the garage after the meeting. I strolled up the street and ascended the steps to the law office.

As my hand reached for the large silver gavel door hand, I could hear the distinct sound of humming coming from the other side of the glass. It grew louder when the door swung open. It was Bea. She was in the best mood I had ever seen her in. She was humming 'Zip-adee-doo-dah' at the top of her tone-deaf voice.

"'Why Bea, you are positively glowing,' I said. 'What happened? Did you finally get laid?' I quipped as I approached her desk. She didn't flinch or break her song, but pointed up with the tip of her pen, which was a sign to me to go up to Jamison's office straight away. So, I dropped the baseball off on my desk and left the company of her F-flat minor, Disney-induced coma and stepped into the insecurity of an upwardly moving elevator.

"There is something disturbing about getting a sinking feeling while moving in a straight upward motion. It's like realizing the inevitability of an impending crash and being fully aware you are no longer in control—much like an arrow must feel being pulled back before the archer's shot. I steeled my nerves against my increasing anxiety and clung to the rail in the elevator.

"When the elevator opened on the eighth floor, Leslie sat head down engrossed in her paperwork—the door of Jamison's office was standing open—no doubt for me. 'Go right in,' she said without looking up, but I could feel her watch me walk by her from above her horn-rimmed glasses. Now I was really worried. I straightened my tie and brushed my lapel in a nervous effort to shed my dread and then stepped into his office.

"There were two gentlemen with him sitting at a table to one side of his eminence office. They rose to their feet as I entered the room. Mr. Jamison looked me in the eye. 'Jacob,' he said. 'This is Mr. Bishop from the law offices of Tomlinson & Tucker and his client, Mr. Embers.' I smiled at the two men in an effort to set a relaxed tone and reached out to shake their hand. It was like greeting a statue on Easter Island—nothing.

"I cleared my throat. 'What can I do for you, gentlemen?' I asked as I approached the table. My eyes fell on Mr. Embers and his clenched fists and reddening face. He was a man struggling to hold himself back. Jamison glanced over at him and then back at me to see if I had picked up on his hostility. Mr. Embers leaned in and whispered something to Mr. Bishop. Mr. Bishop drew a deep breath. 'We have something here we were hoping you could shed some light on,' he said.

'I will do what I can. You see, I had originally contacted the building inspector, a Mr. Gravis. He was the one who did the inspection of the West Palm Estates. He—'

'Eh-hmmm,' Jamison shook his head. 'Um,' he paused, 'that's not why they're here, Jacob.'

'No?' I puzzled. 'I was told that someone from the New York Life & Trust was here to see me. I thought it was about the West Palm Estates case.'

'No,' said Mr. Bishop. 'We've come about your counter divorce suit on behalf of Francis Embers.'

'Oh, that,' I said.

'Yes,' answered Mr. Bishop. 'We have here the terms of her abandonment suit you submitted to my client.' Mr. Embers leaned in and whispered once more into Mr. Bishop's ear. Mr. Bishop threw a hand up signaling him to remain calm. 'We have something here which concerns both you and your client, Mrs. Embers.'

'Well, I'll take a look at it, but I can tell you right now, our stance on the matter is firm,' I said, taking an aggressive tone. Mr. Bishop raised his eyebrows in surprise.

'Humph!' scoffed Mr. Embers and he grumbled something into his attorney's ear, which sounded like, 'Hesh-maring-mag-zute.'

"Mr. Bishop place his left hand on his client's shoulder to steady him and then pulled a manila folder from his briefcase he placed it on the table and slid it in front of me. 'You should have a look at these, Mr. Sullinger, before you make such statements.' Jamison's silence sounded off a warning in my skull.

"DANGER! DANGER! Doctor Robinson, DANGER!"

"I struggled to keep my composure, but casually picked up the envelope and squeaked out, 'What...what are these?'

'Pictures, Mr. Sullinger,' said Mr. Bishop.

'Pictures of?' I questioned. 'Are they of your last trip, Mr. Embers?'

'Hardly, Mr. Sullinger,' said Mr. Bishop. 'They were taken at my client's residence while he was away in Indonesia.'

"My hands began to sweat and my throat became a token of Death Valley as I struggled to swallow my own tongue. I peeked into the envelope so as to protect the contents from Jamison. I saw nothing but skin. "You needn't hide them, Jacob, I've already seen them,' said Jamison.

"I slowly pulled the pictures out, but could only look at them from the corner of my reluctant eyes. They were pictures of Fran holding my boner as she pushed me on to the elevator and others were of me tucking her breast back into her dress as I dragged her drunken body backward. *How...? How did they get these?* My mind raced back and forth like and animal in a cage starving for an answer. Then, I saw it: the Salvador Dali painting in the background, and remembered the stranger who always seemed to be on his phone whenever I brought her home. *Shit!* My brain screamed beneath my cold sweated calm.

'Do you have an explanation for these, sir?' Mr. Bishop asked.

'Well, I...I...I never—I mean, we never. We may have had a few drinks, but...but, I mean really, we... If you want to know the truth, she... She was the one...'

"Mr. Embers collected his nerves. 'That's a nice suit, Mr. Sullinger. Where did you get it?' his voice rumbled with suppressed rage.

"I looked down at the *ME* on my lapel and stammered, "I had it made...uhm, special...It was a joke, you see...It's ME...Get it...ME?' I laughed in a desperate attempt to grease my way out of this mess.

'It's mine! It stands for Mitchel Embers, you idiot!' he howled, pointing to the ME embossing on his own lapel.

"Mr. Bishop steadied his client for the third time and then looked across the table at me. 'Mr. Sullinger, the private detective that took those pictures is willing to testify in court that you spent the entire night at the Embers' residence on no less than two occasions. Are you still willing to go through with your countersuit? Do you know the consequences of sleeping with your clients?'

"Jamison threw up his hand. 'Gentlemen. The law offices of Simon & Neubauer do not want such a blemish on our otherwise sterling reputation. Let me assure you, I have already set in motion the process to have Mr. Sullinger disbarred and removed from the plaque outside. His things will be gone from the premises within the hour and Mrs. Embers will be forced to find other representation.'

"A smug look came across Mitchel Embers' face as I shrank back into his suit and fell back into the chair behind me. 'I think this ends the proceedings, don't you?' asked Mr. Bishop.

"Mr. Embers answered with a grunt before declaring, 'I want reimbursement for that suit as well, it's worth more than your severance, I'll bet.'

"'Severance?' Jamison questioned as he looked down his repugnant fat nose at me. The two men left the room and closed the door on my career behind them. Jamison towered in silence over me, fuming though his flared nostrils, waiting. A moment passed before he finally said, 'Why are you still here?'

"I glanced up at him and then slithered out of my seat and started the dead man's walk out of his office and down the black and gold laced marble floored hall to the elevator, a man traumatized by what seemed to be a miscalculation on my part. Fran's husband really was meticulous in everything he did. The suit felt three sizes too big and far too hollow.

"When the elevator opened, it was empty. I stepped inside, pressed the first-floor button, walked to the back and leaned my head against the wall as it descended. The bell sounded on the first floor with an almost mocking of my soul and the doors opened to laughter as Beatrice stood there waiting for my disheveled arrival. Her laughter echoed up the elevator shaft, amplifying its humiliating effect on my psyche.

"I turned and walked past her like a ghost recently disenfranchised from its once prominent life, swung my office door open and saw the cardboard box setting on my desk. I then looked back at Bea sitting with her arms folded, smiling. Then she dismissed me with a wave of her hand and continued singing, 'Mr. bluebird on my shoulder.'

"I kicked the door closed and began to collect my things in a numb, incoherent malaise. *My Stephen King book, my stapler—no, no, that's not mine, my Rolodex—yes, I'll need that*, I thought. *My copy of the Journal, my...* Then my eyes landed on the baseball in the plastic bag and I paused for a moment. I reached into the bag and pulled it out. It rested in my hand uneasy and smooth. The stitching worn, but firm and slightly faded.

"My thumb grazed over the signature. Even though it was a forgery, it didn't seem to devalue the ball and for at least one little girl, it didn't matter. *What's in a name?* I thought. *What makes one name worth so much and another worthless?* I shrugged my shoulders, and put it back in the bag and placed the bag into the box. Then I threw in a ream of paper, four pencils, my Baseball Hall of Fame coffee mug and coaster, and the copy of my degree from off the wall.

"With my briefcase and box, I shuffled toward the door like a man walking the last mile. Thoughts of what it took to get to that point floated to the forefront of my mind: *late nights in the library—four years of college, three years of law school, exams, applications, interviews, internships*, all of it wasted in a single day. My soul gave up a great sigh as I opened the door, slunk past Bea's desk, and out the double glass doors. 'Don't let them hit you in the ass!' she said, as the doors swung closed behind me.

"Once I descended the steps on to the street, I was struck by the empty feeling of the busy traffic and pedestrians, of how the buildings seemed to tower over me in their cold arrogance. All the people marked by their status-seeking garb were still blissfully unaware their lives were tenuously stitched together with the lies they have told themselves. The gray skies and wide streets seemed to draw the joy out of my imminent success, even from the very marrow of my happiness.

"All this manic anxiety came to a screeching halt when I looked down the street to my shiny red Aston Martin, which was at that moment being hoisted on to the flatbed of a tow truck. 'Hey! What the fuck do you think you're doing with my car?' I yelled. The tow truck driver stood a good eight inches taller than me with greased back hair, a pinstriped shirt with a name tag that read Lance, and a mouth full of chewing gum. He looked at me and smiled while the hum of the hoist raised my car backward onto the bed of the truck.

'I said, what the fuck do you think you're doing?' I repeated.

'Impounding it,' he said without flinching.

'Why? There's still time on the meter.'

'Don't know…got a writ here,' he said, waving some papers in his left hand. He was obviously a man of few words and fewer thoughts.

'A writ? From which court? This is an import, you idiot!'

"He stopped chewing for a second and his face turned to stone. 'The DEA wants this car.'

'The DEA? What the hell could they want with it?'

'Well, they don't exactly tell me those things but usually, it's because it was used to smuggle drugs into the country.' He reached into his shirt pocket and handed me a card with an address on it.

'What's this?' I asked.

'The address of the impound yard. Anything you got left to say, you'd be smart to say it to them. Now, fuck off, before I beat the crap outta ya and stuff you in the trunk.'

"The trunk, the trunk, I thought about where I had put the suitcase with the five hundred thousand dollars in it. *Oh GOD, the money is in the trunk!* My brain screamed as I flew into a full-blown panic attack. 'Hey…hey, wait a minute, um… Lance, I got something I need to get out of the trunk first. Can you let me grab it really quick? I'll pay you, if you do.'

'What kind of fool do you take me for? That might be what they're looking for. Now, piss off before I call the cops myself.'

'All right, all right, I'll pick it up later, but I'm writing your name down to file a complaint.'

'Well then,' he said, 'you'd better spell it right. It's G-e-t L-o-s-t P-u-n-k. Got it?' He then set about chaining the car down to the deck of the truck.

"I glared at him with all the hatred of a bastard child. 'You better not scratch it, or so help me, I'll make sure they take it out of your paycheck, you fucking rube.' I turning toward the bus stop and walked the short distance to the corner, set my box and briefcase down on the bench and rifled through my pockets for what was left of my money. There was three dollars and eighty-five cents. The bus schedule read two seventy-five for a bus ride to Yonkers, which left me a dollar ten to my name. If it weren't for the money I had given Jack White and the suitcase in the trunk of my car, I would be destitute.

"Fifteen minutes later, the bus arrived. I gathered the remnants of my disheveled career, got on the bus, and took a seat in the back to hide the shame of my situation. The thought of the 2.5 million was the only thing holding me together at the seams. The suitcase in the trunk of my car, on the other hand, was a matter of intense concern. Whatever illegal gain the car was used for will most certainly point a suspicious finger in my direction, once the $500,000 was found.

"I have got to get it out of my car tonight, I thought. I looked at the address on the card. It was 408 Twelfth Avenue along the waterfront, a straight shot from Candis's apartment. With only my wit, my phone, and a dollar ten, I was going to have to find a way to get to the yard, get inside, find my car, unlock the trunk, get the suitcase, and get out without being seen. It was reminiscent of the two weeks of B&E Uncle Matt put me through when I was fourteen, the thought of which made my hands sweat like a Bolivian goat herder on his wedding night.

"The bus arrived two blocks from Candis's apartment and I got off. As I walked along the sidewalk, I became aware of a strange smell in the air. It was the smell of burning trash. A plume of soft gray-white smoke rose from a trashcan outside Candis's apartment. I approached it cautiously and looked in. The trashcan was filled halfway with clothes—my clothes—now shredded and set ablaze and slowly being consumed by the flames.

"The baseball that I had so carefully fashioned into the copy of her father's copy rested in the middle of the fire. There was no doubt left in my mind—my charade was over. I no longer had a place to stay and all I had left to wear was on my back. The irony of the stolen suit I wore was not lost on me in the least. I tossed my briefcase and the box of office supplies into the fire, keeping only the bag with Candis's prize baseball in it. I walked quietly to her door and hung the bag on the doorknob and walked away.

"There was only one way this day could get any worse, I thought as I wandered back to the bus stop. At that moment, my phone rang out from my inner coat pocket. I pulled it out and looked at the number. It was Jack White. My hands began to sweat. Fearing the worst, I hesitated, but surrendered to curiosity with my fingers crossed, I answered. 'Hello?' I said with a shaky voice.

'Jacob…my man!' Jack answered. 'There's been a bit of a setback on your investment.'

'How much of a setback?' I asked, holding my breath.

'Well…' There was an extended pause.

'Well, what?' I snapped. 'What kind of a fucking setback, Jack? Don't tell me you lost my money! You better not have lost my money, Jack!'

'It took me by surprise too. I mean, I've never seen anything like it before. That stock I told you about. It did exactly what I thought it would do, it took over eighty percent of the market, but then…something happened that I didn't expect.'

'And what was that?'

'A company stepped in and bought both failing companies, combined them and bought the property rights to the area around the Donte properties, and just like that, the Donte properties had no beach access. They dropped in value and plummeted on the market.'

'What! How far did they drop? How much did I lose?'

'Well, that is why I'm calling. Did you have any more where that came from?'

'What? You lost it all?'

'Not all, but nearly…I meant you might be able to buy a happy meal or something.'

'I'm fucking dying here and you're making jokes?'

'Um…that wasn't a joke, I'm afraid. I'm not kidding, I was at the golf course courting a new client when the collapse took place. You know what it's like when you got a fat one on the line, you got to take the time to reel them in.'

'I don't fucking believe this. I give you 2.5 million dollars and you lost it all in one day? What kind of broker are you?'

'It wasn't my fault, the company that took them over was a real power player. They deal in insurance and real estate.'

'Okay, if they were so big, what's their name? Maybe I've heard of them.'

'Um…Darkstar or something. Yeah, yeah, that was it, Darkstar Inc.'

'Darkstar Inc.? God damn it! Is this some kind of cruel fucking joke? That's the company I got the money from in the first place! Augh!' I cringed in frustration. 'Okay, now hear this, you sad sack of horse shit! You will take whatever is left of my money and you will work whatever mythical magic your ego still has and earn back my fucking money, or so help me God, I'll take that happy meal and stuff it in a very unhappy place! Are you reading me?'

'Hey asshole, I don't have to take this shit! You signed a contract. You knew the risks coming in. If you want to play with the big boys, you got to roll big. You rolled, you lost—end of story. I will mail you your $3.52 and that will end any further discussion. So, go fuck yourself, you trumped up little twit!' Then the line went dead.

"I was stunned. I could feel every nerve in my body twitch with anger. My head raced with all the rage of a caged gorilla. I couldn't breathe. It felt like I had a piano on my chest. I walked the streets aimlessly until late afternoon, lost in a mindless depression. The world seemed to spin wildly around me. Like the center of a black hole, I felt the turning of the universe and the weight of the cosmos pushing down on me. I was a singularity, a point of less than zero value. It was a breathless moment in my life, a moment when you can't find any good reason to breathe. Yet, I lived, like it or not.

"I wandered into a small park overlooking the Hudson River, where children played on a playground in the safety of the watchful eyes of their parents. They looked so happy with their innocence still intact, their future still undefined and the hardness of the world still padded by the caring of their families. It seemed any thought of success on my part was made in self-delusion. *I never had a chance*, I thought.

"I slipped my hand into the pocket of my coat. There was an object in its depths. It was round and flat like a coin, but larger. I pulled it out and looked down. It was a red poker chip, the one I had picked up from the ground the day I met Monsieur Diabolus. His number embossed on the face of it gave me a glimmer of hope. How it got into my pocket, I had no idea, but as long as I had his number and an ability to play a great hand of cards, there was still hope. *So, he wants to play hard ball*, I thought. *Well, I got five hundred thousand and a poker face he'll not soon forget.*

"I stuffed the chip back into my pocket and took out the card with the impound yards address. The yard was only a couple miles down the road I was on. My wandering feet found their intent and I headed straight for the yard. I couldn't do anything until nightfall, but I knew I would need time to scope it out and come up with a plan. I hadn't had to break into anything since I was fifteen. I might be a little rusty.

"When I arrived at the yard, I looked at my phone to check the time. It was 6:37. There were still lights in the upper windows of the building, so I knew I had plenty of time to cautiously case the place. Slipping my phone into my shirt pocket, I walked along outside the ten-foot fence scrutinizing the yard until I had spotted my shiny red beauty. It was only three cars in and fifth car

208

from the end. Not a bad spot from where I stood, it was far enough from the light to still be inconspicuous.

"I plucked my keys from my pocket, aimed the remote at my car, and pressed the trunk button. The trunk popped open with a light chirp. "Yes," I hissed beneath my breath. The top of the fence was lined with razor wire I would have to contend with and street lights were at every corner of the yard.

"I chose the light that was adjacent the building in the alley, picked up a few rocks and threw them at the bulb until I had knocked out the light. *Yeah, you still got an arm,* I thought to myself. *This is where I'll get in, at the darkest corner of the yard. Now, how to get past that razor wire? A pair of bolt-cutters would sure come in handy right now. It's time to peruse the neighborhood, maybe there's a hardware store nearby.*

"Making my way down the block and then the block after that and two more before, I found a small hardware store getting ready to close. I stepped inside. 'We're just closing,' the clerk said, motioning me back outside.

'It's okay,' I said, 'I just need to use the bathroom. It won't take me a second. Promise. I'm dying here.'

'Well, all right then, but don't take all night.'

"I spotted the tool section and strolled quickly down the aisle as I adjusted the waistband on my trousers. Spotting the bolt cutters halfway down the aisle, I snatched up a short pair, opened their handles, and slipped them down my pants so they rested on the inseam. 'Where are you going?' the clerk shouted. 'The bathroom is that way!' he said, pointing to the back of the store.

"'Ha! Sorry,' I laughed. 'I'm always get turned around in stores.' I darted to the back of the store and into the restroom. Once inside, I secured the cutters by slipping them beneath my underwear, making sure to avoid the family jewels, fastened the button, and zipped up my fly. I flushed the toilet for effect and washed my hands before stepping back into the store. 'I sure appreciate that; my bladder was about to burst. I shouldn't have had that forty-ounce soft drink with dinner.'

'Yeah, yeah, yeah. Come on, let's go, I want to get home before the game comes on.'

'Oh, yeah, I forgot about the game tonight. Have a good one.' I said as I slipped out the front door. The clerk bolted the door behind me and I turned and walk calmly down the street. I buttoned my coat and forced my fists into the pockets while I quietly walked the four blocks back to the impound yard.

"When I got there, I strolled past it once, being sure to check the office windows and surrounding doorways for any onlookers. I walked down to the light on the farthest corner and crossed when the light turned green, and then ambled back up the street and into the alley behind the yard. Taking my place beside the dumpster there, I waited for nightfall.

"I unbuttoned my pants, unzipped my fly, pulled the bolt cutters from their precarious spot, and slipped them into the hollow of the dumpster mount. Then I crouched down next to it and sat on the ground. Leaning back on the wall full of graffiti left by some new age vandals, I quietly watched for any movement in the yard across from me. I watch the traffic, the pedestrians, the windows of the impound building and most of all, I watched my car.

"From where I sat, I could just see the back of it and the thin dark line of the open trunk. The knowledge of the void and the suitcase within its depths and money setting just inside tickled my imagination. Though my eyes were open and fixed on the back of my car, I could see the cash in the forefront of my mind stacked neatly in rows and bound with blue rubber bands. The yard was still and the lights in the upper widows went out one by one. Street lights flickered to life as shadows spread into evening and the traffic thinned to a stray car every few moments, but still I waited.

"I pulled my phone from my shirt pocket and checked the time; it was 8:35, and still I waited. I watched the last car pull out of the impound yard parking lot and turn down the street, but still I waited. I waited for some unknown tell to expose itself to me. I sat there clutching my phone as if it were going to give me the courage I needed to pull this off.

"At nine o'clock, I slipped my phone back into my shirt pocket, rose to my feet, pulled the bolt cutters from the face of the dumpster and stepped across the alley. I stood behind the darkened street light and reached up with cutters to the top of the fence and clipped the wire. With each snap, the razor wire sprung backward a little along the fence, until I had made a three-foot gap at the end nearest the wall.

"Laying the cutters on the ground, I took hold of the fence with both hands and began to climb. Two cars on the road slowed as they approached the traffic light and stopped. I froze and waited, watching to see if they had noticed the giant Armani spider near the top of the fence. The light changed and they pulled away none the wiser. I continued my ascent. At the top, I slung my legs over the side and lowered myself down.

"The yard was large—about the size of a soccer field—not large enough to make escape easy if I had to run though. The cars were parked too close together for me to walk between. I would have to climb over them or go around. I opted to climb the '79 Ford Barracuda' that was parked behind my car. The owner probably wouldn't even notice the scratches on that puke green paint job. *God, some people just have no taste*, I thought as I placed my foot on the bumper.

"I climbed onto the hood on my hands and knees and up the windshield. I could feel the metal buckle beneath me as I slithered on top of the roof of the car. The cars were parked back bumper to back bumper, so it was just a matter of slipping onto the trunk of one car and opening the trunk of mine. Since I was already on my stomach, the maneuver didn't take much effort. It was a short belly glide down the back windshield, a one-foot scoot to the edge and there I was, face to face with that beautiful void I had been staring at all night.

"Reaching my right hand out, I began to pull the trunk open, when a bright light hit the lot and the cars I rested on. Once again, I froze and watched as a car going north had turned into the impound parking lot. It came to a stop and a man got out and went into the building. I watched as the lights in the windows lit back up as he moved through the rooms. Then the door to the yard flew open and I cringed. 'I damn near messed up tonight, didn't I, boys? Yeah, the boss surly would've had my ass if I had left you guys inside all night,' he said as he stood in the doorway. 'Well, what you waiting for? Go on, you guys are on duty, now get out there.'

"I heard the jingle of keys on a chain or something and then the door closed and the lights went off in the building again. I watched as the man left the building, got back into his car and drove away. I drew a sigh of relief and slowly lifted the lid to the trunk of my car. *Ah, there she is*, I thought as the suitcase came into sight. 'Hey beautiful, come here often?' I smirked beneath my breath. 'What do you say we get out of this place and you can slip into something more comfortable, like a mutual fund or a high interest saving account,' I said as I slipped my fingers into the handle of the suitcase.

"It was at that moment that I heard a sound that snapped me back to my childhood. It was the sound of hard nails on a hard surface. My mother used to make it when she tapped her press on nails on the counter top. A low rumble started over my right shoulder and was joined by another in what became a song I would call Growling in Harmony by Wolf-gang I'm-a-dumb-ass Dohtard. I wrenched my head to the right to find a German Shepherd and a Doberman Pinscher standing on the roof of the car next to me.

"'Shit,' I said as I pulled the suitcase close to my body. It must have offended them, because they started doing two things: drooling and barking. I jumped to my feet and leaped to the next car and scrambled to the ground. They took off after me, but had no traction on the cars, so they tumbled down and hit the ground running. I scaled another car and they followed me from one to the next, so I jumped down and ran around the lot trying to get enough space between them and me to allow for a getaway back over the fence.

"They followed me on the cars at first and then took to the ground, which forced me back on top of the cars. I began to talk to them as I leaped from car to car. 'Come on, guys, give me a break, I'm in a tight spot. I need the money. I swear I won't come back if you let me... Umph!' My right foot grazed the hood ornament of a Lincoln continental convertible and I went flying forward into the rag-top, which didn't bear my weight. My upper torso hung through the hole as my butt stuck up in the air. Something black flew out of my shirt pocket and landed on the backseat of the car.

"'Oh, no! My phone! Crap!' I exclaimed. Quickly, I launched my right arm out toward it and stretched my fingers in a bid to grasp hold, but it lay just beyond my fingertips. Then I felt the shooting pain of a set of canines being buried into my left buttock. 'Ahhhh!' I screamed. 'You son of a bitch.' I swung the suitcase around me and its steel frame hit the dog's head with a thud and he went flying onto the other cars. 'That's it,' I said. 'Phone or no phone, I'm getting the fuck outa here.'

"I pulled my body up and jumped over the hole in the top of the Lincoln, skipped across the next two cars, and slung the suitcase over the fence into the alley. Then I sprinted toward the fence and flew onto it like my name was Rocky the Flying Squirrel. My hands had reached the top when I felt the sharp teeth latch on to my calf and then slip to my pant leg, hang there, on the tatters of the material, and violently flail about. There was a *Rip*, and my leg was set free. I flipped my bottom half over the fence and slid down the other side. When my feet firmly hit the ground, I turned and gave both of their barking faces the finger. 'Not tonight, bitches,' I said. 'You guys just got served.'

"I collected my bolt cutters and suitcase and left the dogs with the choice last words... 'Go suck a chihuahua.' And I walked back down the alley with the bolt cutters in my left hand and the suitcase in my right. I sought out the shadows and the solitude of the back alley. The suitcase had two combination locks, one on either side of the handle and a solid stainless-steel case with a reinforced seal. I, on the other hand, was equipped with short strong bolt cutters and the determination of a professional safe-cracker.

"I felt sure the locks would succumb to my need. The alley was still and the doors of all the buildings were locked and bolted. I rested the case on the ground and examined the locks in the light of the full moon. They were a four-number combination. Thinking back, I tried to come up with combinations I felt sure Diabolus would have used. There were all manner of sixes, fives, nines, and sevens, but the locks proved stubborn so, I tried prying it open by placing the teeth of the cutters in the groove of the seal and twisting the handles.

"I slipped twice and began pulling on the lip of the seal, but the cutters had created a sharp edge and I split my fingers open at the attempt. My frustration boiled over and I began beating on the case as hard as I could with the cutters. With grunts and groans, I swung until my breath was deep and my arms were numb and completely spent. I fell to my knees in front of the damn thing, tugging my hair and cursing beneath my breath.

"'That son of a bitch knew! I don't know how he knew, but he knew. Here I am, broke as a broke dick dog with a suitcase full of money that I can't get into. Hey-ah!' I yelled as I swung the cutters at it one last time. They made a loud 'crack' when they collided with the case and fell to one side. The case sat there unopened. Reaching into my pocket, I grasped the poker chip in my hand and stared down at it. The number on the chip seemed to mock me. *Even if I have his number*, I thought, *I don't have my phone anymore.*

"'God damn you, Diabolus!' I exclaimed, clenching the chip in my fist. Then I took a deep breath and sighed, rose to my feet, picked up the suitcase, and slowly left the alley.

"The events of the day and the late hour were weighing on me hard and there was literally no one I could call and nothing I could do but walk the city streets in a delirium of mindless thought. The cut wire on the top of the fence, the open trunk, and my phone resting on the backseat of the Lincoln Continental meant I had to put some distance between myself and the impound yard, but I didn't know where to go and I had no money to get there, short of what was in the suitcase.

"After walking for what seemed like hours, I turned down a residential street full of tenement buildings. There, behind the trashcans and concrete staircase, I made a bed of trash bags. I opened one of the cans, slid my suitcase in and laid a bag of trash on top to cover it up, and then curled up in a corner and fell asleep."

Jacob drew a deep breath and sighed. He turned his face away from Dr. Kessler. "Do you think we could finish this tomorrow? I'm kind of tired."

"I suppose," said the doctor. "You have been talking for three hours now, but we still haven't touched on the reason you're here."

"You mean you don't know?" asked Jacob.

"I know why your Great uncle Walt came to the hospital, but his case was different from yours in many ways."

"In what ways?" asked Jacob.

"Well, for one thing, we haven't had to use insulin therapy on you yet. Walt used to get so bad, we had to take restraining measures and insulin shock therapy just to calm him down."

Jacob scowled at Dr. Kessler. "My god! Doesn't that cause seizures and coma? That's a little extreme for a man of his age, don't you think?" exclaimed Jacob.

"Maybe, but sometimes we have to use extreme measures," the doctor explained.

"Extreme measures? You mean like the ones you use on those poor souls on Zed Wing?"

"Zed Wing! How do you know about Zed Wing? You didn't go down there, did you?"

Jacob fell silent a moment and scowled, and then grumbled, "Never mind how I found out, I just don't like the idea of you doing things like that to my Uncle Walt."

The doctor shrugged his shoulders. "Yes, but it worked. It calmed him down."

"Sure, torture usually does work when you're trying to elicit some behavior you think is warranted." Jacob's words bristled with sarcasm.

"I see. You're not happy with how we managed your uncle Walt's *problem*." The doctor folded his arms and stared over at Jacob.

"Yeah, and I bet you charged him for this so-called *therapy*. Didn't you? Well, I'm sure glad I don't need *therapy*. Because I'm broke—you can't get blood from a turnip. You won't get much from me… And that's another thing…you haven't discussed the fees for this little resort."

The doctor became restless in his seat. "Well, we…we can discuss that later. Right now, I want you to concentrate on recalling the events which brought you to the hospital."

"I get the feeling there's something about my Uncle Walt, you're not telling me."

"Your uncle was very special to me," said Dr. Kessler.

"That well may be, but there's something else here that smells like guano and I don't like it."

"You don't have to like it, Jacob, but you do have to deal with it." The doctor's smug glare descended on Jacob like a straitjacket. "If you cooperate, you can find the answers you seek and you can put it all behind and get back to your life. If not, you're just a slip of the lip away from Zed Wing yourself."

Jacob stifled his frustration and, with locked jaw, grumbled, "Life? What life? I have no life to go back to." He fell silent and fumed beneath his folded brow. "All right, all right," he blurted out, "I will finish this next time, but I don't see how it's going to help. Can I go now, *your highness*?"

The doctor gestured to the door with his hand. "I want to see you tomorrow, Jacob…ten o'clock."

"Yeah, yeah, yeah. Don't you have any other patients to *Fix*?" he growled as he stormed out of the office. Dr. Kessler sat in the echoing silence of the empty room, scratching his chin as he listened to Jacob storm down the hall. Jacob walked with his teeth clenched and fists tight. He disappeared into his room and closed the door behind him.

Safe inside, he began mumbling to himself as he paced within the space between the beds. "He thinks I don't understand what's going on. He thinks I don't know, but I spoke to Gabriel, I saw the archangel Michael, and I know who Diabolus is. I can feel his hands on this place," he said as he looked around himself. "Sure enough," he repeated, "I can smell his scent all over this place. Yes, yes… If nothing else…I know that smell." Jacob fell to the floor next to the bed and wrapped his arms around his legs. He folded his knees in tight to his chin and began to cry. "God help me, I can feel him here. He's hanging over me."

Jacob was so focused on his pain, he didn't hear the door quietly open when Boo entered the room. Boo stood gazing down at Jacob's broken form on the floor for a moment before saying anything. Jacob slowly became aware of his presence and looked up. "Gabe, is that you?" he asked. Boo shook his head, knelt down on the floor, and put his arm around Jacob's shoulder. "I can feel him, Boo. I know he's here," said Jacob.

"Who's here, Jacob?" asked Boo. "Your uncle Matt or is it Diabolus?"

"Yes," was all Jacob said. He leaned into Boo's shoulder and whispered, "It's like a weight in my head pulling me down. Will it ever go away?"

"I don't know, maybe…maybe not. No more than mine will, I suppose," Boo answered. "But that's the fight we've inherited from life. Like it or not, we have to stay strong."

Jacob took a deep breath and wiped the snot from his nose with his sleeve. "I guess, I've changed. I used to like that smell."

"What smell?" asked Boo.

"The smell of money," said Jacob.

Boo didn't understand Jacob's answer, but he didn't question it. "Come on," said Boo, "I'll buy you a cup of coffee. I've got some good news."

A glimmer of hope shone in Jacob's swollen eyes. "I could use some good news right about now." Boo helped Jacob to his feet and patted him on the back and they both walked to the courtyard while Boo told Jacob about his day with his sister, about his trip to the museum of art and the family picnic at the park. It did Jacob good to hear about the reunion and his spirits were soon lifted. "There's something else, Jacob," said Boo, "I think I'm ready to go home now. I'm ready to go back to the world of the living. I've been dead for so long, I'm ready to live again."

Jacob glowed with enthusiasm. "I knew this was coming. I couldn't be happier for you. I think I know what you mean. I've been living on the other side of the grave myself. It's where all of my family are now. There is no one left in my life to reunite with."

"Well, I won't be your captain any more. That's all behind me now, but you have a brother for the rest of your life, Jacob. I will come and visit you as long as you are here," said Boo.

"Do you mean that?" asked Jacob.

"Of course, I do. I'll visit every week, if you want."

"I don't mean that," said Jacob, "I mean, do you really think of me as a brother?"

"Absolutely," said Boo. "Beneath the skin, we are the same, you and I, and there is no brother better than a brother you've been to battle with," beamed Boo. "I'll be there for you inside this place or out. You are kin now."

Those words rang like a bell deep in Jacob's heart, for he had heard them once before and he knew they were sincere. "When are you leaving?" asked Jacob.

"Tomorrow morning," Boo answered.

"So soon?" Jacob asked.

"I know it sounds extreme, but I feel I have a lot of lost time to make up for. Suddenly, I want to give back to my family, my community…the world. I will still be coming here for therapy, of course, but there is so much to do, so many changes I can begin now. It's like life has opened itself up to me and I am ready to receive all it has to offer." Boo's voice bristled with excitement, the sight of which made Jacob snicker. Boo blushed and shrugged his shoulders.

"Look at you," exclaimed Jacob. "You're a Captain of your own life." Boo waved off the notion but held his chin up. "You are my hero, you know?" Silence fell like ballast from a rising balloon. "Before you go, I need to tell you something—it's something I haven't told you or anyone yet."

"Sure, what is it?" asked Boo.

"It's the strangest part of my life, I'm afraid. I've told you about my childhood and about how I met Diabolus, and how I lost my job, but I didn't tell you what brought me here to the hospital, about the game, or about Michael, or Gabriel…or my tree of being."

"Tree of being?" Boo said. "Something tells me this is no ordinary story."

"I'm not here by accident," said Jacob. Boo placed his hand on Jacob's shoulder.

"Come on, I know a place where life grows in a circle." Jacob took a deep breath and they both rose to their feet and started off to the now well-worn path toward the garden.

The Reckoning

They walked in silence to give Jacob time to summon his courage, but also to put some distance between them and the other patients. Once they arrived at the garden, Jacob took a deep breath through his nose. The scent of the garden was intoxicating and the sound of trickling water across the rocks at the base of the fountain tickled the imagination.

Jacob stood before his great uncle's mandala garden of life and a wave of regret hit him like a Louisville Slugger. The memory of Uncle Walt hung thick in the air with the fragrance of the flowers, like a friendly ghost who haunted him. God how he loved the memory of the man. Jacob stood, blank-faced and shaking his head. "What?" asked Boo.

"Oh, it's nothing. It's just…" he paused. "I let him down," said Jacob.

"Let who down?"

"My uncle Walt. He had such high hopes for me, and I let him down." Jacob's lips curled in disgust.

"I thought you hadn't spoken to him since you were thirteen. How do you think he knows how you turned out? He couldn't have known anything about how you turned out," exclaimed Boo.

"Oh, he knew, he knew…he knew because of my tree of being. I planted it when I was twelve and it was the last thing I saw before I came here."

Jacob looked longingly toward the pond beyond the garden, and so they continued their walk to the bench beside the pond. "Do you remember the story of the tree I told you about? I am connected to that tree; it reflects my spirit into the world…be it good or bad."

"Yes, but I thought you were speaking metaphorically." Jacob shot a cold look at Boo. "You mean it's real?"

"That is not even close to the strangest part of my experiences," said Jacob as he glanced over at a thick shadow beneath a willow tree. "I want you to promise me you won't laugh at anything I tell you. These things might seem crazy, but you have to believe me, they are as real as you or me."

"Jacob," Boo said plainly, "look at who you are talking to. I am here for you, brother. Talk to me."

Jacob took a moment to collect his thoughts. "Well," he said, "after I lost my job at Simon & Neubauer, I lost the 2.5 million in a bad investment, and then I had lost my phone and my car. I wandered the Manhattan streets with 500,000 dollars in a suitcase that wouldn't open, a tattered Armani suit, a head full of regret, and a feeling of life closing in around me. I knew I had fucked up. I had become something I wasn't supposed to be. At three o'clock in the morning, I neatly tucked my briefcase into one of three trashcans, covered it up with a bag of trash and sprawled out in the corner behind a concrete stairwell of a tenement building on walker street.

"When I think back, it seems like a dream. That's how they found me— like voices out of the night."

"Who, Jacob?"

"My reckoning, I guess. The ass kicking I should have gotten when I was young. They came as if they were part of a bad dream I was having. I remember a distant conversation carried on in the midnight air. I was asleep, of course. I had been completely spent by a day of loss, a day of grieving and a day of mindless wandering. The trash bags I laid on might as well have been a feather bed as far as I was concerned. I was six feet deep in dreamland when these voices floated into my subconsciousness. The first one was bold, but submissive...

'You were really somthin', Josh. I bet she never saw that coming, huh?'

'Ha, yeah, right! She had a lot of nerve showin' up at your bachelor party after what she'd done.'

'Ha, yeah, that bitch better tell her little fuck toy Tony to stay away from me, if she knows what's good for him. I'm marrying Jammie. I don't care what he thinks. He had his chance, he fucked it up. Now she's mine and I don't care about his two-timin', highbrow, Long Island, prep-school, silver spoon eatin' ass. She's mine now! Whoohoo!' A scream echoed down the narrow dimly lit streets. Footsteps shuffled in the darkness beyond the reach of the street lights.

'Hey, hey Josh, is Jammie's sister datin' anybody? I mean, do ya think I got a chance?'

'Shut up, asshat. She's only a sophomore in high school.'

219

'So what, she'll be a junior next year, won't she? Old enough to spread, don't you think? Your first was a junior, wasn't she? Hahahaha!'

'Can it, Joey, you touch her and I'll have to jack you up—on account of she's Jammie's little sister and all. You'd better stick with that cougar you've been fucking with.'

'Hey, hey what's that?'

'What's what, moron?'

'I mean that, that homeless guy sleepin' behind the trashcans. Is he for real? This is our street, ain't it?'

'Yeah Josh, let's wake him to the reality of crashing on our street.'

"There was a rush of footsteps that came in fast and a moment of silence, then some snickering and then, WHAM. The crushing blow of a Nike shoe spun my head sideways and they all started yelling. 'Get him, Josh…I'll fuck you up, you bum…somebody grab him and hold him; I want to kick him in the balls!'

"They pulled at my clothes and I felt my body being lifted off the ground, so my immediate reaction was to curl into the fetal position. I heard a tear and I dropped to the ground. This brought retribution raining in from all sides. A battery of fists and feet pummeled my face, back and gut. The taste of blood began to fill my mouth, but I couldn't do anything.

"Then one of them said, 'Somebody find me a board, I'm going teach this fucker a real lesson.' I squinted through my fingers to try and get a look at their faces between the fist blows, but it was no use. In the midst of the chaos, a siren rang out in the distance and it got steadily louder. The streetlights began to flicker wildly up and down the street. Shadows came and went and came again, until their volley of punches slowed. 'What the fuck is that?' I heard one say. 'Something just pushed me in the dark.'

'It wasn't me.'

'Well, it wasn't me.' The lights flashed again and when they came back on, one of them was on the ground, and still the distant siren grew louder. 'Look Josh, we'd better get out of here. Someone called the cops and I…I can't go downtown again. My dad would kill me.'

'Yeah, look, it's just a bum, let him go.'

'Okay, okay,' said Josh. Then he bent down and grabbed me by the shirt. 'Listen here, shit stain. You got lucky tonight. I better never see you on my street again, you hear?' I nodded in submission and he shoved me back down.

As the hint of flickering blue and red lights tainted the darkness, they slipped away, back into the silence from which they came. I lay there coughing and spitting out the blood from my nose and throat. I pulled myself tighter into the corner behind the cans and watched a police car drift slowly down the street."

"Wow," said Boo. "So that's why you're all bruised up? What did you do then?"

"I sat there, staring at the empty street until I finally fell back to sleep. The sun was shining bright the next morning when I finally woke up. It was the sound of the trash man coming up the street which woke me. From that point on, I made it my mission to find Diabolus and get the briefcase open. In my mind, he owed me and I was going to get my money back—by hook or by crook, as they say.

"So, I retrieved my briefcase and started off toward the center of Manhattan—to the *Inferno Room*—to take my life back. Several hours later, I found myself standing in front of the two enormous closed gates to the Inferno Room and a simple script paper that was taped to the door. Closed for remodeling.

"'Remodeling… Remodeling?' I kept repeating to myself. 'What in the world would need remodeling? It's a brand-new building. It wasn't even here a month ago.' I could feel a growing despair in the pit of my stomach. It was a growing deficit of the useless being I had become—a negative in a world of positives. Just a few days before, I was the master in commander of my universe, and now I would be lucky if I could find a bus token.

"There was another growing concern in the pit of my stomach, and that was my stomach. I hadn't eaten since the previous morning, so with a full head and an empty gut, I walked the streets of Manhattan. I thought about stealing the money from a sleeping homeless man's hat, but then I realized, I was homeless too. It didn't make sense for one hungry man to steal from another, it would be like moving the pain next door, as opposed to getting rid of it.

"I looked at the man sleeping and for the first time, I noticed the lines of his face, the texture of the skin, the wrinkles around his eyes and mouth and realized that in order for those creases to line his cheeks and eyes, he must have been happy at some point in his life. It's funny, you know—what you think about when you're all alone. I could tell this man hadn't spent his life worrying about his worth. This was a face that had known laughter and by the looks of it, it was a fair amount.

"I shook my head and wandered down to the park along the waterfront. There, I slid the case under a bench and sat, and watched the ships float by the Statue of liberty.

"*Give me your poor, your tired, your weary,*" I thought out loud. A scoff bubbled up from my pitiful state. I had become all of these. The waning afternoon sun glistened on the water as gulls swooped down at some morsel floating on the surface. I began to think about the water—how deep it was? How cold? How strong were the currents? How long it would take for a man to die if he found himself floating in the river? Would it be painful?

"My thoughts then drifted to a point beyond the statue, to the distant Jersey shore, to the docks where the Staten Island Ferry moors, and to the place where my childhood died. A sleeping token of that child awoke in me and urged me to return, and but for the lack of money or subway ticket, I would have. It was then that I heard the sound of soft shuffling feet, the smell of a lamb and felt the presence of an old man who took the seat beside me.

"I was so bereft with self-pity I didn't even acknowledge his presence. 'Well,' he said, 'what did you do with the baseball? Did you sell it?'

Without even turning my head, I said, 'Nope—gave it back.'

'Oh…I see. Probably for the best anyway,' he said as he slid a gyro into my lap. My head dropped and the corners of my mouth ascended.

'How is it you always know where to find me?' I smirked as I glanced over at that crazy old man.

'I don't really. I just go where the wind takes me. Today, it took me here, and here you are.'

"I nodded and picked up the food. 'Then I am grateful for the wind today. Thank you.'

"He smiled. 'Good, good. That's how it starts, you know—small, like a seed—one simple act of gratitude can change the world.'

'Well,' I said as I stuffed the gyro into my mouth, 'I guess I shouldn't be surprised. You did tell me you would meet me on the other side.'

'No, no…We're not there yet, Jacob,' he said. 'You have one last journey to take. If you return, I will be there waiting for you.'

'If I return?' I asked softly. 'What do you mean *if* I return?'

'Well, some don't. Some choose another path, but I will be there, nonetheless.'

"Turning my attention back to the distant shore and feeling the pangs of my predicament, I could barely groan out a reply. 'You always talk in riddles I can't understand. I don't think I can deal with it right now, Okay? I lost my job, my money, my car, my clothes, and my phone and I'm only about a flapjack and a *Yankee Doodle Dandy* from losing my mind. I'm sure you understand, don't you? I can't deal with this right now, but thanks for the food—really—I mean it. I really appreciate the meal.'

"The old man nodded and set the rest of the gyros down on the bench and then he rose to his feet. He turned to walk away, but stopped, and without turning back, he said, 'I wouldn't throw the wrappers out until you've checked them thoroughly, if I were you.' He then casually walked away.

"I looked down at wrapper of my gyro and found a subway pass stuffed between the folded napkins. So many questions filled my mind. *That old man always seems to be a step ahead of me. Why is he always following me around? Why doesn't he pick on someone else? What did he mean some choose another path?* I shook my head and watched him walk away. *Still, he came just in time.* I thought as I wrapped my mouth around the gyro.

"After another hour of watching ships, I reclaimed my case and made my way to the nearest subway tunnel and took my place in the throngs of people going back to New Jersey. My ear was bent by the sound of an older couple laughing in the distant corner of the subway landing. I glanced over at them briefly. They were a homeless couple—or so they looked like to me. A crocheted shawl hanging over the woman's shoulders and the man's tattered coat and pants gave them away.

"This didn't seem to put a dent in their disposition. They were sharing some canned soup from the vending machine and carrying on like they didn't have a care in the world. It was then I noticed their faces, the creases and lines which had marked the passing of time and the cruel nature of life into the fabric of their skin. Yet, there was such a strong light which shone in their eyes.

"It was a brief thought—a flash of consciousness that recognized both the suffering of life and a source of strength within it. *How could this be?* I thought. *The two things should be at odds with each other. How could suffering and happiness dwell in the same house?*

"As this thought sank in, I became aware of a teenage boy moving through the crowed landing toward the front. He had a dark gray hooded sweater, ragged jeans and old Converse shoes. Once again, there was something about his face which was branded onto my frontal lobe. His disheveled light-brown hair hung over swollen red eyes. His fists were clenched tight in his coat pockets as he pushed his way to the front of the landing in a bid to be first on the train. His lower lip trembled and his head held down as he slipped between people standing in his way.

"I couldn't help myself; I followed him through the crowd until I stood just a few feet behind him. I watched him step to the very edge of the landing and wait for the train. A rush of air from the tunnel and the clattering of the tracks echoing from the darkness marked the train's arrival. The boy stiffened his stance and leaned out over the tracks. He blinked his eyes a couple of times and then closed them and let his body fall forward. I could feel my heart pound within my chest. My hand flew out on an impulse and caught the boy's hood and snatched him backward into my arms as the train pulled in. 'Don't,' I said. 'Just don't.'

'Let me go!' he screamed. 'Let me go!'

"I held him tight until the train had come to a complete stop, then I released my grip on the boy. Frightened and somewhat stunned, he struggled out of my arms and stumbled away though the crowd and up the stairs to the street. I took a deep breath and steadied my nerves. Onlookers stared at me with strange ambivalence, either judging me or admiring me, but saying nothing, as it was their nature to not get involved.

"When the doors opened, I took a seat close to the door and watched the other passengers file onto the train. Their faces began to ring clear to my eyes. Like snapshots in a photo album, my memory took note of their expression, posture and dress and filed it away as a moment in time—a moment in their lives. It would've been meaningless to them, but it wasn't to me. For the first time in my life, I noticed how the human face showed their entire life in the eyes and the lines and in the posture of their body and smile—or lack thereof. It was a study into the depth of human character. It was the first time I had even cared to notice. I wondered what my face said about me.

"Fifteen minutes later, the train stopped and the doors opened on the New Jersey side, and I stepped out to a three hour walk to Liberty Marina. As I walked, the sky grew overcast and a strange brisk wind came in from the southeast. I could feel the lost memory of my childhood drawing me toward the bay and with every step, I felt the imminent storm approaching. Still, for some reason, I had to do this. There was something about that place I could not deny.

"I reached the bay by 8:30. The sky was shedding the last rays of its crimson-orange light and a dark gray-purple consumed the horizon like a medieval shroud falling on the distant shores. I stood on the edge of the dock, staring at her—an icon on the water—proud and somber in her silent fortitude. She gave me such assurance of heritage, a strength of promised future tense. Then lightning struck in the distance and I was reminded of the coming storm and of the dream of her crashing into the bay.

"I was overwhelmed with grief. I lifted the briefcase to my chest and cradled it in my arms. The time to take stock of my life had arrived. I could feel the strain of the money pulling at my heart through the case. It was here that my life turned, and I accepted the fate someone else chose for me. It was here, I would either find myself or lose myself to the winds of a bitter heart. It was here, I was going to rise or fall.

"With no one to meet and no one who cared, the shadow of worthlessness fell over me—I had reached zero. I stared into the water and the reflections cast my memories back into my face. 'Uncle Walt,' I whispered to the waves, 'you were my only hope. You were my only family, and I failed you. God damn it. I failed you.'

"I couldn't take it anymore. My eyes began searching the ground for stones. I scoured the surrounding shore for rocks to line my pockets; anything of size and weight. 'This is it,' I muttered to myself, 'no more excuses, no more lies and no more...' I glanced down at the case. 'You...' I scowled. 'It's all because of you.' I looked out across the water. 'Maybe, it's time to be rid of you,' I said, and I swung my arm backward, preparing to sling it into the river. At that moment, a voice came from behind me.

'I wouldn't do that, Mr. Sullinger—you'd miss your chance.'

"I froze where I stood and slowly turned around. A gentleman stood in front of me that I didn't recognize. Without hesitation, he gestured with his right hand to a large boat moored at the dock. 'Right this way. Mr. Diabolus is waiting. The game can't start without you.' I pulled the case back to my chest in a moment of weakness and followed him eagerly to the gangplank."

Jacob paused his story for a moment as Boo sat there gripped in silence. Jacob bent over and picked up a round stone from the ground and rolled it between his fingertips. He looked at Boo. "Have you ever thrown a stone into the water and wondered how it felt to sink so fast?"

"What are we talking about, Jacob? Did you try to...?" he stopped.

"No, not quite...or at least I don't think I did. Ha," Jacob scoffed. "That's just it, I don't really know if I did or I didn't, but I know how it feels to sink so fast the pressure forces the air right out of your lungs." Jacob leaned back and threw the stone into the lake with a strange far off look in his eyes.

"He mentioned a game, what game was he talking about?" asked Boo.

"A poker game—seven card draw—the only game Diabolus plays."

"And the money?"

"The money? The money wasn't really what we were playing for, but you probably guessed that."

"Okay, there you were standing in front of his yacht with your case in your hand..."

"I think I had been playing this game ever since I was thirteen years old. Win or lose, it didn't matter at this point, I literally had nothing left to gamble with but that case," said Jacob.

The Games We Play

"I stood before the gangplank in a moment's hesitation and gazed at the magnificence of the ship. It was large private boat with big lighted windows, an upper deck and a full crew. Flags from every country hung from a line that stretched fore and aft from the center bridge mast, and the shiny white hull gleamed like pearl in the dock lights. Two seamen waited for me at the other end of the gangplank.

"I felt a nervousness settle in my stomach as I took those first steps onto the ship. I tightened my grip on the case and greeted the two men with a cold stare when I reached the other side. 'This way, sir,' said one of them, so I followed him along the rail across the deck and through the double glass doors at the back of the boat.

"The furnishing inside was, of course, second to none. The walls were done in dark walnut with a fine gloss finish. A lavish sofa and chairs in red leather with mink and sable lining sat facing the open view the glass doors afforded. A full bar in white oak and ebony lay waiting to pleasure any thirsty traveler with a toxic cocktail.

"My memory flashed back to the devil's brew I had imbibed a few weeks earlier. I could still almost feel the effects it had on me. A mahogany bookcase sat along the starboard wall with rare first editions of classics and ancient folk stories from the Middle Ages; there was even a book on the rise and fall of ancient Crete. The ceiling was painted in the image of an old map complete with tides, depths and currents. The floor had been tiled to look like a starry night, with the Milky May, and a lighted crescent moon centered under a coffee table of thick glass to magnify its presence in the room. It was as if the world had been turned upside down.

"I was so taken in by the opulence of the boats interior I forgot to follow the steward. 'Ehm…this way, if you please, sir. Monsieur Diabolus is waiting.'

"I followed him down the hall and down a brass spiral staircase to a large room with gold curtains and a single round table beneath a chandelier. There, sitting in a tall-backed purple velvet chair sat Monsieur Diabolus, a lit cigar between his fingers and a shit eating grin on his face. 'Ah, Mr. Sullinger. I knew you would come. Some people, you know, you can count on.'

"I sputtered out a few meager words. 'I couldn't get the case open.' His smile grew larger.

"'Come, sit down. You look as if you've had a turn for the worst.' I shot him a dirty look. 'Is this all that is left of your fortune?' My brow fell even deeper between my eyes. 'No matter, we shall play for this then. Let me see the case.'

"I took the only seat opposite from him and reluctantly slid the case across the table. He stood it on its end and looked down at the two combinations on opposite sides of the handle. He reached into the breast pocket of his vest and withdrew a small key. He slid the two combinations to the right and the left with his thumbs to reveal keyholes. A cheap smirk glazed his face when he slipped the key in and unlocked the latches. He then laid the case down, slid it over and opened it up in front of me.

"I exhaled a great sigh. The generously stacked hundred-dollar bills wrapped in rubber-bands sat in even, crisp, motionless rows of future longing. My hands began to sweat. Then, I looked up at him. He pulled his cigar to his mouth and took a long drag.

'Can I go now?' I asked beneath my breath.

"Diabolus stood towering over me, glaring down in condemnation. 'What do you think? You did call the number, and here I am.'

'But I thought—'

"'You thought?' he said without hesitation. 'I know what you thought. You thought you could get the case opened and then take your money and leave. You're not a stupid man, Jacob. You know how this works.' He slipped his hand into his pocket and pulled out a deck of cards, and then began to sift them with his left hand. I took a deep breath and leaned back in my seat.

'All right then,' I said. 'Deal the cards. I still got some game in me.'

'Oh, I know,' he said, 'in fact, I was counting on it.' He snapped his fingers and the door opened and my jaw dropped at the same moment. The vision that walked into the room was none other than the Asian beauty. I could feel my blood begin to surge south. Her ivory skin in the dimly lit room gave off a soft glow of its own and the emerald satin dress fit just tight enough to spark the primal imagination. Her scent, which now lives in my more seductive dreams, floated around the room, saturating it in honeysuckle and lilacs.

"I closed my eyes and breathed her in, to the corruption of my soul. She had remained an irresistible phantom, the ghost of my desires. Diabolus chuckled at my obsession and watched with amusement the nature of my torment as he blew a puff of white smoke across the room. I was fully aware of her purpose there; she was a deliberate distraction from the game. I would have to focus like my life depended on it. 'She's beautiful, is she not?' he said.

"I choked back a laugh. 'That's putting it mildly,' I said under my breath.

"'Look at her face. The lines, the symmetry, her bone structure…she is a work of art.' I tried not to look, but my eyes were draw to her with such longing. 'Her name is Tanlan, she came to me as a little girl bereft of her own face, homely as it was. Of course, I took her in. Now she is a paragon of beauty.'

'She is breathtaking.' I felt the words slip through my lips.

"'Ehm,' Diabolus cleared his throat. 'That was a long time ago. Would you like to see what she looks like now?' He took a deep drag on his cigar and blew it into her face. The smoke rolled forth like a great storm across the ocean and collided with her features. She turned her head slightly in disgust. As the cloud mingled in her midst. I watched her face transform into the face of a rotting corpse. Her eyes withered away, her nose collapsed, and the cavity of her mouth shriveled to a hollow, devoid of teeth. She writhed in pain as the thought of her own mortality caused her great suffering.

"My heart fell. I knew she was a slave here now, enslaved by her own vanity. A wave of fear moved through me when I realized what we were playing for. Diabolus glared across the table at me. 'Yes, Jacob,' he said, 'you're in deep water now…enough small talk,' he declared, and he slapped the deck of cards in front of her. 'Time to play your hand, Jacob. Give Mr. Sullinger some chips.'

"Tanlan took the case from the table and placed it on a beautifully carved curio cabinet that stood against the wall. She took a hundred thousand from the stack of hundreds and counted out as much in chips, and then set them in front of me. Diabolus received twice as much.

'Planning to lose a lot tonight, are you?' I quipped.

'Let's just call it bait for my quarry,' he remarked.

"She shuffled and dealt the cards with machine-like accuracy and the cards landed face down in front of me. I took a hundred-dollar chip and threw it into the pot. 'Ante up,' I said.

'The ante is a thousand at this table, Jacob. I like a slow kill, but I don't have all night.'

'All right then, a thousand,' I said, throwing a five hundred and four one-hundred-dollar chips in.

"I lifted the corner of my cards and then watched his face for any tells. He didn't even look at his cards, but threw a ten-thousand-dollar chip in. I had a pair of nines and a jack, so I matched him and scrapped four cards. Diabolus met my stare with cold defiant disregard, as one would disregard a mosquito or bothersome fly. He then threw three cards on the table.

"He glanced at the new cards when they landed in front of him, shot a look at his dealer, and then back at me. A smile came to my face. And I bet his ten thousand and he raised another twenty. He called and I laid down a full house, three nines and two jacks. He flipped his two pair over, and I pulled the chips in, snickering at his kings over fives. 'This is going to be easier than I thought,' I gloated.

'The night is still young, Jacob.' And he leaned back in his chair.

"I spent the next hour and a half watching him close when I thought he was bluffing. In that time, I had won most of the hands and was beginning to feel confident I could take him. Hand after hand, I led either by three of a kind or two pair of face cards to his sevens or tens. Then, I received a windfall with the first deal of eight, nine ten, jack.

"I bet fifty thousand and passed off the other three cards as calmly as a Sunday drive. He matched me and received four cards, then I saw it. His nostrils flared just slightly when he looked at the cards and he threw in another fifty thousand. I acted like I didn't notice and called. He was bluffing and I had the straight to prove it. Diabolus gave a snort and crushed out his cigar in a nearby ashtray. 'I must say, Mr. Sullinger, you are proving to be most entertaining. It has been quite a while since I have had such an adversary.'

'I have no complaints,' I said, raking the chips in. It had only been an hour and a half, and I was already up a hundred-fifty thousand.

"Diabolus rose to his feet and walked to the curio. He lifted a glass from the curio and reached for the bottle which sat on a silver tray. 'Will you join me in a glass of brandy? It's from the south of France. A small winery there has distilled the essence of the heavens. I must declare, it has become a weakness of mine.'

'I think I will take a pass; I barely remember the last drink you gave me.'

"'Suit yourself, but it is a brandy unmatched in this world,' he said returning to the table. He sat back down and gave a glance to Tanlan. She shuffled the deck and passed out the next hand and the game commenced in earnest. Once again, I came out strong with two pair ace high and then he took the next hand with four queens. We volleyed back and forth for another hour and a half, neither gaining over the other until a moment when a large swell hit the boat. It heaved and dropped with such force, Diabolus had to steady his glass.

"He did so without fanfare or even acknowledgment of the fact—as if he had been expecting it. A low rumble in the distance and the soft ringing of a buoy upon the water signaled the onset of a coming storm. We played on as the ship tossed gently back and forth. My three queens beat his two pair. His full house beat my kings over sevens. My straight beat his three jacks, his flush beat my four tens, and all the time the boat pitched higher and higher. With each hand, I watched his face.

"By now, I had established without a doubt his *tell* and I played it for what it was worth. Tanlan dealt the cards, and with a glance, I knew I had an easy win. It was a king high full house with a pair of tens. I stayed cool and slid seventy-five thousand into the pot and took no cards.

"Diabolus took a deep breath and I saw it. His nostrils flared ever so slightly before matching me and tossing another fifty thousand in. He took three cards and added another ten thousand into the pot. We stared at each other for a long moment before I called him. An irreverent smile slithered across his face as he rolled his cards over to reveal a Queen high straight.

'You must have thought you saw something, Jacob.'

"I gestured with a nod. 'Yeah, you could say it was something like that,' I said with all due respect. I was at ground zero—a hundred and thirty-five thousand down in one hand and no true tell in sight. I swallowed that bitter pill and played on as the cursed bell rang clearer and louder above the storm, and the waves boar their full weight against the hull. The next two hands smiled on me before the weather really turned bad.

"Diabolus had finished his drink but nursed yet another cigar until the air was foul with its smell. I glance up at Tanlan, my insecurity written all over my face. She looked back at me with a glare devoid of emotion. It wasn't a look of hatred, or malice, but one of complete indifference. She was as cold as a coffin.

'What are you waiting for?' asked Diabolus. 'Deal the cards. I don't have all night.'

"Tanlan shuffled once again and the cards came to rest in front of me. By now, I was scared to look, but Diabolus would have none of that. 'Come now, Jacob,' he said. 'Your time is nigh.' I picked up my cards and cringed inside; there were only a pair of deuces. Tilting my head slightly and raising my eyebrows, I pondered a bluff.

"I threw in twenty thousand and asked for two cards, as to not overplay my hand. He quickly matched me and took three cards. I received my two and graciously threw another fifty into the pot. Diabolus paused a moment and stared at me. I raised an eyebrow for dramatic effect. He leaned back in his chair took another long drag of his cigar before calling me. I shrugged it off and threw my deuces on to the table. He smiled confidently and chuckled, puffing his stogie. 'You have a strong poker face, Mr. Sullinger. I am enjoying this game immensely.'

'I'm glad,' I remarked, 'I wouldn't want to disappoint.'

"He motioned to Tanlan, and the game went on. By now, the ship tossed in every direction. The chandelier swung around above our heads like a pendulum ready to fall and the bell on the buoy rang out across the water like a siren's song. The next two hours passed like years as hand after hand I watch my stack of chips dwindle away. I cashed in another hundred thousand and then another, until there was only twenty-five thousand left.

"When Tanlan dealt the cards, I had but a whisper of a chance. I picked up my cards and felt the rush of confidence which only a five-card straight can bring. I quickly slid twenty thousand into the pot. Diabolus shrunk back a little and hesitated. He then matched and slid three cards over. Tanlan dealt him his three and he glanced over at my remaining chips.

"He carefully counted them and threw exactly twenty-four thousand onto the table. I looked again at my cards. *How sure was I of this hand? This queen high straight staring back at me?* I looked over at him—*what are the odds he got the three cards he was hoping for?* I slowly pushed twenty-four thousand into the pile. After a long moment, he flipped his cards over to show a king high flush. My shoulders sank, but I couldn't accept defeat. 'Let's play one more hand, shall we?' I said.

'Really Jacob, you only have a thousand left. What have you left to prove?'

'Nothing. That's just it. I have nothing left, not even my pride. You will have all of me, or you will have none of me. That is how it's going to be.'

'You have a thousand, you should cut your losses,' he said as he reached for his coat.

'Fuck losses, play me or accept that you're not the card man you say you are.'

Diabolus stood there a moment steadying himself against the swaying of the boat.

'Play me, damn you.' I scowled at him in a defiant stare. I then looked over at Tanlan and then back at him. 'You don't own me yet,' I said. He glared back at me as if I were a fool not worthy to speak such words. He braced himself against the storm and then returned to his seat. 'One hand, played as is,' I said.

'"Agreed,' he said, and he then nodded to Tanlan. She shuffled the deck while looking over at me. She then dealt the cards face down and waited. Diabolus didn't even look at his cards, but watched me pick up my hand. I got a surge of smug confidence when I glanced down at my hand. The bell ringing in the harbor grew loud and obnoxious in my head, but that didn't matter now, because I held a hand which couldn't possibly lose. The cards were not in order, but the royal flush was unmistakable. I glanced up at him with a defiant smirk on my face.

'You haven't looked at your cards, Monsieur Diabolus. Have you lost your desire to play?' I quipped.

'Not at all, Jacob. I am only aware of the fact you have nothing left to bet with. The night is over, Jacob. You have been weighed and measured, and you have been found wanting,' he said as he rose to his feet.

'Oh, no you don't, you shyster. You pick up that hand and play me. I would bet my soul on this hand.'

'Ha!' He laughed and a loud clap of lightning followed. 'Your soul?' He mocked me with a cold glare. 'Tell me, Jacob, is there anyone in your life whom you love more than yourself? Daniel had this, at least.' I thought for a long moment, my mind frantically searching its archive for anyone who meant more than life, but there was no one I loved more than myself, I had to concede.

'No,' I squeaked out. 'There is no one,' I said lowering my head.

"'So, when you die, all that you love dies with you... Pity. Then I need not gamble for something that is already mine,' he said. He stuck his cigar into his mouth and began to laugh. His laughter rang out like the bell in the distance. He took his coat and hat from the hooks on the wall, placed his hat on his head, slung his coat over his shoulder and left, closing the door behind him.

"I laid the cards down face up on the table and stared at them. 'But...I could have won...I could have won,' I said under my breath. My heart was in a state of collapse. There was nothing left inside me. Tanlan had vanished the second Diabolus left the room, as did all of the chips and cash. I was left alone in a ship tossed about, like a cork on the water.

"A huge swell collided with the boat and it rolled on to its side throwing me and my chair to the floor against the corner of the room. The ship rose and fell hard. There was a loud crack and a sheet of water burst into the room and swept across the floor. I tried to collect my thoughts, but all I could think about was that stupid last hand and the empty case now floating on the floor. I struggled to my feet and staggered to the door and shook the knob violently, but it was locked.

"The water was rising fast. Then ship pitched again and I was thrown against the stairwell. As I clung to the rail of the spiral staircase and watched the table sink beneath the water, I pondered my options. *The way I came had glass doors*, I thought. So, I quickly climbed the rail and scrambled up the stairs. By this time, the ship listed so far to the right, I was nearly walking on the wall as I made my way toward the back of the boat.

"Another wave turned the boat upside down and as in some cruel joke the map which was the ceiling, had now became the floor and the floor, still beaming of the starry night, hovered over my head. The waterline was now almost all the way up the glass doors and streaming in from around the frame. I picked up a barstool and hurled it at the doors. They shattered into a thousand pieces and the bay rushed in to greet me. I took as deep a breath as I could hold and sank beneath the swirling tide.

"Down, down I went through the broken doors and away from the sinking ship as it pulled me into the plummeting depths. The pressure of the deep pushed against my chest, forcing bubbles from between my lips, but my lungs held and I struggled with all my limbs toward the surface.

"When I reached the surface, the waves crested over me. I coughed and gagged in the swirling wash. All was black, but the city lights in the distance and the bell that had plagued me, still rang clear and loud. It was at that moment, I realized it was becoming louder and louder. At first, my thoughts were of Diabolus and the bell calling me to join him, and then it occurred to me where I was in relation to the buoy and the motions of the tide. I decided to swim in the direction of the buoy in hopes of having something to hold on to until I was rescued. It was the only plan I could come up with.

"Each time it rang, I swam toward the sound as hard as I could until I could see it in the turbulent darkness. Exhausted, and weak, I struggled up to the buoy and slung an arm around one of the three braces that made the arch for the bell. The sound was deafening, the water cold and my plight hopeless. I cast a longing look to the lights of the Brooklyn Bridge and thought of Rosalinda. I could still see her face watching me from the hall of her grandmother's house. I had nothing left to give. There was nothing left to say. All of my life simply slipped through my fingers like her silky auburn hair.

"As I hung there desperately trying to block out the sound of that bell, I pondered the question of my life and its meaning. *Why was I still living? Why was I even trying to stay alive? I had nothing to go back to, or even anyone to run to. What was left for me but an empty life of shallow pursuits? I had nothing to show for all my hard work, but I also knew who was to blame.* My grip loosened on the buoy and I let myself slip into the bay. I watch the lights of the city disappear behind the waves and heard the sound of the bell fade beneath the water."

Jacob paused his story as he looked out over the stillness of the pond.

"What happened?" asked Boo. "How did you survive?"

Jacob shrugged his shoulders and scratched his head. "That's just it… I don't really know. I remember sinking and letting go…of everything, you know? Letting go of life and struggle—and disappointment and—and emotion—and finally, even letting go of breathing. I just didn't even care about taking another breath anymore. Nothing seemed to be worth it. I saw only black, so therefor I became black. I was as nothing, so I felt no loss…and…and that's all I remember."

"That's all?" asked Boo.

"Well, there are vague memories, fragments really, but I can never be sure of what was real anymore."

"Okay, tell me what you think you remember, then," said Boo.

"Okay, well, let's see," Jacob said focusing on the moment. "I remember something pulling on my arm and rising." A moment passed as he thought. "And I remember feeling someone's arms wrapping around me. A warm feeling came over me, like being wrapped in a thick blanket, but the blanket wasn't real. It was a warmth which can only come from within. It was the warmth of love—a complete love. You know?"

"I don't think I understand," said Boo.

"Okay, let me put it another way," said Jacob. "Think back to your childhood. Was there ever a time when your mother held you close and you felt in your heart of hearts, as true as true could be, you were completely and fully loved?"

Boo thought for a moment and then smiled a deep genuine smile and then gave a nod.

"It was like that. That's as close as I can put it," said Jacob. "I woke up face down on the asphalt in my own puke, listening to someone mumble to themselves behind me."

Where Angels Go

"Who was it?" asked Boo. "Wait, don't tell me...It was that crazy old man who followed you around. Wasn't it?"

"At this point, I had no idea, but yes. It was. He was rummaging around inside a dumpster talking to himself."

"'People don't know,' he said. "They don't know the value of the stuff you can find in one of these things. Look, look here. Here's a perfectly good London Fog coat. Sure, there's a hole in the pocket and a mustard stain on the collar, but it seems to wear just fine.' I lifted my head from the ground and coughed up the river on to the ground. Then I heard him climb down from the dumpster. 'Ah, you made it,' he said.

"I coughed again and choked out the words, 'Made it? Made it where?'

'The other side,' he said. 'I told you I would be here, and here I am.'

'The other side of what?' I asked.

'The river, you gooseberry. We were standing on the Jersey side. Now we're on the Brooklyn side. What did you think?'

'I guess I thought...I thought...Oh, never mind,' I said waving him off. 'How did I get here?'

'Mikey saved you—you were pretty messed up,' he said. I nodded in agreement.

'Where is this Mikey now? I don't see him.'

'He's standing right in front of you. Only, you can't see him because it's not allowed.'

'Oh, I see,' I snarked. 'I guess I will have to take your word for it. Won't I?'

"The old man took a couple steps to the right and leaned in and whispered beneath his breath, 'What do you think? Well, yeah, but you could make an exception just this once. I don't think he will mind, considering.'

'Oh, all right Just this once.' I heard someone say in a soft voice.

"'Tell me, Jacob,' said the old man, 'can you see the lights of Manhattan across the river?' I raised my eyes, and for a split second I could see the lights of the skyline shimmering in the dark like a million motionless stars, but then a shadow fell over me and there was nothing. I strained at the distance trying to see something—anything—but there was only black. I scooted back a few feet and brought into focus a huge shadow of a man.

"He was twice my height with what seem like wings stretching out on both sides. There were slivers of bright light shining gold and white from behind him, as if he were standing between me and the radiance of the sun. His mighty wings flexed before me and then he vanished, leaving me staring at the traces of dawn and the Manhattan lights. The old man smiled down at me and my puzzled face. 'It's okay, Uriel,' he said. 'It's not for you to understand.'

'How do you know my name? Nobody knows my first name,' I said. Glaring up at him.

'It's a fine biblical name, Jacob. I have a biblical name too. My name is Gabriel, but you can call me Gabe.'

'I...I don't get it,' I said. 'Why did you save me? I have nothing to go back to. I have no money, no home and no family left. I have lost it all,' I lamented.

'Yes, but just look at what you've found. You've found a great place to start over and since you know where you went wrong, you know what mistakes to avoid. Now that's good news. Come on, let's get something to eat.'

'Where are we going?' I asked.

'To Angelo's,' he said. Then he leaned in close and whispered, 'It's where angels go.'

'I can't go there. Rosalinda will see me,' I panicked. 'I have no money.'

'You really don't understand, do you?' he said shaking his head. 'It was never the money she was attracted to. So, come on.' He held out his hand to help me to my feet, but I waved him off.

'I'm not dead yet,' I said as I stood up.

'That's the spirit,' said Gabe. 'Never surrender.'

"We walked the empty streets as the sun rose behind us and the smell of the docks mingle with the morning dew and steam rising from the sewer drains. Our footsteps echoed off the buildings and disappeared into the alleys. 'What's it like?' I asked.

'What's what like?'

'Heaven. What's it look like? You've seen it, haven't you?'

'Oh yes, I've seen it, but I couldn't begin to tell you, because I don't think you would understand.'

'Try me,' I said.

'Well, it's not a destination as you are thinking, but it is a place. It's a place where you disappear because you love so much—a place where the happiness others feel is more important than the pain you feel. It's a place in time when you no longer cling to things of this world, but live in an everlasting moment which exists in the hearts of others. You see, it's not an easy thing to explain.'

'It sounds wonderful,' I said.

'Well, here we are,' he said as we came to a stop in front of the neon sign. It flickered a couple of times before giving off its beautiful pink and blue glow. 'Look, they're just opening up.'

'Can't we come back later? After I've had a chance to clean up. I can't go in looking like this.'

'Okay, where do you suppose you'll go to clean up?' he said.

'Good point.' I sighed. 'I guess it's now or never. God save me, this is so embarrassing.'

'This is what he saved you for, Jacob. Suck it up and learn to let go of that pride. It wasn't working for you anyway.'

"I held the rail of the stairs to the restaurant door tight in my right hand and gritted my teeth as I ascended the steps. The door opened and we quietly stepped inside. Rosalinda was crouched down behind the waitress station fetching plates from the cupboard. I stood in silence looking around the room. There was a young black girl of eleven or twelve, sitting in the booth next to the kitchen door. She had no plate in front of her, nor was there any silverware on the table. She glanced over at me as if to say, what are you waiting for? Gabriel motioned with his head. 'Well, go ahead. She won't bite.'

'Who is she?' asked Jacob.

'Go introduce yourself. I have to go now, but I will see you again in time,' he said.

'In time for what?' I asked. He turned and walked out as quietly as we came in.

"As I walked toward the table, there came a scream from the waitress station and the sound of shattering plates. 'Jacob!' screamed Rosalinda. 'What the hell happened to you?' Rosalinda ran to me and threw her arms around me, kissing my face and weeping. The kitchen door swung open and her three

239

brothers stood gawking at my bruised and battered form. 'What the hell did you do to him?' Rosalinda screamed at them.

'Wow! No, no…it wasn't us,' said Saul.

'Yeah Rosa. Honest! We never laid a hand on him,' remarked Franco.

"'It's okay, Rosa, I'm all right. Your brothers had nothing to do with this. This was my own fault,' I said soaking in her affection like a cat. Rosalinda cradled my head in her hands. Her tears washed down my face. I held my hands up in a weak effort to stop her, but secretly, I was relishing every single sensation of her soft fingertips and warm kisses.

"'Come on, sit down over here,' she said, walking me over to the corner table by the kitchen door. 'Esci da qui, teste di blocco. Torna al lavoro,' she said as she slammed the door in her brother's faces. I sat down and slid into the booth and looked across the table at the young black girl and then back at Rosa. 'Let me get you something to eat, Jacob. How about some calzone? I think we have some tortellini left over from last night.'

'Can you bring an extra plate for my new friend,' I asked? Rosa paused a moment.

'An extra plate?' she remarked.

At that moment, the young girl spoke up, 'Oh, that's all right, I don't want anything, you go ahead and eat, Jacob.'

'Never mind, Rosa,' said Jacob. 'One plate is fine.'

'Okay then, one plate it is,' she said with a smile, and she disappeared into the kitchen.

"I sat there looking across the table at her. She was a strait-laced girl in a light blue striped dress. Her eyes were deep brown with a light of strength in them. She had a no-nonsense air about her, but a kindness in her smile. 'So,' I said awkwardly, 'what's your name?'

'Hope,' she said. 'I'm your guardian angel. I'm here to keep an eye on you—until you get your wings.'

'My wings?' I chuckled. Somehow, the thought of me having wings had never entered my mind.

'Sure. Why not you?' she retorted. 'You are as entitled to your wings as anybody. I am here to help you make decisions. Well, the tough ones anyway.'

"Rosalinda appeared from the kitchen with a cup of coffee, a plate of tortellini and a basket of rolls. 'You are a saint, Rosa. You know that? An absolute saint.' Rosa sat the plate and rolls down in front of me and handed me the cup of coffee.

'You have to tell me what happened to you, Jacob. I want to know who did this to you.'

"I shrugged my shoulders and shot her a hapless smile. 'It's a long story, Rosa, and I'm not quite sure where to begin. It's safe to say, I've learned a lot in the last forty-eight hours.' I glance over at Hope and she beamed and nodded in agreement. I sat there and ate my fill as Rosa caressed my hair and looked into my eyes longingly. We talked about the old neighborhood and about her grandmother. We talked until we got to the question, what next? For that, I had no answer. 'I don't know,' I said. 'I have no family left—not since my great uncle passed. My parents died in a car accident five years ago and there is no one left in my family tree.'

'Why don't you go back to your Uncle Walt's house? It may do you some good, Jacob—to see the old place, I mean.'

'I...I don't know,' I said. 'What do you think?' I asked as I looked across the table at Hope. She gave a firm nod. Turning back to Rosa, I said, 'Okay, do you feel like a road trip? I lost my car too. Actually, I've lost everything. I can't even pay for this food.'

'Oh, Jacob,' said Rosa as she caressed my cheek. 'You know, I would never charge you. Of course, I'll drive you down to your uncle's house.'

'Can we bring Hope?' I asked.

"'I wouldn't go anywhere without it,' Rosa answered. 'Just let me tell my brothers we are going.' Rosa slid out of the booth and opened the kitchen door. 'Hey blockheads,' she belted out, 'I'm taking the car for a few days. You can catch a ride with Uncle Vinnie. Don't wait up for me, I'll call you in a few days—okay?' I could hear them swearing in Italian from the other side of the door, but she wasn't deterred in the slightest. 'Ah...chiudi la bocca,' she yelled. She turned to me and said, 'They said it was fine, take as long as you need.'

'They did? Why am I not convinced?' I laughed.

"Rosa blushed and took my plate from the table. 'Let me get my coat and bring the car around front. I'll meet you outside.' She took the plate into the kitchen and I grinned at Hope.

'I like her,' said Hope. 'She reminds me of my mother.'

'Yeah, I do too. Actually, I have secretly loved her my whole life, but I've never been able to tell her.'

'You should tell her,' said Hope. '"That is something she needs to know.'

'Ah, she can do better than me,' I grimaced.

'Still, you should tell her.'

'Maybe,' I said, 'maybe someday when I grow some guts.'

"A car horn sounded outside and Hope followed me to the street. Rosalinda sat in the driver's seat of a rust colored 1998 four door Lincoln Continental convertible with white interior. I walked around to the passenger side and opened the rear door. Rosalinda watched me with a strange curiosity. I closed the door and opened the front passenger side door and climbed in beside my Rosa in the front seat. 'It's a long way, Rosa, are you sure you want to go?'

'Shut up and give me the address so I can plug it into the GPS on my phone.' I looked into the mirror and saw Hope with a smirk on her face.

'I can't thank you enough, Rosa. I will pay you back. Honest…when I get my life back, I mean. I won't forget this,' I said.

"She glanced over at me lovingly and turned on the radio. 'Let's do this right,' she said and she slipped a Journey CD into the player. We rocked and sang the eight-and-a-half-hour trip away stopping only for lunch and rest stops. Once we arrived in Clay County, West Virginia, we drove through the town of Clay.

"The route we took led past the Clay County home for the mentally ill, which stood only a mile and a half from Thicket road, the road that led to Tanglewood. I could feel my stomach tighten up when we turned right onto the long country road that led out of town. Soon we came upon the short stone wall which marked the boundary of the property and the end of our journey. It stood like a permanent placeholder separating my childhood from the rest of my life.

"The long winding drive inched me back in time, closer to the childhood I had abandoned. The pangs of those regrets showed themselves in the form of trembling hands. Rosalinda noticed and slid her hand over mine and gave it a squeeze. 'I'm right here, Jacob,' she said. 'I'll come with you if you want.'

'I think maybe I should do this alone,' I said.

'Okay, I'll wait in the car,' she answered.

"I looked up the drive to the old house as we approached. The windows and doors were boarded up tight and the shrubs around the house were all overgrown. The paint was peeling and the screen door was in disrepair, but the smell of the woods and the honeysuckle vines were an unmistakable reminder of my great uncle's presence. It was as if his ghost was hanging around the old place, waiting for me to return.

"We pulled up to the front door and I got out of the car. I slowly walked up the stairs to the long wide porch. His tall backed wicker chair still sat to the left of the front door. I could hear the echoes of the argument he and my father had the last time I was there. The white lace curtains still hung in the windows. I could see them between the cracks in the boards. The shadow of a scared thirteen-year-old boy probably still darkened the corner window frame. I peered into the window, but the dirty glass and the darkened room afforded little view of the interior. I drew a deep sigh and turned back toward the car. 'I don't think anyone lives here now,' I declared.

'It don't matter,' said Hope, 'you know what you came for. Get to it.'

"Rosalinda sat quietly waiting for me to decide what to do. 'I'll just go around back then. I want to pay my last respects to Uncle Walt.'

"Rosa gave a nod and I began to follow the cobblestone path around the house. It led beneath a rose-covered arch and through a small gate covered in ivy to the back yard where Uncle Walt's garden was still flowering among tufts of overgrown grass. The roses were in desperate need of pruning and weeds lined his flowerbeds and in between the cracks of the walkways. I took the long path still worn into the dark earth by Uncle Walt's many visits to the family graveyard, beneath the towering willows.

"Quietly, I approached and stood just outside the yard staring at the gravestones. With a heavy heart, I took those next steps toward the back where I knew Robert's remains were laid to rest and sure enough, there it was, a tall gray stone with the words Walter Thomas Sullinger, 5 August 1949 to 20 January 2017. The words, *a sower of seeds in a world of needs*, etched below his name. I stood in a reverent silence trying to say something. Then I glanced to my left and saw Gabriel standing near the stone wall. 'Go ahead, Jacob,' he said, 'tell him what you've got to say. Get it out of your system.'

'Um, here I am,' I began. 'I'm sorry it took so long. I...I didn't mean for things to turn out this way. I didn't mean to stray so far from you and Georgia. If I could take it all back, I would. There are so many regrets I have. All I can say is I'm sorry. I know you can hear me.' I began to sob. I fell to my knees before his grave and wept, pleading, 'I'm sorry, I'm sorry, I'm so sorry.' Then I heard a voice from over my shoulder.

'It's all right, youngin'. He knew you would come back some day.'

'Georgia?' I exclaimed.

"'Yes, child. I'm still livin' here. Your great uncle left me the guesthouse in his will and told me ifin' you ever come back, I wasta give you this.' She held out an envelope in her right hand. I looked over at Gabriel cautiously. He nodded and gestured with his hand. I rose to my feet, wiped the tears from my eyes, and took the envelope. It was a letter from Uncle Walt. It read:

Dear Uriel,

If you are reading this, it means you have come home in search of answers. In all honesty, I must say, answers are always hiding in places you never want to go. Do you remember the pagoda that stands next to the doors of my greenhouse? If you lift the roof, you will find the key. Enter the greenhouse, but know this; whatever you find, didn't change my love for you. This love abides with me always—even now.

Your uncle and your sole champion,
Walt

"I stood there, stunned and amazed by his sense of devotion. 'He loved you very much, you know,' said Georgia.

"I looked at his grave and shook my head. 'What a remarkable man,' I said.

'Yes, he sure was, Jacob. That's for sure,' said Georgia. 'I took care of your uncle for thirty-five years. I have never met another man like him. I was his nurse, you see.'

'His nurse?' I glanced over at Robert's grave and remembered Uncle Walt's words about the devil among the gravestones. My mouth opened, but nothing came out.

'Go ahead, Jacob,' said Gabriel, 'Ask her. It's what you've been wanting to know.'

"I took a deep breath and asked, 'Georgia, what did Robert die of?'

'He killed himself, Jacob. He took his own life on that tree over there,' she said pointing to one of the great willows.

'Why?' I asked. 'What was so bad?'

'He had the same problem your uncle had and he just couldn't handle it,' she said.

'What was it?' I felt the hesitant words squeaked from my lips.

'Schizophrenia,' she said plainly. 'They both were schizophrenics, Jacob. I helped Mr. Sullinger with his medication.'

"My shoulders sank under the weight of this knowledge. I bit my lip. Georgia watched me take a long, slow look at Gabriel standing near the wall. He smiled at me warmly. 'The truth is like a bitter pill, Jacob,' he said. 'If you can stomach it, it can help you build a better life. These are the words which will serve you best.'

"I didn't want to hear them, they stung my heart as they sank in, but I knew they were true. The thought of the Clay County Mental Hospital flashed into my mind. 'What'll I do now, Gabe?' I asked.

'This is goodbye, Jacob,' he said. 'I have taken you this far, the rest is up to you.' Then I watched his image fade until the willow limbs that hung behind him danced in the breeze, and he was gone.

"Georgia watched me as if she shared the vision, but only shook her head. 'Come on, Jacob,' she said. 'You and your lady friend can stay with me tonight and you can go to the hospital tomorrow.' She stepped up and put her arm around me and I felt that old melancholy feeling of home. I looked down at the letter in my hand.

'There's something I have to do first,' I said. 'Why don't you show Rosa and Hope to the guesthouse and I will be along shortly.'

'Okay, Jacob. If you want to be alone. Supper will be waitin' when you get back,' said Georgia.

'Thank you, Georgia. You were always so good to me,' I said.

'I told you then, I means it now; you are kin to me, boy. Nothin' gonna change that.'

"We walked together until we reached the top of the garden where the grapevines grow wild. She took the path to the front of the house as I wandered between the rows of concords and Romulus vines toward the greenhouse. It stood at the end of the rows, dark and ominous, like a secret in its sanctuary. The afternoon sun was grazing the treetops and except for a persistent woodpecker, the birds had settled in for the ensuing evening.

"When I reached the greenhouse, I pressed my face against the glass in hopes of gleaning some view, or at least to see the green of the foliage I remembered. It was dark and unforgiving. I took the large lock that bound a chain between the doors handles into my hand and passed my thumb across the keyhole. The pagoda Uncle Walt wrote about stood to the right of the two glass doors. I stepped over and lifted the roof of the pagoda. The hinges creaked with the rust of a decade, but the inside yielded a ring full of keys.

"I took the keys and returned to the doors. Sifting through them, I tried them all one by one until the tumblers gave a click and the lock popped open. I slid the chain from the door handles and tossed it to the side. Placing my open palm on the door as I took hold of the handle gave me the illusion that I was prepared for what was inside.

"Pushing past the fear, I pulled the door open and peered into the dark. I was hoping to find green leaves and overgrown flowers, but instead, there was death. Everything was dead, dried and collapsing under its own weight. Spiders had taken up residence on the branches of what used to be beautiful vines of hanging blossoms. Even the carnivorous plants were but a shell of brown folded leaves. There were black stalks like roots jetting up from the ground everywhere. They bore no leaf or fruit, but stood in the presence, even the center, of every plant. As if they drew their nourishment from other plants.

"This was my uncle's most precious house, his most prized plants. The building was set up to keep them at the right temperature, the perfect moisture. *What could have killed them?* I thought. Following the walkway, I came to the place where Uncle Walt's precious orchids once grew. They were like dried straw in barren earth. A black stalk had twined its way around them. I reached down and touched a stalk of the orchid and it crumbled in my hand.

'No,' I whispered to myself. 'How could this be?' There was broken glass strewn all around the ground and the fading light of day shone through to the soil. It was then that I glanced to my right and beheld the only living thing in the greenhouse. It was tall and dark and reeked of dead flesh. It was my tree; the tree I had planted when I was twelve. It had grown through the roof and stretched its toxic roots throughout the greenhouse.

'No!' I screamed as I beat my fists on its trunk. 'You can't be me! I would have never done this. God no! Not me! I don't want to be...I don't want to be...me.' I fell to the ground beneath the tree and dug at its roots screaming, 'I'll kill you, you son of a bitch! You took the life of others so carelessly, so selfishly! I will take yours!'

"Jumping to my feet, I ran out of the greenhouse, down the path to the shed where Juan and Pedro kept their tools. I fumbled though the keys and unlocked the shed. Frantically, I searched the shed until I found something to kill it with. I snatched up the gas can and a lighter Juan had left and ran back to the greenhouse. I emptied the gas can on the trunk of the tree and lit fire to the dried remains of Uncle Walt's flowers.

"Backing away, I watched the flame consume the tree first and then spread to the surrounding plants. 'Yes,' I yelled. 'Burn, burn…you sorry excuse for a human being. I will never be you again. Do you hear me, Uncle Walt? I will never be like that person again, I promise.'

"Stepping back outside, I watched it from a safe distance for a few moments, and then left it to burn. I walked back to the guest house and joined Rosa, Hope, and Georgia. That night we had dinner and talked and laughed and later that night, I slept like a baby."

Jacob ended his story and Boo was stunned. "Wait, what happened next?"

"Next? Well, the next morning I asked Rosa to drive me here, and here is where I'll stay, if I don't sort things out."

"What if you can't?" asked Boo.

"I don't know, really. Maybe my life will always be this way, shifting from one state to another, never really knowing what is true or…"

"So, Diabolus was real? Or was he…" asked Boo.

"That's just it, I don't know," said Jacob. "I can't tell. It seemed real, but there are gaps in my memory that I can't explain. I don't remember being pulled from the water…or where the rocks I had put in my pockets went. There are too many questions to dismiss any of it."

"I tell you what," said Boo. "I will come back and visit you in a couple of days. We can come here to talk until you feel better."

"Thanks, Boo. I really appreciate that," said Jacob. "I can't talk to the doctor. There is something about him I don't trust. He seems to have no end of time for me. You could say, he has taken too strong an interest in my case."

"Why is that strange?" asked Boo.

"I have no money. Have you ever heard of a doctor who works for free?"

"Ahh, I get your point," said Boo. "Well, as my mother always said, it'll all come out in the wash. That's for sure."

Jacob laughed and rose to his feet. "Look at me. I've taken up enough of your time with my sob story. You've got the rest of your life to catch up with and I don't want to stand in the way of progress." Jacob gave him a hug and patted him on the back. "You're the best friend I've ever had, you know."

Boo smiled and gave him a salute. "Don't give up the fight, Jacob."

Jacob saluted back. "I won't if you don't," he said. Boo smiled and walked back up the hill.

The Disciple

Jacob spent the next three days avoiding Dr. Kessler and wandering around the hospital. He thought of slipping into Zed Wing again, but ever since he had mentioned it to Dr. Kessler, there has always been at least one guard in the security office. There were moments he felt sure he was being watched either by Gabriel or Diabolus, he wasn't sure. His lack of trust only entrenched the lonely feeling of abandonment within him.

With every passing day, he gained a deeper understanding of Uncle Walt's son and his predicament. A wall of isolation was closing in around him and if he didn't find some resolution soon, they were going to find him swinging from one of these trees. He visited his uncle's garden and the duck pond as many times as he could, but only when he knew Dr. Kessler had a patient to interview. Dr. Kessler frequented the gardens as well, probably to look for him. The doctor had a strange obsession with Jacob's case, and it left him uneasy.

On Saturday, Boo appeared at the gate. He had a big brown bag in his right hand and a generous smile on his face. "Boo!" Jacob exclaimed. "I can't tell you how much I miss you. This place is a mortuary without you here. Nobody wants to play shuffleboard in the halls with bedpans and crutches, or tie yarn to Mrs. Baklava's walker."

"Ha!" Boo laughed. "I used to love that one. Hey, I brought lunch. What do you say we eat lunch on the patio with our old friends Freud, Skinner, Piaget, and Pavlov?"

"Sounds like a winner, what did you bring for lunch?" asked Jacob.

"You'll never guess," exclaimed Boo. "Egg salad sandwiches and tapioca pudding."

"Perfect," said Jacob, "they can have the leftovers."

They walked around the left side of the hospital and took a seat on a bench at the end of the patio. Boo took the sandwiches out and passed one to Jacob and then leaned back and took a big bite of his sandwich. "So how is it out there?" asked Jacob.

"I tell you, Jacob, it's good to be alive again. I'm still having those dreams, but I don't feel alone any more. I have my family to help me," said Boo.

"Yeah, family helps," said Jacob.

"How are you doing?" asked Boo. "Any progress?"

Jacob shrugged his shoulders. "You know how it is, two steps forward—"

"And three steps back," answered Boo. "Well, you know what I think? I think the hell with it. You're going to have to face those demons whether you're in here or not, right?"

"I guess," Jacob answered.

"Why don't you kick it in the butt and check yourself out. You're wasting a lot of life sitting in here and you sure ain't going to tell that Dr. Kessler. So, why don't you call that lady friend of yours and get the hell out of here. There is little to no love in a place like this, and what you need right now is to be with those who truly love you."

"I suppose," Jacob stammered. "If she's still waiting. She has probably gone back to Brooklyn."

"You never know until you try," said Boo.

Jacob sat there musing about the possibility and fingering his sandwich. Boo suddenly snatched the sandwich out of Jacob's hands and threw it at the bust of Sigmund Freud, hitting it right in the face. "Come on, Jacob," said Boo. "The worst thing that could happen is you wind up with egg on your face, and it's not as if that's never happened before."

Jacob laughed. "Okay, okay…you win. I'll call Rosa this afternoon…I was going to eat that, you know?"

"No worries," said Boo. "I brought another one…actually, I brought one for all six of our faces. Ha, ha, ha," he laughed.

Jacob laughed out loud. "You had this all planned out, didn't you?"

Boo gave a smirk and shrugged his shoulders. "Maybe," he answered. "I'll never tell."

They finished eating and calmly walked back to the gate where Boo's brother was waiting in the car. They stood there an awkward moment until Jacob said, "Go on, get out of here. I don't want to be responsible for holding you back."

Boo threw his arms around Jacob. "I'm looking forward to a time when I can see you whole," he said. "You're almost there. Don't give up. That's an order, Private. Do you hear me? Don't give up."

"Yes sir, Captain. I hear you loud and clear," said Jacob. They gave a quick salute and Boo climbed into the car. He waved goodbye as the car pulled away, and Jacob was once again left on his own with Boo's words echoing in his skull.

Jacob looked around the hospital and saw the patients roaming the grounds, the halls and the game room. They were watching TV alone, walking alone and talking to themselves. It began to occur to him, a mind left to itself will turn inward on itself. A flash came to his memory of *Alister Stromwell* standing at the window of his room on Zed Wing. He remembered pressing his face against the glass to find him staring out of the widow through the only hole the ivy didn't cover.

"He was looking out," Jacob said to himself. "He was trying to see the world outside of his pain...I get it!" he exclaimed. "I get it!" Jacob began laughing as he ran through the halls of the hospital. "I get it! The song of life!" he proclaimed. "I will sing it for you, and you and you," he said pointing to the other patients. "You, my flowers...my seedlings, you will awake. Awake, you sleeping sunflowers. Yours is not a world of me, but a world of we...a world of us. Show yourself a new world, a world of possibilities. The possibilities of a world where my problems don't matter. You heard me. They don't matter. Oh God, how those words ring out sweet to my ears. They don't matter to someone with a full heart!"

Jacob ran out of the front door, down the steps and collapsed on the lawn laughing. The late afternoon sun was shining and the grass tickled his ears as he laid on his back. Suddenly, he noticed how alive his senses felt. The grass seemed greener, the sun brighter, the birds sang louder and the world seemed to turn beneath him.

Jacob spent a long moment or two staring up at the bluest sky he had ever seen. He marveled at how, no matter how hard you try, you couldn't take it all in. "It goes on forever," he said to himself. "This is amazing, I need to tell someone. I need to tell Rosa."

He jumped to his feet and ran back inside calling, "Alice! Alice, where are you!"

Alice had gone to the records room and was returning with an arm full of files when she was ambushed by an exuberant Jacob. He swept her off her feet and swung her around. "Gracious, Jacob!" she exclaimed. "What's gotten into you?"

"The sky, Alice, the sky. Did you see it?"

"What's wrong with it? Is it falling, Chicken Little?" she quipped.

"No silly, it goes on forever." Jacob gently set her feet back on the floor.

"You're crazy," she exclaimed. Then she quickly cupped a hand over her mouth. "I'm sorry, I...I didn't mean to say that."

"Yes, Alice, I am. Isn't it great?" Jacob said laughing. "Hey, I need to use the phone. Can I? Can I please, please, pretty please, with sugar on top? I promise it won't take long."

"Yes, yes. If it means I can go back to work. Just don't let the administrator see you," she said.

"Oh, thank you, Alice. I'm nominating you for sainthood this year, just as soon as I can get the Pope to take my calls."

"Well, I won't start writing my acceptance speech quite yet then," chided Alice "What are you waiting for, you know where the phone is and how to get an outside line. Get to it."

Jacob sped down the hall to Alice's desk and snapped up the receiver. He fumbled a little when he dialed Rosa's number, but recovered and cleared his throat while he waited for her to answer. "Hello," her soft voice resonated through the line.

"Hi Rosa, it's me, Jacob. I think I'm ready to come home now."

"Really? That's great, Jacob. I bought some clothes for you at the local Goodwill. They're not too fancy, but I think they will fit you," she said.

"Thank you, Rosa, I hadn't thought about that. I guess that shows you where my head has been," he joked.

"When do you want me to pick you up? Do you want to leave right away?"

"No, it's getting late in the day for that now. How about in the morning at nine?" he asked.

"Nine it is, I will see you then, Jacob," she said softly and hung up her phone.

Jacob put the receiver back and took a deep breath. "God, I love that woman," he said to himself. Alice sat down at her desk and place the files in a neat stack in front of her. "Well, Alice," he said plainly. "This is my last night here at the hospital. I'm leaving in the morning."

"Shouldn't you tell the doctor? I mean, did he release you yet?" she raised an eyebrow at the notion.

"Nah, he'll find out soon enough. Won't he? I'm just kidding, I'll tell him tonight before he goes home." Of course, Jacob had no intention of talking to the doctor, but Alice didn't need to know that. Jacob took a piece of paper and scribbled Rosa's name and number on it and gave it to Alice. "Give this to Boo for me, will you? It's Rosa's. He can get ahold of me by this number." Jacob then walked to the courtyard for one last dinner.

The next morning, Dr. Kessler was waiting outside Jacob's room when he woke up. "You weren't going to tell me where you were, Jacob?" asked Dr. Kessler. "After all, we've been through? You are my favorite patient, you know?"

"Really?" asked Jacob as he pushed past him down the hall, "and why is that?"

"I thought we were making progress, weren't we?" asked the doctor, keeping step.

"I don't know," said Jacob. "It felt to me like we were going around in circles."

"Well, these things take time, Jacob. We need to resolve them slowly. It can sometimes take years to resolve a person's issues." Jacob shot a disgruntled look at Alice as he walked by her desk. He knew who the mole was in this particular case. Alice just smiled and hummed a little tune to herself as she worked.

"Ha!" Jacob mocked. "My issues may never be solved and you knew that, didn't you?" The doctor fell silent. "If you don't mind, Doc, it's eight forty-seven and I got a date with the love of my life, so sign me out of here and get out of my way."

"At least let me walk you out to the street. I don't want to end this on a bad note, Jacob. I want to be your friend—you know, call me up from time to time and we can go golfing or something."

Jacob reached the street and stopped in his tracks and glared at the doctor. "I don't know what your angle is, doc, but I wouldn't spend a lot of time waiting for that call," he said.

"Wait," said Dr. Kessler. "There is someone you need to talk to. I told him you were checking out at nine and he said he would meet you here."

"What? Who is it?" asked Jacob.

"I think I would rather have him explain," said the doctor.

A huge smile stretched across Jacob's face when he saw Rosa's car coming up the street. "This guy you're talking about better hurry, doc, I think I see my ride." As the car drew near, Jacob looked into the back seat. There were two people riding with Rosa. One was Hope. She was sitting with her arms folded and a look of disgust on her face.

The other sent waves of fear through Jacob when he realized it was Diabolus. He sat with his hands folded on his walking stick and a smug look upon his face. Rosa pulled the car to a stop right in front of Jacob. Jacob's eyes were fixed on the backseat of the car. "What are you doing here?" he demanded.

Rosa spun around to see who Jacob was talking to. Jacob waited for an answer. Diabolus calmly look up at Jacob. "I have come to spend some time with my disciple," he said.

Hope turned to Diabolus. "You hush up," she snapped. "You know Jacob don't belong to you no more."

Diabolus cleared his throat and reached into his coat for a fresh cigar. "I wasn't referring to Jacob," he said without regard.

Jacob opened the car door. "Get out," he demanded. Hope agreed with a resounding "humph."

Rosa and the doctor stared at Jacob curiously. Jacob watched Diabolus step from the car and stand next to the doctor and then Jacob closed the car door.

"Are you all right, Jacob?" asked Rosa. "Are you sure you are ready to leave the hospital?"

"As ready as I'll ever be," Jacob answered. A black sedan with Massachusetts plates pulled up behind Rosa's car and a tall, well-dressed man approached Jacob.

"Mr. Sullinger, my name is Charles Standforth. I'm with the firm of Hobart and Comings," he said holding out his card. "We've been trying to reach you for about two weeks."

"Oh, you have, have you? Well, this is the first I have heard about it." Jacob shot a glare at the doctor.

"Yes, well, that may be, but I represent your great uncle's estate. He was quite adamant you receive your inheritance."

"Yes, I know he had a small shipping business that dealt in antiques or something. Can we do this some other time? I'm trying to get back to my life," Jacob urged.

"That is just it, sir. The shipping industry is an eight-hundred billion dollar a year industry and you uncle's business enjoys almost two percent of that market. With a thousand ships and over a hundred and sixty warehouses all over the world, Sully Shipping has become a juggernaut in the shipping industry. His personal holdings alone gross twelve billion dollars a year," said Mr. Standforth.

"That's great," said Jacob. "Why are you telling me?"

"Because you are his sole heir to this fortune. I have his will right here, but it requires your signature."

"Wait just one minute here," exclaimed Jacob. He pushed Mr. Standforth to one side with his right hand and stepped toward the doctor. "That's why you took an interest in me. That's why my uncle was your *favorite* patient. That's why it was so important for us to be *friends*." Jacob's voice rumbled with anger. He then looked to the doctors left where Diabolus stood chuckling.

"So, he's the disciple you have come for," said Jacob. Diabolus puffed his cigar and laughed. Kessler, Standforth, and Rosa watched Jacob's strange behavior. Turning back to Mr. Standforth, Jacob said, "I'm sorry, Mr. Standforth, but this will all have to wait. I will come to your office in a week or so to sort all of this out. That will give me some time to make a list of charities I would like to donate to—starting with an investigation of this hospital and the living standard of those in Zed Wing."

Jacob glared at the doctor. The doctor's back stiffened at the sound of those words. "Right now, I have a lot to make up for and I'm going to start with Rosa." Jacob walked around the car to the passenger side, opened the door, and got into the front seat. He turned to Rosa, looked her straight in the eyes. "Rosa," he said, "I have always loved you; from the moment I saw you watching me from the hall of your grandmother's house. I have been that scared little boy for too long."

"I have always known," she said. "Jacob, it's that scared little boy I fell in love with. Now, let's go. Georgia is waiting to welcome you home to Tanglewood."

Jacob looked into the rear-view mirror as Rosa pulled away from the curb. Hope's face was beaming like the first sunrise on a new world.

"I'm glad you kept hope with you," said Jacob.

"Oh, Jacob," Rosalinda sighed, "I have always kept hope alive."